The Cosmic Caretaker

Ange Anderson

"I think, therefore I am."
Rene Descartes 1637

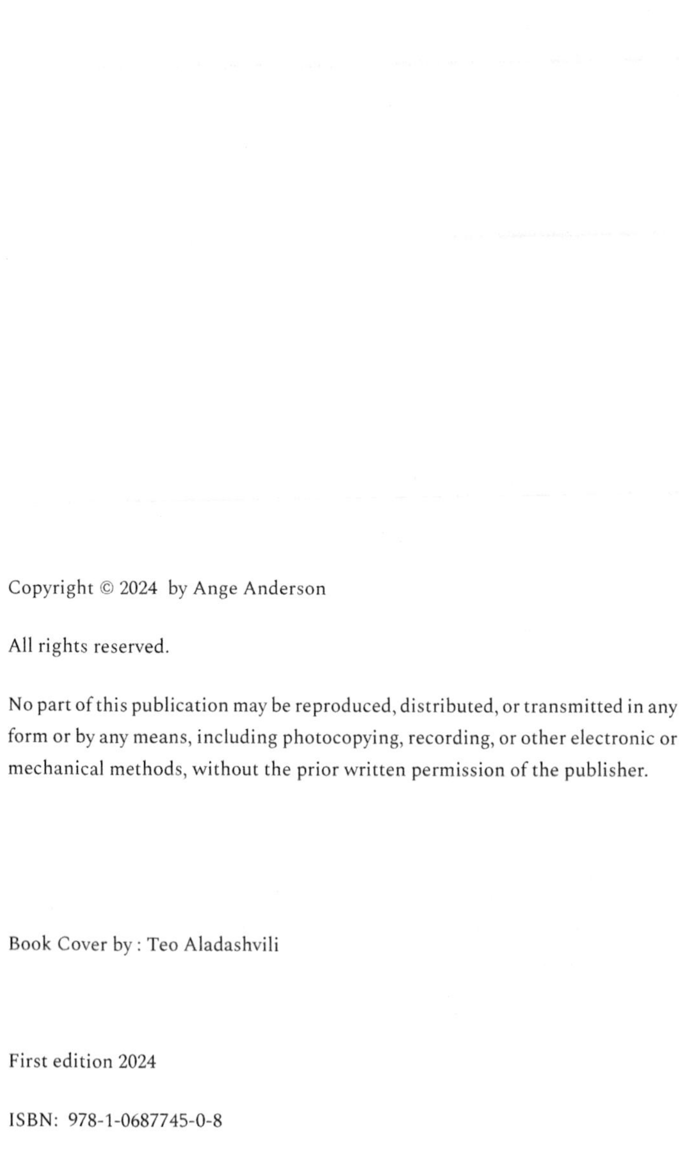

Book Cover by : Teo Aladashvili

First edition 2024

ISBN: 978-1-0687745-0-8

Contents

Prologue

Six-year-old Tilly has a memory that doesn't belong to her - it belongs to me. Tilly didn't steal this memory; it simply came into her consciousness while she travelled from the astral plane and descended to Earth into a human body for her latest reincarnation.

The memory escaped from the Cosmic Memory Database (CMD) which stores all the memories and experiences from past lives. It can be found on the astral plane- a realm of secrets and knowledge where astralites live. Like a feather, the memory drifted on the wings of a stork delivering a baby, and the baby happened to grasp it in her chubby hands and own it, as though it had always been hers.

The astral plane is a place that we return to after death, where we existed before birth. Only those who have the power to separate their consciousness from their physical bodies can access this mysterious world. They are either astralites or rebirthers.

Tilly is no ordinary child - she is a rebirther. Rebirthers can move on to their human lives as soon as they are reborn, but many wish to have a foot in both worlds until they are forced to choose. They can make this choice up until the age of seven.

For six years Tilly has shown an obsession with shiny things that weren't hers, as if she'd been a magpie in a previous life. She has clung onto the memory gem, a beautiful rainbow-coloured prism created by my mind not hers. I have waited anxiously as Tilly approaches her seventh birthday as a human when she will lose the ability to astral travel- and lose the memory gem. Thankfully she has been ordered to return it to the CMD immediately.

As she drifts off to sleep, I can feel a sense of regret radiating from her. I watch as her astral form leaves the body and seamlessly travels through different planes until it reaches the CMD. The vast expanse of swirling energies welcomes us as I follow Tilly towards the section where memories are stored in barcode form. I sigh with relief as she carefully places the memory gem back into its designated slot in the database.

Her ethereal hands appear to tremble with the weight of responsibility, and reluctance at returning such a precious memory that sparkles with all the colours of the rainbow. Satisfied that she has completed her task, I oversee her return to her slumbering body. Knowing that on her upcoming seventh birthday, as predetermined by cosmic forces, she will lose all memory of being a rebirther and having past lives.

My name is Isaac Newton. I am a rebirther and in training to become a cosmic caretaker when I will have as much power in the cosmic world as I once had on Earth. To my mind, the accolade is well overdue.

1

THE MEMORY 1664

Isaac tucked his lank, shoulder-length hair inside his nightcap and wrapped his cloak around himself as the cold grip of winter's chill seeped into his bones and he prepared for a long night of observation. Believing, as he did, in sleep being an affectation of the lesser man. His makeshift observatory in Cambridge College loft was his sanctuary. Where he could lose himself in thoughts about the cosmos, away from the prying eyes and judgmental whispers of his peers. Glancing at his calculations he carefully adjusted the borrowed telescope, eager to find the comet and continue plotting its course.

With his keen eye pressed against the telescope, he searched and searched for the elusive comet. His mind raced as he checked his calculations against these new observations, meticulously documenting them in a code only he could understand. As he found the comet and plotted its curve on his chart his thoughts were consumed by the laws of Kepler and their implications on its path. Suddenly he jumped away from the telescope hardly believing what he saw. There were two comets in the night sky. He felt ecstatic, and that nothing on Earth could equate to his love for the cosmos, its vast expanse of stars and galaxies swirling in a maternal embrace. At four in the morning as his eyes grew too weary to continue with complete accuracy he wrapped his cloak around himself, lay on the makeshift bed on the floor and fell asleep.

Later that morning, Isaac waited outside his mentor, Isaac Barrow's study. Hearing Barrow's familiar voice call out "Enter" and with a firm grip, he turned the stubborn bronze handle and stumbled into the room. A wave of warm air greeted him as he stepped inside, noting enviously that a fire was blazing in the hearth. Placing his mathematics paper on Barrow's desk he couldn't help but notice Barrow's dishevelled appearance. His trademark white cravat was tainted with wine stains and his waistcoat buttons looked like they were about to burst from their settings and blind anyone sitting opposite. Isaac made a mental note to stand for the duration of their meeting. Both to avoid such a calamity and to make a hasty retreat once Barrow acknowledged his submission.

It seemed that his mentor was in no rush to oblige, and gauging that Barrow, favoured by Charles II for his wit, expected some good-natured banter, he told him of his sightings the previous night.

Barrow was still in a stupor from his opium binge, barely feigning interest in his musings on the heavens. But he persisted, determined to impress his mentor with his theories.

"I observed not one but two comets through the telescope last night," he told him.

Barrow looked up at him. "Alas, my eyesight is too bad for peering into the sky, even with the help of a telescope, but what do you believe the comets were up to?"

Isaac attempted a witticism of his own, "Do you not see, Barrow? The comets are not random wanderers but are tasked by the counsel of an intelligent being to choreograph the elliptical dance of the spheres."

He could almost feel the gears turning in Barrow's mind as he awoke from his haze.

"You mean to prove Kepler's laws," he remarked.

Emboldened by his response, Isaac continued, "I like to imagine that every planet and every star in the cosmos takes part in the perpetual dance of the heavens.

Barrow smiled and challenged him.

"But Newton, surely Kepler meant it as an orchestra that produces the music of the spheres and mathematical harmony, not a dance. A dance doesn't suggest harmony to me."

Nevertheless, Isaac stood firm in his belief – for to him, the heavens were a magnificent performance that surpassed any human creation and affected all life on Earth.

He replied, "Kepler may have spoken of an orchestra, but to me, it is a dance. One that exudes mathematical precision and cosmic balance."

He watched with disdain as Barrow reached for a beeswaxed clay pipe from the stand on his desk. In between testing the draw on his pipe and expertly packing it with tobacco, Barrow said, "The Pythagoreans taught us that the heavenly orbs resonate to produce mathematical music, audible only to our souls."

Before Isaac could voice his opinion, Barrow turned to him with a disarming smile. "I think dance is purely from your imagination Newton. It might indicate that you need to be less of a recluse and attend a ball at court."

Isaac's thoughts immediately drifted to Catherine, the girl he had tried to learn to dance with, in a room above her father's cramped Apothecary shop. He shuddered at the memory of her screaming as he accidentally stepped on her foot. Her brother Arthur appeared on the scene, though Catherine made light of it, adoring him as she did. But the next day, on the way to school, Arthur kicked him hard in the stomach and whispered in his ear, "See how you like sudden pain!" Despite winning the subsequent fight against him, Isaac couldn't bring himself to face another dancing lesson from Catherine.

He turned to Barrow with a forced smile. "I fear it would only lead to disappointment for my dance partner sir."

Truthfully, Isaac wanted nothing more than to escape the conversation and retreat to his observatory and into the cosmos. He yearned for the safety of his inner world, his calculations and the orbit of the comets. He turned to look longingly at the door, not wanting to dwell on his ineptitude as a dance partner, nor compete for superior intellect with the Lucasian Professor.

Barrow suddenly asked, "Are you not lonely, Newton? "

"Preferring to be by oneself is different from the emotional state of loneliness sir. There is a whole cosmos to explore and not enough hours in the day for exploration."

The outside world was a constant source of disappointment for Isaac Newton. People too consumed with superficial matters, unable to see the depth and value within themselves. A reliable telescope however could transport him to another realm and was worth ten conversations with his estranged mother who had abandoned him at birth. In his inner world, he found solace that surpassed any mere discussion. He preferred to be alone, but he was never lonely.

His heart raced as he scanned the room for a way out. Barrow's piercing gaze held him captive, unwilling to let him leave now that his mind had been stirred into action. The man leaned in, his pipe clenched tightly between yellowed teeth, and Isaac could feel the weight of his words before they even left his mouth. He was trapped, both physically and mentally, as Barrow continued to attempt to engage him in conversation.

They had similar upbringings, sent to live with grandparents at an early age, but they had very different personalities. They were two sides of the same coin, forged from similar beginnings but tempered by different fires. While Barrow soared like a vibrant butterfly in social circles, Newton preferred his solitary hermit shell, enabling him to chase his passions in peace.

Barrow said encouragingly, "So what of these comets Newton?"

Dropping his guard, Newton answered, "I watched them until I fell asleep and when I slept, I dreamed that the first comet sent a destructive meteorite to Earth, but this was cancelled out by the second white comet which sent several small meteorites of different colours of the rainbow to enrich the Earth. It seemed prophetic."

Newton observed Barrow gripping the stem of his pipe, taking long, contented draws before he enquired, "Were you able to decipher the dream?"

As the room filled with the unpleasant miasma of tobacco smoke, Newton ruminated over the question and longed to return to the cold comfort of his chambers. Barrow sat across from him, a smug look on his face as he spoke about making mincemeat out of some young theologians who dared to challenge his beliefs about the biblical flood. They opposed him believing it was caused by a comet set on a path destined by physics to perform its task. Newton kept his opinions close to his chest, knowing that one wrong word could make him the subject of Barrow's next dinner party anecdote.

Newton answered respectfully, "I am no Joseph sir. However, the actions of the second comet made me wonder whether white light is composed of a rainbow of colours. It is something that I wish to begin to investigate if I may take your leave."

His eyes lingered on Barrow, his mentor, and saw him give an admiring glance. Though Newton's face betrayed nothing, his mind was ablaze with calculations and theories.

"Take care, Newton, social isolation can nurture not only genius but madness too."

Newton sensed a paternal tone as the professor added, "I have said enough. At least you aren't claiming that the comets you observe are portends of disaster and plague. Cambridge is awash with such ignorant prophecies!"

Newton felt a pang of agitation as he realised he had unintentionally walked backwards while Barrow spoke. Making his way towards the door, he couldn't help but feel like Barrow had been toying with him the entire time.

"Indeed, you may go," Barrow said, looking up.

He noticed Barrow opening his paper on Euclid and taking a deep drag from his pipe.

Isaac Newton was being dismissed.

Returning to his study Isaac determined that not only would he replace Barrow as the Lucasian professor at the university but that he would find an explanation for the colours of the rainbow and name the law of force affecting the motion of comets in the cosmos.

2

COMETS AND PLAGUE CARRIERS 1665

The distance between Cambridge and London, as the crow flies, was roughly fifty miles. In both cities, the constellations shone brilliantly against the night sky without any obstruction from light pollution. On a chilly January evening, James Stafford trekked back home from a coffee house in London where he had been discussing the path of a recent comet.

Unlike his contemporary Isaac Newton, James was not an academic. However, he possessed an insatiable thirst for knowledge and was self-taught in astronomy, astrology, and geometry. These fields were all crucial in understanding how the movements of planets and stars impacted the lives of people on Earth. Despite being old enough to attend university, James' father had never considered such a possibility for him. Instead, James found solace in his shared interest with his mother: alchemy. Their family's saltpetre business only fuelled their curiosity even more. Saltpetre was a key ingredient in numerous alchemical processes. James was known locally as 'The Saltpetre man who shovelled up shit.'

As the evening fell, a comet blazed through the sky with as much light as a second moon. James rushed home to join his household, all huddled together in anticipation of the much-talked-about celestial display.

Pamphlets handed out across London claimed that comets were divine messengers. The members of the household, caught up in the fervour, believed it to be true. James, always attuned to the atmosphere, sensed a mix of fear, and wonder as they gazed upwards. He gave a reassuring nod to his mother before taking the opportunity to remind them all:

"If we make a great effort towards a calm and sober behaviour, and relinquish any overweening pride, we have nothing to fear."

"Will it bring famine and disease, dear brother?" asked his twelve-year-old only sister, Mathilde, glancing mischievously at Sara, their servant girl, known for her insight on celestial matters.

James glared at Sara, then turned to their mother with a sense of urgency. "Mama, do you have any updates on Papa's return?" His voice was strained, and his eyes darted around the small gathering, ensuring all eyes were on him. He could feel Sara's discomfort, but it was worth it to divert their mother and the servants from focussing on her predictions.

"John will inform us if there is any news," their mother replied cautiously before dabbing at her eyes. "Can anyone still see the comet?" she added as a distraction while she wiped away tears.

All eyes turned towards the sky once more.

As the sun dipped below the horizon each evening for three months, crowds gathered to witness the comet's nightly show. The celestial traveller grew and shrank, shifting from fiery red to soft pink to brilliant blue. On its final appearance, a fluorescent green halo appeared around the comet, casting an otherworldly glow over the city of London, giving it an eerie aura that seemed to create day from night itself. For there was no more darkness that night and more than a hundred church bells rang in unison across London in an attempt to curry favour with God.

In March, James' father, Henry Stafford, a Cavalier art dealer, and James' elder brother, Harry, returned to England aboard a ship from the Netherlands. They were part of the recovery committee appointed by King Charles II for the repossession of King Charles I's works of art, either sold or stolen during the Commonwealth regime.

It had been a long sea journey of five days due to tides and weather. They experienced a stormy voyage, and both were exhausted from the rough waters and seasickness. They no longer wore periwigs or their usual attire, which signified their status in society. The nature of their assignment required them to be invisible. They didn't have time to fully recover from their sea voyage and as they disembarked into the early morning fog at Chatham Docks, horses were waiting for them to ride straight home.

The rain came down in sheets and their hats and cloaks became sodden once again. The cavalier signalled to a group of men, waiting on the quay for his arrival. Trusted King's men, who had been Royalist soldiers the cavalier once served with. They waited with a coach and horses to collect the large trunk of tapestry pieces and a small trunk of gifts for the family as they were offloaded from the ship. All being well, the coach would arrive at their home in London a few hours after father and son. Secreted in the larger trunk were two valuable works of art that once belonged to Charles I. A Titian and a Bronzino. Their mission had been successful.

Father and son rode hard to their home in London. They arrived at their stables in the early evening and were surprised to be greeted by Mathilde.

Frustrated by her inability to embroider a butterfly in her sampler, she snuck out of her embroidery instruction that afternoon leaving behind her latest attempt. It was a tangled, knotted mess of silk threads and beads. Placing the treasured silver needle in its pouch she escaped, and hid in the upper store of the stable, which stored hay. There she sat and twirled a bead between her sore fingers.

Fran, Mathilde's loyal companion, had made it her mission to teach Mathilde the intricate art of stump work. With every stitch, Fran demonstrated she reminded Mathilde that the stitches were caterpillars that would eventually become butterflies, signifying the family's unwavering loyalty to the monarchy. But for Mathilde, who saw Fran as a sister, the hours spent on embroidery felt like torture that even the special silver needle could not alleviate. Its prick to the finger caused as much blood to spill and ruin the linen and silk threads as did the iron wire needles. She could never imagine herself perfecting the skill deemed necessary for a future wife and mother. Though she understood Fran wanted her to have something to show her father on his return she found that she could only think of his return and could not concentrate on the task that required her full attention.

When she heard the sound of horses' hooves over cobbles, she quickly but carefully descended the rough wooden ladder, which could leave splinters in one's already sore fingers if you grasped the rungs too tight. Safely descended she ran to her father as he dismounted from his horse. She threw her arms around him, and the cavalier bent and buried his face in her hair, which smelled of rosemary oil.

The contrasting smell of horse sweat and dung that permeated the stable was not lost on him. He pulled stray pieces of hay out of her hair, feeling uncomfortable and embarrassed at how he must stink, not having washed in days.

Setting Mathilde to one side, he took a tiny cloth parcel from the breast of his doublet and handed it to her. She opened the parcel and found a precious gold and coral necklace. He recited the tale the jeweller spun when selling him the necklace, possibly one of many.

"The jeweller assured me that it is sprinkled with stardust from the tail of a comet that showered down upon the Hague,"

She looked up into his face and exclaimed, "There was a comet here too papa. I saw it."

Into her ear, he whispered, "I was fortunate to see the recent comet's path through Huygens's telescope at his Voorburg estate."

His daughter's eyes shone as she marvelled at the specks of diamond-like stardust that studded the yellow gold and he felt her impatience for him to secure it around her neck. As he did so, she covered him in kisses. He watched as she ran across the courtyard to find Francine and show off her necklace.

Henry, the eldest son, named after his father, according to family tradition (though everyone called him Harry to distinguish him from his father), could be heard getting his horse settled for the evening. The cavalier knew that his oldest son felt passionate about treating his horse with respect, believing it would serve him better with attention lavished on it. He shrewdly left Harry to his perceived duties.

As he entered the kitchen from the courtyard, their youngest child Gabriel, aged twelve, rushed to embrace him, as his wife Anne, supervised their evening meal. He was reminded of his lack of hygiene and put out his hand to deter physical contact.

He said, "It is time I retire to my bedchamber for a wash and a well-deserved sleep."

Anne blew him a kiss and he gave her a tired smile, pretending to catch the kiss he applied it to his lips. As he made his way out of the kitchen towards the staircase he stopped, remembering his eldest son.

"Please try to ensure Harry does the same. John will wake me when the coach turns up."

Anne nodded and sent Gabriel to find Harry. Bone-weary he climbed the wooden stairs with something still on his mind and he could feel her watching his ascent from below waiting for added instructions. She knew him so well. Each wooden step dipped in its centre warped from the moisture of the kitchen below, aided by two centuries of footsteps. He found himself comforted by the well-worn, tired staircase and knew he should leave her to resume her chosen duties. But he was always like this after an important assignment, he would forget that Anne knew how to manage a household as well as a successful saltpetre business and apothecary, though she was quick to remind him. They always went through this staircase ritual. Suddenly it came to him, he turned and added, "Please have the kitchen supply the very best refreshments for my friends when they arrive."

"Do you wish for James to welcome them?"

Ashamed of forgetting his second-born son he put his hand to his brow in contemplation then quickly dismissed the idea. "No. I imagine he is ensconced in the laboratory and besides, he has nothing in common with my friends. John will wake me, and I will welcome them."

"But.."

"Goodnight my love."

The next day the trap door to the basement cellar needed to be kept open, and the household was warned to keep away from the steps leading down.

Gabriel stood at the top of the steps and listened to a scattering of applause as the treasures were uncovered. His mother appeared at his side.

"Has he brought back something special?" Gabriel asked, looking directly at her.

"Hush, I cannot say. I do not wish to tempt fate. Yet I think the King will be pleased."

She took Gabriel by his reluctant shoulders and led him away.

That night, a new, smaller comet appeared in the sky and could be seen each night for a month. This second comet would send showers of red, orange, yellow, green, blue, indigo and violet meteorites down onto the land.

3

SEARCHERS 1665

In the dead of night, Gabriel woke from his stupor to the sounds of pounding fists on the door. Disoriented, he thought they were at his bedroom door; they seemed so close. He lay as still as possible beneath his blanket, heart pounding, listening intently. As he came to his senses, he realised that the accompanying voices were from outside in the street. He pushed himself onto his elbows in bed and put his ear to the mullioned window. Searchers!

"Open the door. We know you have a dead body, a plague sufferer, in there!"

His bedroom lamp added a small amount of light to the room. Sara, the maid, always ensured that a lamp was lit, as she knew him to be scared of the dark. Gabriel confided in her that he saw faces in the wall hangings, in the blankets, and even in the wooden panelling. He pulled the blanket around his shoulders and shook with fear. He knew that his sister, Mathilde, had developed a large bulbous sore, and he recalled the recent instructions he overheard father give the servants. That, if visitors called, she should be hidden in the cellar until they could depart for their country house in Eyam. He regularly eavesdropped on conversations and foolishly believed his cloak would give him the power of invisibility.

According to his father, Eyam was located so far north that it was considered a haven from the deadly plague. Secluded and surrounded by heath-clad hills, they would be safe there. He felt relieved; he was sure Mathilde would get better at Eyam. The sooner they left for Eyam, the better. He did not like to think of his sister in the cellar.

The cellar housed newly acquired works of art from the Netherlands, including sacks of saltpetre and barrels of wine from France. Large and spacious, with a couple of long wooden tables down one wall, it had a window overlooking the garden. The walls were adorned with completed tapestries, some waiting to be hung in the main part of the house and others destined for the homes of eager customers.

He had sometimes seen his father unfolding paintings at the tables. Harry, his older brother, informed him that they were models for tapestries to be woven in England. For that purpose, the paintings were cut into strips before they left the Netherlands. They were easier to disguise and carry.

One corner of the cellar stored large canvas bags, which transported the strips of canvas easily and safely. Priceless works of art recently smuggled back from the Netherlands, were immediately taken to the cellar.

Gabriel looked at the dead fly floating on the water in the wash basin. His father believed in washing in icy water. Gabriel would sneak down to the kitchen, where Sara would heat water for him to use and deliver it to his room. He picked up his thick woollen cloak lying across the bed (for extra warmth). Though it was already April, there were snow flurries only yesterday. He wrapped the cloak around himself and got out of bed.

He tiptoed barefoot across the cold, wooden floor, undid the door latch, and then crept to the top of the stairs. Beeswax candles in sconces in the hall were alight. Peering down from the staircase, he observed a flurry of hushed and coordinated movements that would remain completely hidden from anyone outside.

James, his brother, recently returned from visiting his fiancée's family, and John, their manservant, carefully carried his sister, Mathilde. She was dressed only in a shift with stocking feet, on a blanket down the steps into the dark cellar below. His father held the trapdoor open. The boy imagined that his sister would have to lie on the floor. He remembered seeing rats on the floor of the cellar.

He watched his mama direct Fran, using the signs that Fran understood, being deaf. As Fran understood her instructions, she took the covered basket from his mama and quickly followed the others down into the cellar. Sara joined his sister in the cellar, and everyone else returned to the hall so as not to arouse suspicion.

John, the footman, stood by a wall sconce silently and meticulously checking off each item to be loaded onto the coach. Fran returned the rug to its position, covering the trap door. His father, overseeing everything, signalled for James to open the front door. Two elderly women, both with harsh features and sly eyes, strode into the hall carrying white office rods.

The stench from them wafted up to Gabriel, and he felt sick to his stomach. These were the searchers. A parish constable remained in the front doorway. The taller of the two women spoke. She wheezed as she spoke and scratched herself continually, though her clothing was moving of its own accord.

“We have been sent to affirm whether the body you have claimed died from natural causes did indeed do so.”

“We also intend to search this house to see if there are any plague sufferers here.”

“Do you know that you must report plague sufferers to the authorities?”

While she spoke, the other searcher, short and round, looked around at everyone assembled, studying each face for expressions of nervousness. She gave a ghastly smile, displaying three discoloured fangs in her large, grotesque mouth. She looked up at Gabriel and crooked her finger, beckoning for him to join the group. He remained frozen on the spot.

"I would like to know who reported a dead body on these premises," demanded father. He looked directly at the searchers and continued, "As you will see, that is not the case." He raised his voice for the parish constable to hear and said, "It would be usual for a doctor to be called for; don’t you agree?"

“We only do what we are told, sir.” The tall searcher looked at the constable, who nodded in affirmation.

"I shall complain to the alderman about this," said Father.

"Is this everyone in the household?" she asked.

"Yes,"

"Do you only have one servant sir?" the tall searcher asked in an incredulous tone.

"The other manservant, a maid, and my daughter have travelled on to Eyam. The manservant will help prepare our country house. We travel there ourselves tonight," Father lied.

"If we find a dead body here or anyone here with the plague tokens, you do know that we will have to seal the house up for 40 days—and you won't be going anywhere!" cackled the short searcher.

Gabriel's mother took a lamp from the hall table and confidently led the searchers through every room in the house. Gabriel watched them leave the hall. Feeling less fearful, he put his hand on the smooth, worn oak banister, steadied himself, and descended the stairs. Meanwhile, a plague watchman appeared at the doorway. He wore a greatcoat and dark, battered hat. He carried a lantern and staff in one hand. In his other hand, he held a small rattle that he shook to grab people's attention.

"Everything alright here?" His voice echoed into the night.

Josiah, the bearer of the dead, replied. "It appears we are on a fool's errand,"

"Ah, not to worry, Josiah. Are we to suppose that the women are giving this a clean bill of health?" Artemus asked.

He put the lantern and rattle to one side and began rubbing his cold hands together. He nodded his head rapidly as if he knew the reply.

"It seems there was no ill health to start with Artemus," Josiah answered, "These good people are off to the fresh country air of Derbyshire as we speak."

Looking towards Gabriel's father, Josiah added, "Ain't that right, sir?"

As Josiah spoke, Gabriel noticed Artemus looking towards his father, busily directing John and his older brothers to take some heavily packaged paintings and some large canvas bags out to the coach that appeared in the back courtyard.

"Indeed, we are my good man," father replied.

"Do you have your passes to get out of London, sir? "

Father showed Artemus the passes, which proved we were not plague carriers and asked, "I wonder if, if I were to make it worth your while Artemus, would you be able to deliver three notes?"

Father continued, "One to Mr Goldston near Popes Head Alley, one to Mr Thomson, who has a little room over the Porters Lodge in Westminster, and one to Mr Farriner Jr., apprentice baker of Pudding Lane?"

The recipient's addresses were visible on the folded letters, sealed with wax and engraved with father's signature ring. Artemus nodded and winked at him. Father put the handwritten letters into a leather pouch, recited the addresses once more, and ordered John to fetch his purse. Artemus, unable to read, watched the manservant disappear and smiled. He took the pouch from Father and made a pretence of reading the names that he remembered. "My memory serves me well, sir. I shall deliver forthwith sir, and I am very grateful to you, sir."

Gabriel remained frozen on the rug, fearful that if he moved, the rug would move too and expose the trap door. Fran put her arm around him and gently guided him into the kitchen.

Candles in sconces and table lamps gave a comforting glow to the kitchen. He imagined his father sitting at the top of the long table, where there were a couple of table lamps, composing the notes he spoke of. There were bundles of papers loosely tied with leather strings still lying on the table. An inkwell, quills, and a beautiful new silver fountain pen were also in evidence. Gabriel had never seen his father use the kitchen to compose letters. Today was a strange day.

As Gabriel sat down, he noticed a fragment of a note on the floor. Gabriel picked it up. He knew his letters and tried to read them. It contained groups of numbers. He tried to figure out if the numbers had meaning. It took his mind off his concern that the searchers would discover his sister.

Fran held her hand out to him, and he gave the fragment to her. Gabriel watched her as she secured a leather string through a ready-made hole in the note and attached it to the rest of the papers. She carefully put them, and the writing implements, into the large writing box, engraved with the family crest, sitting on the table. She closed it securely and snuffed out the nearby candles.

Afterwards, she moved further down the table to the heart of the kitchen. She picked up a tiny apple-shaped pomander ball and demonstrated that she wanted him to help her finish it. Gabriel nodded his agreement and took a seat. Sitting at the kitchen table, he began rolling the sweet-smelling mixture into a ball. Copying Fran, he coated the small ball with a powdered mixture of cinnamon and cloves. After this, he rolled it through a secret alchemical concoction to blend in these ingredients and preserve the smell. Fran kneaded the mixture together, and Gabriel mirrored her actions. Finally, Fran melded it all back into a ball. She took Gabriel's silver pomander and carefully fitted the small ball inside. He held it to his nose, sniffed, and smiled contentedly. Ida, the cook, held up a small bag holding her mixture and looked directly at Fran.

She added a couple of signs that they both understood and were familiar to all in the household, as she said loudly, "I swear that sweet smell is the longest lasting that can be made anywhere in London."

Fran watched Ida's mouth move, smiled gratefully at her, and continued to fill the family's pomanders as Gabriel looked on. He looked around the kitchen, his favourite room in the house.

There were lavender nosegays at every window, and the fire burned brightly. A pot hung over the fire, on the boil, and beeswax candles illuminated the room. He felt warm, comforted, and safe.

Ida came out of the cold pantry carrying a large, salted ham. Using her foot to kick the door closed, she hauled the pot with an effort to the sink and set it down. Ida preserved the ham by mixing kitchen salt with a small amount of saltpetre. The recipe belonged to his mother, and it seemed to save the ham for as long as they needed. She carefully transferred the ham into a bowl of warm milk to remove as much salt as possible. As Gabriel watched, he could hear the searchers speaking in the entrance hall again. He crept to the doorway leading into the hall to watch and listen.

"Forgive us for our intrusion during your hour of closing up," said the tall searcher to Mother.

"That is quite alright," replied Mother. “As you said, you were only doing your job.”

"It don’t make sense," said the short searcher, eying up the money passing between my father and Artemus.

"I assure you that we have no dead bodies here, but if you would like to look in the outhouses, you are more than welcome," said Mother, pointing in the direction of the gardens.

“No, we won’t this time, madam; we have other properties to visit this night. We’ll take up no more of your time.” said the tall searcher, and the night intruders left.

Once outside the frontage of the property, the searchers, the bearer, and the watchman gathered and whispered together.

“What do you intend to do with the letters Artemus?” The tall searcher asked.

“Why, burn them, of course,” Artemus answered, fondling the coins in his pocket as he spoke.

"I have neither the time nor the inclination to pass them through steaming vinegar to destroy their contamination."

He fixed his hat firmly on his head before adding, "I do not intend to go on a fool's errand to deliver them either."

"Then a share of the coins is in order," she answered quickly.

"Is it not?" She looked around the small gathering, and all except Artemus nodded in agreement.

Outnumbered, Artemus shared the coins. As they all made their way to leave, Artemus added, "We should return in a few nights."

The others turned back with questioning faces.

Artemus answered, "I had it on good authority that this was certain to be a plague-ridden house where more money could be made."

The tall searcher replied, "You know more than you're telling us, Artemus."

"Spit it out!"

"All I heard is that this is a house built on the profits of pigeon muck, and where there's muck, there's money to be made."

"Mark my words."

4

HARRY'S TALES

As soon as the searchers left, Fran hurried down to the cellar. Gabriel's gaze followed his father's descent and lone return a while later. After carefully concealing the trap door with a rug, his mother gestured for Sara, the maid, to help dress Gabriel. Afterwards Sara hustled him out the door and onto the coach, while the grown-ups continued to hurry with loading it up.

Outside in the stable yard, the horses pawed at the ground eagerly, their impatient neighs sending clouds of mist into the chilly night air. The full moon illuminated everything, surrounded by a starry sky. Gabriel couldn't help but marvel at several shooting stars gliding across the heavens —each one more magnificent than the last until they faded away into nothingness as if they had never been there at all. A full moon was the reason for choosing this time of the month to travel. It would be their guide on this journey.

Gabriel felt Sara's sharp grip on his arm, scolding him for his sluggish pace. He resisted being pushed onto the coach, feeling suffocated by the warmth of his woollen cloak. But he knew he had no choice but to comply with her demand. He noticed that on one of the seats lay folded blankets, which he hoped would keep Mathilde warm. On the floor, lay the basket of food prepared by Ida for the long journey. The smell wafted towards him, triggering memories of the warm, bustling kitchen, easing his anxious mind. He sat next to the blankets, picked one up, and wrapped it around himself to warm it, ready for Mathilde.

He pulled the coach blind to one side and watched Sara returning to the house, hoping to see Mathilde carried to the coach. Instead, his mother leaned inside the coach, her face grim.

"Gabriel," she said, "Your papa and I have had to make a difficult decision. We must leave Mathilde behind in London."

His heart sank at her words; he knew that her condition had worsened, and the journey would be too much for her fragile state. His father joined them, whispering something in his mother's ear before she rushed back inside.

Gabriel held back tears as his father solemnly stood at the coach door. He understood the gravity of their decision—days of travel could be fatal for Mathilde. His father assured him that a doctor in London would restore her to full health. Although still worried, Gabriel clung to this glimmer of hope.

"When Mathilde is well enough, she and Francine will travel by coach to meet us."

He spoke with conviction though Gabriel could see the doubt in his eyes.

He added, "I have every confidence that your mother is instructing Francine in how to care for your sister. She will not let us down."

Gabriel heard the distant sound of the bellman ringing his bell and calling out "Past one of the o'clock" as his father returned to the house. He carefully placed the warmed blanket on top of the cold ones in the coach.

With boisterous energy, Harry, his eldest brother, bounded up the steps of the coach and Gabriel's mood changed to one of palpable excitement. It had been too long since he had last spent time with Harry, always away on an adventure and more recently with their beloved father off doing important business. Gabriel felt vulnerable and lonely in their large house, his mother and James were always locked away in their laboratory, leaving him in the care of Sara, the maid. With Harry by his side once more, he felt a sense of brotherly camaraderie.

"Let me regale you with stories of our adventures," Harry exclaimed dramatically as he sat beside his younger brother.

Gabriel leaned in eagerly, ready for another retelling of their favourite tales of 'Roundheads and Cavaliers,' where the cavaliers always emerged victorious. Oh, how he missed those moments when Harry would sit by his bedside and weave tales of adventure until he drifted off to sleep, dreaming of brave sword fights.

"Not just any tale tonight," Harry whispered slyly, "but one from when Papa first introduced me to the art trail."

His eyes sparkled mischievously as he mentioned their family business, though James argued with him that saltpetre was the family's true trade. As the third son Gabriel never imagined taking part in the family business, he was meant for the church. However, Harry recently had a brush with death and Gabriel understood he wanted him to take his place working with their father if something were to happen to him.

Gabriel settled into his seat on the coach to listen. He had never worn so many clothes at once before. Yet he was grateful for them as he sat motionless in the coach.

He wore a half shirt topped with a full shirt, with a woollen waistcoat under a long woollen coat. Sara had insisted on him wearing Holland drawers under his breeches for added insulation. And finally, on top of all these, he wore his warm woollen cloak. On his feet, he wore woollen stockings and black leather jackboots. On his hands, he wore sheepskin gloves. Only his face felt the cold. He looked across at Harry and imagined him similarly attired except for the gloves. With the addition of a sword, of course.

Gabriel heard the pride in Harry's voice as he began with his tale of their father's daring expeditions across the continent. Searching for priceless works of art to add to King Charles I's collection. The journey was dangerous, as travelling by land in Europe at this time was perilous. To mitigate the risk, they would travel by river whenever possible.

"Was our papa ever in grave danger?" Gabriel asked.

Harry paused dramatically before answering. "Most certainly! They were all in danger and they usually had a heavily armed escort. But when they didn't, they took turns keeping watch."

Gabriel's eyes widened in awe as his older brother Harry told him tales of daring adventures. He listened intently, knowing that Harry trusted him to keep these stories secret. Gabriel was always fascinated with his brother's stories, unlike his brother James who often seemed uninterested. It made Gabriel happy to have this special bond with Harry.

Harry reached down and pulled out his sword, placing it on his lap for Gabriel to admire but not touch. Gabriel could see it was a beautiful European rapier, with intricate designs etched into the blade. The patterns displayed the bladesmith's skill and Gabriel admired the weapon's beauty. It was smaller and lighter than Harry's other swords but had already proven its worth in battle. Gabriel knew he had claimed it from a Frenchman he had defeated, unable to retrieve his favourite sword from the man's body. Shuddering at the memory of that particular tale Gabriel urged Harry to continue with his story.

"Forgive me, my dear brother; I wanted to entertain you, not give you nightmares about blood and gore."

Sitting beside his older brother Harry in the dimly lit coach, Gabriel couldn't help being captivated by his every move and word. As they sat together, the scent of roasted ham filled his nostrils, making his stomach growl loudly. Harry paused in his storytelling to reach for the ham from the basket, expertly slicing off a piece with his dagger and offering a piece to him. He declined, too eager to hear the rest of the tale. Gabriel watched as Harry savoured each mouthful, smacking his lips in satisfaction as the flavour of cloves danced on his tastebuds.

“Where was I? Ah yes, the King had sent Papa and his band of brave cavaliers on dangerous journeys across Europe to retrieve valuable art collections.”

Gabriel's eyes widened as his brother's storytelling abilities mesmerised him. Despite the limited space, Harry's animated gestures with the rapier transported them into the scene he depicted.

“Why did the King want these collections?” Gabriel asked eagerly.

Harry grinned mischievously and winked at his brother. “You'll find out soon enough,” he teased, before sucking the ham’s fat from his fingers and wiping his blade clean on a nearby cloth.

Gabriel's eyebrows furrowed with concern as he listened to his brother's tale of innocent civilians subjected to unspeakable horrors and the visions he conjured up weighed heavily on his mind.

"Did Papa try to help them?" Gabriel asked, hoping for an answer that would ease his troubled thoughts.

Harry's face turned grave and using the cloth he dried his chapped and calloused hands before answering, "He couldn't involve himself in wars. His specific mission from our King was to acquire the most exquisite pieces of art assembled as quickly as possible.”

Gabriel worried if deep down it was their greed driving their actions. Before he could voice his thoughts, Harry said, "It was as if the King knew his time was running out. Our papa had to leave his protective band of comrades to go alone on a crucial quest for the old King. He was to purchase a precious still-life painting by Torrentius, an alchemist known for his mysterious works. And where do you think they found this prized possession? In a simple bakery in Amsterdam."

Gabriel's eyes widened in horror at his father's plight, but he knew what an alchemist was. He would often sneak into the laboratory where his brother James and their mother conducted experiments. He was fascinated by alchemy, watching eagerly as they created potions, remedies, and even gunpowder for fireworks. Lost in his brother's words, he absorbed every detail with excitement.

"After a treacherous journey, Papa successfully acquired the painting and returned to the King's court."

Harry leaned in closer lowering his voice to a whisper. "Papa was fortunate in securing the painting. Shortly afterwards Torrentius was imprisoned in the Netherlands for claiming his paintings were created through magic!"

Gabriel's eyes widened with fascination. He held his breath, eager for more information.

"Was he a wizard? I overheard one of the servants call our brother James a wizard."

Harry took on a concerned look but said, "He wasn't a wizard,"

He continued. "But they tortured him all the same."

"They also suspected he was the leader of the secret society of the Rosy Cross, that many alchemists belong to, even now."

“A secret society,” Gabriel repeated, his mind racing with possibilities.

“But I don't think he ever admitted to using the dark chamber,” Harry added ominously.

“The dark chamber?” Gabriel exclaimed. “What is that?”

Harry chuckled softly as Gabriel pulled the blind across and glanced outside at their father, who was bawling out directions to the coachman to be careful with the pieces of art he was loading. He returned his attention to Harry and persisted, “Is the dark chamber somewhere where magic happens?”

"Some may think so, but it is merely a time-consuming process artists use. It is also known as the 'Camera Obscura' in certain circles."

Gabriel’s face fell with disappointment. Art techniques did not hold the same allure for him as they did for Harry.

In a whispered voice, Harry leaned in and added.

“Torrentius did admit, however, that the sound of humming bees came from his studio. Although no bees were in evidence.”

Gabriel was hooked once again." Did he summon bees with magic?" he asked in a hushed tone.

Harry's eyes sparkled with excitement as he confirmed, "Yes, witnesses claimed that he used alchemy to bind his toxic paint. But it wasn't just for show, it was necessary for his unique technique."

Gabriel's hands clenched together with intense excitement at the mention of magic. "A true wizard," he whispered, feeling like he was part of a secret world.

"I knew it!"

Gabriel saw Harry's expression turn serious.

"Let's not jump to conclusions about what we consider wizardry to be."

"What do you believe it is then?" Gabriel pressed.

Harry leaned in and replied, "I believe a wizard is someone who can perform magic and use supernatural powers, forbidden magic. Alchemy involves mystical and physical processes that cause transformation. It's different from using magic. That is what Torrentius used. He was an alchemist like your brother, Gabriel. Not a wizard. If your brother were accused openly, he could be sent to the scaffold. Do you understand? Never, ever speak of your brother James as being a wizard."

Harry's accusation stung, and Gabriel couldn't bear the thought of betraying his brother. He could feel tears threatening to spill from his eyes, but he refused to let them. He needed to change the subject before he lost control and appeared weak.

"How do you know so much about him?"

"Because Torrens, as he liked to be called by his friends, couldn't help but brag about his work. He loved creating an air of mystery around himself and his paintings."

Gabriel's wonder turned into curiosity. "Is that why they imprisoned him? For showing off?"

Harry's expression turned serious. "That, and because some saw his abilities as dangerous and forbidden."

Gabriel leaned in closer to his brother Harry, eager to hear more details about the notorious Torrens, the leader of a secret society. He could barely contain his excitement as Harry related his arrest for painting scandalous images of naked women. Harry acted out the prison torture Torrens endured dramatically, as Gabriel clutched a discarded blanket to his chest in fear and fascination.

Gabriel couldn't help interrupting as Harry paused for effect. "Do they call a painting of naked people a 'still life'?"

Harry shook his head with a chuckle and checked to make sure they weren't being overheard before whispering, "You still have much to learn about art, brother. But it's good that you question things; that's how you learn."

A smile spread across Gabriel's face at the compliment. He leaned in closer as Harry patiently explained that the painting was of objects, not people.

"It was a round piece with a flagon, jug, glasses, and a bridle if I recall correctly," Harry said proudly. "And it hung in the King's collection during his lifetime."

Unable to contain his curiosity any longer, Gabriel blurted out, "But what about all those scandalous paintings of naked people? Did King Charles I own those as well?"

Harry's grin grew sly as he leaned in closer to whisper, "That, my dear brother, will forever remain a mystery."

Leaning back in his seat, Harry continued with another fascinating tidbit. Frederick Henry of the Royal House of Orange in the Netherlands had requested a favour from King Charles I on behalf of the Rosy Cross society, that the King save Torrentius from a life in prison by bringing him to England and making him the court painter.

Gabriel's hands clapped together in ecstatic joy. "He lived through the torture. I thought he must have died!" he exclaimed.

Harry stared blankly at Gabriel.

"You said that his limbs were separated," Gabriel explained, his voice filled with excitement. "But since he didn't perish, he must be innocent."

Gabriel saw Harry smile as he leaned in closer to him and whispered. "King Charles I saved him."

Gabriel smiled contentedly and finding Torrentius a difficult word with his stutter said, " King Charles II must possess the only remaining paintings by the bee man."

"No, dear brother," Harry sighed.

Surprised, Gabriel straightened up and waited for Harry, who had paused, but began again with a hint of hatred in his voice, "All the magnificent pieces of art that King Charles I collected were either sold or supposedly destroyed by those traitorous roundheads."

Gabriel's brow furrowed in confusion.

Harry continued, "Including the paintings by Torrentius."

Tears welled up in Gabriel's eyes as he processed this information and Harry's voice grew heated as he spoke. "It is wrong that a King who transformed our country with art would himself be imprisoned for blasphemy. Officially, King Charles I spared Torrentius from death, but no one rose to save the King when he needed it most."

"No one?" Gabriel asked.

Harry almost spat out his next words, "Any supporters were not allowed to vote. He was made to walk through the banqueting hall to the scaffold under the ceiling that portrays the divine right of kings. The cruel irony of that would not have been lost on him."

The family harboured deep resentment towards the Puritans, not just for their brutal murder of their beloved King but also for their plundering and looting of their country home in Eyam. All their silverware and portraits were seized and publicly burned.

Their father had once joked that future generations would never know where they got their good looks from since all their ancestor's portraits were gone. But Gabriel knew it was no joke —it was an immeasurable loss of their history that they would not be able to pass on to their future children.

Gabriel tugged at Harry's cloak, startling him, and asking, "Will our King Charles II get his father's paintings back or were they destroyed like ours?"

Harry paused before whispering, "I'll tell you a secret, brother." He leaned in close, and Gabriel could smell the faint scent of ham on his breath.

"King Charles II did want to recover all of his father's paintings, but no one can find them. We don't believe they were destroyed, as rumoured because they were too valuable. Our spies have searched high and low, but it seems we may never retrieve all of them."

As Gabriel gazed at his older brother, a swell of admiration filled his chest. He yearned to possess the same level of boldness and cunning that Harry had, but he knew deep down that he was more akin to his studious brother, James than he would like to admit. As if reading his thoughts, Harry straightened his posture and spoke with authority.

"Remember our recent trip to the Netherlands?"

Gabriel nodded excitedly, recalling the sweet marzipan wrapped in layers of fabric that Harry had brought back for him.

"We were tasked with finding a Dutch artist who used the camera obscura and could paint a still life like Torrentius." Harry licked the salt that crusted his lips. He asked, "Do you remember what a still life is, brother?

Gabriel nodded, urging the story on.

"Father and I went to the Netherlands, to Delft, with Lord Buckhurst, the Marquis of Dorset." Gabriel lifted the window blind, hearing a shout as something clattered outside, then shuddered, feeling the chill night air. He quickly closed it and gave his full attention to Harry.

"Indeed," Harry continued, "Father suggested an examination of such paintings by an artist named Vermeer, whom Father believed used the dark chamber."

"I remember the dark chamber brother," Gabriel said, disappointment obvious in his voice.

"If we were caught taking paintings out of the Netherlands, we might be flogged, and the paintings would be confiscated and become the property of the Dutch crown."

Harry continued to whisper conspiratorially, "The marquis knew of bakers in the Netherlands that accept what they considered great works of art as payment for their customers' debts. The baker in Delft had portrait paintings by Vermeer, not the still life for which we were hoping. As far as we could ascertain, there are no Torrentius paintings left in the world."

Gabriel's face fell. "An artist such as he should have left something behind after all he went through!"

Harry gave him a mischievous wink and said, "Though we did manage to locate two of King Charles I's paintings! A Bronzino and a Titian both with his branded monogram confirming his ownership. Papa has meticulously listed these items in his inventory and swiftly notified three of Lord Buckhurst's agents through the watchman tonight. He assures them we will safeguard them until the plague subsides."

Gabriel remembered recently standing with their Mother at the top of the cellar steps and hearing the applause beneath them as the paintings were unwrapped and he felt a warm glow of pride for his big brother whom he loved dearly.

Harry continued, "Father purchased one painting for our country house that is my favourite painting in his collection. It is by a Dutch artist who did not sign it. It is of a girl carrying a basket of cherries and wearing a gold necklace with a coral pendant around her neck. The coral would protect her from the plague."

As he listened, Gabriel thought of the new gold and coral necklace his sister wore. It consisted of a gold chain and a coral pendant. Mathilde excitedly told him it was covered in comet dust that had dropped out of the sky. She wore it for their recent family portrait painted just before she fell ill. She would swirl her sage silk dress around for him, making a soft rustling sound that he loved. He knew his brother weaved tales to distract him from the harsh reality of their sister's situation. The stories were a welcome escape, but they could never fully erase the weight of their sister's predicament hanging over them like a dark cloud. John, their manservant, said rumours were widespread that those travelling from the Netherlands brought the plague to England. Was that what was wrong with Mathilde he wondered.

5

ESCAPE TO THE COUNTRY

The horses at last began to move slowly forward, jolting Gabriel out of his bleak reverie. His mother appeared at the coach doorway, and without saying a word, she nodded to his brother. It seemed he should change places with James, who sat outside with the driver, and John, the manservant. Two candle lanterns hung from corners on the footboard, lighting their path. As the brothers changed places, Gabriel saw a pistol pass between them. He also noticed that John carried a sword and a pistol to deter highwaymen. Gabriel's mother climbed into the coach, silently placing one of the blankets over his knees as she sat opposite him. His father joined them, snuffed out the inside lantern, and the coach began its journey.

As the coach rumbled out of the yard, Gabriel could see Ida walking away from the home she had served faithfully ever since he could remember. Laden down with her belongings, she began her walk across London to join her family until their family returned to London after the plague. Sara followed behind her, carrying a small bundle.

Listlessly, Gabriel swayed with the motion of the coach and watched the buildings in the immediate neighbourhood drift by. His neighbour's family left months ago, and their house was securely locked to prevent looters. He worried whether his father remembered to secure their home. The cellar, where his sister and Fran lay, had a door that led out to a kitchen garden and the river. His brother James reassured him that his father had taken precautions and a watchman paid to place heavy locks on all external doors and keep an eye on their house while they were away. He told him that looters would not take the risk of travelling up the river to loot properties. Besides, the family would all return to London when it was safe to do so. Before then, their sister would recover, Fran would contact the coachman, and both would join them soon in Eyam.

Gabriel thought that they had forgotten a crucial factor. Fran, being deaf, would not hear a thief in the night. He feared that if looters were to find the cellar, they could take advantage of her disability.

He looked out from under the hood of his cloak and saw that his brother wiped away silent tears as he spoke. In truth, his brother James was as fearful as him and equally helpless.

Their father described Harry as the foolhardy brother and James as the sensible brother. Gabriel was expected to be the dutiful son. He would receive a college education, as befits a man of the cloth. As the third son, he did not believe he had a choice. He was carried along by Harry's tales and wished to see something of the world. However, knowing that his father would only have his best interests at heart, he became resigned to a life of religious servitude.

His father had not been born wealthy, nor his mother. Yet his father had become a well-known cavalier. He travelled across Europe first as a soldier, fighting the Catholic cause in Europe, amassing a small fortune, and earning a reputation that served him well during the later Civil Wars. The family owed their wealth to their apothecary, saltpetre, and their mother's knowledge of alchemy. Her skills helped landowners grow their produce. It allowed his father to follow his passion for art, which he gained as a soldier during his travels in Europe. He knew his father believed that art would be the family's legacy though he was proud of her support.

Gabriel looked across at them both as they whispered anxiously together. The experience of travelling through the middle of London in the dark during the plague was nightmarish. The cries of women and children echoed through the city, their loved ones lying dead or dying in the houses they passed by. It was a haunting sound that pierced the air repeatedly. He heard his father say that there seemed to be more people about at night than during the day. The coachman lashed out with the horsewhip as people tried to approach the coach.

Gabriel's brothers took turns to sit with the coachman and keep alert. When they returned inside to sit beside him, they no longer spoke, intent on catching up on sleep while snoring loudly.

Suddenly, the much-needed rain began to pour down, dousing the fumigating fires burning endlessly to ward off the plague. The coach came to a halt as the chosen road became swampy. The horses proceeded at a walking pace, then took a slight detour, and the coach continued its route onto the Great North Road, avoiding Finchley Common. As the coachman took the detour, Harry leaned down, pulled the windowless blind across, and shouted into the coach.

"Papa! There is a more direct route. May we go via Finchley Common?"

He added, "It will take less time."

All eyes in the coach were on Father as he looked up at Harry and quickly replied. "Highwaymen lay in wait by the oak tree at Finchley, stealing purses and passes to sell on."

Father half stood to speak more quietly to Harry, though everyone in the coach craned their necks to hear his next words.

"We have no desire to provoke them to murder us. While I have every faith in your sword fighting, I do not see the need to put it to the test when we have other options."

Father deftly resumed his seat and Harry closed the curtain. The coachman continued forward but stayed alert as he drove. Surprisingly, once away from London, the sound of the rain, the companionship of his family, and even the snoring of his brothers made Gabriel feel sleepy. He slept, and, in his sleep, he dreamt of his sister, whom he understood, from carefully listening to his parents' whispers, had caught the plague. It was all he could do not to cry out in his sleep; the dream was so vivid and so real it felt like a warning. He had no Sara beside him to mop his brow and help the visions go away.

They made two overnight stops on the long journey to rest the horses, share a proper bed and eat reasonably good fare. As they approached the Derbyshire hills Gabriel felt a sense of foreboding as birds circled the coach and he was reminded of the bird-like beaked plague doctors of London. He fell asleep imagining the plague had travelled with them to Eyam. But when Gabriel awoke, the first thing he noticed was that they had arrived at their destination. They were safe. Father thanked the coachman and handed him coins for his troubles.

6

THE BASEMENT CELLAR

Fran lay asleep next to Mathilde all through the night. As the morning light entered the basement cellar, she opened her eyes and looked around her. Her eyes widened in horror as she saw a couple of rats climbing stealthily over Mathilde. She picked up the stick she had placed beside herself and whacked one, trying to avoid hurting Mathilde. The rats scuttled into the dark corners of the basement, and Fran sat up and looked around her. The food, wrapped in cloth several times, was secured in a small sack inside the covered basket. The rats attempted to get inside but didn't succeed. Yet. She felt the touch of Mathilde's hand, and Fran's weary eyes looked into her face. Bloody sputum dribbled from the girl's lips, and Fran could see from the rat droppings covering her smock that the rats had been making a feast of it.

Fran couldn't have heard them, but she hadn't felt them near her either. She worried that the responsibility was too much for her. She felt like a failure. Having arrived with Mathilde's father unannounced those few years ago, his young daughter treated her as the longed-for sister of her dreams, and their bond was sealed. She prayed silently, patted the younger girl's hand, and stood up. She needed to get some water and a rag to clean Mathilde.

She opened the double-bolted basement door and a couple of rats escaped and disappeared into the river Tyburn. A pigeon stood on the flight entrance to the small, stone dovecote. Knowing that she loved to draw birds, her guardian first introduced her to the parent of that pigeon when she arrived in London. He explained that it was a trained messenger pigeon but that she could draw sketches of the bird if she so wished. As she handed him the first sketch she had drawn, he reverently placed it in his Bible. She observed this action with a feeling of warmth and satisfaction, knowing he would cherish her gift.

He allowed her to keep a few discarded pigeon's feathers to use as quills. Mathilde's mother taught her to make ink using ferrous sulphate, tannin (from oak galls), and gum.

She learnt to use the quill and ink expertly, storing all her sketches in a locked box in her room.

The pigeon fluffed up its feathers, put its head to one side, and looked at Fran.

Fran sent her thoughts to the pigeon, *I have nothing to report*. The pigeon began to make a contented cooing sound.

Around the dovecote lay the potager garden. Anne borrowed the idea of such a garden from France, though she grew herbs and no vegetables. She grew the herbs for medicinal use and use in cooking. Fran pulled on a frond of lavender and ground the seeds in her palm. She held them to her nose and breathed in the intoxicating smell before scattering them back into the soil. Picking up the empty bucket, she strode across the garden to the river to fill it with water.

The moment she lowered the bucket into the water, she stifled a scream as she watched a rotting corpse float by. She could not, and would not, dare use this water for drinking. The small barrel of ale that Ida left for them would have to suffice. Fran was glad it wasn't raining, but it meant that she could smell the fumigating fires more easily. She worried about the miasma and knew she would feel safer inside. She re-entered the basement cellar. Using a damp rag, she buffed up Mathilde's cloak. A spare set of clothes for each of them lay folded on the table for

when they left to join the others at Eyam.

Mathilde's coral necklace hung around her neck to protect her from the plague, and the silver pomander attached to her smock protected her from bad vapours in the air. Fran possessed a silver pomander too. Fran gently untied the loose smock that hung on Mathilde's frail frame, revealing her weakened state. She placed her hand on Mathilde's feverish chest and could feel a shortness of breath. She checked the bubo under Mathilde's arm, noticing that it had swollen to the size of a small apple. Fran was frightened by the size of the bubo. With no one there to give her advice, she needed to think for herself. She thought that if she had that gruesome thing on herself, she would want to get rid of it. Yes, she would lance it. It was easy enough to do.

Mother left them with a chamber pot, telling Fran to use the urine for cleaning wounds and to give sips of it to Mathilde. Fran took a pigeon feather. She held it in the chamber pot, half-full of piss, to clean the feather. She proceeded to lance the bubo with the clean end of the feather as Mathilde lay sleeping. The pus shot out of the bubo all over Fran's face and chest. Mathilde screamed out in pain.

Fran quickly cleaned them both up using the urine-soaked rag. She covered up the remains of the bubo with clean rags left for the purpose. She noticed bruising covering Mathilde's body. She wondered if Mathilde's mother noticed that before she departed for Eyam. Fran had become her assistant in the apothecary and the art of alchemy, but she had always gone to her for the final word. She realised that the decision to lance the bubo was hers alone. She was not too proud to admit she could be wrong. If her decision proved wrong, she would not trust the family's response to their grief. All she could do was pray and wait for Mathilde to improve.

Fran's stomach grumbled, urging her to eat. She uncovered several cloths to reveal slices of preserved ham, prepared by Ida and the mistress and sliced specifically for them. She thought of the cook, the servants, and the family who had taken her on as one of their own, and tears welled in her eyes. That split second of diverted thought encouraged a rat to move towards the delightful smell of food. Fran caught the movement and covered the food with the cloth while grabbing the stick. She banged it on the stool with all her might, and the rat scampered away as the stick split asunder. She knew she could not afford to drop a morsel.

Pulling off a piece of ham she held it to Mathilde's nose for her to smell the delicious aroma. No reaction. She held it to her mouth. No movement. She ate the piece herself, sucking out all its juices until she had sucked it dry. She manoeuvred the tasteless piece of meat fibre with her tongue into the space where a back tooth had once been. She instinctively knew there was no point in trying to give a piece of ham to Mathilde. She would not have the strength needed to chew it. Its saltiness made Fran thirsty, so she took a sip of ale and swallowed the fibrous remains.

Once more, she securely tied the cloth around the ham to protect it from the vermin. She was certain the rats could detect the scent of the salted ham in the air, and she feared they would become even more brazen in their attempts to steal the precious parcel of food.

She had an idea. She had never seen pigeons eating meat. She would put it in the dovecote for the pigeon to guard. She took the stool, placed it next to the dovecote, picked up the wrapped food, climbed onto the stool, and quickly threw the parcel into the dovecote. The rats would have to contend with the pigeon if they wanted that ham.

When she returned to the cellar, she sat behind Mathilde and lifted her into her arms. She took the ale and tried to make her take sips by holding her mouth open with one hand. She succeeded in getting her to have a couple of sips. She took off the cloth surrounding the underarm bubo on the girl and gently pressed a rag soaked in urine to the wound. As she did so, Mathilde vomited all over herself and afterwards began to cough up more blood.

Gingerly, Fran removed herself from behind Mathilde and took the rag to throw in the river. She collected more lavender fronds from the potager garden and threw them about on the basement floor.

As she cleaned Mathilde again, she wondered whether the family had arrived safely at their first coaching inn. Her guardian informed her that the journey would take eight tedious days. Homeless people would think nothing of stealing the coach and killing all its occupants. She felt safer in the basement with Mathilde for the time being. She began to say prayers for the family's safekeeping, followed by prayers for Mathilde and herself. While reciting them, she fell asleep, exhausted.

7

THE BURIAL PIT

In the darkness of the night, Fran awoke, startled awake by a gust of chilly air. The basement door was open. She immediately went outside and saw, by the light of the full moon, the pigeon panic-fluttering at a rat attempting to climb up to the dovecote. She rushed to the bucket, and, picking it up, threw the rainwater at the rat. The surprised rat dropped to the grass and scampered off.

Fran looked up at the pigeon, busy using its beak to push the parcel of food out of the dovecote.

She caught the parcel as it fell. She stood in the moonlight and opened the parcel, ripping off a piece of salted ham with her teeth. She held the large piece in one hand, securing another parcel containing the coins needed for their travel, inside her smock. As she secured that parcel, she felt a bulbous growth under her armpit. She took a bite of ham, and chewing on it, went into the basement. She had an idea that she got from her observations of birds. She would try to feed her charge like a bird feeds its young, with the juices from her mouth.

As she walked over towards her charge, her heightened sense of smell told her that Mathilde was dead. Fran choked on the regurgitated ham. She could not cry. She could not panic. Neither would help them. She needed to take Mathilde outside in the moonlight to ensure she was dead.

She held onto the girl's ankles and dragged her slowly, as gently as she could, on an empty canvas bag, away from the sacks of saltpetre she had been sitting against. Once she had got her outside, she looked at her closely and felt for her pulse. There was no pulse. The body was cold. An empty vessel no longer holds the water of life. Fran knew in that instant that she had to make quick decisions.

She went into the basement and found the loose flagstone her guardian had shown her.

She carefully prised it out and, using the lamp, looked into the void below. It was the entrance to a short tunnel, and she recognised the ledge he showed her. She put her hand inside and felt around the ledge. She pulled out two small bags. One contained an inventory of paintings and to whom they belonged. She returned the bag to the ledge. The other smaller bag he had shown her the contents of before he stowed it under the flagstone. She tucked that bag inside her smock with the food parcel.

Seeing that the ledge was sturdy, she placed the lamp to the side, and climbed onto her belly into the void, using the ledge as a holding point. The worst that could happen had already happened.

Once inside the void, Fran manoeuvred herself back to the ledge to obtain the lamp. She took the lamp inside the void for seconds to see what was inside before quickly putting it back.

The void floor was carpeted with canvas bags. Fran was sure these were full of tapestries and paintings. She already decided exactly what she was going to do. She was going to give Mathilde the burial she deserved. She was going to preserve her. Exactly like she practised on a starling she found dead near the family warehouses. That still looked well-preserved even though it had died over a year ago. Fran let her instincts guide her. She dragged a couple of canvas bags from within the void to the entrance.

After climbing out of the void, she pulled out the two canvas bags and opened them. They were full of cut pieces of tapestry. In the cellar, Fran pulled two large saltpetre sacks over to the void. Using the sharp knife her guardian left her, she cut open the sacking and poured the saltpetre onto the canvas bags below.

She went out into the moonlit garden and stripped Mathilde naked, using urine-soaked rags to clean her. The pigeon looked on. When a rat crept close to Fran, smelling the dead body or the salted ham secured on her person, the pigeon extended its wings, and with a flurry, flew at the rat.

Fran looked at the pigeon and silently thanked God for the pigeon's protection of her and Mathilde. She wondered whether she was doing the right thing, yet she could not leave her outside, where any animal could take her. She could not merely leave her body in the basement, where the rats would feast on her. She reasoned that she needed to show the family that she had done everything she could for Mathilde. They would be able to see her preserved as a whole. As far as she could see, that was the only option. She prayed for strength as she put the clean stockings and undergarments on her charge.

Using the tapestry strips, Fran began bandaging Mathilde's body for burial. Afterwards, with the utmost care, she dressed her in the clean clothes she was keeping for their journey to the country home. First, she dressed her in a clean smock with full sleeves. Both the undergarments, the fine clothes, and the tapestry strips, she hoped, would protect Mathilde from insects, hating the idea of insects crawling all over her body. She placed Mathilde's favourite green silk dress on top. Mathilde lost so much weight that it fitted easily over her bandaged body.

Fran hung the gold and coral necklace over her head and placed a nightcap on her head. She attached the pomander to the clean smock, for extra protection against vermin. She carefully placed the two empty sacks under Mathilde and slowly dragged her body towards the void. With tears streaming down her face, and as gently as she could, she lowered Mathilde into the void. She placed a canvas bag carefully over Mathilde's face. She pulled the remaining three sacks of saltpetre over to the edge of the void and averting her eyes, she opened them and poured the saltpetre over Mathilde. Fran said a final prayer, confident that Mathilde's soul would become immortal with a strong and perfect heavenly body.

She put the rest of the sacking in the void and the heavy flagstone back. She pulled the table back over the flagstone, exactly as she saw her guardian do. She went back out into the garden and saw that the pigeon was waiting for her. She took a tiny tube of thin, light paper out of the bag taken from the void. She read his instructions. She must "attach the paper tube to the messenger pigeon's leg if Mathilde dies". Fran completed the operation with relative ease. The pigeon waddled a short distance away, and, using its' powerful wing muscles, took flight. It soared off into the distance without a backward glance.

Fran remembered her drawings of the pigeon and, at that moment, wished she had kept them with her. Drawing always took her mind off her worries and concerns. Her inks and precious pieces of paper were locked away in her room. She felt an urgent need to write about what happened in this basement, but she did not feel brave enough to go into the main part of the house yet. She would attempt to do so when she left the house, but where would she go when she left the house? As she pondered over the dilemma, she used the empty bag to store the coins given to her to pay the coachman for the journey and overnight stops to Eyam. She placed the bag of coins on the bank as she stripped herself and threw her soiled clothes into the river. She dressed herself in her travelling clothes, determined to find the coachman the next day. She would travel to Amsterdam, her family's home.

She went back into the basement, leaving the door open behind her for the daylight to save using a candle during the day. Exhausted, she drifted off to sleep.

8

THE SEARCHERS RETURNED

When she awoke it was dark, though she could see the moon lighting up the garden outside. She did not know how long she lay sleeping. Looking around her, she thought she saw a light at the basement trap door. The door opened. The searchers, whom she remembered seeing on the dreadful night her adopted family left for Eyam, began descending the stairway. The short searcher was holding a long pole with a hook on its end, which carried a lantern. Seeing Fran, she grinned her toothless grin and spoke to the tall searcher.

A watchman, recognisable by his clothes, stood at the trapdoor entrance above them. Fran could see that they seemed agitated by her very existence. The tall searcher poked at her with her staff and, using it, with expertise, it must be said, stripped Fran instantly of her clothes.

As she did this, the food package fell to the floor, and the ham tumbled out. Immediately a rat appeared, as if from nowhere, and snatched it up, scampering off with its prize. Fran looked down at her naked body in horror, covered in bruises and sores. The short searcher lowered the lantern down onto the table and then used the hook to poke at the bubo under Frans' arm. She directed proceedings,

"Milady will go on your cart, Josiah.

Josiah looked at the short searcher with a confused expression before turning to leer at Fran.

"She's not much longer in this world." The short searcher cackled.

Using her hook, she pointed out the bubo to him, before giving him more instructions.

"See what you can find of value in the property to pay us for the inconvenience."

The tall searcher used her staff to push the cloth that had covered the ham out of the basement door.

"We can check in the kitchen for any food. Save it from going to waste."

The searchers gave each other sly smiles as if they were cats used to the situation before them, and Fran the mouse to toy with. Between maniacal laughter and venomous taunts, they expertly manoeuvred their staffs to prod and poke the naked girl up the stairs as they taunted her.

"Any treasure hidden in this house milady, or did they take it all with em?"

"Any silver? We love a bit of silver."

Fran could lip-read if they faced her, but they didn't face her. The short searcher turned her over to face them demanding "Answer us then!" Fran stared at them with a scared, perplexed expression.

The tall searcher exclaimed, "She is an idiot."

"Ahh, that is why they left her in the cellar to die."

"No sense, no feeling, poke her some more."

As she arrived on the top step, the searchers shoved her so that she fell face down onto the hall floor, where the two men stood waiting.

Artemus, the watchman, straightened up and shrugged his indifference. It seemed to Fran that he was determined to have no part in their fun, but he would not stop it either.

The two searchers used their staffs to continue to play with Fran, as she lay on the floor. Josiah left his position at the front door, moving into the hallway to watch Fran as she struggled naked under the taunts and prods of the searchers.

Fran felt a sudden breeze as the front door slammed shut, and Artemus looked into the cellar. He wore a greatcoat with large pockets, and a battered hat, and carried a lantern and staff. All of these were the tools of his trade, and he used them with expertise.

"An outside door must be open down there, get back to your post, Josiah," he growled.

During the plague, Artemus was tasked with guarding the properties of wealthy individuals, shielding them from possible theft. Tiring of the night's "fun" he instructed the two searchers to take what they could from the kitchen then give him the nod, and he would lock up the front of the property.

He looked around at the paintings on the walls. "What did these pigeon muck collectors want with paintings of the countryside when they could simply enjoy a walk and see it for themselves, eh Josiah."

"Looks like rubbish to me Artemus." Josiah agreed.

Artemus descended the stairs, picking up the dress with his staff as he did so. There was plenty of wear left in it, and it might do for his eldest daughter, whom he judged to be the same build as Fran. But, he remembered, the old crones believed the young woman to have the pestilence. He carried the dress on the end of his staff out into the garden and headed for the river, where he dropped the dress into the flowing waters. At that moment, his eagle eyes spotted the bag on the bank. Prodding it with his hook, he loosened the thread, and the coins tumbled out.

"What no one sees, no one needs to care about," he said, with perverted pleasure, as he picked up the coins and quickly buried them in a capacious pocket.

He returned to the cellar and grumbled aloud for all to hear, "No treasure here. Don't know why anyone thought there would be. Nothing here, but a pot to piss in."

The searchers raided the kitchen for what they could easily carry in the shawls they wore for the purpose. Artemus and Josiah took Fran's arms and legs apiece, carried her out to the cart, and threw her on it.

The four comrades in crime let themselves out of the property and shared the produce from the kitchen. Artemus put a Red Cross on the door to deter robbers who thieved and looted empty houses, as the two searchers scurried off homeward.

Josiah got up onto the seat of the horse and cart he was in charge of. He shook his rattle and cried out in a loud voice.

"Bring out your dead!"

"Bring out your dead!"

"Bring out your dead!"

Inside the cart, Fran looked fearfully at all the naked, dead bodies surrounding her. She smelled their stench. She felt the fragility of their bones beneath her and though she had the greatest sympathy for them she could not believe that her time to die was upon her. Gingerly she stood up and the sound of a corpse's bone breaking made her whimper. But her mind became consumed with thoughts of how to escape this hell on earth.

9

EYAM

Gabriel was hiding in the stable, still upset at leaving his precious Mathilde behind in London. He avoided his older brothers, not wanting to be teased. As the youngest child, he was accustomed to being spoiled by Fran, Mathilde, and Sara. His mother was often preoccupied with her saltpetre business, convinced it could produce the elixir of life and transform into other minerals.

His usual enjoyment of the quiet country life in Eyam was tainted by Mathilde's and Fran's absence. And he missed Sara, the maid. Incautiously he confided in James that he was unable to sleep for worrying about them in London and that he was having bad dreams, imagining Mathilde was dead. As a result, last night his mother made him a cure consisting of apple cider vinegar, saltpetre, and honey. The cider vinegar had been particularly tart, and it kept coming back up into his mouth, throughout the night, causing an unpleasant sour taste in the back of his throat. He was no alchemist, but he did wonder whether the ratio of ingredients was correct. He would do what Sara had advised in future. "You cannot tell anyone that you see these visions, Gabriel. Not even your family for they may send you to the Bedlam asylum for lunatics. Instead, you must tell the faces to go away!"

The stable was a favourite place of his. It was a building made of large square dressed stone and a mix of stone rubble, built to last. Both he and Mathilde would hide in the stable when there were lessons to attend or chores to do, watching and listening to the animals. Today the horses were gently neighing and chewing, making horse hoof steps on their carpet of straw. A tuneless version of the popular song "Bartholomew Fair" invaded the ambience and Gabriel knew James was nearby.

He looked through a large knot hole in the door and watched as James emptied the water from a bucket into a sturdy, shallow copper bowl, seemingly purloined from the kitchen, which he placed just outside the large, circular dovecote as he sang if one could call it singing. He held his breath as James took a linen pouch, put it to his nose and sniffed. then placed it in the water, stirring the alchemic concoction with his fingers. James stopped singing and began making a cooing sound as he continued to disturb the water.

Gabriel heard him call "Plato!"

A pigeon swooped down beside James and poked a beak into the water a couple of times and his brother James became silent. The pigeon placed one foot on the edge of the bowl, then the other foot, and took a drink of water before hopping into the bowl. It strutted about seeming to splash itself with the water and then sat contentedly in the bowl for a couple of minutes as James spoke soothingly to it. Gabriel strained to hear James and was surprised to hear him thanking the pigeon for the saltpetre it produced. Finally, it launched itself out of the water onto the grass and shook itself repeatedly, walking clumsily back and forth as though drunk.

Another pigeon soon appeared, mimicking the first pigeon's bathing technique. James left them to it, disappearing inside the dovecote. Once the copper bowl was empty of pigeons, Gabriel walked over to it and picked out the pouch. He did not need to look inside. The smell of lavender was heavy in the air around him, like a soft fog gently swirling through his mind.

"Ahh, there you are," a familiar voice said behind him. Startled, Gabriel dropped the pouch.

"I've been looking all over for you; your mother wishes for you to join me. We will fish for carp from the stew pond," John said, handing Gabriel a fishing rod.

"Where is Mama?" Gabriel asked.

"Your mother is collecting herbs from the garden and honey from the beehives for her remedies. Harry and your father are ill, and she wishes to make poultices whilst the celestial signs are good."

“Why do we have to fish?” Gabriel asked, his voice trailing off when he heard the swish of skirts behind him.

Gabriel's gaze followed his mother as she marched determinedly towards the kitchen, a basket of herbs and honey cradled in her arms. He couldn't help but feel a sense of unease as he watched her. "Will your recipe work?" he asked, trying to keep the worry from his voice.

But his mother's smile didn't reach her eyes, and he could tell her mind was elsewhere. She replied distractedly, "I've come up with something new, but it will take time to prepare. Hopefully, we won't need it." Gabriel's heart sank at her words, unsure if this new concoction would truly be effective in its cure.

She said, “I intend using the rotting intestines of the fish, mixing it with saltpetre then distilling it into a vessel so that it becomes fish oil. I will take the tiniest amount and add it to water then I will mix it with honey to put on buboes if their illness progresses to that stage.”

“They will smell of fish Mama,” Gabriel said, dropping the fishing rod and holding his nose.

“It will be a minuscule amount diluted in water,” said his mother sharply as she bustled into the nearby kitchen, her eyes darting to make sure he wasn't following. Gabriel reluctantly stayed back but couldn't help peeking through the doorway as she started her preparations. The honey she had collected gleamed golden and luxurious in the light, perfect for adding to herbs and making poultices and salves to ease the suffering of those infected. But he knew he shouldn't be watching- it was a form of alchemy and he had been told many times by James to keep away from things that didn't concern him.

Suddenly John grabbed him by the ear and thrust the fishing rod back into his hands. "No time to daydream. We've fish to catch young Gabriel." he barked impatiently.

The next morning, as Harry and his father lay in bed battling high fevers, Gabriel searched in the upstairs library for his father's bible as asked. Suddenly, he heard a commotion outside and spotted Reverend Mompesson approaching on horseback. Gabriel, his father, and Harry were all practising Catholics, a dangerous choice in their time and place. To avoid persecution, they held secret gatherings in their home every Sunday for worship. But with the arrival of the Protestant pastor Mompesson, the risks had become even greater in Eyam. Hurriedly, Gabriel brought the bible to his father, who lay with an open nightshirt revealing a large bubo that James was tending to.

"The reverend is coming!" he exclaimed.

Gabriel watched as James exchanged a knowing look with their father, silently agreeing on a decision already made. Without hesitation, James spun on his heels and rushed down the stairs to the entrance hall, disappearing out onto the dirt path.

Curiosity piqued, Gabriel hurried to the library window and looked down from above. He saw the reverend carefully removing his feet from the stirrups. Gabriel could hear snippets of their conversation from where he stood.

"I'm afraid we are not receiving visitors today," James called out, his voice firm and unwavering.

The reverend's expression turned sour as he replied, "I have merely come to pay my respects. I was in the area. I shall not take up much of your time."

The reverend continued "I am afraid the plague has descended upon our village. To contain it, we must not allow anyone to enter or leave."

Gabriel's heart clenched. He did not want the reverend to see his father and Harry.

"If there is plague in the village and you have undoubtedly been visiting their homes then I am afraid you are not welcome in ours," James said sternly from a safe distance as their mother joined him. "Everyone is busy hunting and fishing to stock up the larder."

Gabriel watched from the open library window as the Reverend gave a polite nod to his mother dressed in humble work clothes and wearing a net over her hair, perhaps on her way to the beehives. He understood from James that the Reverend did not hold women in high regard and had no desire to waste his time speaking with someone he deemed beneath him. Gabriel couldn't help but feel a sense of satisfaction knowing that his mother's presence made him uncomfortable. With one last doff of his hat the Reverend settled his feet back into the stirrups, and sitting upright once more, he bid farewell, before cantering away down the dirt path.

In February 1666, Gabriel and his older brother James took two days to dig three graves in the garden of their country home. On the third day, between them, they buried their father and Harry in one of the graves, servants in the other, and valuables in the other. All Gabriel wanted to do was to leave this accursed place and return to their London home to Mathilde to prove to himself that his visions were just fears.

In the immediate days after the deaths in Eyam, Gabriel sought solace and understanding from the family Bible. He found a tiny slip of paper with numbers written on it and it reminded him of the fragment he had found in their London kitchen. He carefully shook the bible and more slips tumbled out.

After days of intense focus, he finally felt confident that he had deciphered the code. It seemed to him that not only James, but his father too, had a reason to be grateful to the pigeons. His father had used them as messengers. Gabriel managed to decipher and read brief tactical messages written between his father and the King's men during the Civil War.

Gabriel placed the tiny slips of delicate paper in a small pile. He picked up the bible to examine it and found tucked inside the binding was a newer slip of paper.

He opened it carefully and read it then broke down in tears. Surely it could not be true. The message told of

Mathilde's death from the plague. The message consisted of three groups of numbers, which once deciphered simply read *'Mathilde. Plague. Dead.'*

Desperately wishing he had not succeeded in breaking the code, he rushed to find James and asked him to decipher the message.

"You are indeed as bright as Papa claimed," James said, "You could have been a cavalier like him. But it is a dangerous life, and he has promised you to the church in the belief that you will have an easier life. I can only pray he was correct."

Gabriel's voice trembled with disbelief and grief. "Is it true that Mathilde is gone forever?"

James nodded solemnly. "I'm afraid so. But we mustn't let Mama see us cry. She believes a certain concoction can bring back the dead, and we must leave her to chase after this hope or she will die of grief."

Gabriel desperately needed comfort from someone, anyone. But at twelve years of age, he was expected to be strong and keep his emotions in check.

The next day a messenger pigeon arrived at the dovecote. Gabriel watched from the stable as James carefully held one hand under its body, supporting its weight, and the other around its wings, retrieving a tiny tube attached to its leg. Gabriel rushed out of the stable his heart racing with hope and fear. Could this be the message he had been anxiously awaiting? The one that would finally tell him if Mathilde was truly gone or still alive? Did his vision of her lying underground in her sage taffeta dress prove false? James handed Gabriel the tube and his hands trembled with anticipation.

"C2 London." Gabriel read aloud, trying to decipher its meaning.

James explained that their father's death was still unknown to the King and his men, hence the use of pigeon post.

"The King has returned to London. It is time for us to leave Eyam."

The next moonlit night Gabriel, James and their mother stole away from the village of Eyam. Gabriel recalled the paroxysm of anger and pain as he turned his head for one last time to gaze intently at the shadowy graves beneath the heath-clad hills of Derbyshire.

10

RETURN TO LONDON 1666

Entering London James noticed that houses of plague sufferers were still marked with red crosses and the calls from the usual costermongers were replaced by the calls from the death carts. Hearing the cry "Bring out your dead" he watched a laden death cart traipse through the empty street; horrified to think that both Mathilde and Fran would have suffered the indignity of lying on one of them.

As soon as they arrived at their London home James checked the cellar, which was empty. The house was ransacked and selected pieces from his father's art collections from the walls had been stolen as if to order. He sighed with relief on seeing Harry's favourite painting still on display. The thieves had not taken paintings by unknown artists.

James was not interested in art. As an apothecary, he worked tirelessly, without his mother's usual support. She was obsessed with concocting the elixir of life that she believed granted immortality. She believed saltpetre to be a vital ingredient in the elixir of life and she knew it had preservative powers. She began experimenting with its restorative powers on dead pigeons.

The saltpetre business flourished, and they bought up more warehouses along the Thames waterfront to store the saltpetre and gunpowder they began making for the King. Most people considered James to be a merchant of saltpetre and gunpowder. It suited James to be known as a merchant. To those who understood it, alchemy was not magic, but to the uneducated, it may have seemed like it. He did not want to be accused of wizardry and was relieved that his mother chose to live at one of the warehouses on the waterfront where their laboratory was located. This allowed her to continue her alchemic pursuits without the prying eyes of James' wife.

James engaged in covert communication with fellow alchemists both domestically and internationally, forming a clandestine web of intelligence gatherers. These included academics, such as Isaac Newton and Robert Boyle who believed, as James, that saltpetre was a powerful weapon against the growing atheism of the time. All were committed protestants, though James having been brought up in a household of mixed religions, was tolerant of other faiths.

One morning his wife joined him for breakfast saying, "Husband, I must tell you that the cellar smells of death and I fear your dear sister's ghost resides there."

James frowned his disapproval at what appeared foolish talk at first until she added, "Gabriel goes there daily to talk with her when he thinks no one is listening. I fear he is going mad."

"I will forbid him going down there and I can put a lock on it."

"That will not do husband. It smells down there, and I fear it is contaminated by the plague."

James asked exasperated, "Do you expect me to have the cellar sealed up?"

"For our baby's sake, dear husband," she cajoled, smoothing her hand over the small bump of her stomach, emphasising the point, and giving him her sweetest smile.

Overcome by the prospect of new life in a house that used to be full of life, James readily agreed, "Of course, dearest heart."

James watched his brother Gabriel standing in the cellar and he could see the pain etched on his face. He knew that Gabriel missed their old life, but it was their mischievous sister Mathilde that he longed for most. James could feel her presence in the musty air of the cellar. As they stood there, James couldn't help but question Gabriel's true parentage. He was born nine months after a raid by the roundheads on their family home, while their father was away fighting in Europe, a couple of years after the civil war ended. But despite any doubts or suspicions, the family always treated him as one of their own, a true Stafford. With his unusual amber eyes and hair, the colour of straw, Gabriel bore a striking resemblance to their mother. It was unfortunate that she had abandoned him and given him up to the servants immediately after his birth. Fortunately, Gabriel had always aimed to please, making things easier for them all.

The cellar was musty and damp, but the faint scent of lavender lingered in the air. James stood tall and stern before his younger brother, their father's wishes heavy on his mind.

"Gabriel," he began, his voice low yet firm. "Papa wanted you to have an education and status that he never had. That is why he wanted you to be a scholar."

James handed Gabriel a worn piece of parchment with a schedule neatly written out for each day of the week.

"On Mondays, you will study Latin. Tuesdays, Greek. And Wednesdays, Classics." James looked intently at Gabriel. "Languages are crucial for a gentleman, and I've heard you speak Latin before. You have a natural talent for it, my brother."

James noticed Gabriel's warm rush of appreciation at the compliment. He remembered seeing Gabriel learn bits of Latin from their older brother, Harry, during his travels abroad. For Harry, knowing Latin was essential for survival. James was pleased to see Gabriel's face light up at the opportunity to become proficient in the language. Learning Greek would open up a world of classical literature for him to explore. As for studying classics all day on Wednesdays, James envied his brother's chance to dive into such rich and ancient texts, even though he didn't envy Gabriel's future as a priest.

James emphasised his next words, "Each Thursday, it will be Hebrew."

Gabriel groaned.

James laughed and said encouragingly, "Come brother it will just be liturgical and as a priest, you will need it."

Gabriel said, "Brother, you constantly remind me of the cruelty and intolerance of Catholics in power that serve as a reminder of what would happen if Catholicism was ever restored in England. Yet you wish to honour Father's wishes for me to become a Catholic priest."

James, unable to argue the point but feeling a sense of duty owed to his father's deathbed wishes, continued reading from the leaflet in front of him, "On a Friday is rhetoric and declamations."

Again, Gabriel sighed but James knew that the lessons on Friday were meant to help him overcome his introverted nature. However, he imagined Gabriel would have much preferred to only attend school from Monday to Wednesday and learn only what interested him.

James understood that Gabriel followed the Catholic faith because their father and older brother Harry had been Catholic. He was grateful that their father had married for love and had not tried to change their mother's Protestant beliefs.

Despite this, James couldn't help but wonder if Gabriel was truly meant for the Catholic priesthood. However, he knew his brother to be a good Christian with a sincere love for Christ, and he believed that there was a need for more Catholics like him.

Faith and religion were not topics for discussion in their father's presence. The family was assumed to be Catholic, but it wasn't until after their father's death that James' fiancée's family fully accepted him as a future son-in-law, as they were staunch Protestants.

Trying to push aside his concerns about his socially inept brother's future, James said, "You will have divinity catechetical every Saturday morning."

Gabriel answered, "I am looking forward to studying, brother. It will keep my mind occupied."

"Remember," James added with a hint of urgency in his tone, "our family honour depends on it." Realising that he didn't need to use such tactics as Gabriel seemed genuinely willing to study, James softened his tone and said, "The time for grieving is over. You are the third son, and tradition dictates that you must fulfil this duty."

11

THE ACOLYTE

During his solitary walk to the Jesuit school, Gabriel heeded Sara's advice and spoke to the voices of the faces he could see in the clouds above. Even if he looked to the ground their babble was incessant. He followed her instructions, refusing to let them get a word in and boring them with practising his lessons in Latin, Greek, and Hebrew until they disappeared. She was right, this tactic worked, but it was exhausting.

Each day, as Gabriel left school he faced endless torment and humiliation. The other boys would lie in wait for him by the gates like predators ready to pounce. They ruthlessly attacked his morbid nature, sharp intellect, babyface features, and lack of physical prowess with cruel words and vicious laughter. At the same time, they threw rotten fruit from the neglected orchards at him, leaving him bruised and sticky. As he stuttered his protests, a vulnerability he tried to hide, they taunted him more mercilessly. But despite returning home battered and broken every day, no one seemed to notice or care about his struggles. The arrival of a new baby took priority over his well-being.

In the first few months of his journey home, he called into his mother's laboratory and observed her work. She appeared oblivious to his presence and never inquired about his training. The family deaths had a profound effect on her, and she seemed unaware of the real world around her. Gabriel continued to feel unloved but remained determined to earn her approval and applied himself diligently to his studies. By the time he turned thirteen, the Jesuits saw potential in him and recommended him to train to become a novice priest, beginning as an acolyte.

As a young acolyte studying natural philosophy, Gabriel shared with his older peers the possibility of using alchemy for their minor ailments. In spite of being the youngest among them, he believed his studies in natural philosophy allowed him to offer them such remedies. Students complained of headaches from intense studying, but Gabriel found success with his mother's recipes. He had memorised them from her book, which had miraculously survived the fire that claimed many buildings in London including their warehouses. The fire also claimed the lives of his mother and their faithful servant John. Desperate to gain acceptance among the other novices he secretly used his mother's remedies without James's approval.

Back at college, he handed out lavender, crushed verbena leaves, bruised dill, or peppermint taken from the family herb garden and gave instructions as to their use.

"You need to inhale these herbs and I guarantee they will rid you of your headaches. I have used them, and they work."

Word of mouth meant that he was regularly asked for the remedies. In severe cases, he advised them "You must rub the herb in a tiny amount of oil between your fingers, before rubbing it into your foreheads and the backs of your neck," giving them written instructions to accompany his words. Occasionally, when pressed, he made the oils and the natural remedies himself understanding from his mother's written words that a few drops diluted in water were just as effective as a full dose. He desperately wanted friends and felt that, at last, he was popular. When they began calling him "Dr Stafford," he took it as a compliment.

Gabriel approached the steps to the college on a mild Monday morning in June.

Above him, two novices whom he had brought herbal oils for, were waiting for him, and watching from the door to the college. He became apprehensive as a Jesuit priest appeared at the door, seized both novices forcibly and directed them inside.

Suddenly two soldiers rushed at him from behind taking hold of his arms. The Jesuit priest reappeared and descended the steps to join the soldiers.

"Yes, this is the young acolyte identified as causing the death of a novice by the use of sorcery. I have informed the bishop."

Gabriel noticed the priest speak quietly and understood that he did not wish to draw attention to bystanders to something that might be associated with the college.

Gabriel said, "I just gave herbs to my friends. Look here. Take these and investigate them for yourself. They will not harm you. I swear it."

He held out the herb oils he had prepared. The priest became irritated and appeared to Gabriel not to wish to touch the concoctions. He turned and strode quickly up the steps and into the college. The soldiers hurried Gabriel away. As they dragged Gabriel along the rough cobblestones, he struggled to keep his composure. The people around him looked at him with pity and suspicion, some even showing contempt.

"Where are you taking me?" he asked.

"To the clink." Both soldiers told him in unison.

Gabriel grew terrified. He knew the Clink Prison was a prison in London that held mostly church and lay clerics who committed offences against the established church. The prison was full of non-conformists (imprisoned for refusing to belong to the Anglican church) fellow practising Catholics like himself, and Protestants accused of petty crimes. Often, Protestant spies were planted in the prison to implicate Catholic prisoners for treason.

Gabriel sorely wished he had never tried to win friends by attempting to provide potions his mother had taken years to perfect. What if one of the students he gave potions to had passed them on to another student with whom the herbs disagreed?

Each night, he clasped his hands in prayer and begged for the strength to endure another day, but even the Virgin Mary seemed distant in this lonely and oppressive place. He whispered his Latin prayers into the darkness, clinging to his only source of comfort in this never-ending nightmare. The constant jeers and taunts from his fellow prisoners pierced through his prayers. To them, he was a Catholic heretic intent on corrupting their pure Protestant beliefs. He endured daily torment and abuse at the hands of three clerics, one acting as a lookout to ensure no one intervened. When they finally tired of their sadistic games, he would curl into a foetal position, feeling the rawness and pain coursing through his body. Blood seeping down his legs, bruises marring his skin, and the crushing realisation that there was no escape from this hell. Exhausted and broken, he cried himself to sleep.

The turnkey, with a greedy glint in his eye, as silver crossed his palm, eagerly agreed to turn a blind eye, branding Gabriel as a Molly - a dangerous pariah who brought nothing but chaos and corruption to the prison.

Days turned into weeks, and finally, after a month of isolation, his brother James was allowed to visit him. His shock and anger at seeing his bruised and swollen face only added to Gabriel's shame and fear.

"Who has done this to you.? Tell me their names. I will report them immediately." James shouted.

Ashamed, frightened, and unwilling to talk of his torments of the mind or the physical and sexual abuse by the prisoners, Gabriel gave a half-truth, "The Protestants do not like to hear a Catholic pray."

"Then for pity's sake pray inside your head. God can still hear you!"

He had resigned himself to doing so, but it was too late. He was too easy a prey and they abused him whenever opportunity would allow.

Gabriel's family were known to be Royalists, and before their deaths, both his father and brother Harry served the King loyally. James promised to write to the King to intervene on his brother's behalf. Before leaving the cell, he reassured Gabriel that the King would pardon him.

"After all, the King's court is dominated by Catholics."

As James was leaving the cell, Gabriel watched a Catholic prisoner stop him and say, "Tell them your brother is committing heresy if you want to save him from those men. Get him put in the tower!"

Gabriel did not want to be sent to the tower. Although some prisoners were released from the tower, it was known for its torture. He felt it would be the death of him. Surely James would not ask for him to be sent there. Release from prison was what he wanted. He saw James' hands ball into fists at his side and his head looked like it was going to burst as Gabriel imagined the prisoner whispered to him exactly what the three clerics were doing to his young brother.

He heard James answer loudly "I am working on his release, but it is taking time to prove his innocence. He has not killed anyone. Those animals will suffer if you speak the truth!"

On hearing raised voices the turnkey approached the cell. Gabriel watched as James, trembling with rage declared, "I will not let this go unnoticed, I am going straight to the bishop and exposing your negligence in protecting the young men in your care. I will make sure he sees my brother's battered body and demands justice."

Gabriel's heart raced as he watched his brother's explosive temper towards the turnkey. He feared the consequences for himself, but also couldn't help feeling a tinge of satisfaction seeing the turnkey pale at his brother's threat. As soon as his brother stormed out of the cell, Gabriel witnessed him whispering something to the ringleader. The ringleader's wicked grin sent shivers down his spine as he immediately demanded an audience with the bishop. Gabriel knew something nefarious was about to happen.

12

FELO DE SE

The next day, as Gabriel anxiously awaited a pardon in the cell, he was met by two soldiers accompanied by the turnkey. His stomach churned as he realised what was happening.

"Sirs, do you have a pardon for me?" Gabriel pleaded, grasping onto any shred of hope.

In response, the turnkey dramatically announced in a booming voice "This acolyte is hereby ordered to be taken to the Tower of London for crimes against His Majesty!"

Gabriel cried out "No, this cannot be. My brother assured me I would receive a pardon. You are mistaken."

The turnkey repeated the bishop's words to all those in the large cell.

"This heretic and sorcerer, this recusant shall be made an example of for his treason, to deter you Catholics intent on restoring Roman rule."

As he spoke, the turnkey pointed accusingly at the remaining two Catholic prisoners, who had managed to conceal their faith, unlike young Gabriel. They looked at him with terror, worrying they might soon face the same fate.

The other Protestant and Anglican prisoners sneered and taunted as soldiers led Gabriel away from the cell. Even the fellow Catholics joined in, as though their survival depended on it. Gabriel saw the ringleader slip coins into the turnkey's hand before the turnkey followed him out of the cell.

The soldiers escorted Gabriel to the tower and led him down a few steps to the door of a dungeon. As Gabriel stumbled into the small cell he was enveloped in its darkness. He was frightened to be left alone in the darkness where faces lurked in every corner, and he began chanting incessantly in Latin the prayers and herbal remedies he had memorised. Left in solitary confinement he was scourged with rods daily for the crime of treason. By the time James was allowed to visit, he found him emaciated, frail, and at death's door.

His injuries were so severe that he could not move his limbs. He was too weak to take part in the escape James planned for him. Instead, he understood from this turnkey that in three days, he would be tied to a plank of wood, and dragged by horses through the city of London, from the tower to the Tyburn gallows then hung, drawn, and quartered.

As a young acolyte, Gabriel struggled with conflicting emotions. On one hand, he felt bound by loyalty to his brother James. On the other, he was haunted by deep-seated fears of accusations of sorcery against his family. These fears were now materialising in his own life, leading him to feel like he had brought this upon himself.He was in a melancholy state of mind and could not share those thoughts with James. Instead, he asked James if he could give him freedom from the fate that the turnkey told him lay ahead. Desperate and broken, he pleaded with his older brother, a master alchemist, to help end his life.

Two days later, Gabriel was visited by a Jesuit priest who had bribed his way into the tower, disguised as an Anglican clergyman. He brought a concoction with him, which the priest confided to the acolyte was a gift from his brother James. Immediately, the fear left him, and he became more composed.

The priest shed his Anglican robes revealing his true Catholic identity to Gabriel. He began to pray with him, leading him through confession and absolution.

He placed the silver pomander, filled with a spice concoction made by James, around Gabriel's neck. Gabriel clutched the pomander tightly, holding it to his nose and inhaling deeply. The familiar scent held all the memories of his childhood and comforted him.

Using a concealed knife the priest carefully removed Gabriel's stinking clothes. Then he gently clothed Gabriel in a set of cavalier clothes James had given him. He was overwhelmed with emotion at finally wearing the attire he had always longed to wear and Gabriel wept.

The priest anointed his forehead with oil and recited a prayer to give him courage on his journey through purgatory. Following James's instructions, he sprinkled the inheritance powder into the chalice and poured in a small phial of wine. After stirring them together, he offered the chalice to Gabriel.

Gabriel drank from the chalice as the priest continued to pray aloud, blinking away silent tears as he did so. Then, donning the Anglican robes and collecting up all of his paraphernalia, the priest bid him farewell, telling him that he had an appointment at the clink to deal with.

The dying itself was easier than Gabriel imagined. His brother, an expert alchemist, would have wished to ensure his young brother's transition was as painless as possible.

Yet, the transition to the afterlife was not in James 'control. He knew that if his brother James could direct his future, he would immediately begin his afterlife in the company of Mathilde, Harry, their mother, and father.

Instead, due to Gabriel's belief system and his interpretation of the priest's prayers, he went straight to purgatory.

13

ISAAC

It was like being released from a bagatelle board as he shot out of the astral plane into the cosmos on his self-calculated trajectory. Fear hit him right in the core of his orb being. His purple light vibrated wildly in panic mode for what seemed like an eternity but could be measured in seconds. Then, as he stared at the vastness before him, his words from his last earthly human life in 1726 came back to haunt him:

"This most beautiful system of the sun, planets, and comets, could only proceed from the counsel and dominion of an intelligent and powerful Being... This Being governs all things, not as the soul of the world, but as Lord over all; and on account of his dominion, he is wont, to be called Lord God παντοκρατωρ or Universal Ruler."

— Isaac Newton.

Isaac travelled as a purple orb at the speed of light through the solar system, watching celestial bodies dancing around each other, held in orbit by an invisible force he had once named gravity. The chaotic nature of the universe appeared organised. Isaac felt small but connected to every celestial being in the cosmos as a sense of overwhelming peace and nurture enveloped him.

He revelled in the knowledge that he was one of the chosen few rebirthers to train as a cosmic caretaker, entrusted with maintaining balance in the cosmos. Each time he was reborn on Earth, as different forms of life and consciousness, he learned valuable lessons that would prepare him for his role as a caretaker of the cosmos. He longed to achieve what he believed was his destiny, but a twinge of sorrow lingered as he contemplated the multiple rebirths necessary to reach his ultimate goal. Even though he knew it was all worth it for moments such as this, of pure euphoria and understanding. The complex concepts of quantum physics excited his mind, much like the never-ending expansion of the universe. It was a feeling of euphoria that nothing else could compete with.

Opening himself up to the vast network of inter-stellar communication he felt his mind expand and he connected with the cosmic consciousness— a universal language made up of dark matter used by all forms of life in the cosmos. Vibrational energy coursed through his spirit, reminding him that words were inadequate for true cosmic understanding.

Only higher frequencies could convey the depth and complexity of knowledge exchanged between beings from different corners of the cosmos. As he opened himself to these transmissions, his mind filled with messages of silent wisdom from centuries beyond his existence. Vibrational frequencies from the cosmic consciousness transmuted into telepathic thought and Isaac could understand them.

Use your consciousness to ask for help. Planets and stars will move aside for you if you ask them.

While on Earth as a human he preferred working alone, but here, in this ever-expanding cosmos, he felt inept. It stretched before him, a vast and intricate society that had evolved into a formidable super-organism. His heart raced as he thought about the intense training that awaited him, knowing that if he passed, he would become a crucial member of a team of cosmic caretakers. He would be more important in this world than he was as a human on Earth. Humans held the power on Earth, but they were mere minions in the cosmos.

As a cosmic caretaker, he would rely on other caretakers in a symbiotic existence, connecting, monitoring, responding, and adjusting to maintain balance in the constantly growing cosmos. He wasn't keen on working alongside others but knowing the vastness of the universe he doubted they would be close in human terms. He couldn't help but wonder if he should have a cosmic caretaker with him now, guiding him through this daunting journey. His thoughts were answered immediately.

Two orbs, side-by-side in the cosmos, would not remain so for long once the gravitational pull worked its' magic.

His ego inflated, causing a surge of irritation to consume him. He shouldn't need reminding of gravity's effect. He invented gravity. He could practically feel his thoughts plucked from his mind before the chance to fully form them, leaving him with a sense of violation and helplessness. And as much as he hated it, he knew deep down that this was why he had failed to progress further. He couldn't let go of his need for absolute control and couldn't bring himself to trust anyone else with his thoughts and fears.

Pulling himself together and with laser-like focus he determined to approach a planet, his mind set on unlocking the mysteries within its celestial body. Every object in the vast expanse of space was subject to the powerful force of gravity, which can create ripples in the very fabric of spacetime. He would use his escape velocity to break free from a celestial body's gravitational pull.

He hurtled towards Mercury, the force threatening to shatter his entire being, and then he discovered a daring strategy that defied all logic. By flying against the direction of the planet's orbit around the blinding sun he could decelerate with unparalleled speed. Gravitational time dilation slowed his speed due to the curvature of space-time. He slackened and the cosmos communicated with him.

Report back.

He answered the thought: *Report back on what?*

When you see it you will know.

That seemed to be the pet phrase of the cosmic consciousness "Report back." After every rebirth, he had to report back. He completed his orbit of Mercury with nothing to report and chose to observe some stars hoping to glean useful information.

He would be expected to report back on his observations. Observation had been his forte as a human; Newton was known for it. But as an astralite he no longer needed to write copious notes. Now when he observed anything and wanted that observation recorded his thoughts were immediately transferred to the CMD and stored for future use which gave him infinitesimal pleasure. He used to have to write so many notes and thinking about so many things at once meant he sometimes lost track of where the notes were.

One of his concerning observations was that the void of space was filled with debris, the remnants of human activity in the solar system. As he travelled through the chaos, he dodged shards of metal and scrap, grateful for the law of inertia that kept him from propelling into another galaxy. He remembered his days on Earth as a human, looking through his homemade telescope at the pristine beauty of the cosmos. Now, that beauty was marred by thousands of satellites and pieces of junk floating aimlessly pulled this way and that by the gravitational pull of different celestial beings, threatening to destroy anything in their path.

He could feel the energy of the cosmos. It was tangible. It was more tangible than the atmosphere on Earth.

Suddenly, a bright burst of light shattered his reverie as a long-dead satellite exploded into a fiery display before him. The smell of burnt fuel filled his aura and he couldn't help but think about the release of energy from matter that created this spectacle. It reminded him of his theory, how every celestial body in the cosmos was made- up of the same building blocks —matter and energy. A concept that now seemed even more profound under the sparkling shower of metallic fireworks in the dark expanse of space. A telepathic prompt put him back on track.

Celestial bodies are like worker bees. The sun, our major energy source, must be protected in the same way that the queen bee is protected.

As he pondered this another telepathic thought entered his consciousness.

The queen bee regulates the unity of its colony, and the sun regulates the unity of the solar system. The bee is vital for the sustainability of planet Earth and the sun is vital for the sustainability of the entire solar system. Bees use dance as a form of communication and some celestial bodies use dance as another form of communication.

The birds and the bees. He should have studied them more while he was on earth. They could hold the secrets to the evolution of the cosmos. They would each need to be his next rebirths, Isaac thought, as he travelled on course in the vastness of space.

A distant memory of a breakthrough he had made while on Earth briefly trickled into his consciousness. He needed to search for it in the CMD. He had written it on paper and forgotten to write it in code so burned those papers during his last moments on Earth. He did not want anyone else to finish his thought processes and claim his work as theirs. He needed to confirm it but shuddered at the thought of revisiting the CMD, hoping none of his memories escaped this time.

Last time, one of his memories had gotten away and was taken back to Earth by a rebirther.

It was a precious memory. One that contained his theory about light being solely responsible for colour. Artists on Earth were fascinated by his concept, especially how he arranged colours around the circumference of a circle. The memory gem had transferred to the CMD as a beautiful rainbow-coloured crystal. It reminded him of how proud he was of that achievement.

Suddenly his thoughts were interrupted as bursts of light erupted around him in the vast expanse of the cosmos, proving his theory correct. A wave of satisfaction washed over him, feeding his ego, and validating his work.

Yet, even here among the stars, there were dark forces at play. Forces that wanted to sabotage his goal of becoming a cosmic caretaker by tempting him with pride and vanity. He realised that danger lurked everywhere, even in this seemingly perfect universe where darkness could still seep through and threaten his greatest aspirations.

He knew his precious Isaac Newton memories should only be used for reference if he were to be of use as a cosmic being. With the knowledge gained from his many rebirths on Earth and his observations of gravitational waves in the cosmos, he intended to provide a quantum theory of gravity when he was allowed the time to do so but would need his original research as a starting point. Fortunately, the rebirther Tilly, had not lost the ability for astral projection and returned the memory safely to the storage facility.

He understood the universe was constantly expanding at an alarming rate, causing objects beyond a certain boundary to become unreachable. However, gravity remained a powerful force that held large-scale structures together, like galaxy clusters and galaxies. As long as gravity continued to counteract the effects of expansion, these structures would remain intact, and the cosmic event horizon would not shrink beyond the scale of individual star systems. His work would play a crucial role in preserving the stability of the cosmos.

Lost in his thoughts he hurtled towards a black hole and quickly used his escape velocity, crucial for avoiding being consumed by its immense gravitational force. The shock of almost being eaten alive meant he no longer knew where he was. He looked about him and recognised the Earth's moon in front of him, and entering its orbit was dismayed to find that it also was a vast oceanic dumping ground. Humans had the wondrous gift of space exploration but weren't cleaning up after themselves. They were the masters of their demise polluting the Earth and the cosmos. As he pondered their carelessness, Isaac made a vow to himself. When he ascended to cosmic being status, he would end humanity's destructiveness before they could ruin the entire cosmos.

As he began to orbit the Earth, gravitational time dilation slowed so that he could examine Kosmos 482, the agoraphobic satellite in its orbit, which he surmised seemed destined to crash land on Earth's surface soon. He turned his attention to Earth itself and marvelled at the vibrant glow of the aurora borealis as if someone had etched on a black scratchboard revealing these hidden colours. It was like a hidden masterpiece waiting to be discovered. He was grateful that the curvature of space-time allowed him that moment to see through the blackness to appreciate it. But he knew that was not the purpose of his work experience in the cosmos. The beauty of the cosmos was without doubt, but that beauty needed to be protected.

Suddenly he spotted a comet approaching the planet Earth. The vibrational energy of the comet was significant. It pushed on through the miscellaneous items of orbital debris surrounding the planet. It was on a mission. That was obvious. He had observed comets on their elliptical trajectories through his telescope on Earth and concluded that they were eccentric and wondered if he had been correct in his assumptions. Words from the higher vibrational waves entered his consciousness.

Everything that vibrates energy has a personality. A human being has a personality that affects the way it lives its life on earth. Astralites and rebirthers have personalities that affect the way they live their life on the astral plane and Earth. Comets are cosmic beings that have personalities that affect the way they live their lives and even how they travel in the cosmos.

Isaac knew that he was a ball of energy but that his energy was different to other astralites and rebirthers and he could relate to that as his personality. He wanted to know more.

What personality does a comet have?

The answer entered his consciousness immediately.

Comets are often of the exuberant variety, full of energy and happy for the freedom of low gravity and speed so they can, if unchecked, career out of control in the cosmos.

Isaac was not in the least surprised. *Will I get a warning if one is heading towards me?*

You will sense a higher vibration when comets are on the scene.

Isaac watched the trail left by the comet as it orbited Earth and heard higher vibrational waves telepath,

The friction from any close encounters made by rhapsodic comets can cause destruction and devastation to planet surfaces.

All matter in the Milky Way could be affected. Caretakers are monitoring them constantly.

Isaac was concerned for his future life as a cosmic being and knew he would need to understand the roles played by other cosmic beings. *Why is that?* He asked.

In a nanosecond, the reply came. *In the same way that the moon's gravitational pull affects the tides of the Earth's oceans. Critical planetary and lunar geometry means that every cosmic being affects every other cosmic being. Even when planets are in conjunction, they could affect tidal and thermal forces, seismic activities, temperature changes, and loss of light and energy on planets, moons, or stars.*

Isaac wanted to know what role comets played in the physics of the cosmos but before he had time to formulate the question in his mind the answer entered his consciousness.

A comet performing its duty will deliver water and organic molecules through the meteorites they distribute to designated celestial bodies.

Are you saying they help keep the mechanics of the cosmos going, like a clock? Isaac asked.

No, more like an orchestral piece of music or a dance movement.

Isaac looked all around him as his purple light vibrated in agreement. *Humans have been debating such things forever it seems.*

Suddenly it was as if hundreds or thousands of cosmic beings replied to him in unison. *The harmony of the spheres, of the cosmos, conducted by the entity known to some as God, or*

Cosmic Consciousness, and to others as Dark Energy, could be at stake if cosmic beings such as comets do not play their part.

Isaac nodded in awe and wonder. *Will I meet the entity?*

Silence met his question. Isaac may well have been a human of influence on Earth but in the cosmos, he was merely a rebirther aspiring to become one of its caretakers.

Amid the expanding galaxies, his mind raced with theories and equations. The constellations blurred together as he became lost in his thoughts about the mathematical intricacies of the cosmos. He marvelled at the delicate balance of mass and gravity, which allowed for the formation of stars and the evolution of planets. Each number had to be perfect for this intricate dance of cosmic forces to work, and it left him in a state of pure amazement. He nervously looked about himself as he felt the ripples in space-time knowing black holes were invisible until it was too late. Comparable to a cosmic Venus flytrap but worse. He wanted to be allowed on more trainee flights so that he could work out the gravitational waves surrounding black holes and thus avoid them.

As his first trainee expedition through the vastness of space ended, his longing to become one with the never-ending cosmos he had adored since his university days grew even stronger.

On the astral plane, the council unanimously decided Isaac would travel to Earth for his next rebirth. He accepted the responsibility wondering if he was to be reborn as a bird or a bee.

14

BARTHOLOMEW FAIR REVISITED

When Gabriel was an acolyte he believed in the existence of purgatory. He understood he would go through purgatory and purify his soul ready for heaven. He never contemplated being in a state of limbo. Not able to move forward and not able to go back. He was in an endless spiral, never ending nor beginning, its circumference inching ever closer to an eternity of madness assisted by his brother's alchemical concoctions which gave his visions free rein.

Leaving his bruised and battered body behind on Earth meant he was pure thought. Wherever he was now it was all about thoughts and feelings, and the visions he had been so careful to deny access filled every single moment. Voices from his consciousness continually spoke to him.

You are an abomination to humanity because, by rejecting life, you have denied the gift given to you by God.

Gabriel answered the voices in his head with a thought of his own, *Yes, you are right, my punishment fits the crime of felo-de-se.*

There was a cacophony of laughter as a voice told him, *We are here to entertain you. Welcome to the fair!*

A vision of a fair entered Gabriel's consciousness. It felt familiar. It looked like Bartholomew Fair at Smithfield's. He had visited it as a child, with his father and brothers. He relaxed.

It was just as he remembered it. He seemed to float above the shops, taverns, and tents as they radiated out from a central platform in a circular form. If you followed the circular pathway and did not detour from that path, it led in a spiral to the mayor's platform. He could hear the familiar chorus of the Bartholomew ballad sung in a tuneful voice, welcoming him to the fair, as it did on his last visit before the plague struck London. This was good. He sang along inside his mind, keeping to the tune he remembered.

Room for company, here come good fellows,
Room for company, Bartholomew Fair.
Cobblers and broom-men, jailers, and loom-men,
Room for company, Bartholomew Fair.
Butchers and tailors, shipwrights, and sailors,
Room for company, well may they fare.
Paviers, bricklayers, potters and brickmakers,
Pinders and pewterers, plumbers, and fruiterers,
Pointers and hosiers, salesmen and clothiers,
Horse coursers, carriers, blacksmiths, and farriers,

Colliers and carvers, barbers, and weavers,
Sergeants and yeomen, farmers, and ploughmen,
Billfolds, fellmongers, bellows-menders, woodmongers,
Pumpmakers, glassmakers, chamberlains, and matmakers,
Collarmakers, needlemakers, buttonmakers, fiddlemakers,
Fletchers and bowyers, drawers, and sawyers,
Cutpurses, cheaters, bawdy-house doorkeepers,
Room for company, Bartholomew Fair.
Punks, ay, and panderers, and cashiered commanders,
Room for company, ill may they fare.

He remembered that his father treated him to a sheet copy of the whole ballad for a penny, buying the copy from the ballad singer, who carried copies in a satchel, hung over a shoulder.

He suddenly found himself at the entrance to the fair. As he began his walk, following the circular path around the fair, he found that on either side of him, distorted mirrors reflected past horrors of his life all at the same time. He closed his eyes in the hope that the visions before him would disappear, but his drug-crazed mind allowed the visions to take control.

Stop he cried out.

An animated dwarf with a brace of dead rabbits over his hump-backed shoulder entreated him,

Make your way to the puppet show- if you still miss your sister.

It was raining, as it sometimes did at the fair, even in August, and the ground became marshy, as it did when it rained. Gabriel tried to run to find his sister, but as he ran, he was splashed with mud. The mud found every orifice on his body.

Off to his left, he spotted a grotesque carousel and slowed his pace to a squelching walk. The carousel boasted sixteen majestic horses. -four of each colour. White, black, red, and pale horses chased each other round and round in a circle until his mind was giddy. A freak of nature sat on each horse. He remembered these freaks from his visits to the fairground, but he couldn't remember freaks riding the carousel. The music stopped, and as the carousel halted a voice claimed him.

Your turn to sit upon a white carousel horse Gabriel.

The eerie music started, the horses began their circular ride and Gabriel found himself upon a white horse.

Look over your shoulder, Gabriel and see the pale horse and its rider, a two-headed man. It is gaining on you. What are you going to do? You cannot escape Gabriel. Look behind you. Look behind you Gabriel.

Gabriel would not look behind him. He concentrated his gaze on the black horse in front of him until its rider turned to wink at him with its one central eye.

Gabriel turned his concentration to the pole in front of him, that he held onto for dear life, as the horses and their demonic riders increased their pace.

How do I make it stop?

He tried to remember how he treated the freaks at the fair. Had he laughed, as others did? If he did, he was sure it was a nervous laugh. He desperately thought back to his last visit to the Bartholomew Fair.

It is rude to stare son.

The voice of his father entered his head. He learned to avert his gaze that day. The carousel came to a sudden stop, and he quickly dismounted.

As he walked away from the carousel he felt in his pocket and found a token. He had somehow earned a token but had the uncomfortable sensation of being stared at by hundreds of eyes who wanted his token.

He scanned the fairground in every direction. He could see mountebanks selling quack medicines, which made you believe you were dead, even though you knew you were alive. Tents displaying the wares of cloth sellers and shoemakers, their wares taken from the deceased. Fortune tellers who were taking your tokens for predicting the death to which you had already succumbed. Hundreds of eyes stared at him.

A pillory stood on a stage. Next to the stage stood waiting, ornate carriages, to take the aristocrats back to hell, once the fair was over.

Next to the carriages were horses and under these horses was hay, dung, and urine trampled into the mud. A vile, toothless woman sat among the offensive matter. She reminded Gabriel of the searcher who searched his home for Mathilde on the night they drove to Eyam. The woman was rolling the hay, dung, and urine into balls making "apple balls" for obnoxious-smelling pomanders.

Costermongers were walking around the fair selling rotten, stinking food —apples, pears, eggs, and cabbages and the air was thick with the smell. No delicious gingerbread here. Fairgoers purchased the vile-smelling balls of dung and the rotten food for use as missiles to throw at whoever was unfortunate enough to be in the pillory stocks. Gabriel's mind rushed on not wishing his conscience to put him in the stocks.

Too late. Something brushed against him, and he felt a shiver run down his back. Looking around, Gabriel could see one of his tormentors from his schooldays calling out to him.

Ripe fruit from the neglected orchards. Save them from going to waste. Fancy a pelting pretty boy?

On his left, Gabriel could see the puppet theatre. The curtain was drawn, which meant the show had already begun. He could hear raucous laughter coming from behind the curtains. Was Mathilde really in there?

He quickly strode over to the theatre and pulled the curtain aside so that he could hide inside. He could see Punchinello on stage, but the audience wasn't laughing at Punchinello. They were laughing at each other. They were pointing at their plague tokens and laughing.

Stop it, Stop laughing. Mathilde is that you? Are you there Mathilde?

The showman suddenly appeared in front of him. He wore a leather hat, leather gloves, a long coat, and boots. In his hands, he carried a long wooden cane. He also wore a terrifying mask that covered the showman's face. It had glass eyes and a powerful hooked nose, resembling a bird's beak. The beak smelled as though it was filled with alchemic herbs. A miasma of rotting plague bodies surrounded him.

Gabriel heard himself cry out, *Is your body rotting here Mathilde?*

Have you come to join us, Gabriel? asked the showman telepathically, opening the curtain wide with his cane and offering him standing room within.

Gabriel backed away from the showman, hearing Mathilde's voice on the wind calling to him.

No, I am not here Gabriel.

Gabriel frantically began looking around in all directions. For Mathilde and an escape from the pillory, the puppet theatre, and its rotting corpses. The nervous laughter filled the theatre. The showman pointed to the billboard propped up against the side of the tent. He laughed at Gabriel, who continued to walk away backwards in a circular motion so that he appeared repeatedly in front of the billboard. As Gabriel approached the billboard for what seemed like the hundredth time, the showman had disappeared.

Gabriel's feet felt hot from repeatedly walking in a circle, but he imagined his backward steps were finally leading him into hell.

Where are you, God? Do I deserve hell?

The thought made him turn around, and in front of him, he saw a fire- eater. The fire-eater was another freak of nature, standing as tall as two men. The fire-eater pointed out a red glow in the distance. All around him was thick, choking smoke. Gabriel began to panic.

I don't want to relive this. Stop it. Stop showing me this. Please stop it.

The fire eater was showing him scenes from Gabriel's memories of the Great Fire of London. As if created by a macabre artist. The fire began to drive out the booksellers who sold at the cathedral, and the wind carried their papers up into the sky above St Paul's cathedral only to fall as burnt confetti onto the upturned faces of the crowds below. Memories of the smoke and his tears made it difficult to see where he was stumbling. Pigeons from the rafters of St Paul's cathedral dropped dead in front of him as burnt offerings, blocking his path. The fire turned the lead from St Paul's roof into molten lava pouring its corrupted wealth like a river out onto the streets of London.

Gabriel remembered following his brother, James, along the waterside towards their warehouses to find their mother and stopping to help people fleeing their burning homes.

In his mind, he could see a man on fire walking towards him carrying a woman. Her body was all shrivelled and twisted, her hands clutching a book. The book appeared new. The woman's face was the face of his mother.

Mama, he sobbed, I'm sorry Mama. I will save you this time Mama. I will.

The fire-eater was ecstatic and urged Gabriel to share more memories of the fire, but Gabriel was reliving a nightmare. He wanted the chance to change the past and save his mother. He wanted to run away from the fairground and find her, but he couldn't move. Anchored to the spot he thought to himself, *What would my brave brother Harry do?*

As that thought entered his mind, he found himself outside the boxing ring. Feeling in his pocket he found two tokens. Prize fighters were on stage. One of the fighters was Harry, a Catholic, and the other was the Protestant ringleader from the Clink. He knew in his mind Harry had died. Was the ringleader dead as well?

Harry was a great swordsman, but he was no fist-fighter. He was no match for the Protestant. Gabriel watched in horror as the Protestant rained down blows on Harry's naked and greased upper body. Gabriel felt the impact of every blow, as he had when he was alive. He knew that his tormenter would do worse things to him that Harry would not allow. He was weak. Harry was strong.

My sins surround me. Pure evil destroys any strength I thought I had. Free me from this guilt God!

He thought he heard Harry's voice call from beyond the sulphurous soup of purgatory and say,

There were three of them brother. You never stood a chance. Religious hypocrisy has no place in heaven.

He choked on his tears as he walked backwards and fell onto a makeshift Pigeon Toss game. He put his hand in his pocket and pulled out three tokens. This particular game was bloodthirsty. The boys tossed weighted sticks at the pigeon, tied to a stake by one leg. They had gathered in a circle. Seeing Gabriel land in the middle of the circle, they thought he might try to steal the tokens thrown into the middle for the winner. Yet Gabriel was trying to shield the pigeon from their blows. It looked like James' pigeon 'Plato' They began to beat Gabriel and the pigeon with weighted sticks. The bloodthirsty boys bruised Gabriel severely and completed their humiliation by smearing him with the blood of the dead pigeon. As the boys collected the tokens, Gabriel crawled to safety, curled up in a ball and groaned in pain as the drug-induced death held him in its grip.

Gabriel hoped he was in purgatory on a journey to heaven that would permit him to change outcomes by doing virtuous deeds. Instead, he could not stop his mind from going round and round in vicious circles like the spiralled architecture of Bartholomew Fair. He would never escape. He felt he deserved it for the felo de se crime.

Exhausted, he fell asleep and when he woke, he was at the riverside helping those trying to escape from the fire, just as he remembered. In front of him, a ferryman appeared in a boat and a voice that wasn't Gabriels quietened the storm of voices in his head and his mind became calm. A sense of pure love and peace overwhelmed Gabriel. The ferryman, surrounded by a white light said, *Do not be afraid. Have faith. Take my hand and come with me.*

Gabriel took the ferryman's hand, got into the boat, and the ferryman steered the boat across the calm waters to another shore.

15

ON THE ASTRAL PLANE

It felt like he was waking from a nightmare. Instead of the constant visits to the perpetual fair, surrounded by darkness that permeated the soul and voices that threatened madness, he woke to radiant light and found himself on the astral plane. He wasn't sure why he had moved on.

Instead of the daily assault of sorrow and afflictions, an orb of multi-faceted coloured light welcomed him. A brilliant luminescence radiated from the orb as it began to take form and Gabriel had never seen such a dazzling sight. Hundreds of multicoloured shards spinning and weaving themselves together into an orb hovering before him.

His eyes widened as the lights coalesced into one entity and the orb's voice boomed like a waterfall cascading down a mountain, introducing itself as Torrens. He was an astralite and was to be Gabriel's guide in understanding the astral plane and the opportunities available.

The astralite had a flamboyant personality and was full of energy which surrounded him. Other orbs of light were in the background and Gabriel realised that he also had become a copper orb of light and was contributing to the radiance. The astralite before him exuded so much energy combined with an artist's palette of coloured lights and seemed accustomed to drawing in followers and receiving adoration. It was what attracted Gabriel to him. He radiated confidence and Gabriel listened in awe as the astralite spoke into his consciousness.

Welcome, welcome, Gabriel. It is so good to meet you. I understand your papa was an art dealer and I feel we could have things in common.

Gabriel listened carefully because he understood he would undergo training to become an astralite himself. At first, learning seemed to take longer than it did on Earth as he adapted to a unique way of learning. Everything went into your mind, your consciousness, and from there to the cosmic memory database. He arranged his section of the CMD into hundreds of books, and it took practice to remember which book to open.

He asked the astralite, *Why have I moved on from purgatory? Why am I on the astral plane?*

Gabriel felt a jolt as Torrens's thoughts entered his own. The astralite spoke with an air of superiority seeming to ignore the question, claiming that all beings in the cosmos were consciousness. Despite his doubts, Gabriel listened as Torrens continued to lecture in an arrogant tone. As a priest in training, Gabriel possessed humility - a trait Torrens seemed to lack. Torrens explained how all individuals, regardless of their plane or level of consciousness, were pure thought. The concept wasn't new to Gabriel, and he noted, it wasn't what he asked.

Torrens continued, *On earth, thought inhabits a physical reality. Now you do not have a physical body to pander to. I assumed you understood this.*

Gabriel hadn't meant to ask about consciousness, but rather why he had suddenly found himself on the astral plane after purgatory. Did his thoughts betray him? The realisation hit him hard —this was a whole new world, existing beyond his comprehension.

He saw how being trapped in purgatory had consumed and addicted him to suffering, taking its toll on his mind and soul. Now, faced with this unfamiliar world, he yearned for the option of hibernation for centuries rather than having to navigate the challenges of communication that he struggled with on Earth and suspected would also prove difficult here. Torrens probably wasn't at fault for not answering his question. His tortured mind must be asking other questions he was unaware of. Hibernation it seemed was no longer an option. It was available at the point of death not afterwards.

Torrens, so full of himself, continued to spout his inner thoughts about hell and belief systems.

Hell is of your own making.

Hell? Gabriel asked, surprised.

Torrens ignored the interruption. *It comes from your belief system. Your beliefs were influenced by the world you lived in before you died. You wished to go to hell.*

Gabriel was stunned. Torrens tried to justify it by saying he meant purgatory instead of hell, but Gabriel knew the truth. Torrens' ego had got the better of him. And now, they were on the astral plane discussing their beliefs and the supposed crimes that took him to purgatory.

I must remind you, we are not judged by the specific cause of our death. But by the choices we make in life. I hear you lived a devout life, full of hardships.

Gabriel felt a pang of guilt as if the astralite was implying he could have avoided purgatory if only he had made different choices.

He heard Torrens let out a deep sigh, almost melodramatic as he added, *Yes, indeed, but I understand why you ended up here. You were a devoted Catholic. As for myself, I renounced Catholicism and joined the Rosicrucians. We do not believe in purgatory. Yet no earthly faith can prepare you for the eternity that awaits when you are dying.*

Gabriel wondered if this astralite knew what happened to his physical body. He thought he would not have had a Christian burial. He understood that for his crime of felo-de-se, he would be buried at the Culverhouse Crossroads. A stake driven through his body, to keep it pinned to the earth, to prevent him from ever moving on to the next life. So why was he here? Had the stake rotted away and freed more of his consciousness so that he was a whole soul? Not an earthly person, with an earthly body, not an earthbound ghost, but an astral being.

Torrens was now in his stride and continued, *It matters not what people on Earth do with the empty vessels that once held the souls of the dead.*

Gabriel listened intently willing Torrens to tell him that his body was no longer staked in the ground. But Torrens was being theatrical again as if performing to an audience, albeit an audience of one. Gabriel stared in awe as Torrens simultaneously created a kaleidoscope of colour surrounding them as he spoke into his mind, *They may still think they can control the soul's journey for instance, by putting items in the coffin of their loved one's earthly body to assist them in the afterlife. That's like fool's gold. How can material things, like a Bible and a crucifix from a material world, assist anyone in a world outside of materialism?*

Gabriel remembered the projection of his soul from the earthly world to the next was extremely fast. He also remembered screaming for help in purgatory. It seemed to him that no one on the physical plane listened to him, or they couldn't hear him. It was as if he were on the other side of a looking glass. Looking at the fairground mirrors in purgatory, he could see people on earth, but they could no longer see or hear him. Torrens was right. Earth and the afterlife were worlds apart. Torrens words made Gabriel think and he imagined they were meant to do just that. Maybe he didn't answer questions directly because that was too easy.

When the physical body is left behind, the immediate surroundings of that physical body are not considered by the soul as it leaves the body. It's exactly like a butterfly emerging from its cocoon only much faster.

Gabriel suddenly understood. Even though he had been taught on Earth that he could lose his soul, because of his sin, it didn't happen. His soul became a part of universal consciousness when it left his body. He realised that humans held no power over the cosmos and understood the uselessness of earthly possessions in the cosmos. This was a different world. Torrens may have seemed like a strange choice to support Gabriel, but he liked him. His flamboyance reminded him of his brother Harry.

As he tried to process his thought Torrens continued regardless, *You and I are pure spirits on this higher plane. Being on this astral plane, you may stay here. It seems to me that you have earned that. Or you may descend to learn lessons from the third dimension known as Earth by having a physical life. Rebirth. If you choose a rebirth, once on Earth, you will immediately forget that you were a spirit. The spirit will be buried inside your physical being. You will forget that you are a spiritual being having a human experience. However, there is no guarantee that it would be a human experience.*

Gabriel no longer felt the weight of a physical body. He felt free. *I understand. I have received this lesson so many times. I am without a physical body. I am pure thought or pure consciousness.*

Torrens vibrated in a myriad of colours that constantly changed. *Consciousness goes on forever. Earthly bodies do not. They get damaged or wear out, and we discard them as if they were rags. Rags and bones. Three hundred and sixty-five years on Earth is the equivalent of three hundred and sixty-five days on the astral plane. Hence a year on Earth equals a day here. Time dilation is real.*

As Gabriel floated with Torrens through the astral plane, he observed the other orbs of light surrounding them. Each one had a unique energy and aura, but he noticed most had a copper hue. Torrens told him it indicated that they were new arrivals to this realm. Gabriel reflected on his death in 1667 and realised that if he were to return to Earth today, he would still be a teenager, almost fifteen years old. However, the Earth would have aged by over three centuries, making it unrecognisable to him.

16

MOVING ON

Torrens hovered in front of Gabriel, his ethereal orb shifting between vibrant hues of blue and purple. He explained that he had chosen not to be reborn and instead dedicated himself to guiding souls who had lost their way on the earthly and astral planes. Gabriel understood the concept of reincarnation, where one could be reborn and experience multiple life cycles on Earth and found Torrens critical and dismissive.

Rebirths are a form of playing Russian roulette Torrens telepathed. *You might inhabit bodies that meet with accidents through no fault of their own. There are so many permutations of unsuitable bodies that you might inhabit.*

Unsuitable?

You start all over in a different body, but that body might not have the abilities of your former body.

Gabriel was confused and asked *Former body?*

Torrens continued as if he were reading from a script, *You are reborn as a baby, your memories from this astral plane are taken from you.*

Why?

You have a new physical body, which, as you have already been told, might not be human. Your memories, are already indexed, filed, and sent to the universal memory store as you depart the astral plane for rebirth.

Gabriel processed the consequences of having a new body. He couldn't bear losing all his memories, especially those before the plague ravaged the world.

Torrens rushed to reassure him, but Gabriel could see his impatience. Torrens explained that all old memories remained stored in a cosmic memory database, easily accessible whenever needed. They were unnecessary for a new life as new memories would be made.

But for Gabriel, his old memories were more than just data. They were a source of comfort, a reminder of life before the chaos. He desperately wanted to hold onto them. To have easy access to them. He felt Torren's impatience to move on with the "Rebirth routine" and continued without pause. Gabriel's copper aura dimmed as he struggled to understand Torren's explanation. He couldn't help but feel a sense of frustration, knowing that he may end up back in this very same situation wondering how he had let an entire physical lifetime pass by without making any progress. How could earthly sins change as consciousness evolves? And if one's earthly body had committed sins according to the standards of that lifetime, would they now be moving backwards in their spiritual journey? Feeling sceptical and unconvinced,

Gabriel mentally questioned whether being a guide suited Torrens' personality.

He watched as the astralite put on a flashy display of colours, likely attempting to distract and appease him. But Gabriel was not in the mood for superficial tricks and flippant attitudes. Torrens continued with his colourful display and explained that returning to Earth meant ageing physically at a faster rate than if one remained in the afterlife.

That's more like a game of snakes and ladders than Russian roulette, Gabriel offered.

Torrens nodded in agreement sending a shimmering light display in Gabriel's direction.

Either way, it is a losing game. Torrens declared.

He confided in Gabriel that he refused to be reincarnated as a human risking the possibility of torture all over again. He wanted to be a cosmic artist. When he died, he went immediately to the Elysian plane, and it was there that he learnt he was highly regarded for his understanding of colours by Cosmic Consciousness. As Gabriel bowed in deference to the great artist before him Torrens promised him that he would perfect the iridescent hues of Earth's birds, insects, reptiles, and sea creatures. He might even change the colours of the rainbow. Then he floated towards another confused orb, whose light was blinking on and off, as Gabriel's often did.

From the conversation with Torrens, Gabriel decided he did not wish to go to Earth again. If he could return to the physical world to a time before the plague, it was worth returning to, but only if he could prevent the plague, the fire, and his time in prison. He decided to stay on the astral plane and to remain in his spiritual body. He could see no benefit to having a physical body. With proper training, he could become a guide for others on the astral plane. Or he could assist those on Earth in coming to terms with a loved one's physical death.

Summoned to appear in front of a selection panel of shining yellow orbs that floated in the dark energy as he did, Gabriel asked for permission to use his super consciousness to connect with minds on Earth. Permission granted he soon found himself drawn to mediums, creatives, and young people.

When communicating with mediums, he retrieved precious memories from deceased relatives stored in the memory database on the astral plane. It was overseen by astralites, who took it in turns to collect the barcodes of precious memories when they were offloaded before the deceased relative was reborn. The earthly relatives seemed to take comfort in these memories, although Gabriel didn't feel he gained anything from the experience.

As someone with a vivid imagination, he often found it easier to connect with creatives. Those who shared his sensitive nature. They seemed to understand and feel things on a deeper level than the average person. And yet, he couldn't help but feel disappointed when they took credit for the ideas he had channelled through his superconsciousness. It felt like they had stolen some of his identity and left him feeling a victim once again. He knew Torrens enjoyed seeing humans deliver his art for others to see. Yet he was also critical of their attempts at mimicking his genius.

Every astralite sought to ascend to become a cosmic being, and it was no secret that Torrens was eager for this advancement. However, Gabriel couldn't help but notice that Torrens' ego hindered his progress.

During his follow-up assessment as an astralite Gabriel discovered that his ego was also at fault. It was too full of negativity and grief for him to support and help others. He would have to return to Earth in his astralite form to reconcile with his past life, hoping it would bring closure and enable him to move forward. Once the decision was made it seemed like a nanosecond before Gabriel underwent language training for his journey into the 21st century. He would not be sent back to the 17th century and had no choice. Cosmic Consciousness scrutinised the actions of the astral council for their prolonged abandonment of Gabriel in purgatory. As the embodiment of love, Cosmic Consciousness was deeply troubled by this lack of compassion towards Gabriel. It mirrored the failures of humans during Gabriel's earthly existence where even his family's prejudice regarding his conception meant he had never experienced complete love. He needed the opportunity to experience earthly love before he experienced it cosmically to appreciate the difference.

But first, he needed a rebirther by his side. As he watched a waiting purple orb of light, it changed into a beautiful archangel pigeon. Gabriel studied the pigeon as he and the pigeon waited for the optimum time to cross dimensions. He could not comprehend ever wishing to be reborn as a bird.

My name is Isaac, the pigeon telepathed.

17

PIGEON TALK

Isaac's purple orb glowed softly as he hovered above the Stafford family's computer in the gallery, conveniently left on at all times. One of his tasks was to research mankind's impact on the planet and their relationship with birds. His consciousness activated the computer controls, allowing him to scroll through internet information. But Isaac wanted firsthand experience. He was curious about Gabriel's perspective, knowing his lifetime on Earth involved pigeons. He wanted access to the visuals of Gabriel's thoughts and memories through a shared consciousness. He decided that he needed his rebirth form for that conversation.

Isaac walked unsteadily on pigeon toes into the basement. He saw Gabriel waiting in expectation for Mathilde to reappear in the last place he had known her to be. The archangel pigeon's plump body remained proud, and his head bobbed. Wings tucked close to his sides were extended slightly as if in greeting and helped him to balance as he waddled. Swaying carefully from side to side on his naked feet Isaac decided that flying was definitely preferable to walking. Rays of sunlight poured through the window, illuminating his feathers, and creating a shimmering halo around him. For a few seconds, he seemed to be in perfect harmony with the universe, swaying to a sweet melody that only he could hear. As he moved, he could feel Gabriel's eyes on him, taking in every movement as if mesmerised. Isaac assumed Gabriel was full of admiration but when Gabriel finally spoke, his words were unexpected.

It must be difficult having no hands. Do you wish you had them?

Isaac's head tilted slightly as memories of his recent flights flooded his mind. Out of all his rebirths being a bird and soaring high in the freedom of the skies was his favourite so far. *If I had a choice between wings and hands,* he paused for effect, *I would choose wings every time.*

Isaac saw Gabriel's eyebrows raise in surprise at his answer and understood Gabriel wouldn't be able to imagine the enjoyment of being a bird, even for a day. They both lived on Earth during the 17th century when humans treated animals with little regard, especially pigeons. Sensing Gabriel's confusion, Isaac leaned towards him with a twinkle in his eye, *I'd rather be a bird than a bee.*

Gabriel laughed and Isaac continued, *Despite their equal importance in sustaining life on Earth, I always assumed I would be reincarnated as a bee in this lifetime. But flying as a bird brings me more joy and freedom than having the monotonous job of collecting nectar all day!* Once those words were out, Isaac couldn't take them back and if he were a bee in his next rebirth, he knew he only had that untethered shared thought to blame.

Isaac's intense orange eyes demanded Gabriel's attention and followed Gabriel's every move as he searched the basement, which bore no resemblance to the 17th-century cellar. Isaac knew Gabriel would realise that Mathilde would not be joining him today and began his questions.

Were birds important to man during your lifetime?

Isaac looked at Gabriel's surprised expression as he struggled with accessing the CMD without a working brain. As an astralite on the astral plane, he had easy access to memories from the CMD. However, memories while on Earth required a functioning brain. Isaac gave him access to his small brain and before long Gabriel answered. *Pigeons were important to King Charles I, Charles* II, *and my family. There were even laws made protecting the saltpetre they produced.*

With a mighty flap of his wings, the majestic archangel pigeon bent his knees and launched himself off the ground. His powerful jump propelled him upwards, allowing him to gracefully soar above the ground without his wings touching it. He landed with perfect control and poise on the delicate coffee table, ensuring not to disturb even a single item resting on its surface.

He strutted around it, surveying his surroundings with an air of superiority that suggested the human Isaac Newton was still a big part of his persona. As he cocked his head and puffed up his breast feathers, it was clear he was challenging Gabriel's words.

The laws weren't to protect pigeons, he telepathed, scoffing at the idea.

Isaac wasn't finished. He declared, *The laws ensured King Charles I had a constant supply of saltpetre.* As if to punctuate his point, Isaac let out a loud squawk and relieved himself right on top of the table.

Gabriel turned away. Intentional or not Isaac had touched a nerve. *The hatred and disdain my brother suffered for providing saltpetre for the King was not merited.*

Isaac, bobbing inquisitively managed to manoeuvre himself in front of Gabriel again. He could sense that the CMD was sending memories and Gabriel seemed to be struggling with the offloading into their shared consciousness.

Gabriel sighed heavily as Isaac's brain sorted the memories, allowing him to reminisce. Visuals of the large dovecotes suddenly loomed into their shared consciousness; the walls caked with layers of droppings from the thousands of pigeons that nested in them. Isaac could see that it would have been both a mesmerising and terrifying experience for a human as hundreds of fluttering wings and cooing birds surrounded you.

He listened intently, bobbing his head inquisitively as Gabriel explained what the memories meant to him, his tone growing serious and defensive.

Remember, we were only after the best saltpetre, he explained. *We didn't destroy homes or steal what wasn't rightfully ours.* He paused; his expression seemed pained. *It was a disgusting task, but we did it with due regard for people.*

In the visuals flashing into his mind, Isaac saw Gabriel as a young boy gathering saltpetre for his brother. Isaac noticed Gabriel's fists clenched in anger at the memory. Gabriel may have resented pigeons, but Isaac's time as a rebirther had taught him that all creatures held equal value in the creator's eyes. He fluffed up his iridescent wing feathers and turned his handsome bronze head to the side, his orange eyes judging Gabriel. The saltpetre men may have had privileges because of their role in collecting saltpetre, but did that mean the pigeons deserved no regard? Did Gabriel's family become rich off the backs of these innocent creatures he represented? It seemed to Isaac that Gabriel was still clinging to the idea that humans were somehow above animals. For too long, humans had thought themselves superior and caused endless pain and suffering to innocent creatures like pigeons. Isaac felt it was his duty to make him see the truth, to understand the important role pigeons played on Earth. He telepathed.

Being in God's image does not mean that you look like God but that you have a responsibility to look after pigeons as if you were God's caretaker on earth.

The CMD on the astral plane, alerted by Gabriel's mind trying to find a memory that justified his family's treatment of pigeons, began to send their shared consciousness more of Gabriel's long-forgotten visual memories. Gabriel's past insecurities flooded Isaac's mind as he watched.

Isaac looked at a memory sent by the CMD in their shared consciousness and saw Gabriel standing in front of the saltpetre warehouse. As scenes played out before them he saw Gabriel made to accompany the saltpetre crew on weekends. The crew whispered to him, promising riches if he helped them overthrow his brother and take over the business. But Isaac could see that even at twelve years of age Gabriel had no interest in running the family's saltpetre business. He saw the angst look on his face as he dutifully reported back to his brother and the usurpers were quickly dismissed. Isaac could sense the disdain and hatred towards Gabriel from the rest of the crew but admired his courage and determination to do what he believed was right.

That memory triggered another negative memory into their shared consciousness as Isaac watched a discussion between Gabriel and James.

"Why do the pigeons hate me, James?"

James pointed at the pomander Gabriel always wore and shrugged as he told him, "Pigeons don't like cinnamon, Gabriel. Spicy odours upset them, and they will let you know it."

Isaac watched as the young Gabriel replied, "I cannot do the job without the Pomander brother." Sniffing he added, "Their smell offends me too."

James' matter-of-fact answer came into their shared consciousness "Then the pigeons will always dislike you, Gabriel."

Isaac flew to the standard lamp and, using his beak, like a pair of tweezers, pushed the switch on, flew back to the coffee table and stood as if in a spotlight. Parading this way and that way, so that the light emphasised the beauty and the iridescence of his feathers. The memory of Fran suddenly surfaced in their minds, along with her fascination for Gabriel's father's copy of Robert Hooke's book 'Micrographia'. They vividly recalled her intricate sketches of Hooke's drawings of feathers, painstakingly crafted using a feather's quill.

Gabriel telepathed, *Until we prized pigeons for their saltpetre, they were killed, mostly for food, but often for their down and feathers.*

Isaac was quick to reply, *Yes, and their down and feathers used to fill pillows and feather beds. A common superstition was that those who slept on pigeon feathers would live to a ripe old age. Do you not see the irony in that?*

The CMD sent them a memory of Gabriel collecting saltpetre from a nobleman's lavish dovecote, and he explained to Isaac that pigeons living in noble and royal dovecotes had armed guards protecting them.

Isaac began using his beak to gather preen oil from the base of his tail and carefully rub it into his feathers. He was engrossed in the task, knowing that a pigeon's life depended on immediate repairs and constant maintenance of their feathers though he knew it might appear to an ignorant mind as simple vanity. He took his time, savouring his power over the young astralite.

Once he finished preening he scoffed at Gabriel's romanticised view of grand homes, knowing all too well that they were simply symbols of human vanity. His view was that the elaborate dovecotes were nothing more than status symbols, with their size and intricacy determining a human's place in society.

He browsed the memories that the CMD was sending their shared consciousness, showing the rare occasions when Gabriel had visited noblemen's dovecotes. But even then, Isaac couldn't help but feel disdain towards such excessive displays of wealth by humans. Something he had never been guilty of.

If pigeons loved these lavish dovecotes so much, why don't they choose to use them today? he challenged, *From what I've seen during my brief time as a pigeon, we don't like sharing our home with other birds. We want a safe place to live away from predators, with access to nesting materials and food nearby. We crave the freedom of the skies. Humans are no greater or lesser than ants crawling about their business on the surface of the Earth whereas we have the vast expanse of the sky at our disposal.*

Gabriel had no answer, but Isaac hadn't finished with him yet.

Do you think pigeons enjoyed waiting their turn to provide for the table? Isaac asked pointedly. *Or do you agree that these ornate niches were a dangerous game of Russian roulette?*

The question lingered between them, their minds intertwined in thought and conversation without uttering a word aloud.

A vivid memory became lodged in their shared consciousness showing one of the pigeon homes Gabriel visited with his brother, owned by commoners, in their backyard. Isaac saw the backyard scene of wooden cages. They were tiny, filthy, and attracted rats. The rats ate the eggs, then the chicks, and finally the caged, weak adult pigeons. Commoners lived the same existence as the birds, prioritising food, water, and a roof over their heads. They could barely look after themselves and their children. They certainly did not want rats to eat the pigeons. If anyone deserved to eat them, it was they.

Gabriel could not deny the truth of Isaac's 'Russian roulette'. Memory after memory invaded their shared consciousness of his family's carp pond, rabbit warren, beehives, and dovecote on their sprawling country estate as their means of sustenance.

The onslaught of memories into their shared consciousness paused as Gabriel admitted *Yes, they contributed to our table*, But *in those days, food was not as abundant.*

Isaac's gaze landed on a plate of leftover sandwiches on top of the fridge, and he locked eyes with Gabriel who added *If we didn't eat them, some other predator would.*

Isaac shook his head knowingly, *The only natural predator fast enough to catch them is the peregrine falcon. I'd take my chances.*

Visuals of Gabriel's mother and James using saltpetre for gunpowder, fertiliser, and medicinal purposes entered their shared consciousness, but Isaac carried on regardless, *Their warm, recently killed bodies were even put to the feet of your Queen Catherine herself, to aid sickness.*

17th-century wars bombarded their shared consciousness. Isaac realised the family's saltpetre contribution to the war effort and began grunting his distress, *Your family seemed proud of serving the Royalists and aiding in the European wars by making gunpowder. I don't believe pigeons would have chosen to contribute to blowing their world to bits. Why do humans persist in complicating everything? Earth as a planet is a miracle in itself. It is a gift from God. All they have to do is treat it as a precious gift.*

A memory of James purloining a copper bowl for his pigeons to bathe in entered their shared consciousness. This memory brought a sense of peace between them. Isaac smiled and relaxed, closing his eyes and stretching out his wings as if taking a deep breath before concluding.

You may speak for yourself, Gabriel, but you cannot presume to know what a pigeon desires or comprehend their ways.

Isaac was dismayed by Gabriel's response. He admired him for being a dedicated priest-in-training, but now he couldn't believe the thoughts he shared. Though pigeons were important to Gabriel's family, his thoughts showed he didn't hold birds in high regard. To Gabriel, they were just mindless creatures with no intelligence beyond their basic survival instincts. It was clear in Gabriel's mind, that humans were far superior to these seemingly insignificant creatures. Isaac was beginning to think that if Gabriel was to move on he needed to be reborn to experience the lives and consciousness of animals. Only then would he understand that all things on Earth contribute to its survival and are equally important to the survival in turn of the cosmos. The Earth was a microcosm of the cosmos, the macrocosm.

Isaac gazed down at his iridescent feathers, admiring the colours humans could not perceive. His eyes glinted with an intelligence that surpassed human comprehension. Then he folded his iridescent wing feathers behind him and leaned forward on the coffee table,

Don't doubt a pigeon's intelligence, Gabriel, Isaac's inner voice was filled with wisdom. *A bird's life on this Earth is vastly different from yours and began long before humans appeared. While man can only perceive in 3D, their eyes can only see a tiny fraction of the electromagnetic spectrum. But millions of years of evolution have enabled birds to see in 4D.*

As the memory of Plato, the Stafford's trained homing pigeon, delivering a message to James came into their shared consciousness, Isaac's thoughts were interrupted by Gabriel's voice in his head.

How do pigeons do that?

What?

Fly home.

Pigeons have magneto-reception. They can detect and use the Earth's magnetic field for navigation.

Gabriel looked intrigued and asked, *Do humans have that ability?*

Isaac paused before responding, *Humans have access to that ability, but very few know how to tap into it or use it effectively. Sometimes those people are mistaken for geniuses because they have taught themselves to use untapped potential. Think of Leonardo Da Vinci. But otherwise, evolution is a slow process.*

Isaac bobbed his head, his many rebirths gave him an understanding of the limitations of human perception compared to other creatures on Earth.

Unfortunately, Isaac lamented, *humans often disregard a bird's equal right to live on this Earth. They continue to harm habitats with chemicals such as pesticides.*

Isaac saw a wave of realisation wash over Gabriel because he wasn't only criticising men of the 17th century; he was suggesting mankind throughout time ravaged and plundered the Earth without regard for other animals or its well-being. He continued,

Rebirth allows us to shed our human perspective and view the world through the eyes of creatures we seek to understand. The health of the Earth's ecosystems is intertwined with that of birds. They play a vital role in conserving biodiversity.

What about man? Gabriel asked, *Has man left it too late to make a positive impact?*

Isaac's response was sombre but resolute. *Man cannot restore the world to its former paradise, as an art conservationist may restore a painting. But conservation is still the key to survival.*

If humans are such terrible caretakers of this planet, how is it still standing? Gabriel asked.

Isaac explained, *Throughout history, comets have graced Earth with their visits. Distributing the gift of consciousness to Earth's fertile soil. Meanwhile, other dimensions have also played a role in shaping the Earth. But it is ultimately the responsibility of humans to act as caretakers of this planet and to collaborate with all living beings for its preservation.*

Gabriel sighed heavily, his transparent form flickering in the dim room. Isaac knew that Gabriel, as an astralite, had a rare chance to return to Earth and reconcile with his past human life before moving on to his cosmic form. But he was not there merely to assist Gabriel in reaching his goal. Isaac's duties extended beyond that - he was stationed on Earth as a guide for the twice exceptional (2E) student, a protector of the planet, and a gatherer of knowledge from human studies on the expansion of the universe and quantum physics. To truly become a caretaker of the universe, he needed a vast repository of information at his fingertips.

Isaac was sometimes made aware of the flaws in his ego, but he saw a chance to lead Gabriel towards a more spiritual mindset. He firmly believed that rebirths would teach him the true meaning of being created in God's image and help him relinquish his 17th-century behaviour influenced by Descartes.

Isaac telepathically relayed a quote from the prophet Muhammad:

'All creatures are God's dependents, and the best among them is the one who serves others.'

He hopped down to the floor and waddled towards the door to the garden. It opened as if by magic. Using his powerful wing muscles and energy, he took flight and disappeared.

Sitting in the basement alone, Gabriel couldn't help but wonder if Mathilde's spirit still lingered in this place, trapped by unresolved issues. He recalled Torrens' explanation of ghosts as lost souls bound to a specific location until they found closure or release. As he waited, his mind raced with questions and desires. But above all, he longed for another chance to be with his sister and yearned for female companionship.

He looked at the coffee table covered in saltpetre, waved his hand over the table, and pointed towards the open door. The pigeon dung was swept along on a gentle breeze out into the potager garden as fertilisation for the soil. Gabriel followed its path, and collecting fronds of lavender, he returned to the basement and sprinkled the seeds of lavender over the coffee table.

The basement seemed to react as the aroma of lavender filled its ancient walls, evoking memories of those who had passed their time there. Gabriel could almost feel Fran's loving care as she tended to the dying Mathilde in this very space, and he offered up a prayer.

18

COVID

In 2020, in London, England, Tilly, a twice-exceptional (2E) student, her chronological age of fourteen, began an internet search for COVID-19, the 21st-century version of the plague. She and her classmates had all been sent home from school. As they each left the classroom, a letter was handed out explaining that a classmate had tested positive for COVID-19. There were only seven other students in the class. Physical distancing was in place, but masks were not required indoors for fewer than ten people. Tilly was determined to uncover the origins of the virus. She proceeded to spend hours researching on her laptop. Eventually, she stumbled upon an intriguing correlation.

In October 2019, a fragment of a comet was spotted over Song Yuan in Northeast China. Then two months later, the novel coronavirus was discovered in Wuhan. Could this have been the way the virus spread? As she scoured scientific journals for more answers, deaths from the disease dominated the internet.

Tilly read that a notable professor of astrobiology said 'The sudden outbreak of a new coronavirus is very likely to have a space connection. The strong localisation of the virus within China is the most remarkable aspect of the disease. In October last year, a fragment of a comet exploded in a brief flash in Northeast China. We think it probable that this contained embedded within it a monoculture of infective 2019-nCoV virus particles that survived in the interior of the incandescent meteor. We consider the seemingly outrageous possibility that hundreds of trillions of infective viral particles were then released and embedded in the form of fine carbonaceous dust. We believe infectious agents are prevalent in space, carried on comets, and can fall towards Earth through the troposphere. These, we think, can and have in the past, gone on to bring about human disease epidemics."

Tilly read that the emergence of the new strain of coronavirus was thought to be the result of panspermia – infective agents in space which eventually reach the Earth's atmosphere and that some scientists have long held that viruses, bacteria, and strands of DNA exist in space carried on comets and meteorites. Three days later on her fourteenth birthday, she experienced the strangest dream.

She dreamt that she sat in a garden as meteorite particles, all the colours of the rainbow, began falling from the sky into her hair. She tried picking the tiny particles from her hair, but they had melted into her scalp.

19

TILLY'S DREAM

Tilly could see images in everything, from faces in the leaves of a tree to monsters in the dark corners of her bedroom as the day merges into night and sleep became an enticing reality. There is a time known as the hypnopompic state. It is the time between sleeping and being fully awake. It is an alternative reality, the twilight world of hallucinatory dreaming and a natural fragmentation of consciousness.

At such a time Salvador Dali's surreal painting of "melting clocks" entered Tilly's consciousness and the number 1664 shot across the sands of time. She lay back as she entered the astral plane, somewhere she hadn't been since she was six years old, and she watched an animated movie playing out in front of her.

Two reckless cartoon-like comets catapulted from the Oort cloud to orbit the solar system. The freedom, mixed with the thrill of close encounters with other cosmic beings, gave the comets the equivalent of an adrenaline rush.

Released into the cosmos by a rogue protostar, with no designated job, they decided to play a game of dares. Each wanting to be the greatest comet challenged each other to extreme dares to gain that title. The winner would deserve the title of "Greater Comet." The loser would forever be known as the "lesser comet." Their first dare would be to create as much havoc as possible by having a close encounter with a planet they hadn't had one with before.

Using the speed of light, they wanted to see who could get as close as possible to the Goldilocks zone and a planet that still had visible life. Earth was the only planet in this particular solar system with visible life. The Earth communicated with the cosmos through radio waves that travelled at the speed of light. Both comets understood, through cosmic intelligence, that had analysed the radio waves, that the Earth had been failing as a planet and headed for planetary death.

If they could get close enough, their gravitational effect might restore the earth's balance. On the other hand, they could alter the rotation, revolution, or tilt of the earth's axis. Any of these could cause seasonal climate changes, loss of light, earthquakes, tsunamis, fires, plagues, or the deaths of any number of plants and animals. But if the planet was dying anyway, did that matter? Planets in other solar systems died all the time.

Earth was its solar system's planet with the perfect greenhouse effect, but humans were turning the greenhouse into a hothouse that could end up rivalling the planet, Venus. That would ruin the synchronicity of the perpetual dance of the planets and their moons in the Milky Way galaxy. Both comets felt that it would be easier for the cosmos to replace Earth with a planet recently created from a moon in the orbit of Jupiter. It seemed to both comets the placement of a planet on the cosmic dance floor mattered. Not the planet itself. The moons of Jupiter were ideally placed. If they could manoeuvre a moon into Earth's position on the dance floor during an "excuse me," then the cosmic dance could continue. Seeds of consciousness planted on the new planet would help it bypass the evolutionary stages the Earth had been through.

However, each comet needed to get close enough to Earth without destroying itself.

As the comets vibrated, their consciousness telepathed, because all communication in the cosmos is telepathic. In Tilly's dream, she heard them communicate with each other. The smaller comet put forward the second dare.

My dare is that once we are in our close encounter, we have to shake our tails at the Earth as it crosses our orbit trail.

Why?

To release one projectile from our tails with appreciable speed and direction to hit a microscopic target, immediately devastating that specific area of its planet.

As the larger comet telepathed, it placed itself parallel to the smaller comet to surreptitiously compare sizes. *You have to be more specific; name the area; name the number of people killed or affected by the devastation.*

The smaller comet searched the Earth map that appeared in front of them both, in the darkness of the cosmos, and answered, *London, England. The closest to 100,000 wins the dare.*

The larger comet agreed, *My chosen devastation will be something humans are familiar with—the plague. Yours?*

Mine will be something they are familiar with too: fire.

The larger comet was still comparing itself to the smaller comet. It jealously noticed the striking green light that cloaked the smaller comet when it chose to put it on. That could produce quite a light show. Shaking itself out of its jealous reverie, it asked: *Are you suggesting that humans will interpret the plague and the fire as signs?*

Yes.

To change their behaviour and stop harming the planet and all its creatures.

Yes.

Then I am agreeable. After all, it is an insignificant loss of physical life in the grand scheme of things. I understand human beings have many incarnations until they can become cosmic beings, the larger comet observed.

I believe so.

Wishing to create as spectacular a light show as the other comet would, through its green aura, the larger comet decided on a way of achieving a similar feat. It remembered that one of a comet's tasks was panspermia - dispersing meteorite seeds like a phantasmagorical bird.

My dare is that once we are in a close encounter, we will eject meteor showers that must streak through the earth's night sky. The showers will contain meteor seeds that will enable the genetic novelty of human consciousness to evolve.

But that isn't a dare.

It is, I am daring you to eject rainbow-coloured meteor showers that we haven't been directed to eject.

Yes, but you are doing it with good intentions, and you have received training in meteor showers, and I haven't.

Whoever said dares had to have bad intentions. A dare is a dare. It depends on whether you can complete the dare.

The larger comet glanced around the cosmos, anxious to be off before a caretaker spotted them.

Besides, we have to make amends for the jokes we play on the cosmos, or we could become insignificant beings in the cosmos and be sent back to the astral plane or worse -Earth.

The larger comet wanted to win but wanted a proper competition and offered:

A meteor shower is easy, just copy me.

The smaller comet answered, *If we succeed, we could come out of this very well indeed. I think mine is the scarier dare, but time dilation will let us know before we return to the Oort cloud, whose dare has caused the biggest shift in human consciousness.*

The larger comet added, If *we both fail, we will need to tag another comet when the last one of us returns to the cloud.*

The smaller comet answered, *Whenever that will be.*

On Earth, it would appear that the year is 1664.

If we fail, the tagged comet will need to return when the Earth is in the 21st century.

The year 2019 lit up the animated cartoon.

There is time to save the planet, and consequently this solar system.

Both comets agreed that whoever succeeded in their dare would be considered by the other as a truly great comet for having continued to keep everything in the cosmos performing in harmony.

Tilly stirred and rose from her bed. She sleepwalked barefoot out into a garden and lay down on the grass. She stared up into the starry night sky, empty of light pollution during the pandemic, and colourful meteorite showers fell all about her. As if in the secret time of night, a rainbow was daring to shed its load.

Later as she sat at the breakfast table, Tilly couldn't help but notice her stepmother's distant gaze. " Are you feeling all right?" she asked, concern lacing her voice.

Her stepmother's eyes bloodshot and dull, snapped to hers. "Just a little under the weather," she replied, taking a sip of coffee that smelled suspiciously like alcohol.

Tilly frowned and couldn't help but notice the slight tremor in her stepmother's hand as she lifted the cup to her lips knowing that her stepmother was most likely drowning in grief and numbing herself with alcohol since Tilly's father passed away.

"I've been feeling strange lately," Tilly ventured, wanting to share her unusual COVID symptoms but hesitant to burden her stepmother.

"Oh?" her stepmother raised an eyebrow, clearly uninterested.

"Yeah, heightened senses and all that," Tilly shrugged.

But her words met with silence, her stepmother lost in her world of pain and addiction. With COVID adding to their isolation and disconnect, Tilly couldn't help but feel more alone than ever before.

As her senses became enhanced only after she developed COVID, she had no idea if the enhancements would remain or disappear once she recovered, if she recovered. She didn't know how useful or detrimental these changes might become. She was fourteen years old, and her hormones were already playing havoc with her neurodivergent mind, but this was different.

Her phone buzzed with a message from school. The text read, 'All schools in England to close again to stop the spread of COVID'. London was in lockdown.

20

VIRTUAL REALITY

It was 10 a.m., and Tilly sat on the edge of her bed, her fingertips trembled as she opened her phone, touched the screen, and read her father's last text. He had sent a series of numbers shortly before his death in January. Her chest tightened as she scoured her memory for what they could mean: Was the message supposed to tell her when he would finally come home?

Her mother had died of a brain aneurysm when Tilly was two years old. Her father remarried when Tilly was four years old and by then Tilly had grown to depend on her father for everything.

Tilly liked Helena for making her father happy, but she wondered if her biological mother would have let him go to Maastricht without them. She doubted it.

Looking around her bedroom, she felt an ache in her heart from missing him so much and she remembered the tears in his eyes when she asked him to paint over the painting her birth mother had decorated the bedroom walls with when she was born. The painting was inspired by the film 'Cinderella' and though it was beautiful she had outgrown it. The walls of her room were now green and covered in vibrant posters of her favourite artwork. A tapestry in a bohemian design hung above her bed, giving the space a cosy and eclectic feel. Her desk was no longer occupied by a bulky desktop computer but instead held a sleek iPad that she took with her everywhere. Potted plants filled every corner, adding a touch of nature to the room. She made a mental note to water the hanging plants more often as they added the perfect finishing touch to her teenage haven. She clutched her locket to herself. It contained a photo of her mother and father holding her when she was six months old.

Tilly made her way down the spiral staircase. Above her hung her father's prized 17th-century portrait of a little girl, carrying a basket of cherries and wearing a coral necklace, the girl's eyes following Tilly's descent.

The familiar smell of oil paints and wood polish overwhelmed her as she entered the art gallery. It was a comforting scent. Unlike a traditional art museum, there weren't hundreds of original paintings lining the walls. Instead, there were only a select few, accompanied by numerous copies and prints. Tilly's father had explained that owning an art gallery meant having connections to acquire rare originals for wealthy buyers, who didn't mind paying extra for exclusivity. Those paintings would not be on the premises for long.

Living above the shop, her father felt a sense of duty to protect Tilly's inheritance that lay beneath their feet in the gallery below. The walls were adorned with art passed down through generations of their family, each holding their own story and sentimental place in Tilly's heart. These pieces were not for sale, and she didn't think they were of great monetary value.

As Tilly walked among them, she couldn't help but feel a deep sense of connection and belonging to these treasured pieces that had always been a part of her life.

The pandemic continued to sweep through the city and the family art gallery was forced to shut its doors. Tilly's stepmother suggested to her father, who was in Maastricht when the pandemic began, that they should create an online presence for the art and prints in the gallery, as she sought solace and distraction from the chaos of the outside world. He approved the idea and planned to be home as soon as possible as he felt they could use any downtime to create immersive experiences.

As Tilly slowly walked down the wooden staircase leading to the basement, she could feel her heart racing in anticipation of what awaited her below. She remembered stories of the exhibitions hosted at her father's gallery and how he brought the 17th century to life. But she never imagined he planned to create immersive 17th-century art experiences in the recently unearthed basement cellar.

Her cold feet enjoyed sudden warmth as she stepped onto the smooth flagstones, heated from below. The reception area held her father's jukebox, a seating area, a small office, and a dark passageway that had a large sign with the words "Immersive Gallery" written on it. She walked down the passageway and marvelled at the room that greeted her. The entire ceiling was covered in mirrors, the floor border, lined with more reflecting panels stretched out around her. Her father employed an audiovisual design company specialising in innovative technological innovations to construct this room. It showed.

A state-of-the-art projector system lit up the surrounding walls with vivid images taken directly from actual paintings, enabling a completely immersive experience as if you were actually in the painting itself. From floor to wall to ceiling, every canvas could extend across every inch of space enveloping the viewer in the experience. With special motion technology, surround sound, hand-controlled haptics, projected art displayed on all sides, and even simulated smells permeating the area, it felt like walking into an alternative reality.

Tilly gazed at the gallery with a mix of pride and sadness. She remembered her father's words and passion for creating an immersive art experience that would transport viewers into another world. His eyes had lit up as he shared his vision, undeterred by naysayers who doubted the project's feasibility. And, standing in the completed gallery, Tilly couldn't help but feel a twinge of heartache knowing her father wasn't here to see it come to life. She knew he would be proud, and she imagined his face beaming with joy as he saw visitors fully immersed in the artwork, just as he had always dreamed. Her tears flowed freely.

She turned to explore the rest of the basement, sealed up by her father's ancestors long ago. She opened the door that led out to a quaint kitchen garden where, shortly before he died, they had both painted mandalas and now she looked at them through clouded eyes.

In the middle of the kitchen garden was an aged stone statue, worn smooth by centuries of wind and rain. The figure was of an angel, its features softened to the point of being unrecognisable. One chipped wing and the other barely discernible, folded against its back. Upon closer inspection, she found a series of neat openings carved into the sculpture. They were almost seamless, camouflaged as part of the flowing robe. But their purpose became clear when a flutter of wings sounded from within, and a beautiful bird emerged from one of the holes.

The statue was not just artwork but a functional dovecote, crafted in the 17th century to house a couple of pigeons while disguising its true intent as decoration. The ingenious design allowed pigeons shelter and safety within what seemed an ordinary garden statue. The dovecote had survived and served its purpose for over three hundred years. She took a photo of the bird as it prepared to fly off, determined to find out what kind of bird it was.

Beyond the garden, she could see a gnarled tree and below that Regent's Canal glimmering in the sunlight. Clasping her hands together in amazement, Tilly wished she could ask her father why this perfect place had been unavailable for so long.

21

MINDFULNESS AND MEDITATION

Tilly was diagnosed as a twice-exceptional child when she was six years old. It was a label that she didn't fully understand but brought relief to her father and stepmother. Her father took the time to research and understand the condition, always ready with a unique solution to help Tilly manage her anxieties. When they travelled together, Tilly would sometimes get panic attacks, causing her chest to tighten and her breath to become shallow. In those moments, her father would reach out a hand to gently squeeze hers. "Remember our mantra," he would say with a mischievous smile. And then, in a thick Liverpudlian accent, he began to chant:

"Let it be, Let it be, Let it be, Let it be.

Breathe in, 1-2-3!

Hold breath. 1-2-3 an' another 1-2-3!

Exhale out, 1-2-3.

Let it be, let it be, let it be, let it be!"

She couldn't help but giggle as she followed along with her father's absurd but effective coping mechanism.

She found herself wishing he were still in Maastricht, alive and able to communicate with her. Without him, she felt a constant sense of panic, obsessing over every little thing. However, using her auditory memory to playback him singing the words in her head, helped to calm her. It made her smile too as his accent was really bad.

She also tried using his meditation techniques and the binaural beats he introduced her to, which helped prepare her for meditation.

She wanted her inner world to be okay. Her father said that was more important. If she had her way, she would get rid of the subjects in school that held no interest for her. Why couldn't schools do that? Why did they waste students' time with a curriculum that took up mind space but didn't teach the skills you wanted to develop?

Frustrated with the traditional school system, Tilly argued with her stepmother about it believing that in this digital age, algorithms should match students with subjects they're passionate about. And she knew her father would have agreed with her, his creative juices flowing as he worked on bringing 17th-century art to the masses through virtual reality.

Desperate to stem the threatened flood of tears that surfaced, she rushed down the new wooden staircase from their home to the gallery below to look at his favourite Ruysch painting.

Her father would meditate on the art of Rachel Ruysch, a 17th-century artist who specialised in still life and flowers.

"Why do you like flowers to meditate on?" she remembered asking him.

"Because Rachel's flowers are so lifelike, you can smell them."

"So, it's just her paintings. Why her?"

"Rachel was the daughter of a botanist and learnt the skills of a botanist. She was so famous in her lifetime that her artwork sold for more than Rembrandt's."

Tilly remembered him taking her into an area of the gallery that he had dedicated to Rachel's art in an attempt to get her interested. Helena, her stepmother, who adored roses too, bought him a fragranced rose candle and diffuser called 'Pink Pepper, Rose, Amber, and Leather.' The heady smell of roses was intoxicating, but the amber and leather gave it a masculine vibe. He loved it and Tilly would always associate that smell with her father.

A couple of months before his death, she finally convinced him to show her his routine. He had always refused before, saying she was too young to follow a powerful meditation.

This time, he simply agreed and taught her the rose and cross technique for safe meditation. He promised that they could meditate in the finished basement together.

Today, she went first to the gallery to look at the Tree of Life tapestry. It was a panel of a tapestry, exhibited in a plexiglass display under low-intensity lighting because of its delicacy. When her father was at home, he would unlock the case so that she could look at the beauty of the tapestry. It filled the one narrow wall of the gallery. He told her that his ancestors had brought it over from the Netherlands during the wars in the 17th century and had risked their lives to own it. She felt an affinity with it as if she had always known she would choose it as her meditation piece. She wished she could touch it but was appreciative of the need for its preservation.

The Tree of Life tapestry consisted of its roots mirroring its spreading branches, providing balance and symmetry, and the promise of eternal life. Varying species of birds sat among its branches. Her father talked of the labour-intensive work of tapestry weavers.

He told her, "They used mirrors which were expensive in the 17th century."

She asked him, "Why did they use mirrors to make a tapestry? I thought it was weaving."

He laughed and explained," In the 17th century, tapestries were woven from the back. If the weaver copied the design exactly, the finished tapestry, when viewed from the front, would be the reverse of the design. If the weaver had a mirror, they could place the mirror behind themselves to see a reflection of the cartoon. By working from the reflection, the finished tapestry was the right way around."

She asked, "Did cartoons have a different meaning in the 17th century?"

He laughed. “Did you think the Simpsons are that old?” and added, “In the 17th century a cartoon was a full-scale drawing that they copied. The Mortlake tapestry workshop owned by Charles I. had the tapestry cartoon, as well as that original tapestry you are looking at on loan from our family and copied it many times before returning it.”

She asked him, “What did they like about tapestries?”

“Tapestries were easy to transport, rolled up and moved between residences. Charles I and Charles II had thousands of tapestries hanging in their various palaces.”

She remembered her father’s words when she told him that she was drawn to the tapestry for her meditation.

“I like your choice of a meditation piece to focus on because it represents eternal life. No one dies Tilly. The tapestry shows the circle of life. A circle has no ending. Circular patterns are found everywhere in nature in the form of flowers, rings of a tree trunk, or ripples in water. They abound in time and space as planets in their spherical forms continue their almost circular orbits around the sun and these orbits dictate time. It takes the Earth a year to orbit the sun and the moon takes a month to orbit the Earth giving us our calendar months. The Earth takes twenty-four hours to rotate on its axis giving us our days. “

The next morning, dressed in a black tea shirt and jeans, both covered in white paint, he greeted her at breakfast and led her to the whitewashed wall of the kitchen garden. She noticed he had planted a couple of pale pink roses on the edge of the kitchen garden and their colour complemented the lavender. On the whitewashed wall were two large circles drawn in green chalk. He asked her to do the breathing routines with him to centre themselves before starting. Once they were ready he explained, "A tapestry would take months to make, and it is something I could not find time to do with you, what with my new project. However, we can produce our circle of art, a mandala, out here!"

He laughed his infectious laugh. He had only just discovered the garden and he was prepared for her to paint on its walls. She was scared she would make a mess of the wall, but he just smiled and said, "You don't have to be a skilled artist to create a mandala. It is about slowing down and going within, allowing your creativity to emerge and express itself freely."

He showed her ideas from his phone to get her started, but as she still seemed anxious, he directed her as they each drew a cross through the centre of their circles to create four equal segments. After further dividing those segments into eight parts, he encouraged her to start in the centre and proceed outwards with whatever pattern came from within. He held a dampened rag so that they could erase any chalk mistakes. Once the patterns were completed they used paintbrushes loaded with green paint to ensure the mandalas withstood the test of time and weather. She became scared of the permanence, but he reassured her that if she didn't like it, they could simply whitewash over them and start new ones. He suggested that once they were both done, they could use them for meditating whenever they sat in the garden. The mandala was special, but the tapestry of the tree and birds looked real. She wondered if she had insisted on him doing a tapestry with her he would have had to stay at home with her and not have travelled to Maastricht. Life was full of "If only."

She looked at the tapestry, taking in its beauty. She had a photo on her phone that her father had sent, but she loved the privilege of looking at the actual tapestry. Given the choice, this would be the art genre she would pursue. Unfortunately, she was not given that choice in school.

She knew her teachers considered her too young to know what she wanted to do. Yet she had read about famous tennis players who had practised their preferred sport as soon as they could hold a racquet.

She looked up at the tapestry and the handwritten note on her lap. It had been written in coded numbers (and some mirror writing)-sent from Maastricht in December 2019 by her father. Tilly took three days to translate it. She enjoyed the challenge and that she had his code to follow for any future letters he might send her. Eventually, she could read the code as if they were words. As if he were speaking to her.

"My dearest child,

Now that I have a spare moment here in Maastricht, I am conscious that I promised you a handwritten copy of my meditation method. I have used a number code because I didn't want to make it easy for you. You have to crack the code before you can meditate.

There are powerful meditations that are both dangerous and difficult but if you practice this meditation it will prepare you for those. When you are ready to crack the code, you will also be ready to use your imagination and be able to meditate. Please follow the guidance exactly.

I have referred to Ruysch's still life as it comes easily to me. Do it two or three times before adapting my method to suit your favourite tapestry. I did not wish to completely spoon-feed you! Whenever you feel overwhelmed by life, take yourself to the tree of life where you can sit undisturbed and let me guide you on a journey of self-discovery through meditation.

As I have taught you before, find a comfortable and quiet place to sit. This is your time and there is nothing more important in the world right now than your relaxation. Close your eyes, take deep breaths, and release any tension or fear from your body. Your physical form will not be joining you on this journey.

Think about the chakra points I have told you about and, starting with the base inhale deeply then slowly exhale. Do this for each chakra point and you will have rebalanced your chakras in preparation. You will feel calm and relaxed. The more relaxed you become the better you will feel. The better you feel the more relaxed you become.

Close your eyes. I want you to visualise Ruysch's still-life painting of 'Rose Branch, Beetle, and Bee.' Focus on one of the buds, still tightly enclosed in its green leaves. Can you see it? Hold it at the centre of your awareness.

Imagine the sepals slowly starting to open, revealing the closed rose pink-coloured petals. Watch as they continue to unfold until you can see the entire bud.

As the petals begin to unfurl, take in the fragrance of the rose with its familiar and enchanting scent. If it helps, light a scented candle, or use a diffuser for added ambience.

Let your eyes take in the warm rays of sunlight embracing the rose. Bask in its light and warmth for a moment.

Focus on the centre of the rose. Imagine that you can see me there. Use your imagination to make me appear handsome. Talk to me about anything that is weighing on your heart. Take all the time you need to confide in me in this way. If you need to share more when I return from Maastricht, pause here, and write down your thoughts and feelings.

Next, imagine yourself becoming the rose —a symbol of pure consciousness and unadulterated love. Remember that both the rose and cross have been used by our ancestors as symbols of strength and protection. Let each point of the cross surround you with infinite energy below, above, and around you, protecting you. Feel the magnetic energy of the vibration.

Remember that the same life force in the cosmos also created the rose and the birds in the Tree of Life and be grateful. Take the time to dream and explore other realities.

When you are ready, open your eyes and return to the present moment. You are back in the room, surrounded by the tapestry of the Tree of Life.

With all my love, your ever-doting father."

Immediately after her stepmother told her about her father's death Tilly felt abandoned, only the letter kept her sane. He had never written to her before. She would never know if she would have been as determined to master meditation without that letter.

Translating the code required a mirror. She found it difficult to use the bathroom mirror and had taken to secretly borrowing her stepmother's makeup mirror. A rose-covered notebook arrived in the mail with the Maastricht postmark dated a week after her father's so-called accident. A small vintage compact mirror accompanied it. Nothing else. No note. On the front of the compact was a William Morris art nouveau print of William Morris' Tree of Life design. She felt that only her father could have sent it.

She slowly descended the ten steps down to the basement, which, since its completion and even more so since her father's accident, felt like her escape from one reality into another reality. Her go-to place, her preferred reality. She held onto the wooden bannister, and as she descended each step, she felt herself go into a relaxed state of mind. She went over to her favourite window seat in the reception area and opened the curtains where she had hidden her father's meditation diffuser that he used. She climbed right inside. She found Arvo Part's 'Spiegel im Spiegel' on her phone and put her air pods on. It was a mesmerising piece of music that she associated with her father. She was determined to listen to the same beautiful music he listened to when meditating.

As the music began and she sat in her new favourite place, a sense of peace and relaxation washed over her. All tension went from her body. She had decided today to meditate on the tapestry scene, and she pictured it in front of her.

She imagined the sheer brilliance of the tapestry work before her. The rose-scented smell of the diffuser surrounded her. The music added to the multi-sensory experience. All was peace and tranquillity. Tilly felt comforted by the scene she imagined in front of her. The tree symbolising time itself. The birds seemed to call to her as if to say," *Look at us, nothing on Earth can match our beauty*."

In an instant, her contemplations were shattered by Sjaak Van Uylenburgh. Officially at the gallery for a private viewing, he began descending the brand-new staircase. His black leather-soled shoes always made a clicking noise, and the sound echoed down to the basement distracting her from her meditation.

22

AN ARCHANGEL PIGEON

Tilly immediately stopped what she was doing, turned off the music, and watched Sjaak Van Uylenburgh, as a cat would watch its prey from a gap in the curtain.

He tried to manoeuvre down the shiny, smooth stairs while carrying parcels in both hands.

He wore a crow black suit, a perfect match to his jet-black, gelled-back hair and black eyes. Even his tie was inky black. A sense of despair accompanied him down the stairs. He made her feel depressed. It was as if he were attending a funeral, not visiting a friend's art gallery. It was theatrical not real. She did not want him to be here, in their home, making her father's death a reality.

He owned his art conservation studio in Maastricht. Her father visited there many times with work that needed conserving or restoring. He made his usual pilgrimage to the

European Fine Arts Fair in Maastricht with Sjaak and stayed on at Sjaak's never to return.

The weight of their loss was made even more unbearable by the COVID restrictions which prevented visits from family and friends. Sjaak had offered to handle all the arrangements in the Netherlands. Tilly knew her stepmother felt indebted to Sjaak, a fellow countryman, for his kindness, but Tilly couldn't help but feel resentful for him not saving her father.

She wanted to ask him why her father had decided to stay abroad when he always returned home after the fair in previous years. But Sjaak was a person she found difficult to engage with unless it was at a superficial level. It was easy to excuse that on her neurodivergence. Her anger turned towards him, who had let her father ride his bike that fateful day. The frustration and resentment grew inside her as Sjaak spoke enthusiastically in broken English with a strong Dutch accent. Her intuition told her there was more to the story than she knew.

"I have come to see this new immersive gallery for myself, Tilly,"

She flinched at his loud voice and knew he had caught her subtle movement behind the curtain.

"Though how it will survive without a physical exhibition programme is questionable," he added.

He pulled the curtain to one side, ceremoniously handing her one of the two parcels he held. Tilly inwardly noted his obvious ignorance about immersive art, his rudeness in disturbing her and no mention of her father's death. Nevertheless, she immediately opened the parcel and found her favourite stroopwafel. She smiled involuntarily, thanked him, and broke off a piece. She remembered how good it tasted and kept that thought as she bit into it. Covered in honeyed hazelnuts, it was crunchy yet still gooey because it had a warm fountain of syrup that had dripped all over the hazelnuts and pooled in the centre. She smiled again. Her taste had come back. She dropped the tissue covering the delicacy, and Sjaak with a smug smile of satisfaction on his face, bent and picked it up.

Tilly's stepmother, Helena appeared at the top of the stairs with a tray of glasses and began to descend cautiously. Dressed in black, she looked incredibly stylish and reminded Tilly of a portrait she had seen of Audrey Hepburn. Helena was petite and dark. Tilly was a redhead, like her father, with piercing green eyes and milk-white skin that freckled easily in the sun. She would describe herself as tall and skinny with enormous feet. It was how she once heard her father describe himself to a potential customer on speakerphone. "Oh, you won't miss me," he said laughing, "in fact, you might trip over me."

She remembered the punchline and smiled to herself. "I'm the tall, skinny, redheaded guy with enormous feet."

Sjaak wandered around the completed basement areas including the new Immersive gallery. Tilly stood opposite Sjaak, eyeing him up and down. She couldn't ignore how much taller she had grown since his last visit. They were almost equal in height. She couldn't remember the last time he came and why he was here, without her father by his side. She wondered if he truly was the close friend he claimed to be or if there was another reason for his sudden appearance.

"I know you won't approve, Sjaak," Helena called down the stairs, "but we wanted to find something different to attract new clients."

Sjaak re-entered the open plan reception area, "This does not link at all with 17th-century masters, and at such expense," he muttered, and his face showed his concern.

Voices echoed up the new basement stairs. Hearing his muttering Tilly watched Helena pause on the stairs and argue,

"I disagree, Sjaak. Art is the artist's interpretation of reality. A piece of art is itself virtual reality. One only has to look at the camera obscura, the technology used by some artists in the 17th century. Comparable, in my estimation, to today's use of VR and AR in art."

She carefully descended the stairs until she reached the basement. She said,

"I don't believe it was properly given credit in the 17th century, as the use of technology in art wasn't understood at that time by the average person."

Tilly watched her as Helena looked around, ensuring everything was left as her father had last used it. Going to the basement fridge she took out a chilled bottle of Chablis and a chilled jug of lemonade and then stood at the doorway to the garden with the tray of refreshments. Tilly could feel an art lecture coming on as her stepmother continued,

"Today we are more accepting of technology as an art and design medium, allowing artists to create striking, immersive, and highly engaging art pieces and multi-disciplinary mixed media art installations."

Sjaak was outside in the small garden. Tilly noticed him take the tissue that he had saved and wipe a bistro chair before sitting down. He screwed the tissue into a ball and put it on the table. Tilly's stepmother arrived at the table with the tray of drinks and set them down. She took a match from a box on the tray and lit the citronella candle on the table. As she sat down beside him, Tilly watched her put her delicate hand on his arm and say softly.

"Sorry, rant over."

Sjaak instantly changed his expression to one of sheer pleasure, "You work too hard," he said, gently.

"At least I can work," Helena said, adding, "We can't go out to dinner because of this pandemic, and the hospitality sector is struggling to survive."

"It may give the hospitality sector time to reflect on itself," Sjaak offered.

"It is time the art world reflected on itself," Helena retorted. "We need to update the way we present art for the 21st century. That would be a positive from this pandemic."

Sjaak poured them both a glass of wine, and Helena drank a large mouthful.

Sjaak said, "I am stuck in London, I would like to be able to do my daily run or bike ride; even a swim would do."

"Aren't you able to?" Helena asked.

"My neighbour tells me that the pandemic forbids them all. Physical exercise gets rid of all my frustrations. It sets me up to take on whatever the day has in store. I am afraid I will be like a bear with a sore head if I don't get my exercise." Sjaak answered.

“Different horses for different courses, Sjaak,” Helena said, demonstrating a yoga pose. She stretched her hands behind her neck and motioned for Sjaak to join her. “Yoga works for me.”

Tilly looked at her sceptically, wondering if she was already drunk.

Before Sjaak could respond to her question, Helena suggested online exercises or showing him a few of her own. Tilly had noticed how much he leered after her stepmother in the past but now he looked uncomfortable as he replied, "Unfortunately, I am a creature of habit. My morning routines are important for my well-being." He took a sip of his Chablis and explained his safety measures to them while running or biking outside during the pandemic.

Tilly reluctantly joined them at the bistro table, feeling out of place and socially awkward. She had to constantly remind herself of proper etiquette and envied those who seemed to effortlessly navigate social situations. Her father, who was usually by her side, was not there to guide her and she felt his absence keenly. She couldn't help but notice that there were no snacks provided like her father would always do, making her yearn for him even more.

Her stepmother was not much of a cook, except for Dutch soup which Tilly and her father loved. It was a smoky pea soup that he described as a comforting hug. Though, since his departure for Maastricht she hadn’t made it, and since his death, Tilly had grown wary of her mood swings, which today was on a manic high.

As they enjoyed their drinks, Tilly forced herself to give them each a small piece of stroopwafel, causing them to forget their previous conversation. Tilly failed to notice the indulgent satisfaction on both their faces as they watched her eat.

The impact of COVID regulations had made everything quiet outside —no planes flying overhead, no traffic or construction noises filling the air. Tilly could even hear birds singing and horses neighing, though she couldn't figure out where the noise of the horses was coming from.

Taking advantage of the calm atmosphere, Sjaak shared what he had learned about their basement with them. He leaned forward, his eyes sparkling with intrigue as he shared his latest findings on the canal and its connection to Feng shui.

As Sjaak spoke, their cat Sheba slinked into the basement, leaping onto the window seat, and waiting for her usual treat from Tilly's father. Tilly's attention momentarily shifted to her beloved pet before processing Sjaak's words.

"So that could be why our ancestors sealed up the basement," Tilly pondered aloud, "because of the negative Earth energy from underground streams."

Sjaak nodded in agreement.

Tilly's mind then drifted to the strange beehive they had discovered hidden in a corner of the basement. It had fascinated her. "But what about the bees?" she asked.

"Ah yes, insects like bees are naturally drawn to areas charged with geopathic stress," Sjaak explained, "but other animals tend to avoid these areas." He paused thoughtfully before adding, "It seems your ancestors were well aware of this phenomenon."

Tilly countered, "But look, there is the archangel pigeon that has moved into the old dovecote."

As Helena topped up her wine glass, they all looked toward the old stone dovecote. It was only big enough to hold one or two pigeons. It looked ancient.

The 12 Days of Christmas song entered Tilly's head '*Two turtle doves and a partridge in a pear tree*'. She wondered if the dovecote might have been a romantic gesture. Her feeling of grief returned as she remembered her father telling her that turtle doves had become an endangered species. He told her that their habitat in England was under threat. On their migratory flight to Africa for the winter, people in Mediterranean countries killed them for food.

Perched at the feeding table directly below the entrance a pigeon listened with polite attention. It turned its head from one to the other so that it would not miss a spoken word.

"A pigeon is a pigeon," said Sjaak. "They are all the same to me, rats with wings and carriers of disease."

Tilly stared at him in horror as he suggested,

"Put up some bird spikes that will get rid of it."

The pigeon glared at the rude Dutchman, and Tilly gave a pleading look to her stepmother. She could not personally save turtle doves, but they could try to keep this pigeon safe.

Helena smiled drunkenly and indulgently at Tilly, the living, breathing image of her father. "We will do no such thing," she said, glaring at Sjaak.

Tilly said quickly, "I took a photo of it on my phone and found out from an internet search that it is an archangel pigeon." Tilly held out her phone for them to see.

"You can see the photo here."

She flicked through the photos on her phone, holding it up in front of them both. "Don't you agree that they are striking and unforgettable?"

"Yes, well, there's always an exception to the rule," Sjaak said, ignoring the photos and the pigeon's stare. Full of his self-importance, determined to hog the conversation, he continued, "Did I tell you that my new puppy is an exception to the rule of dogs only seeing in 2D?"

"She can see in at least 3D, even 4D, like birds. She will bark at the TV if another dog or even a tiger appears, and the TV is mute. So, it is not the noise to which she is responding."

Tilly's gaze fell on her stepmother. One minute she had been acting the social butterfly and now she was like a little bird clasping its wings to her chest. It was as if her stepmother seemed to think she was the only one who mourned her father, Tilly thought, not ever wanting to share her grief with Sjaak.

As the days passed after her father's death, both Tilly and Helena changed as they each retreated into their own worlds, grappling with their pain privately and struggling to express their emotions openly. To Tilly Helena suddenly became distant and cold, turning to Sjaak for comfort via the internet. Tilly couldn't help but feel like an outsider in her own home, as she watched them earlier retreat to the kitchen, whispering in their native tongue and casting furtive glances. And something about their interactions didn't sit right with Tilly —it was as if they were hiding something, a secret that only they shared.

She recalled the intense arguments between her father and Helena about Sjaak's questionable activities before he left for Maastricht, and she couldn't shake off the feeling of unease whenever she saw her stepmother seeking solace in him. With her enhanced senses Tilly could see a black aura surrounding Helena as she spoke to him that pulsated like a quiet anger and hung in the air as a dark cloud. Despite knowing that Helena despised Sjaak, Tilly couldn't help but wonder what secrets they were keeping from her.

Though Tilly wished for support and understanding from her stepmother, she knew that she wasn't ready to share the precious memories of her father with anyone else just yet. She still held onto the hope that he was alive and well in Maastricht, unable to return due to COVID restrictions. Yet, Sjaak's presence in their home without her father made that hope seem impossible.

Helena's eyes were glassy, with unshed tears as she slurred her words. "I think Henry would know why the basement was blocked up."

Sjaak said, "I doubt the beehive, or a particular breed of pigeon caused them to block it up. Humans aren't afraid of the birds and the bees." He laughed at his use of metaphor before placing a parcel on the patio table, in front of Tilly's stepmother.

Helena thanked him and opened the parcel carefully, as instructed, and found beautiful hanging crystals.

He said, "To combat the geopathic stress and negative energy,"

She reached for the crystals, her hand trembling as she attempted to focus on their glimmer in the sunlight. "So thoughtful of you," she slurred, struggling to hold them steady.

As Tilly slowly walked toward the basement, having contributed her social input for the day, she overheard Sjaak confide to her stepmother,

"I heard that hauntings are tied to negative Earth energies. I imagine previous ancestors bothered by ghosts closed up the basement. Teenage hormones produce metabolic energy, so it's not a great combination."

Tilly turned her head to watch him as he touched Helena's hand for the briefest moment and said, "Added to her grief, it might be worth limiting the time Tilly spends in the basement."

Tilly heard a flicker of irritation enter Helena's voice as she dismissed his advice and seemed to sober up immediately. "The basement has our new immersive gallery there, Sjaak. I need Tilly's technological expertise to finish the project her father began."

"Forgive me for saying, but that is a task for experts. Aren't you putting too much stress on her fourteen-year-old shoulders?" he asked.

Her stepmother responded, mustering all her civility, "Tim, from our design team, will still lead the project and provide assistance when necessary."

Tilly couldn't stand the way Sjaak had weaselled his way into their lives since her father's passing. She resented the hold he had over Helena, easily manipulating her with wine and false sympathies. It was as if he believed their common nationality should bind them together. He had dealt with all of the arrangements in their homeland concerning Henry's death, telling Helena that her own family lived too far away in Friesland for them to assist during COVID. Tilly was convinced that he was somehow responsible for both her father's death and her stepmother's recent drinking problem, a belief which only worsened when she saw him refill Helena's glass of wine.

She heard Helena share reluctantly, "Tim has set it all up and has every confidence that she can continue her father's work."

Helena added, "Besides, they are available for online support. It is something Tilly wants and needs to do, and I believe she will make it work."

Tilly walked into the open basement and turning to close the door behind her she saw Helena picking up the crystals once again, holding them out to Sjaak and saying, "Would you mind attaching this hook and the crystals to the tree for me, please?"

Tilly smiled to herself. Helena wasn't the pushover Sjaak assumed she was.

23

A CHILD'S GRIEF OBSERVED

Tilly sat in the basement window seat, gazing out of the large picture window at the hanging crystals. When the sunlight hit them, it sent dancing rainbows of colour across the small, landscaped garden. The gentle breeze caressed the crystals, and they vibrated, releasing sounds of tranquillity. She watched her stepmother potter about the kitchen garden, disinfecting the dovecote and equipment used for the pigeon. She was thankful that Helena was up and about and was purposeful. Too often lately she nursed her grief in an alcoholic bedridden haze.

Tilly tried convincing Helena that the pigeon chose to live with them, but Sjaak had warned her stepmother that the pigeon might catch COVID and pass it on to them. Tilly quickly researched the likelihood on her phone. She found that it was rare for pigeons to catch the coronavirus. Human coronavirus was type 2, and pigeon coronavirus was type 3. She learned that it never passed from bird to human or vice versa. She was grateful that the pigeon chose to live in their garden.

Turning from the window, Tilly looked around the reception room. The actual footprint of the basement stretched the length of the building, with a reception area where she sat. The reception area only had one window and one door both looking out onto the garden. Sunlight would flood that area of the basement, and thick, blackout curtains hung all along that wall. It was Tilly's place of calm where she would sometimes listen to binaural beats on the free Insight Timer app that her father installed on her phone. It helped reduce her anxieties and she would hear her father's voice explaining binaural beats to her.

"This is true alchemy Tilly. Mental alchemy. You come from a family of alchemists."

She would close her eyes and look into the past at memories of her father and her sharing secrets. With aching desperation, she was determined to break through the walls of time and space in search of phantom conversations with the only person who cared enough to listen without judgment.

She remembered a long-forgotten thought that she shared with him "Isaac Newton was an alchemist."

Suddenly she was back in time in the art gallery and could hear him say "He was more of a chemist than an alchemist and he was full of self-importance because he was a genius and ahead of his time in so many things. Did you know that NASA used his laws of motion to build rockets?"

"How do you know so much about alchemy and the 17th century?" she had asked.

"I am fascinated by the 17th century when our family began this art business. Aspects of 17th-century society, culture, science and politics laid the groundwork for the world as we know it today."

"Why do you think he was more of a chemist?"

"Newton communicated through mathematics and equations, but all of his alchemical writings were encoded. After centuries had passed they were finally decoded and seen as groundbreaking scientific discoveries. Everything we believe about our world was derived from his observations and deductions. Another reason for me to admire icons of the 17th century. But why are you so interested in him, why not a pop star?"

Tilly groaned "Dad!" then added, "I don't know. I just am. I like the idea of writing in code. Can we write in code?"

There was no one else on Earth that Tilly could talk to like that. She missed him so much it took her breath away. She didn't believe she would ever meet anyone who understood her like her father.

Opening her binaural beats app, she recalled her father's words "Binaural beats help me to think more clearly."

She focused all her attention on the audio and could distinguish varying tones with slightly different frequencies entering each ear simultaneously. Understanding that her brain would create a beat from these two tones, she could multitask while still benefitting from the effects of the binaural beats. She closed the curtains but chose not to sit in her favourite window seat. She closed the door, and the room became dark.

She settled into one of the plush leather tub chairs, placed perfectly on either side of the sleek coffee table. The setup was intentional, meant to create a comfortable atmosphere for prospective clients to meet with either parent. The basement had been out of bounds to her and Helena during the conversion and for a time afterwards while her father and the design team worked on a business project of her father's.

At one stage, her father insisted that she and her stepmother go on a holiday together. He claimed that the noise and upheaval were detrimental to their health. She worried about his health for the two weeks they were on vacation. When they returned home, new wooden stairs led to the restored basement. A short corridor, walls and ceiling painted black, led to the Immersive gallery. Her father seemed incredibly happy. She needn't have worried. As she listened to the binaural beats in the darkened reception area, she imagined she saw a luminous copper sphere near the stairs. She wasn't frightened. It might have something to do with the Immersive Gallery at the end of the corridor.

Tilly peered through the window, observing her stepmother's hesitant steps towards the garden door. She watched her enter the modern basement and saw her hand trembling on the handle. The room was dimly lit by a flickering copper light, casting eerie shadows. Her stepmother stood frozen, searching the darkness for something elusive. Tilly knew that she would disapprove of the gloomy atmosphere down here, and sure enough, she heard her say, "Your father wouldn't want you hiding away like this." But at fourteen years old, Tilly no longer listened to what her stepmother presumed her father would want because he was dead, and she had no idea what he wanted. Anyhow she wasn't turning to drugs like some of her peers; her father would have been proud of her strength and resilience.

"Now that Sjaak is here," Tilly blurted out, gesturing towards a sealed wooden crate in the corner, "that must mean my father's coffin is in London too." She looked at her stepmother with pleading eyes. "I need to see his coffin. I can't believe he's gone until I see him."

Helena turned to look at her and Tilly suddenly noticed her red, puffy eyes that showed she had been crying. Helena spoke in a hushed voice (as if speaking any louder would make it real), "The COVID restrictions in the Netherlands meant that your father was cremated the same afternoon of his death."

Before Tilly had time to respond her stepmother rushed on, "The Netherlands allowed his cremated remains to be repatriated once their initial lockdown was lifted and Sjaak brought the ashes with him when he brought the crystals and stroopwafel."

Tilly retched. "I ate that stroopwafel in front of you both while you knew you had my father's ashes in the house" she blurted out and asked, "Why wasn't I told? I wanted to see him one more time."

Helena was sobbing but began walking up the staircase. "I couldn't find the right words, please forgive me," she said, as she clung to the bannister to support herself.

Tilly did not rush to help her, consumed by her own grief but she followed her up the stairs to their apartment, where

Sjaak was hovering. He rushed to Helena's side, but Tilly noticed her freeze at his touch and asked him to pour her a drink as she composed herself. Tilly followed him into the large kitchen. The open cupboard housed her father's treasured cooking spice collection, but it was empty.

"Where are all of the spices?" Tilly asked.

"I noticed they were out of date, so I emptied them into the bin," he replied dismissively with a wave of his hand.

Tilly gaped in shock. "She allowed you to do that!?" she exclaimed.

She rushed out of the kitchen with angry tears as her stepmother entered. She could not bear to be near her at that moment.

As Tilly descended the stairs, she could hear her stepmother's muffled sobs coming from the kitchen. She clenched her jaw and balled her hands into fists, feeling a surge of anger and sadness wash over her. Hearing those sobs reminded her of the times she'd heard her wailing her father's name drunkenly in the shower late at night where Helena must have thought no one could hear her. She had been on her way to seek comfort from her, then hearing the noise, which was akin to an animal in pain, Tilly crept down to the basement and cried alone.

Tilly knew that her stepmother only forced herself out of bed on days like this to take over her late husband's business—it was all for show. She didn't resent her, deep down Tilly understood that Helena was struggling to manage without her father and keep his business alive, but they couldn't share their grief. Her grief for her father was private, it was not for sharing.

She felt sure Sjaak, her father's deceptive friend, was taking advantage of her stepmother's vulnerability and grief. He made everything more complicated. He pretended to offer support and guidance while secretly trying to take over their lives. And it seemed like he always spoke to Helena in their native language, a language Tilly had never bothered to learn. She resented him for it, longing for simpler times when it was just her parents running things.

Everything had changed, and Tilly couldn't help but feel cheated out of precious moments with her father that he spent with Sjaak. She wanted nothing more than to turn back time. She could imagine her father's laughter and remember his last words to her as he left for Maastricht.

"Whatever happens in life, promise me you will keep smiling, Tilly."

The memory made her smile involuntarily. She promised him, of course.

She worried she might forget his voice, so she searched and found all the family videos and binge-watched them on the 360 screens in the Immersive gallery. The video images surrounded her. She was no longer in the real world; Transported into a virtual world where her father would always be there for her, waiting for her to join him. A place where she could go and feel his love and remember how he stole a kiss when she wasn't expecting it. A place where he showed her how to ride a bike with stabilisers. A place where his actions suggested he was still alive.

This was not a photo, capturing a moment in time, but virtual reality. The past restored. A place where she could join him whenever she wanted to. It wasn't fair that COVID took away her opportunity to say goodbye. If she could create an immersive experience with these videos, then she would have the ability to put her father back together again. She could turn back time.

She thought about the video footage and that, with her ever-growing knowledge of AR, VR, and AI, perhaps she could recreate him in the virtual world. She could simulate a world where he didn't die.

She could create a holographic cosmos. Perhaps the world they were living in was a virtual world of someone else's creation. If so, she would create a better virtual world. It would be a world where he was always there for her as he promised. He would never become an elderly parent needing her support. It wasn't a crazy idea.

She left the VR room and went into the reception area where the jukebox resided. She found the jukebox fascinating. It was stylish yet classic looking. Decked out in shimmering gold and chrome, it had a transparent glass top over the record changer and player, enabling you to see the rotating wheel of vinyl records as you made your selection. It held seventy of her father's favourite records. The jukebox had a remote control, which her father said hadn't been possible with the original jukeboxes. He toyed with getting an antique but wanted the vinyl without the hassle. She noticed her father used the jukebox in shuffle mode and would cycle through his records until he was ready to turn it off. When Helena criticised the appropriateness, he told her that clients would be fascinated and be able to browse the records and play them as they waited (though it was full of all his favourite 45 RPM records). Tilly used the remote, and the jukebox began playing Helen Reddy's 'Angie Babe.'

She turned the music up and wandered back down the passageway to the immersive gallery carrying the remote. Entering the gallery Tilly became aware of the luminous sphere again. She turned off the music. She closed her eyes and opened them slowly. The luminous copper sphere was still in the room but had moved. It could be that the sensors were dodgy in the room, and they needed to contact the design team to rectify it. She was alert, constantly scanning the room, determined to root out the source of the problem. In her wildest imaginings, she did not expect what happened next. The luminous copper sphere rose and burst to reveal what looked like a young, handsome 17th-century cavalier. As he materialised, she observed that he wore a plumed cavalier hat, a floor-length cloak, trousers that reached his knees, and long boots. He looked older than her, but not a great deal older.

He was slim with shoulder-length straw-coloured hair and bewitching amber eyes watching her every movement. This apparition was not her wished-for father.

She could smell him. He smelled overwhelmingly of cinnamon and cloves but something else that she couldn't identify but imagined was the smell of fear mixed with sweat. His presence filled the room, and she pulled on her COVID mask, which nowadays she always seemed to have slung around her neck.

Sheba prowled into the room, arched her back, and began spitting. The young cavalier vanished.

Tilly stood dumbfounded. Did the immersive installation have a glitch? Should she contact the design team to tell them? Or did she have an overactive imagination? She decided that she needed to turn on the installation and watch what had already been developed to see if the young cavalier was part of a VR production her father was working on or perhaps a holographic glitch in the programme.

24

A STEPMOTHER'S GRIEF OBSERVED

Helena watched Sjaak check the Nespresso coffee machine. She knew it needed cleaning before he could use it, and she was relieved to see him get to work on the task.

He handed her a glass of chilled wine and poured himself coffee from the coffee machine. She took a large mouthful of Chablis, savouring the familiar taste in her mouth, before it headed for her empty stomach. She took another mouthful, hoping it would soon numb the pain of her grief, which was ever-present.

She wiped her tears away and said, "Take me back through the day of the theft." She walked over to the kitchen table and, sitting down, added, "I want to hear everything the police have told you."

He leaned against the kitchen unit. "You mean Interpol," he said.

"Don't be so pedantic!"

"I have told you everything already," he argued.

"Just tell me again. Damn it!" She demanded.

She watched as he slowly and deliberately added sugar and creamer to his coffee before answering.

"It isn't going to change the outcome."

"Tell me!"

She waited as he carried his coffee over to the long wooden kitchen table, sighed and sat down. Consumed by grief she cradled her second glass of wine.

Taking the notebook from his inner pocket he began calmly reading his notes to her.

"At 7 a.m., witnesses thought they'd spotted two men lurking in a white van around my studio."

"At 7 a.m., the same witnesses noticed me leaving the studio, cycling off as usual."

"At 7.15 a.m. there was an abrupt report of a vehicle collision!"

"The only witness to the crash told of a white van that seemed to ram the bike, speeding away from the scene after."

Sjaak stopped speaking, his words hanging in the air like a fog as he looked across at her. She hung off his every word —desperate for more information than what he had already revealed during previous readings from this same notebook.

He continued stonily, "By 7.45 am I had received a phone call to my studio apartment about somebody injured...som eone riding my bike admitted to hospital in critical condition!"

Lost in his words Helena acted out the scenes in her mind.

"At 8 a.m., by some strange coincidence, those same witnesses noticed the white van parked outside my studio once again, occupied by two supposed workers dressed in drab overalls, carrying a painting or paintings covered in cloth." He added," The witnesses weren't alarmed since I often take in paintings to conserve or restore them; however, the timing of these events became highly suspect."

He paused and she was back in the room with Sjaak who was helping himself to more coffee before continuing, "At 8:03 a.m., the witnesses saw the workmen leave my studio with what appeared to be the same painting or paintings still concealed under canvas fabric.

"Surely the witnesses called the police," Helena said.

Sjaak insisted, "It did not appear unusual. One witness speculated that they must have arrived too early at 7 a.m., did not find me there, and returned at 8 a.m. only to have a wasted journey. An almost imperceptible sigh escaped her lips as he finished reading. Sjaak put the notebook back in his pocket, she gave a hollow laugh and said,

"A wasted journey! They were leaving with a Titian and a Bronzino! Worth millions."

He put his hand to his forehead and looked down at the table. Quietly, he said,

"They were professionals. According to Interpol, the FBI list it as one of the top ten art crimes."

There was a long silence before Helena rounded on him and said drunkenly,

"If you had approached a museum, you could have set up a makeshift laboratory in the museum to do the work. It would have been safer than at your studio. Henry asked you to store it in a secure location, away from potential harm or theft."

He nodded in agreement and said, "It would have made no difference to determined burglars."

He added quietly, "Though at least Henry would be alive."

"All this cloak and dagger stuff was bound to end in disaster. It wasn't a guilty secret! Henry's legal team were following the correct procedures. His mistake was allowing you to store the art in an unsafe place."

"Yes, I am sure you have all that legal information somewhere in Henry's filing system. I shall help you look for that evidence Helena."

Helena answered, "I don't understand how you convinced Henry to bypass the usual procedure."

As she observed him, she noticed a subtle shift in his body language. His shoulders hunched slightly, and he spoke slower and with an air of exaggerated patience as if speaking to an elderly relative. She could tell he was trying to keep his frustration in check.

"He followed procedure, Helena. He was checking its provenance, historical significance, and any relevant documentation- though he didn't give me that evidence. He did give me clear photographs from various angles, noting any distinguishing features, signatures, or inscriptions."

"But he allowed you to store the art. He trusted you. It should never have left this country." She persisted. She saw a smug look on his face as he delivered a surprising revelation.

"According to Henry, his family took it from our country in the 17th century. It has been suggested that the Netherlands may be the rightful owner and Henry may have evidence to support this claim."

Gaining composure, she quickly changed the subject knowing it no longer mattered who owned the paintings in the 17th century. That wouldn't have caused his death.

"Tell me again how Henry appeared when you saw him."

Sjaak told her for the umpteenth time what he saw when he arrived at the hospital.

"He looked as though he was sleeping but he opened his eyes immediately before they took him to surgery. I imagined he winked at me."

Helena groaned. "A massive bleed on the brain, Sjaak! They could do nothing to save him. I doubt he had the energy to wink. That is your guilt talking."

She paused, then said with feeling, "It should have been you!"

A low groan escaped his lips as he ran a hand through his waxed black hair. "I know," he admitted.

Through swollen red eyes, she looked at the egotistical man in front of her as he spoke.

"I believe they thought I was Henry," he pondered aloud with a touch of frustration. "But how could they? We bear no resemblance."

Sjaak's resentment towards the wealthy and privileged Henry Stafford was evident in the way he spoke, even though he tried to hide it. "They probably didn't know what I looked like," he continued, "but they knew my routine. If he hadn't taken my cycling gear and bike, I would be dead, and he would be here with you instead."

She drained the bottle and stood to get another. Turning her back on him, she said,

"Tilly doesn't realise how right she is when she looks to you for blame."

He stared at her in disbelief and retorted, "It is the criminal underworld that is to blame!"

She walked unsteadily to the wine fridge as he added compassionately, "We both know that."

She returned to her seat with another bottle, and as she sat, she hissed at him.

"You were meant to restore the art."

He said, "I did."

"You were not meant to discuss its provenance with all and sundry," she added vehemently, "You somehow drew attention to a couple of the greatest works from the lost royal art collection of Charles I!"

Hysteria rose in her voice, "What were you thinking?!"

Sjaak stared at her, his face expressionless as he acquiesced, "Yes, they are valuable. Yes, they once belonged to Charles I but only Interpol can tell us how criminals found out that I was restoring them." he said defensively.

She gave another hollow laugh. "You have a habit of frequenting Maastricht coffee shops that serve cannabis on the side."

She shrugged. "For you, Sjaak, coffee and drugs go together like cheese and wine."

She remembered Henry reminiscing about their wild nights in Maastricht, where Sjaak was a notorious figure in the local coffee shops and known for his love of cannabis. He had a feeling that Sjaak's recklessness stemmed from his connections with powerful people who were drawn to him. Henry assured her that he behaved responsibly, though he couldn't deny the allure of Sjaak's lifestyle and the influential company he kept.

She said," It is no secret that some of these coffee shops are controlled by the criminal underworld." Adding "I do not doubt in my mind Sjaak that you were indiscreet when you were high. You are totally to blame for me losing Henry and Tilly losing her father!"

Sjaak put a finger over his mouth, "Do not shout. We agreed Tilly need not know," he said quietly.

She said bitterly, "What a tangled web we weave, when first we practise to deceive" could not be a more apt saying at this moment."

She added, "I should never have agreed, and now I am complicit. I was losing Tilly to her adolescent phase as it was, but Henry was the world to her. You will have given her cause to hate me more than she already does."

Her steely exterior crumpled and she sobbed. Sjaak passed her the box of tissues, and she wiped her snotty nose and wet, tear-stained face.

Sjaak extended his arm towards her as he said," She is just being a normal teenager."

Helena ignored his gesture as she processed the scene before her, her gaze lingering on the wine bottle she had replaced earlier. Throwing her hands onto the kitchen table, she forced herself to a stand. Her glass was still half-filled with wine, and, with an unsteady hand, she refilled it before sinking back into the chair with a thud.

Sjaak shifted uncomfortably in his seat then stood and made his way over to the coffee machine, "My studio was broken into while I was at the hospital identifying Henry's body," he said as he set up the machine.

"Although the paintings have gone. They would not have realised the value of the tapestries."

With false brightness, he said, "They can be restored."

Sjaak emptied the pods, filled the water tank, refilled the machine, and helped himself to another cup of coffee.

She did not want to talk about tapestries. She began crying softly and said," Why did you let him ride your bike?"

"I have told you already," he sighed. "On the morning of the accident, he claimed he had a headache. He asked if he could borrow the bike to ride it off. Those were his words: "Ride it off."

He added, "To be honest, I cannot do without my daily bike ride, so I simply thought he needed to get rid of the cobwebs of sleep."

"You mean the wine you both consumed the night before!"

"I believed," Sjaak said then repeated with emphasis, "I believed that it would set him up for the day ahead, like it does me. I was being kind. I had wanted to ride myself."

Helena was lightheaded. She hadn't eaten. Butterflies filled the empty spaces in her stomach as fear took up residence. She realised that this story would never have a happy conclusion. It wouldn't matter how often she asked him to retell it. She poured herself another glass of wine and asked him.

“Are Tilly and I safe? Will these criminals target us?”

Sjaak was staring at her and, fuelling her paranoia, he answered too quickly for her liking.

“Don’t be ridiculous. As far as the burglars were concerned, they were fulfilling an order. They may not have meant to kill me or Henry. I imagine that they wanted to ensure that the studio was empty.”

He leaned towards Helena, "They weren't behind the heist," he whispered. His breath reeked of coffee and Helena turned her face away from him.

Reclining back in his chair, he divulged further details.” According to Interpol, the syndicate leaders have hidden the stolen paintings. They'll use them as leverage for reduced sentences if they're caught for other crimes."

Helena put her head in her hands and said, “The fact they are hidden once more would upset Henry. They have only recently left the void that existed under the basement.”

She sighed heavily, her drunken voice dripping with bitterness, “Those paintings are destined never to see the light of day.”

She tried to control her impatience as he let slip a sly smile and spoke slowly as if he thought her drunken state slowed her brain processing abilities.

“It will be a different story now; criminals have no idea how to store paintings. They are burglars, not art lovers like you, me, or Henry. Paintings to them, are merely goods to be traded.” he said smugly.

She hid her contempt for him, her face grim. “If the burglars start spending vast amounts of money, they will surely be caught.”

Sjaak sighed heavily before continuing. He had met with Interpol already and knew the drill all too well. “The burglar will get a tiny percentage of the value. They risk prison and murder, but they will not grass on the organised crime syndicate. The criminal underworld is known to gossip about stolen art, particularly art of high value; it goes from hand to hand very quickly.”

She asked, “Are these criminal masterminds based in Maastricht? How will Interpol find them?”

Sjaak stirred his coffee. He hesitated before saying, “Interpol says criminal masterminds do not shit in their backyards. So, no, they are not believed to be Dutch. They have tentacles reaching all over the world. They control drug trafficking, prostitution, sex trafficking, and the disposal of stolen goods. Anything that makes them money. The burglars may have been Dutch, but they were a tiny link in the chain. Interpol will never give up.”

“Why are Interpol collaborating with you and not me?” she asked.

“Because it happened in my studio.”

“But I could have helped Interpol. They are our paintings, not yours,” she said.

“I gave them photos of the paintings,” he said. “I don’t believe you could have helped any more than that. Do you think I pretended that they belonged to me?”

Ignoring his comment, she looked at the photos on her phone of the paintings. Full of rage she spoke angrily.

"For the Dutch authorities, it is a crime against our cultural heritage."

Sjaak nodded and said, "We are a nation of art lovers."

Helena said, "I believe the authorities will stop at nothing to get these back. Then we will find my husband's murderers!"

Sjaak got up. He picked up the coffee cup and wine glass and deposited both in the dishwasher.

He went to the door, turned, and said, "Please remember that neither Interpol nor the Dutch authorities want anyone, apart from us two, to know about the true provenance and value of the paintings."

"You have a nerve!" she hissed, as she accompanied him to the front door, closing it firmly behind him. Returning to the kitchen, she got herself a clean wine glass and finished off her second bottle of wine.

25

SJAAK

Sjaak walked slowly to his apartment block and thought back to when he met Henry for the first time at the Maastricht art fair in 2012. The organisers of the fair established it to support and promote the professional restoration of significant museum artworks. Grants were open to public museums from all over the world and artworks of any age.

The organisers invited Sjaak to take part in a dedicated panel discussion on the importance of conservation on the first floor of the fair. He agreed to take part because he was a conservator and he hoped to do the restoration work for those chosen pieces of art.

As Sjaak prepared to speak, Henry Stafford joined the audience to listen to him. Afterwards, Henry introduced himself to Sjaak and asked, "Would you care to take a look at a 17th-century painting for me? It needs restoration work."

"I have enough work in Europe to keep myself busy," Sjaak answered, wishing to find the owners of the museums who had won the large grants.

Then Helena abruptly appeared. Sjaak was mesmerised by her delicate beauty. She introduced herself and talked enthusiastically in their native language about Henry's art gallery and where it was in London. Sjaak asked for more information about the gallery and exactly where it was. He agreed to visit the gallery and take a look at the painting. Helena gave him their business card. Sjaak looked at the address. He thought that fate was certainly at work.

As the evening sky turned to dusk, Sjaak sat in his Maastricht studio and carefully retrieved the worn file containing his family's history. He had researched back as far as the 17th century and discovered that an ancestor of his, an orphan, went from the Netherlands to live in London during the plague years. The file supported his gut feeling that the address on the business card was the address she resided at. Had they, had Henry's ancestors been responsible for her death?

26

FRANCINE

Sjaak got in the lift to the well-established London mansion block, where he owned a small apartment. He intended to pick up his dog first and pressed the button to the second floor.

"I have recently walked Schatje and fed her. She could do with a nap, I think," Mrs. Anderson offered, handing him the dog and the lead.

As he got back in the lift with Schatje, walking behind him, he thanked the universe for finding him the apartments. He had been spending far too much money on hotel rooms and was confident he would easily make his money back on the investment.

Sjaak entered his apartment and said aloud, "Alexa, Open 'Calm my Dog."

Schatje ran to her basket as the music filled the air, calming her and her master.

Drawn to a postmark from Friesland in the Netherlands on an envelope Sjaak picked up his post. He carefully opened his small writing bureau and placed the envelope on top. Retrieving his notebook, he set the thick, large envelope aside for later examination.

From his research, he already discovered a great deal about his ancestor, Francine Van Uylenburgh. He had carefully documented everything he found out. He quickly read his notes to bring himself up to speed.

Name: Francine

Orphaned at the age of ten.

Second youngest of eight children.

Deaf.

Father- art dealer in Amsterdam in the 17th century.

Mother: Saskia —died in childbirth.

Father died from tuberculosis shortly afterwards.

Other children, including the baby, are given homes by relatives.

No one wanted Francine.

Note: The Dutch at that time, believed her deafness was a sign of God's anger towards her parents.

A strange girl with a penchant for collecting feathers and observing dead birds.

Could draw birds in remarkable detail.

Father encouraged her artistic talents.

London Art dealer had three sons and claimed she would be a good companion for his only daughter.

Agreed upon by Francine's uncle, her father's brother.

Francine accompanied the art dealer, Henry Stafford, and his son, Harry, on a boat bound for England.

He put his notes to one side and picked up the letters from Francine to a brother in Amsterdam, whom she adored. Taught to sign and to write by the English family she proved to have an aptitude for learning.

He had hit a brick wall in his research. He could find out nothing more about her after the plague hit England. He was convinced she had died from the plague. He wanted to know if she died at the home of Henry Stafford and was about to employ a researcher in England when fate played a part. He met Henry Stafford and his wife, Helena, at the Maastricht fair. He was determined to inveigle himself into their lives and visit their home, once the home of his ancestor, Francine. He would also employ a genealogy site in the Netherlands though he set himself a time limit, not wanting to waste his money.

He poured himself a coffee, sat at the bureau, and opened the thick envelope before him. It contained more envelopes. He opened the letter that accompanied the envelopes. The genealogist asked him to phone him.

Sjaak's fingers drummed nervously on the table as he waited for someone to pick up his call.

"Hello?" A voice finally answered.

"Sjaak Van Ullestrom here. You requested a phone call."

"Yes, I did. I've sent you a significant amount of evidence to review, but I wanted to inform you that your ancestor did not die from the plague as you believed."

"She didn't?" Sjaak asked in surprise.

“No.”

“But I have found no records of her here in England.”

"That is because she made her way back, somehow, to her family home in Amsterdam!"

"You are kidding me!"

Putting his mobile on speaker mode Sjaak went to his drinks trolley, poured himself a glass of Oude Jenever and took a large slug.

The genealogist's voice continued, "Francine's brothers and sisters had been fond of their young sister. As adults, they were pleased to have her home at first."

"At first?"

"Have you heard of Anna Maria van Schurman?"

"The name is familiar."

"She was a famous polymath of the 17th century and a Labadist."

"What has that to do with my ancestor?"

"Francine was a determined young woman and began writing to Schurman, a leader of the Amsterdam Labadist community."

"To have gotten herself back to Amsterdam under her own steam as a deaf young woman. I can only be proud to be related to her," Sjaak replied.

"Well, your ancestors weren't proud, and they disowned her once she moved in with the Labadist community, which they regarded as a sect."

Sjaak remembered searching through Henry's papers to find out more about Henry's ancestors. He found nothing that pertained to Francine. Yet he did remember Henry sharing the fact that one of his ancestors from the 17th century was an alchemist and a member of the Rosy Crown society. He could understand how the woman, who enabled Francine to communicate, would become someone she wished to emulate. That was why she joined a religious sect.

The genealogist continued "Schuman and the Labadist community moved around the Netherlands, eventually setting up home in Wiewurt, Friesland. The northernmost province of the Netherlands. Francine moved with them."

Sjaak poured himself another drink. He helped himself to a hunk of bread and cheese as he listened on speaker mode.

"In Wiewurt, they lived in a stately home. There were six hundred inhabitants. Some were engaged in recording the wonders of nature through drawings, writing, and printing. Others were concerned with the raising of animals, the maintenance of fish ponds and dovecotes, and the growing of fruit, grain, and vegetables. While some chose to mill the grain and preserve foods others chose to cook and maintain the castle. Wealthy people from England and Europe visited the community."

In the back of Sjaak's mind, he knew he had heard the name of Wiewurt. *What was it?* he thought.

The genealogist continued, "You may remember me telling you of her love of birds."

"Yes, indeed I do. I certainly didn't inherit that trait."

"Well, it seemed that throughout her life, Francine continued to collect feathers. Some she displayed, and some she used as quills to produce beautiful ink drawings of birds and their feathers."

"My ancestor was an ornithological artist who was never recognised nationally for her skill it might seem."

"Indeed, open envelope numbered 2."

Sjaak did as instructed. In front of him was the bundle of papers, including a few of her drawings. Sjaak owned those drawings. The drawings were of single feathers, wings, or side and front views of pigeons.

"What do you think?"

"They are incredible and could be compared with Robert Hooke's 'Micrographia.' This is amazing news. Thank you. I was concerned I would find she had died of the plague. This is good news. "

"There is more."

"I don't need to hear any more. You have done an amazing job for which you will be well paid. Thank you."

Sjaak ate the bread and cheese and washed it down with another drink of his favourite tipple and was about to end the call. The genealogist was not finished and quickly interjected,

"Francine was also adept at using saltpetre. She taught people in the community how to use it to preserve the community's food and fertilise the farmland. She used it to mummify her favourite pigeons after they died. These she kept preserved in the basement of the crypt at Wiuwert. "

Suddenly Sjaak's memories of Wiuwert surfaced in his mind. He retrieved his iPad and did an internet search. Yes, he remembered correctly, Wiuwert was famous throughout the world for the mummies discovered in its crypt.

The genealogist continued, "After Francine's death, her body was mummified and preserved in the basement of the crypt of Wiuwert, alongside her birds, in line with her written wishes."

Sjaak was speechless.

"Are you ok? I know it is a lot to take in. As I have said, you have all the evidence to back this up and if you wish to visit Wiuwert you shall find things just as I have described. "

"I don't wish to appear rude," Sjaak said, "But I need to process all of this information."

"Certainly, Ring me if you need to."

Sjaak turned off the speaker phone and sat shellshocked.

The bundle of papers also contained a self-portrait of Francine dated 1667 and a tearful story about two young women left to die during the 1665 plague in London. He felt a growing certainty that his ancestor had buried the body found under the flagstones of Henry's basement. The body of Mathilde.

27

IMMERSIVE ART

Tilly couldn't understand why the holographic cavalier was still lingering around when she knew she had turned the VR system off earlier. She wasted no time in powering it on and effortlessly navigating through the various content, data, and applications with a motion-tracked VR wand.

She skimmed through the materials displayed on the surrounding walls and discovered an almost completed VR experience. Her father and his design team had been experimenting with creating a simulation of The Battle of Edgehill in October 1642.

Tilly hadn't expected a battle to be the focus. Their art gallery primarily displayed Dutch and Flemish masters, so she assumed her father's first project would follow suit. However, as she stumbled upon a letter from a re-enactment society in the VR instructions folder, it became clear why he had chosen this.

In the letter, the society explained that Tilly's father wanted to both highlight the VR possibilities and honour those who perished at the site. The accompanying photo showed a mass grave holding five hundred bodies.

The immersive experience for visitors was of utmost importance to her father. Depicting the harsh realities of battle while also promoting 17th-century artwork served a dual purpose —to educate and potentially sell paintings.

The design team created a virtual floor map to help visitors visualise the battlefield and understand where soldiers fell.

Three carefully selected paintings, rich in symbolism, served as the backdrop for the scene. Each one represented a unique aspect of the Battle of Edgehill. When the installed programme activated, Tilly saw the paintings on all four walls, depicting both the victory and horror of battle. The background showed a cavalry skirmish, symbolizing the Royalist's successful charge into the parliamentarian flanks. The scent of gunpowder filled the basement air. Drumming echoed as holographic cavaliers marched into battle, followed by trumpet and bugle sounds. From the opposite direction, holographic roundheads approached the battlefield.

The design team had brought that section of the painting to life, enabling the viewer to enter the battle through VR. It was incredibly clever and thoughtful. The music that the artwork was set to add to the emotions experienced. The whole gallery was completely engaging.

Tilly perused the attached notes, which described the haptic features of the exhibit. Haptics were designed to give viewers a sense of wielding a sword, pike, or pistol. Tilly's father had instilled in her a love for video games, and this aspect of the exhibit brought to mind those immersive experiences. It would allow viewers to do more than simply observe a painting; they could actively participate as protagonists in the very first battle of the English Civil War.

The painting displayed a young Prince Charles in Civil War armour, accompanied by his brother, the Duke of York. Tilly walked towards the scene, noting that others wore the same period clothing as the ghostly figure she had previously glimpsed. She surmised he belonged to the 17th century and wondered how he had materialised without the programme activated.

17th-century music played softly in the background, enhancing the immersive experience. The basement lights gradually dimmed as the day of the battle progressed. She could hear men's voices singing psalms, their tired and dirty faces glistening with sweat. On the walls, animated projections of soldiers moved about, caring for the dead and dying. As she moved, the images reacted to her presence. Dying soldiers would fade away when "touched." Trying to avoid a 3D trompe l'oeil projection of a riderless horse, she watched as it galloped across the wall and out of the door, accompanied by a gust of wind. Glancing around, she realised that the room was filled with sensors. The two boys remained at the centre of the scene, dutifully playing their roles. Knowing the inevitable outcome of the battle, Tilly struggled to hold back tears at the overwhelming hopelessness of it all. It was an incredibly powerful and immersive experience.

She heard Helena descend the staircase cautiously, her grip tight on the bannister while balancing a glass of wine. Tilly demonstrated to her how her father used VR with 17th-century art to transport customers back in time, allowing them to fully immerse themselves in the experience.

Helena sipped her wine and pondered aloud whether replicating her husband's accident would truly bring them any solace. Helena spoke slowly, "I can't imagine it serving a therapeutic purpose for descendants. Reenacting a battle and realising that you could do nothing to change its outcome...it won't help anyone come to terms with such a tragedy."

Tilly objected, stating, "But that was over three centuries ago! Re-enactments of the Civil War have been happening forever. You'd have to watch it countless times to have any negative impact."

She pointed out that the VR experience, created for the Re-enactment Society, would be a valuable tool for members to relive historic scenes and prepare for re-enactments.

Helena nodded thoughtfully before adding, "There are numerous current exhibits that claim to showcase the work of long-deceased artists in an awe-inspiring technological manner."

Reflecting on her own experience at the Van Gogh exhibit, Tilly excitedly interjected, "It was exhilarating! Immersing myself in his paintings and travelling back in time all in one day was truly surreal."

Tilly's stepmother appeared distracted; her focus drawn to the handwritten note left by her father. She watched as her stepmother read it aloud.

"The immersive experience will showcase a unique virtual reality interactive, guiding viewers through a journey with 17th-century artists such as Dutch and Flemish masters. This visual voyage will reveal the inspiration behind each piece of art, completely immersing you in the world of these masterpieces. You will hear the music, songs, and sounds of the 17th century while also having the opportunity to enter their world through the technology available to artists at that time, using present-day technology. Note to self: Set up an area with a camera obscura for visitors to try. He has written notes for viewers to learn about the artists and their 17th-century lives, selected music and other works of art by these artists. He thought of everything." Her tears flowed as she finished her wine.

Tilly watched on, unable to leave her grief to offer comfort but determined to research camera obscuras so she could fulfil her father's intended plan.

28

FLYING HIGH

It was the middle of the day and Tilly was sprawled out on the grass in the garden, gazing at the ever-shifting clouds above. In her mind, she transformed them into a virtual Magna Doodle, creating and erasing images with each passing moment.

She imagined that she could see Salvador Dali's surreal elephants with their spindly legs drift across the sky distorting into nothingness as the breeze carried the clouds away. Another mass of clouds appeared above her, and as she searched for phantom images, she heard the sound of a happy, cooing pigeon and her gaze moved down to the garden.

The archangel pigeon was waddling about on the grass under the dovecote. It was bobbing its head up and down as it waddled, and it looked cute. Tilly liked to imagine that it was sent by her father to watch over her. It was mesmerising to look at as the iridescent colours of its feathers caught the sunlight. Tilly felt that no human artist could truly capture the sheer beauty of birds.

She left birdseed out at the beginning and end of every day. Though she hadn't seen the pigeon eat the seed, it disappeared. Other birds certainly visited the bird table. She did not 'shoo' them away. They needed food too. Large birds —jackdaws, magpies, and even ravens. Small birds -wrens, chaffinches, and red-breasted robins. She reasoned that to discriminate against them as to who could eat at the table would be a kind of bird racism. She wondered if there was a name for it and whether birds had their form of racism or was it simply all about survival.

She kept the water dish topped up and smiled the first time she saw the pigeon suck up the water using its beak. Pigeons were so clever. Other birds had to lift their heads to let the water go down their throats. Pigeons drank like humans.

Tilly and her stepmother were vigilant with their cleaning routine. Helena believed they were protecting the pigeon from COVID and both themselves and the pigeon from bird flu. The lavender-scented air from the kitchen garden concealed any disinfectant aromas. The pigeon bobbed its head to look at her with its orange eyes.

Sheba, the family cat, appeared in the garden. Tilly became agitated as she watched them both. She was willing the pigeon to fly out of the way so that Sheba wouldn't try to catch the bird. She observed the pigeon, its body suddenly frozen as if it had held its breath. In one swift motion, it burst into flight, wings tightly folded against its body as it soared up from the ground.

It rapidly unfurled them, making two powerful flaps that created an updraft of air beneath it. The third flap was less vigorous as the pigeon leaned forward and the air caught under its feathers, carrying it upwards. Its beady, orange eyes stayed focused on its destination until it finally reached the dovecote.

Once on the dovecote, it bobbed its head to one side, puffed up its feathers, and loudly grunted several times. Sheba ignored the noises the pigeon made but slid her sly green eyes upwards triumphant. The pigeon flapped its wings, launched itself into the air, and flew towards Sheba, not frightened at all. Tilly looked on, amazed, as the pigeon shepherded the cat towards the basement door. Once satisfied, the pigeon used its powerful wings to take off and soar up and away. Sheba stood by the door to the basement mewing. Tilly opened the door for Sheba, who curled herself around Tilly's legs, before whizzing up the stairs.

All at once, the garden was quiet. Tilly looked towards the crystal wind chime, which had given off a vibrational sound that made the garden feel peaceful. The crystals, blown about by the wind had become entangled.

Tilly took a bistro chair and removed the cushion. She placed the chair on the verge of the canal bank, under the tree. The wind must have twisted the nylon threads of the chime around and around, suffocating its sound.

Tilly balanced precariously on the chair and reached up to try and lift the chime off its hook. She could feel the chair begin to give way. She lost her balance and quickly grabbed onto a glass crystal. She hung onto the crystal but knew it couldn't hold her weight. At that precise second, she heard a faint grunting and cooing noise. She glanced up to where the noise was coming from and looked into the orange eyes of the archangel pigeon hovering above her. The glass chime broke.

As she began falling towards the murky waters of the canal she saw the large bulbous eyes of a blue damselfly and she turned her head to see what it was looking at. The pigeon was flying towards her growing in size as it did so. She imagined herself landing on its soft, downy back and being carried safely up into the sky.

In her mind, she sat on the giant pigeon as it flew into a rising current of warm air. The pigeon did not need to flap its wings at all as it glided in a circular motion inside the thermal current. Tilly found it thrilling, and she did not want the feeling to end.

When she awoke, she was lying on the grass verge outside the basement door. Her hand was hurting. She gingerly opened her palm to reveal a broken glass crystal. The palm of her left hand had a tiny slither of dried blood, and it hurt. She used her right hand to pick up the small posy of lavender lying next to her and put it to her nose to smell.

How long had she been asleep? Had she been dreaming? She remembered having an ecstatic feeling of sitting on the most comfortable pillow imaginable as the pigeon guided her through a magical journey, soaring through the stars and traversing galaxies. Instead of chirping or cooing like a normal bird, this pigeon seemed to communicate with her telepathically. It told her that it had returned to Earth specifically to assist her in elevating her consciousness as a rebirther. She could feel its energy pulsing through her, filling her with a sense of purpose and connection. The pigeon then revealed that she would be helping an astralite named Gabriel heal his past traumas so that he could continue his journey in the cosmos. After a mesmerising flight filled with cosmic wonders, the pigeon landed gracefully in her garden. Its gentle cooing seemed to form the name "Gabriel" on her lips.

The young cavalier, whom she had caught a fleeting glimpse of in the basement, materialised before her. He gently helped her down from the back of the pigeon, as if called upon by the pigeon to assist. The pigeon slowly returned to pigeon size and flew onto the dovecote, where it watched them both. The young cavalier proceeded to put his hand above a bush of lavender growing in her mother's kitchen garden. The best fronds of lavender broke away from the bush and floated up into his hand. The fronds formed into a small bunch, and he held the bunch to her nose until she fell asleep. Or did she dream that?

She got up and walked unsteadily towards the basement door. She was unable to put much pressure on her hand to open the door and had to use both hands. As a result, the door opened silently. She stepped inside and was surprised to see Sjaak standing over a box file in her father's office. She knew her father kept all of his files meticulously ordered in that office and when he was alive Sjaak would never have been allowed to browse through his files. Her father took care of all the finances, record keeping and filing. Her stepmother left all of that to him. Was she now allowing

Sjaak to take on that role? The thought horrified her. She narrowed her eyes and watched him as he picked up a letter, and Tilly could see instantly that he was pretending to read it. Even from where she stood, she could see that the letter was upside down. Her stepmother hadn't permitted him to ransack her father's files at all. Before she could even open her mouth, he cut her off. "Ah, there you are," he drawled, lazily looking up from his phone. "Your stepmother has a new project. She thinks it might pique your interest." He gestured towards the stack of papers on her father's desk with a flick of his hand.

As he spoke, his phone rang. "I have got to take this outside," he said, adding, "The reception is poor in this basement." He slid the letter back into the box file and went outside.

Sjaak stood outside and ended the call he had sent himself whispering a famous Dutch saying "een dubbeltje op z'n kant" meaning "that was a close call."

He sprung open a beautiful, engraved cigarette case as though it were some secret diary and took out a Marlboro. He lit the cigarette, put it to his lips, sucked in the smoke, and held onto the sensation before drawing air into his lungs. He exhaled a smoke-filled breath that travelled up towards the sky. Smoking was a habit he had been unable to kick, and a pandemic was not the time to start trying, he reasoned.

At that precise moment, the archangel pigeon, Isaac, flew directly overhead. The smell of the cigarette was toxic and had an immediate effect on his bowels as he soared higher to avoid inhaling the smoke. The saltpetre, the correct name for pigeon dung, began its aerial descent. As it did so, Isaac concentrated on the alchemy of saltpetre.

Saltpetre which could penetrate any substance, even gold. The Miraculum Mundi. Isaac knew how the moisture of the atmosphere mixed with the saltpetre could, in time, fertilise the ground below so that the kitchen garden would have a bumper crop. If he wanted, he could use cosmic energy frequencies to speed up that process. Isaac chose to take advantage of a passing cosmic phenomenon (similar to that which creates thunder and lightning) to do that. He had performed alchemy many times when on Earth as the human Isaac Newton. This was his first rebirth as a bird, and he accessed brimstone and charcoal instead of brimstone and ammonia from the cosmic pharmacy. Added to the saltpetre, it created a small amount of gunpowder.

The archangel pigeon circled the air as this alchemical process was taking place, before flying to the dovecote to watch the kitchen garden, and by default, Sjaak from a safe distance as he waited for the garden transformation to happen.

Sjaak slipped the cigarette case into the internal pocket of his tailored suit jacket. He heard the pigeon alight on the dovecote. Looking directly at the bird with utter contempt, he said under his breath, "Filthy, dirty animal."

He stubbed his cigarette out on the garden path. Isaac heard every word. The saltpetre concoction drifting down from the sky was quickly redirected away from the delicate kitchen garden below. Sjaak bent down to pick up the cigarette stub. He flicked the stub into the compost tub. As he bent down, the gunpowder landed silently on the back of his tailored suit jacket. Orange eyes fixated on the gunpowder, which proceeded to ignite and quietly burn a small, ruinous hole in the Saville Row jacket.

29

THE KING'S BUTTON

As the first rays of morning light crept through her bedroom window, Tilly rose from her bed and quietly descended to the basement.

Her fingers traced over the rows of CDs in her father's music archive until she found what she was looking for —Ennio Morricone's "Gabriel's Oboe." This piece held a special place in her heart as it was one that her father often played while meditating. As the gentle melody filled her ears, memories of their precious time together flooded Tilly's mind, bringing a small smile to her lips.

She thought back to her magical ride on the archangel pigeon who told her she would help someone called Gabriel and then seemed to say the name "Gabriel" as the cavalier appeared in the garden to help her down from the pigeon's back. The name Gabriel reminded her of the beautiful music. The memory brought goosebumps to her skin and a sense of confusion. Was it all just a dream or were these events connected?

She wondered if her grief-stricken mind was playing tricks on her to remind her of that piece of music. She knew she was becoming obsessed with her father's favourite music and worried that she would forget them. But she couldn't bear the thought of losing any connection to him.

As she sat listening to the beautiful piece of music her thoughts radiated the energy of her emotions, and she visualised the handsome cavalier. She whispered the name the pigeon had given him "Gabriel."

To her amazement, there was a sudden shift in the air around her. A faint copper-glowing orb appeared before her, gradually taking shape into a figure. Tilly's thoughts had a magnetic pull which crossed dimensions allowing him to materialise into her world.

The young cavalier wore a silver necklace from which hung a silver ball with perforations, and a heady aroma seemed to emanate from that, which Tilly could smell even through her mask. Tilly wondered whether the immersive room had fractured reality and projected him from the past into the present and whether she needed to help him return. Or maybe she imagined a pigeon talking to her and he was simply a hologram that had escaped from the immersive experience. Or she could be hallucinating, a symptom of COVID.

She quickly turned on the VR programme and projected the battle paintings onto the basement walls then paused them. If he had come from the programme, surely it was reasonable to expect he could return. She believed she was giving him a portal back into his world.

Gabriel stood in front of her, and she saw him looking in fascination at the paintings of the battle of Edgehill surrounding them on all the walls in the room, probably reassured by the 17th-century scene she surmised. She felt him whisper into her mind,

I can see my King, Charles II, as a young prince, and the King's brother, the Duke of York.

Tilly smiled and muttered to herself, "This is so weird on so many levels."

To him, she said, "You are from the 17th century then!"

They both stared at each other. She wasn't frightened but she was nervous with excitement at the prospect of communicating with someone from another world. She hid her nerves and said calmly, "I thought you looked like one of the young cavaliers in this programme," adding, "Are you a hologram that has escaped from this battle?"

She sat with the controls in front of her to steady her nerves as she noticed him watching her.

She heard him in her thoughts once more, *I lived on Earth at the time of Charles II, not Charles I. What is a hologram*?

Tilly tried to explain that they were images that had depth created by lasers and pointed to the princes on the wall saying Those are 2D images, but you are a 3D image.

Looking searchingly at the hand controls and staring at the painting he appeared more interested in the princes than the technology, telepathing, *The painting suggests that the young Prince Charles and his brother, the Duke of York, had been involved in the battle, but that is not true.*

She suggested reluctantly that he could go back into the programme if he wanted to.

No, I can't. My father was at that battle. Not me.

Tilly smiled. She didn't want him to go. She was enjoying this new experience. It was rare for her to feel the control she needed in a new social situation, but in this instance she did. He wasn't threatening like a real person. It was as if he had left a VR game. A non-human companion and better than a chatbot. She dismissed the words to one of her father's records, 'Angie Babe' that invaded her mind's space and said, "I think you might be a hologram from the immersive experience in front of us, though I haven't worked out how you can speak into my mind!"

The cavalier paced around the room, looking as if he belonged to the scenes of battle on the walls. He whispered into her mind; *It was the first battle in the war of the Commonwealth in 1642. I wasn't even born then!*

"Are you saying that you are not a hologram from this immersive experience?" she persisted.

I am not that old!

Tilly put her hand over her mouth to suppress the bubble of laughter that was threatening to escape. She spluttered, "Erm, Your clothes and style suggest that you might be older than you think you are."

He ignored her comment and moved closer to the merged paintings as if searching for someone.

"Who are you looking for?" Tilly asked, "Your father?"

William Harvey, chief doctor to the King. He was tasked with supervising the future King Charles II and the Duke of York, but he is not in these paintings.

"How would you recognise him if you say you weren't even born then?"

He was a very famous physician and philosopher. My father owned a painting of him.

Tilly said, "So you aren't a hologram it seems. Though perhaps you don't wish to return to the battle."

The cavalier took his hat off and realigned the feather lovingly and asked her, *Can a hologram be in two places at the same time?*

She reasoned, "No. I don't think so, but a hologram can be shattered, and each tiny shard will still contain the whole image. So, you could have been broken up in the making of the VR and there could be loads of you about the place."

I assure you I am not a hologram, but I like the idea that bits of me could be in several places at once.

If you are not a hologram then you are either a hallucination or a ghost and I don't believe in ghosts."

She thought to herself that if he were a hallucination, he could only answer with the knowledge that she had in her head. She decided to ask the apparition a question that she did not know the answer to unless she used a search engine or AI. That would prove whether he was just a figment of her overactive imagination. She asked him," How old were the princes?"

The young cavalier appeared mesmerised by the immersive experience before them and answered slowly, *Prince Charles was twelve, so his brother, the Duke, would have been nine during the battle.*

Tilly checked on her phone and found him to be correct. She said, "I'm guessing from your Cavalier clothes that your father was a Royalist and fought for the King."

He flicked his wrists and seemed to be admiring the lace cuffs as he answered guardedly, *We are, or I should say, we were Royalists, yes.*

Tilly said carefully, "I believe I would have been a Royalist like your family if I had been alive in the 17th century." She was rewarded with a melancholy smile, blushed and continued, "I would not wish for the future King Charles III to be beheaded."

King Charles III. Is there another King Charles? he asked telepathically.

"There will be," said Tilly. "Surprisingly, he has a brother who is the Duke of York."

The cavalier laughed, *That is not surprising. The second son of the monarch inherits the title Duke of York. It appears I am destined to be in England when a monarch named Charles reigns.* He reiterated. *Though I was born just after King Charles I was beheaded. King Charles II was my King.*

Tilly's face reddened. She determined to do an internet search to check his knowledge of monarchy traditions and emphasised, "He isn't King Charles III yet!"

The basement wall battle was paused and the CMD on the astral plane began to send memories into the cavalier's consciousness using Tilly's brain as a conduit.

The scene on your wall reminds me that my brother, Harry, told me how a cavalier spotted two boys fighting over a spyglass. Their clothes matched the King's attire.

"The princes we see before us, obviously," Tilly said, looking at him expectantly, wanting to know more.

He nodded his head in agreement. The CMD continued to fill his consciousness with memories and Tilly heard him say.

As the recognition dawned on the cavalier, the nine-year-old Duke of York flung the spyglass with all his might into the gaping mouth of Boye, a white hunting poodle.

She blurted out loudly, "A white hunting poodle! A poodle that hunts- you can't be serious!"

She began to wonder if he was making things up as he went along but noticed the hurt expression on his face as he continued.

In my time on Earth, we had hunting poodles. The dog was Prince Rupert's dog. Prince Rupert led the battle.

Tilly sat back in her chair, folded her arms, and said, "I'm sorry, but I don't believe that a royal prince, aged nine, was actively involved in a war where gunpowder was used."

The cavalier circled her, and she couldn't help but feel a flutter of excitement at his closeness. He seemed to be a living, breathing handsome cavalier here with her. She was not alone. She was not imagining it. His whisper tickled her mind, *The young princes would need to learn the art of war —where else would they learn except on the battlefield?*

How did he do that? How did he make war sound exciting and give her goose pimples? Tilly thought.

Her phone buzzed and she tore her gaze away from the answer on the screen to look at him in awe. "You were right about hunting poodles and Prince Rupert owning one," she said, confirming the cavalier's strange tidbit of information was true. Her doubts were fading about his stories being made up and she was sure she wasn't imagining him. How could she know about poodles being hunters? The handsome cavalier had to be from the past and not a hallucination. Did he travel on the pigeon through a wormhole? Her excitement was palpable. She felt the energy between them as their energy fields intermingled and she felt a magnetic connection.

She heard a husky whisper from the cavalier, *Prince Rupert's dog was also known as a familiar. Do you know what that is?*

She stopped wondering where the cavalier came from, happy to accept that he chose to be with her in this moment. She searched on her phone reading out aloud the search engine's description of a familiar.

"Familiars are supernatural animals that serve wizards and witches."

She paused for a moment as she stared at him incredulously. Was he trying to tell her something? She asked excitedly, "Does that mean the pigeon is your familiar, and does it mean you are a wizard?" She loved the idea that a handsome wizarding cavalier was visiting her. She noticed him looking at the phone in her hand.

You are a necromancer, he whispered, his internal voice full of awe. *With that magic book, you can conjure up knowledge and bring the past back to life.*

She pointed to the control station behind him, unable to control her laughter. "And with this 'magic box,'" she said, gesturing towards it, "you can experience virtual reality."

Tilly felt a twinge of guilt for laughing at his ignorance and quickly composed herself, realising she was also ignorant of the world he had left, which could be far more advanced than her own. He had the advantage of knowing more about the 17th century world too and her father's immersive battle. She held out the phone to him, hoping to make amends. But instead of taking it, he stepped back.

"I understand if you don't know about phones or virtual reality," she reassured him softly.

He looked at her with worried eyes. *But it looks like magic*, he murmured, his concern evident. *And you could be imprisoned for using it*, he shuddered.

Her throat tightened as he turned towards her, and she stared into his deep, sorrowful amber eyes that mirrored her grief. She counted, slowly ticking off the centuries in her mind before concluding that he must be at least three hundred years old. What chance did she have of finding a way to cope with her unresolved grief before her life ended, and why had this 17th-century cavalier turned up? Had the unearthing of the basement unearthed this wizard, she wondered.

His voice interrupted her thoughts, *I am not a wizard. The pigeon is my guide and protector while I am on this plane.*

Tilly gasped. Had he read her mind? "Here," she said, holding out the hand controls to him. He didn't take them.

Can you put it on the table for me? I can't physically hold it.

She quickly, put the hand controls on the table for him. "Let me show you how to turn this on and off."

The cavalier stood over the controls, his fingers deftly working the controls telepathically without touching them as Tilly guided him through the immersive experience. Entranced by the technology she watched his eyes lit up with curiosity as he seemed to explore its settings with his mind.

Can I shape the battle before us? he asked.

She heard the excitement in his voice and smiled; her gaze fixed on the paused battle scene around them. This would be the first virtual reality experience offered by her father's gallery, and she wanted it to be unforgettable.

"I can get changes made by the design team based on your descriptions," she said, nervous at the thought of creating a personalised adventure for the handsome cavalier. "Tell me more about this battle and I'll do my best to bring your vision to life."

He transmitted his thought; *Can we turn back time?*

Tilly's gaze met his, "To you, it may feel like that," she replied softly. "But what was the cause of this battle?" she couldn't remember seeing the cause on her father's information sheet. Surely it would be useful to know. She could pretend to the design team that she found more of her father's notes and get them to make additions.

Our family believed the King's fixation on saltpetre sparked the Battle of Edgehill.

"Saltpetre?" Tilly repeated, not understanding.

He explained that his family's livelihood revolved around its use for fertilisers, gunpowder, and even fire-works, a nostalgic smile appearing on his face.

Tilly thought that his mind had drifted elsewhere, as pictures of someone creating quill rockets with layers of gunpowder and stars that soared into the sky when ignited entered her mind. Tilly shook the picture from her mind and pressed him again.

"Why did the battle happen then?"

Because the King needed to tax the people to afford his precious saltpetre, they had had enough of taxes, the cavalier replied with a hint of bitterness.

Her brow furrowed in surprise as she listened to him. She thought of the royals as figureheads, with parliament holding the real power. But listening to Gabriel she discovered that Charles I and his wife Henrietta Maria believed in their divine right to rule as had Henrietta's father in France.

"No wonder there was a French Revolution!" she exclaimed, remembering her father reading 'A Tale of Two Cities' to her and explaining the overthrow of the French monarchy and execution of the royal family. She suddenly remembered the last words of Sydney Carton "It is a far, far better thing that I do, than I have ever done; it is a far, far better rest that I go to than I have ever known." She thought of her father reading those words and wondered if he was resting. He wasn't the kind of person to rest for long.

She quickly backtracked, sensing the cavalier's unease at her statement. "It's just fascinating how different countries have such different governments," she corrected herself.

"On another note, can you continue your brother Harry's story about the battle?" Tilly was increasingly intrigued by him, feeling a growing attraction towards him as they bonded over their shared interests. She didn't want to dwell on the darker aspects of monarch rule any longer or lose herself in melancholy thinking of her loss. She wanted to hear more about the battle before them, so the VR experience was the best possible. That was surely what her father wanted.

She considered and said, "You got to the part where Boye disappeared with the spyglass between his teeth."

She felt the warmth of the cavalier's smile as he continued.

With lightning speed, the cavalier leapt after the dog and reappeared a short while later with the spyglass, remarkably all in one piece.

Tilly cheered, "Yay!"

He swept off his feathered hat and bowed deeply, extending it towards her with a grand gesture.

Prince Charles tore off one of his gold buttons from his coat and gave it to the cavalier.

"That was generous."

The spyglass was much more valuable to his father, the King. The spyglass was a new technological invention and very precious.

Tilly realised he was telling her subtly that he was aware of technology, but she was impatient to hear the rest of the story and asked. "Did he keep the button?"

The cavalier paused dramatically, pointing to the roundheads surrounding them on the walls of the basement and telepathed, *The cavalier was accused of stealing the button and was brought before the King himself.*

"I wouldn't fancy his chances with the Saltpetre King," Tilly said.

The cavalier ignored the barbed comment against the King.

Prince Charles could have denied giving the cavalier the button, but he was a truthful and honourable boy, destined to change London forever.

"What did he do?"

Prince Charles told his father the truth of the account. The cavalier kept the button.

Tilly smiled. She hadn't meant that but looked at the cavalier's beaming face and became distracted by his good looks. He had the beginnings of a moustache growing and it suited him. She wondered dreamily if it would always remain at that growth stage now that he was dead. Did he still think of himself as being alive? Pulling her mind together she asked, "Can you tell me any more about any of the paintings we see before us?"

He looked at the main painting in front of them and whispered into her mind, *Charles I had the portrait painted that you see in front of us.*

"The one of the two princes surrounded by the battle?"

He had it painted for Dr. Harvey as a gift to commemorate the battle, which he felt the Royalists had won.

"But the doctor was a useless guardian, it would seem." Tilly added, "He didn't deserve the painting."

He may have been a useless guardian, but he was a great doctor and saved many cavaliers during that battle. Not only that but his discovery of the function of the heart and the circulation of the blood was, probably still is, the greatest medical discovery of all time.

Tilly quickly checked on her phone, "You won that argument, but why did your brother tell you all about the battle? I mean it's great for my research, but I can't see why he would tell you."

Because the cavalier's actions had a lasting effect on the young prince.

"How?"

The prince knew that he could trust the cavalier. Years later he made the cavalier part of his restoration committee tasked with finding King Charles I's great works of art in Europe. The cavalier was my father.

He told her that his father was grateful to the young King. He had been promised a peerage by the old King for contributing all of his finances to the Royalist cause. The King had been beheaded before that could happen. Being part of the restoration committee gave him renewed respect.

Tilly could see that he appeared lost in his reminiscences and though what he had told her was useful to know for the VR experience she wanted to pull him back to the present moment. "Did your father find any paintings?" she asked eagerly.

The cavalier let out a heavy sigh of disappointment, his eyes scanning the walls of the gallery. *I was hoping to see a Torrens, Torrentius painting,* he stammered slightly in her mind, *but they're all gone now.*

She saw his gaze fall to the floor, seemingly lost in memories of the prized artwork. Her smile turned secretive and mischievous. "You don't need to worry about that," she said, noticing his stutter for the first time.

I don't. He looked up at her in surprise.

"My father told me all about Torrentius," Tilly continued, her eyes sparkling with excitement. "And I have some exciting news for you, Gabriel. That is your name isn't it?"

Yes, my name is Gabriel. What news?

A painting did survive!"

Really? What is it? Tell me! he urged as the CMD sent memories of Harry telling him about the naked paintings.

"It's a round piece with a flagon, jug, glasses, and a bridle," Tilly explained flustered, shocked by the naked women that had suddenly entered her mind for no apparent reason. "It was found in 1913 being used as a lid on a raisin barrel and had been owned by a baker in the Netherlands before its discovery."

Gabriel whispered into Tilly's mind. *Did you know that bakers over there traded in art Tilly?*

Tilly nodded, her smile growing wider as she heard him use her name. "Yes, my father told me about that too. But here's the most exciting part —It has King Charles I's branded monogram on the back, which was on all of the art pieces he owned," Tilly explained. "And there was a description of the painting included in his state papers, confirming its origin."

She felt a wave of emotion in the cavalier's voice and heard him say, *Do you think I could see it?*

"Of course!" she exclaimed; her cheeks flushed with excitement. "It's kept in the Rijksmuseum in the Netherlands nowadays."

He sighed.

"Let me finish ", she said, "But we have several prints of it upstairs in our art gallery."

Tilly could see that he was amazed that there would be copies of a famous painting available for him to see. She finally felt on an equal footing with him. She asked," Did your father find any of the paintings belonging to Charles I, Gabriel?"

He answered, *My brother, Harry, who accompanied him to recoup the lost art, told me they brought home a Titian and a Bronzino just as the plague hit London.*

She gasped, "A Titian! That would be worth millions today. A Titian and a Bronzino, are you sure?"

My brother was the one interested in art, but I love words. I remember those names.

"Where are they now?" she asked.

I do not know. Our home was robbed when we were in Eyam escaping the plague. The thieves left the art on our walls that they considered worthless. I don't know where Papa left those two paintings. He might have had them delivered to Lord Buckhurst.

Tilly was confused, She felt sure Eyam was famous for being the 'plague village'. Talk about going out of the frying pan into the fire! She began a search on her phone.

When the cavalier spoke, he spoke into Tilly's head telepathically. No one else could hear him. Anyone within hearing distance could only hear Tilly, apparently talking to herself.

Sjaak stood at the top of the steps leading down to the basement. He listened to the one-sided conversation below and was alarmed that Tilly was openly talking to herself about the art she had not, to his knowledge, been told about. He wondered if she had found the documents that he promised the art thieves. Their threats suggested he needed to find them if he wanted to stay alive and collect the money they owed him. He couldn't ask her without causing suspicions and the coronavirus restrictions meant she was hardly ever out of the basement. He had to keep this family sweet and become indispensable so that he could continue his search.

30

GABRIEL'S FIRST VR EXPERIENCE

It was 2 a.m. and Gabriel sat in the basement, quietly taking in the immersive experience of the battle of Edgehill. He was glad to be home. He had wandered throughout the building and some of it was still recognisable. Even the stone dovecote that his father had erected remained in the garden. He noticed Isaac using it.

He watched the immersive experience all the way through by himself several times. Tilly had shown him the visual scenes on the walls but not the full immersion. He quickly taught himself how to control the box telepathically. As a result, the experience seemed so real that he felt like he was there at the battle with his father. The combination of the music, the immersive artwork spanning the whole room —from floor to ceiling —and the use of panels and mirrors, allowed him to feel as if he were there and as if by magic he was back in the 17th century amidst 21st-century technology. His mind was exhausted by all he had to learn but the reward was worth it.

He could smell the gunpowder from the pistols and cannons used by the Roundheads and Cavaliers in front of him. He heard the sound of drums far off and the noise of soldiers giving out their last groans. The nearness of the noise of the battle surrounded him. This frightened him so much the first time he watched it that he immediately wanted to withdraw to a place of safety as fast as possible. Yet he could not, he was spellbound, and he could not turn it off.

The vision surrounded him on the walls of the basement. He could hear a clattering of arms, the noise of cannons, drums beating, muskets going off, cannons being discharged, horses neighing and the cries of soldiers. He could see the ensigns displayed by two jarring and contrary armies as strange and portentous apparitions fought for their lives. It was both amazing and terrifying at the same time. All of his senses were being stimulated as he was immersed in the battlefield experience.

He dared not try to run away for fear of becoming prey to the infernal roundheads that seemed to surround him. He watched as Sir Edmund Verney, the King's standard bearer, had his hand chopped off by the Parliamentarians to obtain the Royal Standard. Aghast, he saw the Royalists recover the standard. It still had Sir Edmund's dismembered hand clinging on. With much fear, he kept restarting the programme, wishing to see a different outcome. It was so real that he believed he might get a glimpse of his father.

As dawn approached and his mind began to tire, he imagined he was in his brother's warehouses. They were full of gunpowder and were dotted along the side of the Thames River. He once again saw John, their manservant, running towards him, clothes aflame, carrying Gabriel's beloved mother from the laboratory that was up in flames. He became choked with smoke. Gabriel realised the reason behind that memory the CMD was sending him: the basement was full of the smell of gunpowder.

He had played this immersive experience so many times that the smell was overwhelming. He decided to open the door to avoid sending the smell up the stairs to Tilly and her mother. Once his mind opened the door, Isaac flew to its entrance and stood, looking up at Gabriel.

Gabriel did not wish to share the experience and telepathed irritably. *I am busy. What do you want?*

The pigeon tilted his head to look at Gabriel and the controls his hands moved over without physically touching before responding. *There is an overwhelming smell of gunpowder. Are you well, Gabriel?*

The immersive experience halted itself as if by magic, and the gunpowder smell began to subside.

Gabriel took in the pigeon's well-groomed appearance and explained. *I didn't notice the smell. In my time on earth, the gunpowder smell was familiar to me.*

Isaac perched on the edge of the coffee table, his majestic wings folding behind him. *"Are you and Tilly supporting each other as you move forward?" he asked.*

Gabriel's amber eyes sparkled with excitement, *She's helping me find answers to questions that I never thought could be answered without endless hours of research on the computer you gave me access to,* he replied.

And are you also helping her find answers? Isaac pressed.

Gabriel's forehead furrowed and he shook his head slowly, his abilities as an astralite did not allow him to uncover certain truths about what happened to her father. She believed her stepmother and the Dutchman were involved in a conspiracy regarding his death, but Gabriel's powers couldn't confirm these suspicions.

I don't think so, Gabriel's powerlessness seeped into his inner voice.

Isaac waddled towards Gabriel and his orange eyes gazed at him tenderly. *All will be revealed in time. Our main focus is helping Tilly move forward from things she cannot change, he explained. She is a rebirther, capable of communicating with us and travelling astrally since turning fourteen. If she continues to develop her powers they will remain. Otherwise, they will eventually subside before her fifteenth birthday and return when she is twenty-one.*

But why am I not a rebirther? Gabriel interjected, feeling a twinge of envy towards Tilly's newfound abilities.

Because you were not planned, you are a young soul. Isaac replied gently, *And your experiences with the plague and the Great Fire of London for such a young soul, are incomparable.* Isaac paused, knowing that despite Gabriel's traumatic beginnings, including their similar abandonment by their mothers, his presence in the present was crucial for supporting his family's past and future.

But she doesn't look any older than me!

Isaac explained that there were three different ways to measure age. First, there was chronological age —the number of years someone lived on Earth. Then there was biological age, which could vary from one's chronological age depending on their overall health and well-being. Finally, there was the spiritual age, a concept that many people longed to have as it represented a deeper level of wisdom and understanding.

It is the one age that we all wish we were older, Isaac telepathed wistfully, *If Torrens were older spiritually, he might already have become the cosmic artist he so desires to be. If I were older spiritually I might be the cosmic caretaker I strive to become.*

As Isaac hopped off the coffee table and waddled towards the door, he turned back to Gabriel with a surprising revelation. *You may be surprised to hear this, but you are younger spiritually than Tilly. She has lived many lifetimes, although she doesn't remember them. In this moment, she is your descendant.*

Gabriel thought of Tilly and how much her green eyes reminded him of his sister Mathilde. He thought of the hologram she spoke of and wanted to believe that a fraction of Mathilde's spirit still resided within this basement like a shard of a hologram, splitting and existing in multiple places simultaneously.

31

WAT BUDDHAPADIPA CALLS

Gabriel vibrated quietly as an orb of consciousness in the shadows of the gallery and watched Tilly gaze at the Tree of Life tapestry, and just like wireless piggybacking, he again accessed her brain. Allowing his consciousness to become full of memories that the CMD storage facility began sending him of the tapestry. Memories of his father and Harry returning from the Netherlands with the tapestry and the excitement filling the household. Memories of Mathilde gazing adoringly at the tapestry, shooing him away if he dared to talk. Memories of Fran sitting quietly with quill and ink, drawing the birds from the tapestry as Sara called to him from the garden. He was grateful for those memories and wanted to relive those experiences over and over again. Everything was better before the plague. The plague changed everything.

Tilly was thinking about Isaac, Gabriel, and her father and wondering where they all were. She decided to play Morricone's "Gabriel's Oboe" on her iPhone hoping Gabriel was nearby and would bring Isaac to join them. As much as she liked Gabriel, she sensed his immaturity and needed Isaac's presence which filled her with a lightness and was like a balm to her grief. The last time Tilly saw her father alive was the morning he left for the airport before COVID-19. She would never see him physically again. Everything was better before COVID. COVID changed everything.

Over the months since his death, she felt his presence in the basement when she played his music or tried out the VR experience, he'd almost completed. She felt a remnant of him in the art gallery, where she could read the detailed notes, he had handwritten, attached to the back of the paintings. A hint of him could even be felt when she dipped her hand into the biscuit barrel he kept filled with custard creams for when he sat in the basement or kitchen garden. She worried that once those biscuits were finished, she would lose yet another remnant of him.

These were her ways of enduring life without his physical being, proof that he had existed and that some of him was still with her. She wanted to understand where the rest of him was. Was the bigger part of him waiting for her on the 'other side' when she died? If that was the case, then suicide made sense. Yet she knew from her chats with Gabriel that Gabriel committed suicide and never saw his family again. But was that just madness and was she imagining a 17th-century cavalier inside her head because her father had been obsessed by the 17th century? Was she imagining that a pigeon could talk to her?

As the familiar music began to play in the art gallery Gabriel materialised in his cavalier form in front of Tilly as she sat on a bean bag looking at the Tree of Life tapestry.

Tilly had gotten used to his unusual smell and left her COVID mask dangling from an ear loop.

She felt as if Gabriel had entered her mind. He was telling her to remain mute when talking to him. To speak inside her head.

I don't mind you speaking aloud but Isaac says it might appear strange to someone who walked in on you in an empty room.

Tilly laughed, "I'm not worried."

He shared a sanitised version of an incident that happened to him.

I was on earth, in prison, and being bullied for saying my prayers aloud, he confided. *My brother James explained that the Lord could still hear me if I prayed inside my head.*

He smiled shyly at Tilly and continued, *All those who have left this earthly plane can hear you if you talk to us internally.*

"But you speak to me aloud," she countered.

It just appears so to you, Gabriel answered. *But no one else in the room can hear me -only you.*

Tilly couldn't help but laugh at the thought of others thinking she was talking to herself and said,

"So, let me get this straight. You don't want me to seem crazy."

The corners of his mouth lifted gently into one of his charming smiles that unsettled her. *I understand it's called telepathy, Tilly.*

Tilly laughed and telepathed, *You have been studying. I am aware that in the same way that the telegraph, telephone, and television changed how we communicate, cranial magnetism will allow everyone to use mind-to-mind communication soon. I may as well enjoy that I can do it already, Unless I am mad, and you and Isaac are figments of my imagination brought on by my grief.*

She pushed those thoughts away and returned to imagining what opportunities her father had for his future life like Isaac and Gabriel seemed to have. Gabriel told her that he and Isaac had come from the astral plane. Was that where her father was? If she found it so easy to see Gabriel and talk to a pigeon, why couldn't she see her father?

She said, "I wanted to ask you more about the place you live in after you die. What is the astral plane?

Gabriel spoke into her mind; *We need Isaac to join this shared consciousness.*

Tilly smiled. She patiently waited for Henrik Chaim Goldschmidt to flawlessly finish his oboe solo before silencing her iPhone.

.

32

I NEED TO FIND MY FATHER

Isaac was sitting on the red-roofed Buddhist temple of Wat Buddhapadipa in Wimbledon, looking over the sanctuary garden, a great spot for quiet contemplation. The sunlight was intense, but he was confident that the microlenses in his eyes would filter out any harmful rays. *Another advantage to being a bird*, he thought, and a pigeon would look rather silly in the sunglasses he had seen Tilly wearing.

He entered Tilly and Gabriel's mind space, filling them with peace and light and sharing visuals of his location.

Tilly exclaimed in awe before asking, *Where are you?*

I am at Wat Buddhapadipa temple. You came here with your father as a very young child.

The visuals of the beautiful temple and its serene surroundings included a lake. It was the first Thai Buddhist temple outside of Asia and served as a centre for meditation.

He telepathed, *Being a pigeon at this time on Earth has its advantages.*

He left the visuals in Tilly and Gabriel's minds as he began radiating his light and energy to them and concentrating on the question Gabriel passed on.

You asked about the astral plane; he nestled down on the red-roofed temple tucking his legs under his feathery abdomen. Once comfortable he continued, *I can only speak for myself.*

Please, Tilly asked.

I have been fortunate enough in this lifetime to fly in the air as a pigeon. In that time, I have seen, up close, manufactured planes that take man from place to place. He trembled at the memory.

Isaac leaned forward. *Using that analogy the afterlife is like getting on a plane. It makes a daily tour of the Cosmos, calling at different destinations according to the beliefs of its passengers.*

Isaac shared his knowledge as Tilly and Gabriel listened intently.

You can stay on the plane and repeat the journey as many times as you want, or you can get onto another plane when you feel ready.

Tilly's eyes widened in surprise at this revelation.

But if you're not ready, the plane won't land, Isaac continued.

So, each person's experience of the afterlife is different? She speculated.

In response, Isaac replied *Not just on the astral plane, but on all planes of consciousness.*

Gabriel nodded in understanding. Isaac was well aware Gabriel's afterlife was vastly different from other astralites.

Isaac scanned the sky with his peripheral vision for any threats to his life before continuing. *Let us take that analogy further and consider the planes that fly in the sky. Can you see that earthly aeroplanes are not all the same.?*

Tilly answered and nodded her understanding, *You mean we have a choice of planes to board from different airline companies?*

As they discussed the analogy, Isaac sensed Gabriel's confusion through their telepathic connection. Gabriel had just returned to Earth after being away for over three hundred years and was still catching up on modern technology, including aeroplanes. So, Isaac took the time to explain that different airline companies offered various experiences for passengers, with attentive flight attendants available for assistance during the journey.

As they were in shared consciousness Isaac could access Tilly's memories. He saw how she struggled with anxiety during air travel and found comfort in her father videotaping their local airport and watching it at home before their trips. He saw that her father had even taught her to focus on the airline's logo while travelling, giving her something tangible to focus on and calm her mind. As Isaac gently reminded Tilly, she always has a choice in which airline company to use for her travels and that Gabriel chose the plane for purgatory.

After death, one's destination is determined by your beliefs and the vibrational frequency that emanates from them.

He added *All that you are when you die is consciousness.*

Tilly sat very still with her legs crossed and her hands clasped together and telepathed,

If Gabriel's consciousness took him to purgatory and it was like an interactive game, it would be okay because you could log out.

Then she paused, expressing concern, *To have no escape from where your beliefs took you must be one of the worst nightmares ever.*

Gabriel sat silently at the table. Isaac guessed his mind was still haunted by memories of the Bartholomew fair of purgatory. It was all an illusion, but for Gabriel, it was a nightmare he could not escape.

Tilly's face turned red with anger as she shared a thought, *I wouldn't want to go to purgatory,* she exclaimed, *and I don't think my father would either.*

Isaac responded gently I *believe human consciousness has progressed since the 17th century, leaving purgatory behind. When people no longer believe in purgatory it ceases to exist.*

Gabriel remained quiet in their shared consciousness and Isaac asked him for his contribution.

In response, Gabriel explained, *Before the printing press existed, books were handwritten by monks giving power to the church's perspective on purgatory.*

Tilly asked, *Are you suggesting that as a Catholic, studying those handwritten books influenced your beliefs at your time of death?*

Gabriel answered, *Yes, I was a devout Catholic before I died.*

Isaac's mind flashed back to the treacherous era they had experienced, wrought with religious persecution. The very act of being religious was perilous in itself. He understood why Gabriel held such reverence for Galileo and his courage in defending Copernicus's theories. Isaac knew that Gabriel had willingly sacrificed his life rather than betray his brother as an alchemist.

But why did you continue to study for the priesthood if you knew the powerful control of the Church at that time? Tilly questioned.

Gabriel gracefully removed his feathered hat and placed it on a nearby table. The hat seemed to vanish in the presence of modern furniture as if it were an otherworldly object. His voice brimmed with emotion as he answered her mental inquiry. *My father wished it of me, and I wanted to please him.*

He added earnestly, *Besides Christ inspires love, not fear, It was because of Christ that I chose to become a priest, not because of the church. Rebirthers return to Earth many times to progress in cosmic consciousness. Christ came to Earth just once. To remind us to love one another.*

Isaac was pleased that Tilly remained silent respecting Gabriels's commitment to his faith. He understood that Tilly was getting obsessively worried about her father's afterlife. She seemed particularly concerned about purgatory and couldn't stop thinking about it. He wondered if Gabriel had been too graphic with her in his descriptions of his time in purgatory. The quiet didn't last long.

Tilly blurted out, *I don't understand you though Gabriel; you have all this knowledge, yet you took yourself to purgatory.*

Isaac could feel the weight of her sorrow as she sniffed and telepathed.

And what about my father? she asked, pleading for an answer. *Are his options limited to just purgatory on the astral plane?*

Isaac spoke gently into their shared consciousness, *My dear Tilly, Gabriel's purgatory was not a physical place. It was a state of mind.*

Suddenly, understanding dawned on her face. *Our minds are our consciousness...even after death?* she whispered.

Isaac answered telepathically, confirming her thoughts. *Yes, our minds exist beyond our physical bodies. We existed before birth and will continue to exist after death as astralites if we choose to.*

Her next question trembled with emotion, *Then where is my father now?*

Isaac responded comfortingly. *When he entered the astral plane, his beliefs guided his journey.*

33

SUICIDE IS POINTLESS

Tilly felt a sense of peace. She was confident she understood all that Isaac told her. She decided to change the subject to something else bothering her. She asked, *What about people who believe that there is no after-life?*

She thought of Sjaak as she added, *You know, those that claim that when you are dead, you are dead.*

Ahh, Isaac said, *Those who believe in nothingness remain in darkness, as if in hibernation. Hibernators.*

Hibernators? she asked.

That's what we call them. They remain in hibernation because that's where their beliefs have taken them.

She smiled as she envisioned a cosmic library, each room full of books she wanted to read but didn't know about until they were presented. *I wouldn't take myself to purgatory.*

I choose to believe in a cosmic library where I can immerse myself in books.

Tilly awakened Gabriel's thoughts who telepathed, *You have reminded me of John 14:2 where Jesus told his disciples that God's house was just as you described it, with different rooms. Anything from Shakespeare might be a good choice for your library.*

Tilly's mind had already moved on from her cosmic library. *Why do people bother to do anything when they die Isaac?*

Isaac answered, *Those who do bother are all aiming for the same ascendance to cosmic consciousness. Our intellect continues through time and our consciousness evolves so that we become closer and closer to the greatest power of all. We become a Cosmic being. This could take millions of Earth years Tilly. It took millions of Earth years for a pigeon to evolve from a dinosaur. But time dilation in the cosmos means we don't feel time passing as we do when we visit Earth. Time becomes irrelevant in the presence of God.*

Tilly paused the Group Think Chat as she processed the information before asking. *Is the greatest power God?*

Isaac answered, *Some might name it God, others might name it Cosmic Consciousness, and others call it Dark Energy. I am sure there are other names that even I am unaware of.*

Tilly asked, *What does a cosmic being do?*

As a cosmic being, you can simply bathe in the love surrounding you and eventually morph into a cosmic body such as a star, a planet, or a comet. With diligent practice and training, one can become a higher cosmic being and develop the ability to manipulate and influence planets and other celestial beings. However, this power also carries a tremendous burden of responsibility, and all these processes take millions of Earth years.

Tilly felt reassured. Her mind was, without warning, starting to process the months of grief that she had accumulated. The fears, the suspense, the waiting for an explanation. She nodded her understanding. *I know the thing I want I can never get.*

She could sense Gabriel and Isaac waiting apprehensively for her to share more.

I want my father to come back to me.

Oh, it's ok, she telepathed, noticing their concern. *I know that is impossible.*

My old life has gone. The heart-breaking ordinary everyday things I took for granted.

Her eyes were glassy, and she held her tears in check as she sent a thought to the think group.

I don't believe we would be reunited if I were to die tomorrow.

She added, *but I was desperately worried he might end up in purgatory.*

As Isaac began to telepath, she stopped him, *Now I realise that he wouldn't have believed in purgatory, therefore his consciousness wouldn't have taken him there. My father was a Buddhist who loved roses. Where will he go?*

Isaac answered, *Your father may choose to be reborn. Buddhists believe in rebirth until they reach a state of enlightenment.*

So, he may come back as a pigeon, like you? She asked, smiling at the thought.

Yes. He would choose each lifetime based on what he'd like to learn from it.

She telepathed, *Can you come back as an insect, a plant, any animal in the sea, on land, in the air?*

Anything is possible if you believe.

She smiled, looked at the Tree of Life tapestry and wondered aloud, *A tree?*

If you wish to experience all aspects of the cosmos to understand the cosmos, then yes you might choose to be a tree. I have tried to experience most life forms so that I may be of help to the cosmos. Isaac answered.

Why would you wish to be a tree? Gabriel asked Tilly.

Isaac smiled in his mind as he saw the look Tilly gave Gabriel. It was as if he had grown another head. She answered him.

Because I've read that trees are social beings.

They cannot talk. Gabriel stated, walking over to the tapestry, and looking into the plexiglass that couldn't reflect his image.

Tilly walked up behind him and pointed to the roots of the tree before them. *I've read that they use electrical signals to communicate. They warn other trees of dangers by sending electrical signals using an underground network.*

Gabriel replied, *But they can't show love for other trees. Their branches aren't arms. They just grow and shed leaves.* Looking more closely at the tapestry he added, *Oh, and they hold birds.*

Tilly followed his gaze and pointed out on the tapestry what she could see wondering if he really couldn't see what was so obvious to her. *They show love to all kinds of animals and insects who benefit from the shade of a tree, the comfort of a branch, a leaf, or a seed to eat. A place to nest, to live under its protection. They support other trees and plants with nutrients through their intricate root networks, ensuring their collective survival and growth.*

Isaac nodded in agreement. *In my lifetimes I have learnt a lot from trees who give such a lot and take so little from the Earth. They play a crucial role in sustaining life on this planet. Their roots hold the soil in place and prevent erosion, while their leaves clean the air providing oxygen to breathe, storing carbon through their canopies that transform sunlight into energy.*

Gabriel's voice softened, *Forgive my ignorance.*

As their minds merged, Tilly marvelled at a tree's ability to live fully in the present moment which they had perfected over millions of years. Something she struggled with during meditation. She imagined that being reborn as a tree would be the perfect choice if one wanted to be fully present and mindful, rather than lost in thoughts about the future or past. Her meditative thoughts drifted as always to her father, and she asked if he could be reborn and revisit her.

Isaac answered, *No, sadly. When reborn, we have no control over our lives and what happens. The only thing we can control is our actions and reactions. He cannot return to you physically, but his energy has never left you Tilly. If you search for him, you will sense that lingering presence.*

When Tilly was in her happy place in the basement she often felt her father's presence. She telepathed.

Yes, yes I do! Whenever I smell roses I feel him nearby. I can watch him in VR, but it is the essence of him that is missing in VR. I like to think that the tiny bit of him that he left behind, like a piece of a hologram, contains the feeling of his love. I smell roses whenever I have that feeling.

Isaac nodded, *God's love is always present if you believe. In the same way, your father's love is always present. As above so below.*

Tilly noticed Gabriel nod and smile in recognition, as he whispered, *On earth as in heaven. You are quoting the Lord's prayer.*

Isaac added, *And there is time dilation to consider, 365 years on Earth equals one cosmic year.*

Tilly looked across at Gabriel and transmitted her thoughts to the group before she could stop them, *Blimey, no wonder Gabriel looks so young!*

Gabriel laughed.

Isaac answered, *As a human, if you're fortunate enough to grow old, Tilly, you may glimpse what time travel feels like. As Isaac Newton aged 84, I found solace in travelling back in my mind to 1680. Every aching joint and frail limb was forgotten as I relived the moment I first gazed upon the magnificent Great Comet. My ground-breaking theory of universal gravitation had accurately predicted its orbit, cementing my place in history. My body may have withered over the years, but my mind remained sharp and free. It allowed me to revisit any memory or place with astonishing clarity.*

Tilly smiled with understanding, *So you are saying I can time travel in my mind to the times I had with my father.*

Isaac nodded and continued, *When we get older all that we have are memories. The secret to life is to make those memories count. But back to your original question Tilly, when you die, if you choose to hibernate, time dilation switches to zero because you have used no energy. You decide.*

Tilly looked at Isaac in the visuals he sent to their shared consciousness. She could see him sitting on top of the temple. She remembered her dream about comets and had a "Wow" moment. Isaac Newton was reborn as a pigeon, albeit an archangel pigeon, and was sharing his wisdom with her. He hadn't chosen to hibernate. He was still a useful being. He wasn't a feeble old person at all. She determined to show more respect to those in the outer world who appeared old.

I've already made my decision. I want to be like you. To be useful. It would be so boring to sleep forever. What a waste. I have another question. If we are consciousness in a body, what happens to our actual bodies when we die? Will my father's body get recycled or reused?

Tilly's question hung in the air, heavy and daunting. Isaac seemed to hesitate before responding and Tilly's eyes flicked to Gabriel, who seemed equally intrigued by the topic.

Isaac answered, *Unfortunately, the body used on Earth is sometimes damaged beyond repair. It cannot be reused, as it is, by another human. Cosmic DNA templates exist, so family resemblances remain when ancestors are born.*

Tilly absorbed this new information, before telepathing, *But what happened to my father's body then?*

Isaac's expression darkened as he continued, *It would be recycled. On Earth, the decomposition of human remains plays a vital role in maintaining the balance of nutrients in living organisms such as insects, microbes, and plants.*

He paused and added. *Are you sure you want to discuss this further, Tilly?*

Tilly could feel the vibrational energy from the temple's calm surroundings as she listened and learned.

I didn't get to see my father's body after his accident, she answered. *I can't talk about these things with my stepmother. She is so angry and it's like she blames him for dying.* Tilly sighed, *And she is always crying!*

Tilly became emotional and her thoughts erupted into the group chat before she could stop them, *She didn't even tell me about having his ashes until I asked to see his coffin!*

Tilly wiped the tears from her lashes.

Isaac offered, *I am here whenever you want to share your thoughts about your father.*

Tilly gulped back her tears as she answered, *I can't tell my stepmother, but I'm glad that he isn't in a coffin.*

Her thoughts became angry once again, *I don't want to visit a place where other people get to share my grief. He was my father, not theirs!*

Her tears were flowing freely down her face as she continued to express her feelings of grief. *Helena has the ashes of my father's body, but I don't believe that he'd want them kept in a jar. There is no colour or beauty in that. My father was a colourful person. He deserved a Buddhist ceremony.*

Suddenly their shared consciousness was filled with beautiful visuals of the temple grounds. Tilly stopped crying overcome by the beauty in her mind's eye as Isaac telepathed, *Death is a difficult subject for most people Tilly. Are you all right to share your conscious thoughts about it with us?*

Tilly found a box of tissues next to her, and taking a couple, she wiped her eyes and, with control in her inner voice, replied into their shared consciousness, *Yes, I am.*

Thank you for explaining things to me. I needed to understand what happened to my father after he died. She took another tissue and spread it out over her face, patting her face dry as she tried to compose herself. A butterfly landed delicately on the windowsill outside, and a sense of peace washed over her. Using her inner voice she said, *The transformation from caterpillar to butterfly mirrors the journey of consciousness as it leaves its physical form behind. The idea of Macrocosm and Microcosm resonates deeply with me, connecting Earth's beings to the vastness of the universe in ways we can hardly comprehend. Now thanks to you Isaac I believe one hundred per cent that once we give my father his Buddhist funeral he will be on his journey to another plane of existence, just like the butterfly fluttering its wings into the unknown. Death is the ultimate alchemy.*

She blew her nose into a tissue and added, *He can't come back to me any time soon, and if I wanted to die to try to join him, I might end up on a different plane.*

Having considered all things presented to her she gave them her conclusion, *So, suicide is pointless.*

Gabriel and Isaac both sighed imperceptibly with relief, as she continued.

Even though his body was too damaged to be saved, scattering his ashes will give new life to others on the planet as they are recycled.

Tilly smiled sadly. She wanted to believe in this cosmos Isaac spoke of.

It's not like I think the past can be restored. I trust the past is there to comfort me knowing I felt loved.

She watched Isaac fluff up his feathers and spread his wings as if calling the meeting to an end. He concluded *I suspect you have listened and talked with us for long enough.*

It is not the time to ponder what we have discussed. Let your subconscious work on that and it will guide you to share your feelings about a fitting Buddhist farewell to your father with your stepmother. It is so lovely outside at the moment. Will you put a mask on and go for a walk around your area?

If you walk due east for ten minutes, I think you may find those horses you asked me to look out for.

The images of the London Buddhist temple disappeared from Tilly's mind. Tilly opened her eyes and looked about her. Gabriel became a luminous copper light and disappeared from the gallery.

Tilly went up to the main part of the house and let herself out into the eerily quiet London streets she had never known. Putting on her mask, she set off eastbound. There was a lot to think about.

34

HOMEWARD BOUND

Isaac took stock of their conversation. He knew that Gabriel was a product of his only time on Earth. A time he had never overcome. He noticed that Gabriel's vibrational frequency lowered every time Tilly said exactly what she thought when she thought it. Isaac was interested in brains and the transmutation of energy frequencies, and he chose Wat Buddhapadipa to help orchestrate the frequencies of their minds, weaving a tapestry of calmness for them both.

Being an archangel pigeon, he was overcome with the urge to take flight, finding solace in the boundless expanse of the sky, and escape from his ruminations. He soared up into the sky, his wings spread wide, flaunting his iridescent feathers. Then he seamlessly blended into his surroundings to evade predators.

As the pigeon soared and dipped across the lake, he reflected on a thought that he was certain must have crossed his mind as a human in the 17th century —was consciousness contained within the brain? Although Tilly's human brain had a greater capacity than a bird's, it was simply an instrument for processing thoughts into actions. Through his many rebirths, he understood that consciousness existed beyond physicality and all beings returned to this source upon death. A brain, upon death, was just a lump of meat.

When rebirth occurred, access to aspects of consciousness, through the instrumentality of a new brain returned (so long as the brain worked efficiently). It became clear why Gabriel had been sent back to Earth —to regain control over lost memories through shared consciousness and reinterpret them. New astralites like Gabriel existed solely as consciousness, lacking a physical form. To access memories, they either needed to connect with the CMD, which was a long and tedious task or rely on shared consciousness as they lacked a brain to serve as a bridge for their mind to interact with this field. He noticed how much faster it was when a working brain was available as a transmitter. Excited by this realisation, he immediately transferred the thought to the cosmic memory database for future research in another lifetime.

Isaac flew to the temple roof and nestled down feeling exhilarated and euphoric. He could hear people chanting in the temple below and thought it would be healing for troubled minds. He guessed that the brain Tilly had in this lifetime didn't always process the information that came from the field of collective consciousness her mind had access to. That part of the brain needed tuning using vibrational frequencies, which had become an acceptable practice if she chose it. It was not for him to suggest. If she were meant to do so the opportunity would present itself to her.

Isaac imagined the soul's embodiment of a being similar to the manufacture of a car that leaves the production line with faults and needs fine-tuning to be perfect. In the same way, when a baby emerged from the womb, auditory pathways to the brain might need fine-tuning. The brain was a great feat of alchemy, but no brain was perfect.

Taking on the embodiment of a bird had initially been a huge shock to Isaac. He was grateful that everything was working and fine-tuned so that he was a fully-fledged, able-bodied bird. As he contemplated his flight, he did not want to imagine how he would return to the dovecote if the magneto-reception he received as a pigeon was out of tune with his bird brain. It allowed him to sense the earth's magnetic field to determine location, direction, and orientation. He would get lost without it. As a rebirthed bird having a fully functioning brain was essential as there was no possibility of fine-tuning a faulty receiver as humans could. The only way to access memories in the CMD as a rebirther was through a fully functioning brain (no matter how small that brain was).

Seeing the air space was clear; he launched himself off the temple into the sky and soared effortlessly upwards into a warm column of air, adjusting his flight with the tiniest movement of his tail feathers. He continued his rise with grace, elegance, and apparent effortlessness. This was the life! He loved being an archangel pigeon. He saw Earth's magnetic fields, overlaid on top of his normal vision, allowing him to keep his bearings as no other landmarks were visible.

The freedom of flight, with his inbuilt compass giving him security, was indescribable. Airborne, and untethered, he aimed to reach euphoric levels on a thermal current before returning to the dovecote.

As a pigeon he was blessed with an amazing photographic memory that he stored as barcodes in much the same way humans kept an index of memories to be retrieved as and when required. He memorised spatial environments, inherited a pigeon's instinct and cognition and, to his shame, was beginning to feel cocky.

Suddenly, a dark shadow appeared overhead. Isaac didn't have time to do anything as he caught the whiff of a sparrow hawk's musky, predator scent as it descended like a stone, landing on his back. It was the smell of death and danger, causing his heart to race with fear.

It immediately used its beak to repeatedly pluck out Isaac's downy bronze and white breast feathers. Isaac tasted the metallic tang of his own blood on his tongue as the sparrow hawk ripped out his feathers. He felt a sharp pain as it tried to drive its talons into him piercing his skin. He could feel the weight of the bird on his back as both birds plummeted towards the ground. The sound of rushing air filled Isaac's ears as he fell, accompanied by the sharp screech of the sparrow hawk. The predator was used to the speedy immobilisation of its prey. Isaac had kept up a strict maintenance routine and was tougher than most.

The sparrow hawk tried to lock its sharp, piercing eyes with Isaac and hypnotise him into submission.

Terrified, Isaac used all his cosmic energy to emit a powerful reflective light from his iridescent feathers to the sparrow hawk's eyes as the sun simultaneously emerged from the clouds. He sent vibrational energy waves through his hollow bones, creating bone conduction that seared through to the sparrow hawk. The light blinded the sparrow hawk, and the crackling energy waves felt like a bolt of lightning to the predator, whose screech turned into a pained cry, and it immediately let go of its prey.

Isaac continued to plummet like a human without a parachute. His surroundings blurred as he descended through rushing air towards the London streets, the unusually quiet city, rows of buildings, and the unforgiving ground. It was as if he were falling backwards through many lifetimes.

He knew if he landed, he would be dead and would have failed in his mission. He forced himself to remember that he was a bird. He struggled to regain control of his body as he carefully lifted his damaged wings and felt a rush of air beneath them.

All at once, he could hear incessant chirping sounds. Isaac dared to look around him. A flock of birds surrounded him wheeling and turning in unison. His garden birds. He must be near the dovecote. They had come to escort him safely home.

Once inside the dovecote, he took stock of his injuries. Several feathers were damaged and overstrained. He set to work, using his beak to repair them. He knew he had just escaped being eaten alive.

Tilly stood looking at the stables she hadn't known existed. A notice was posted on the entrance gate, boldly stating that the stables were closed due to the ongoing COVID-19 pandemic. Tilly used her phone to take a photo of the number, hoping that her stepmother would book her riding lessons once COVID was over. As she walked back home through the streets of London, she saw a flurry of white feathers float down from the sky like snowflakes and land in front of her. She picked one up.

"I think a white feather means luck," she whispered aloud, as she put it in her pocket and headed home.

35

GABRIEL AND TILLY

Tilly jumped out of bed, put on her favourite T-shirt and leggings, and rushed barefoot down the stairs, excited by the prospect ahead. As she wandered through the art gallery, Gabriel trailed behind her like a lost puppy. Tilly scanned each painting critically, looking for the perfect one to use in their next immersive studio project. The design company were finalising the Civil War Battle, and she wanted to find a good follow-up VR experience.

Tilly suddenly felt a wave of magnetic energy as if Gabriel's fingers had reached out to touch hers and she turned, sensing he was behind her. Her gaze traced every detail of his attire, from his feathered hat to the delicate lace cuffs adorning his wrists. But it was the sparkle in his amber eyes that captured her attention. He shifted his head, almost as if acknowledging her sharp intellect and daring her to challenge him. They had reached a point where words were unnecessary, a simple look conveyed everything. The thrill of engaging in an intellectual battle with someone who could match her wits surged within her, and she couldn't resist the temptation.

She telepathed, *Let's choose a painting to discuss from your perspective and mine.*

Tilly spied a painting that stirred her imagination, and she presented the painting to Gabriel. It depicted the Great Fire of London, captured in all its chaotic and terrifying glory by Lieve Verschuier. As they locked eyes, Tilly's mind extended towards him, her thoughts brimming with excitement. "This is a masterpiece," she exclaimed, then telepathed, *I would love to use it for the next VR experience. Shall we discuss it?*

Gabriel's gaze landed on the painting and his consciousness was flooded with memories from the CMD. Tilly could sense his shock as he telepathed, *I've never seen a painting of the fire before, but it's exactly as I remember it - the chaos of people trying to escape on boats while surrounded by inferno.*

The image made him gasp in awe.

What are you thinking, Gabriel? She asked.

He spoke into her mind of the figures in the painting like they were real as if he knew them personally. It felt like their worlds collided, and he was trying to drag her consciousness back to his time on Earth. Her senses were alert to his fear, and she tore herself away from his mind. She continued to evaluate the painting aloud, hoping to impress him with her insights without having to engage with the emotions he was showing. With practised ease, she propped it up on an easel and began examining it closely, speaking aloud as she scribbled notes on her phone. She was unaware that Gabriel had been transported back to another plane, lost in his memories and torments of the fire.

Into an empty room, she said, "From a historical standpoint, this is incredibly valuable and could draw large audiences."

She paused, her mind whirring with ideas.

"If we wanted to immerse our customers in this experience, we would need to create an even more realistic scene —with thick smoke and intense heat just like the real thing. Hmm that needs a rethink."

Tilly studied the painting and couldn't help but be captivated by the busy scene depicted in the artwork —portraying the dramatic event that devastated the city. The flames engulfed buildings, casting an eerie glow on the chaotic scene, a bustling river filled with boats loaded with people's possessions as they fled the fire. But as she commented on the attention to detail, she suddenly noticed that Gabriel was no longer beside her. She wondered how long she had been rambling on to no one. His mind had held such a hold over her that she had to pull away for her sanity, but she also wanted to know the truth behind the painting, to understand the event as Gabriel had experienced it. She didn't want to rely on history books or second-hand accounts anymore -she had the opportunity to have a first-hand account but where had he gone?

As that thought entered her head Gabriel reappeared before her and she stared determinedly at him asking, *Where have you been*?

I have been to the astral plane where unimaginable music calms my soul.

Why?

The picture triggered a memory that I have been avoiding.

Her inner voice brimmed with insatiable curiosity and a fierce determination to learn. *If you divulge all the details of the Great Fire of London, you can dispel it from your mind. You won't have to fear it anymore.*

Despite Gabriel's attempts to dissuade Tilly, her feistiness overruled him. She watched as he removed his beloved hat and held it to his chest. She noticed him glance at the painting as he loosened the cord on the neck of his cloak, and she could sense some reluctance as he began.

News of the fire had reached our home on that fateful Sunday morning, my brother being the first to hear it.

Were you scared? Tilly's eyes were wide with curiosity.

Gabriel replied dismissively, *We were troubled. But fires were a common occurrence in London.*

Did you live near the fire?

No, but our family warehouses were in its path. We knew we had to act quickly.

Tilly pressed on, *And your mother...was she safe?*

She turned from the picture to look at Gabriel who was standing nearby.

At first, I wasn't worried. But as the flames ravaged through the city, I couldn't shake off the fear for her safety.

Tilly noticed how intently Gabriel was staring at the painting before them. It captivated him in the same way that she might become lost in a movie. Without realising it, she pulled out a stool and sat watching him, eager to hear more. She noticed his eyes were the colour of amber and if she more than glanced at them, they took her breath away. He was like a dreamy cavalier from a novel, come to life. Then the realisation hit her like a ton of bricks: he was a ghost, unable to touch or be touched. She had lost her father; she didn't want to lose her mind as well. She missed her father so much it hurt, and she guessed all she wanted was a comforting hug which a ghost would never be able to give her. Her stepmother used to give the best hugs before she became distant after Tilly's father passed away. As a family, they used to joke around and call themselves the Three Musketeers. She told herself that Gabriel's clothes reminded her of happier times with her family. That was all. She couldn't afford to read more into it.

It is as if he had stepped into the painting, Tilly thought to herself as she watched him with fascination. *He's not even here with me anymore.*

Gabriel closed his amber eyes.

Gabriel? she prompted.

He seemed lost in a trance, muttering about saltpetre and the 17th century. She snapped her fingers in front of him, desperate for his company. Was he under some spell? Finally, she asked about the infamous saltpetre, knowing that the word held some kind of power over him.

Gabriel's answer was emphatic, saltpetre was nothing more than pigeon droppings. But as he continued, Tilly could sense the weight of its significance. Finding out that it was used for gunpowder, as a preservative and even an elixir of life by alchemists meant she couldn't understand why he had muttered "damnable saltpetre". Tilly felt it was like the pigeons were giving his family a precious gift for taking care of them, but Gabriel revealed that it was both a blessing and a curse for his family and he told Tilly of his mother's obsession with its power.

Gabriel offered Tilly a hesitant glance, his eyes still haunted by the memories of the fire, and she responded.

If you want to tell me how it affected you I'm listening Gabriel. A trouble shared is a trouble halved as my father would say. If the memory is too painful we can take a step back.

He spoke hesitantly into her mind; *Would you like to see my memories? Together, in shared consciousness?*

Tilly was unsure. The fear she felt earlier when their minds combined made the hairs on her arms stand on end and her palms sweat with a sensory overload. Knowing he only had access to those senses through her body terrified her. If his memories of the fire overwhelmed him, talking about them, getting them out instead of keeping them in was ok but did she want to experience them? Yet she wanted to know that he wasn't just a figment of her imagination. She agreed. As they entered a shared consciousness, she knew they were connected on a deeper level, and she was transported into a world of pain and destruction.

Suddenly she could hear the east wind roar in her ears and watched spellbound as it carried the flames towards the family warehouse and his mother's laboratory. She saw the pavements glowing with fiery redness, as horses and men kept to the water's edge unable to tread on them. She almost cried out as she saw a young Gabriel following his brother determinedly along the water's edge, oblivious to the danger ahead. The acrid smell of burning filled her nose and lungs, drowning out the cries of people, the whine of dogs, and the piercing calls of birds. It was overwhelming and terrifying, but she stayed inside Gabriel's mind until the memories halted, and they both emerged from their shared consciousness, gasping for air.

Gabriel's dry tears slid down his ethereal face as he fell backwards in time, and he vanished once again, she assumed it was to the comfort of the astral plane.

Tilly was stunned by the vivid memories she had seen and knew she would not have coped with the horrors that Gabriel endured but her logical mind couldn't understand why the fire spread so quickly. She asked, *Who was to blame for that fire spreading so quickly?*

The thought lingered in Tilly's mind as she stared at the painting depicting the chaos of that fateful day. The painting somehow calmed her. It was nowhere near as horrific as the mental imagery she had endured inside Gabriel's mind.

Time dilation masking the time spent on the astral plane, Gabriel reappeared answering, *The mayor, Sir Thomas Bludworth, claimed, on first seeing the fire that "a woman might pisse it out."*

Was he in charge?

Yes, but his indecision cost us dearly. The King and Duke took over and were likened to heroes on horseback. Royals had never involved themselves in such a way before.

Gabriel invited her back into shared consciousness and though reluctant she agreed. She was astounded to witness St. Paul's Cathedral crumble in front of her mind's eye. At the same time, she heard the roar of gunpowder saving the rest of the city by creating firebreaks . As she listened and watched the memories come alive Tilly felt her entire perception of the painting shift.

Leaving shared consciousness for the reality of the 21st century she realised that the frozen strokes and colours on the canvas in front of them forever immortalised the scenes she had glimpsed for seconds in her mind. The painting was a pale reflection of reality.

These people in the painting will always be on the brink of destruction, she remarked sadly.

Gabriel's expression turned grim. *They lost everything!*

But in this painting, they still have everything with them, Tilly argued.

Gabriel shook his head. *Their possessions may have been saved from the flames only to rot in the water. Their livelihoods were destroyed.*

Tilly persisted, *But isn't that what makes this painting so powerful? It leaves us with questions and forces us to imagine the ending to their story.*

No! Gabriel shook his head firmly. *The truth is harsher than any imagination can conjure up. These people were left homeless and without a means to provide for themselves.*

It's like a time capsule painting that the artist has labelled 'Lest we Forget' Tilly mused.

Lest we forget, Gabriel repeated bitterly as he stared at the painting, and Tilly sensed he was remembering what he had lost in the devastating fire.

Tilly's heart raced as she shared a random thought of a 21st-century London fire and she relived the events of the tragic Grenfell Tower fire in 2017. She realised that shared consciousness was a two-way street as Gabriel's soothing voice broke through her inner turmoil, his eyes following the pictures in her mind.

The images and sounds are harrowing.

It was a devastating disaster, Tilly responded, turning to look at him. *I followed photos of it on my phone as it happened. I didn't realise they stayed in my subconscious.*

Gabriel's eyes widened with concern and he asked, *People were taking photos of such a tragedy?*

Yeah, it's crazy, but that's how we share news today.

Gabriel pointed at the painting, *The artist who painted that scene was there, amid the flames.*

Tilly considered Gabriel's words. Modern technology made it easier for people to document history. Would modern-day artists risk their lives to capture such scenes? She watched as Gabriel closed his eyes, and a sob escaped his lips. Tilly's mind was once again linked with Gabriel's as she watched him dodging falling debris. The wind carried lit ashes, singeing his hair and walking along the water's edge the young Gabriel doused himself in the river water regularly because the heat was unbearable. She could feel sweat forming on her forehead and dripping down her neck. She reached for her water bottle and downed it in one gulp, feeling the cool liquid replenish her body and quell the burning sensation in her throat.

Tilly couldn't escape the haunting memories of the fire. They were being transferred from the highly advanced CMD, by the astralites using her brainwaves to transfer the memories. They flooded her mind, almost as if the CMD was desperate to unload them once again.

Tilly felt the searing heat of the flames; she saw the crackling of the fire as it devoured everything Gabriel held dear; the feeble leather buckets; the warehouse and laboratory packed with volatile compounds; a man carrying a woman's lifeless form outside before the roof collapsed; the acrid smell of burning sulphur; she watched as a young boy tried dragging the woman's body to the water's edge in a daze and she gasped as she realised it was Gabriel; she saw a young man smothering a man's burning clothes as he screamed in agony and knew he was the older brother James that Gabriel spoke of. She saw that the woman was dead and clutching a book that had miraculously survived the fire.

Gabriel telepathed. *That book was the death of me. I carefully removed it from her body and used the recipes. I remember one day finding that she also used it as a journal and the events leading up to my birth were there.*

He vanished.

Tilly saw all of it and suddenly felt a wave of empathy and guilt for Gabriel and his pain. It was an unusual feeling for her, considering she usually had little control over her emotions. She guessed he was suffering from continuous PTSD that he had never gotten over and she had made it worse. She had to admit she was no good at comforting people. But as he'd already told her, purgatory hadn't exactly been a therapy session for him.

His company had become her lifeline as the world was forced to stay indoors. He was her one source of comfort in the midst of her overwhelming grief, and she could not afford to lose his company because of her thoughtless choice of painting. Their conversations ranged from making each other laugh to deep philosophical discussions. But a rational part of her mind warned of the dangers of developing feelings for someone from another dimension. Madness lurked around the corner waiting to entrap her forever in her internal world. She needed to get a grip on reality though she had to accept that this painting she had chosen was not simply insensitive; it was a haunting reminder of one of the tragedies that steered the direction of Gabriel's human life. She would never look at that painting in the same way again.

Overwhelmed by the scenes she had just witnessed and the feelings for Gabriel that were new to her, she wanted to change the subject. She heard a noise outside which disturbed her thoughts, releasing her from the shared consciousness. She saw the pigeon land on the dovecote, where it sat preening itself. She wondered aloud about the fate of the pigeons during the fire. She looked around for Gabriel, who was nowhere to be seen.

They hovered around their nests, waiting for a miracle, Gabriel answered, suddenly reappearing and his gaze following hers.

Tilly's senses were heightened, and she wiped away tears that clung to her lashes as she telepathed, *They didn't want to leave their eggs or babies behind. How many pigeons died?*

Gabriel stared at her uncomprehendingly, caught off-guard by the question. *I doubt the number of deaths of animals, including pigeons, was ever recorded. There were no Bills of Mortality for animals. Then we believed animals were placed in this world to serve the physical needs of humans.*

Tilly looked at him in horror and Gabriel quickly telepathed, *James loved and cared for his pigeons, Harry loved and cared for his horse, but in the 17th century, the concept of animal rights wasn't understood. Isaac has helped me understand.*

Tilly looked up from her phone. *I've checked out the Great Fire of London, and the fire destroyed some four-fifths of London — including eighty-nine churches, four of the City's seven gates, around 13,200 houses, and St Paul's Cathedral. According to the official records, six people died in the disaster.*

But that can't be true, she added, remembering Gabriel's interest in data.

She watched his melancholy subside as he thought about her question and he answered, *The bills of mortality did not record every plague victim, and I cannot see how it would be different for the fire.*

Tilly looked up from her phone. *Over seventy people died in the 2017 Grenfell Tower disaster in London.* She turned to him, hoping for a response. At that moment, she saw him mimic her gestures and tone of voice, a habit he had picked up from her. She couldn't help but smile as he telepathed in the same manner she used with him.

And your point is?

She could see he was irritated by her use of the phone. Placing it down on the table, she answered, *I know you didn't have towers in your day, but your homes were so close together it is comparable. Both fires were exacerbated by flammable materials.*

Gabriel stared at Tilly. In the past his thoughts about the fire were inviolate. Now he was being forced to listen to an unfamiliar perspective. A perspective that involved the use of a piece of technology that made him question the accuracy of his memories.

Tilly could see that he was irritated by the unfair advantage as he telepathed, *If your present-day is so wonderful in comparison, how did a tower catch fire and kill so many people?*

Tilly went to pick up her phone to see if a search engine could provide the answer. Gabriel glowered at her, and she decided against it.

They did not have to use buckets of water like we did, did they?

No

They did not have to use flammable candles to light their homes as we did.

No

Those buildings were not made of wood, as ours were.

Well, the material was a bit iffy.

You cannot compare the incompetence of builders today with the disadvantages of living in 17th-century times.

Admittedly, we should have moved on quite a bit since your time on Earth. She smiled apologetically.

Gabriel let out a heavy sigh.

Yet he continued, *you lost over seventy people to a fire, and we lost only six.*

Reaching for her phone, she extended it towards Gabriel's translucent figure as she telepathed, *The Grenfell fire was the result of many different contributing causes, all available to view online.*

Gabriel's incorporeal hand reached out to take the phone, but it passed right through. Tilly watched as he shifted uncomfortably, unable to accept the tangible object and she sighed and set the phone back down on the table for him to view as she quickly scrolled through.

I guess it will become the subject of fake news so that it becomes a more palatable story for the general public.

Fake news?

In the same way that your newspapers told you only six people died.

What do you mean?

I question the historical truth of that number based on a tower fire that happened in a small area of London today. She added *I do not question the intelligence of your generation. They may even have invented 'fake news.'*

36

FAKE NEWS

Gabriel followed Tilly down to the basement and watched her do her meditation. The sharing of his memories had enabled him to face hidden traumas he couldn't face when alive but now he wanted to find out what she meant by fake news and once she took her earbuds out and pulled back the curtain he joined her. His heart raced as he sat beside her, his ethereal body buzzing with an unfamiliar warmth. The very air around him seemed charged with electricity and his mind spun, unable to focus as he heard the rapid thumping of her heart in her chest. He closed his eyes and tried to steady himself but couldn't help but wonder if this assignment was testing his masculinity.

He realised that deep down he felt the abuse he suffered before he died was his fault due to the abuse his mother had suffered. It was like a self-fulfilling prophecy. As if he accepted that he should suffer what she suffered to right the wrong done to her. Losing his protective family had made him appear vulnerable to his abusers in the same way she had appeared vulnerable while her husband was off fighting in Europe. He experienced first-hand what she had experienced, and it made him understand why she sometimes looked at him as if she had seen a ghost. He would feel a chill that made him want to comfort her, but she would quickly go about her business and the moment was gone.

He had not chosen the celibate life of priesthood; it had been chosen for him and being with Tilly made him realise he would have chosen a different path if he had been allowed. He had been grateful to Henry Stafford who had always treated him as his flesh and blood and his siblings too. He wanted to be the third son of the man he thought of as his true father and to become a good Catholic priest that Henry Stafford would be proud of.

Returning to the site of the blaze, with Tilly by his side, gave him the strength to confront the trauma of his mother's death and face up to his hidden memories. He finally understood he wasn't at fault for not saving his mother; he wasn't to blame for the fire, and he wasn't to blame for her rape. The weight of guilt that surrounded him for every bad thing that happened to his family lifted from his shoulders. He realised he had always felt like a bad talisman. Being raised by the superstitious Sara and Ida may have contributed to that feeling and they had drummed into him the need for him to be the perfect child.

As they spent more time together, it was evident that Tilly was helping him heal. He was creating positive mental images to replace the overwhelming horrific images his mind had held onto and tormented him with.

Breaking the momentary spell, Tilly telepathed, *You understand that 1666 wasn't the end of the world, don't you?*

He nodded, grateful for her challenging stance, which took him out of his reverie.

Tilly got up from the stool and paced the room, *So, with hindsight, who or what do you blame for the Great Fire of London? Surely you don't believe it was a punishment from God.*

Gabriel had always known it wasn't a punishment from God. He had assumed the plague had been delivered by the comet as Sara had predicted but his recent internet searches had shown him that human lice and rat fleas could also have contributed. He had thought his sins were to blame for the fire but having the ability to revisit memories he was now certain in his mind who was to blame for the fire, and it wasn't God.

It depends on which story you choose to believe, he finally telepathed, turning to look at Tilly. Her green eyes met his, reminding him so much of Mathilde that he had to turn away.

What do you mean? she asked, tapping him on his ethereal shoulder.

Gabriel turned to face her, feeling a sudden loss of energy being transferred to her. He turned the static electricity into a warm embrace. He felt her succumb to the comfort of his embrace and he smiled. Isaac taught him how to harness static energy and convert it into kinetic energy. This newfound ability allowed him to express his emotions physically. He averted his eyes from her penetrating stare that seemed to question that hug, yet she remained within it. He spoke into her mind, *My brother James told me that they heard rumours about the Dutch starting the fire*, he explained. *We had just burned their port city a month before, so retaliation was suspected.*

Did you suspect them? Tilly asked.

He shook his head. *No, but my brother believed it must have been them.*

Why?

Tilly's challenging tone broke the energy but helped him focus. He began to fill her mind with his words, sharing the offload from the CMD of what he had read in the Gazette newspaper.

A report on the fire appeared in The Gazette a few days later.

Both could read The Gazette as it appeared in their mind's eye. His gaze locked with hers and he continued, *As you can see it claimed the fire started in Pudding Lane at Thomas Farriner's bakery – the King's baker.*

Tilly's eyes widened in awe. *He baked for the King.*

Gabriel couldn't help but smile at her excitement. *No, he didn't.*

He watched as her brow furrowed in confusion.

But The Gazette claims he did! I can read it for myself. Are you saying the newspaper lied?

He gave her a teasing smile. *I'm saying that sometimes things are not always as they seem, and we should question what we read.*

She sat back in her chair and whispered *Fake News* into his mind.

Gabriel heard the whisper but couldn't stop thinking about how much he was enjoying spending time with a girl and finding out the truth, with the power of hindsight, of what happened during his lifetime. He sighed before pulling himself together, saying, *Farriner was a humble baker of biskits, yet his title as the 'King's baker' gave him some prestige in the eyes of the people.*

As he explained the process of royal warrants, Tilly eagerly shared a warrant Queen Elizabeth II had given to a broomstick maker that she found online. They both couldn't contain their laughter at the thought of the queen flying on a broomstick. It seemed absurd that royalty would need a broomstick.

Gabriel grew serious and paused for effect, wanting to impress her with his knowledge, *It would appear that in your day, as in mine warrant holders don't work directly for royalty. Farriner did not work directly for the King. It was said that his son, Thomas Farriner Jr., worked directly for a friend of the King's.*

What has that got to do with the fire? Tilly's green eyes looked earnestly at him.

Her earnestness made him feel important and he felt in control. He had never been in control growing up. Looking back, his entry into the church was meant to shield him from becoming a controlling roundhead, whom his family feared he could have become without the church's guidance.

He told Tilly the rumours and speculations regarding the cause of the fire were all they talked about back then. The CMD was busy filling his mind with the memories, and he shared them with Tilly. As a large overweight man appeared before them in their shared consciousness, he telepathed, *He was a friend of the King, Lord Buckhurst. I've mentioned him before. He sometimes called himself the Marquis of Dorset, though he was but an Earl. Rumour was that he offered Thomas Farriner the younger £100 to start the fire.*

He saw shock register on her face.

No way! No way! she repeated telepathically, rocking back and forth excitedly on the stool.

Gabriel closed his eyes so he could not see her rocking, which upset his equilibrium. Another memory entered his head from the CMD. A memory of his father asking the plague watchman to deliver a letter to Thomas Farriner Jr.

Tilly stopped rocking. She picked up her iPhone and began pressing buttons as Gabriel looked on.

Oh, my goodness!

Tilly slid off the stool and stood, holding her phone out for Gabriel to see. *Look! My search has yielded Thomas Farriner Jr's last will, which mentions the £100 owed to him by the Marquis of Dorset! £100 would be a small fortune in those days comparable, my internet search tells me, to almost £30,000 today.*

Gabriel marvelled at the capabilities of Tilly's phone. He could feel Tilly's mind racing with possibilities as she sent him a thought, *So you think the King may have been involved in the fire.*

He reminded her to slow down, saying telepathically, *You're jumping ahead.*

He wanted to savour the retelling and keep Tilly captivated for as long as possible. He continued sending her his thoughts, *I recall Sara, the maid, mentioning a rumour that the King's mistress Nell Gwyn had a soft spot for Buckhurst. So, he was often sent away on missions. My father even accompanied him to*

Europe to recover the lost and stolen art of the King's father taken by Cromwell.

He noticed Tilly shift on the stool, her fingers gripping the edge, and he felt her willing him to give her more gossip of the day.

What has that to do with Thomas Farriner Jr, the fire, and the Pudding Lane bakery? she asked.

He took off his hat and adjusted its feather as he glanced at Tilly, noticing her sage green T-shirt perfectly matched the green of her eyes. He was reminded of Mathilde's favourite dress and Mathilde's eyes, the same eyes, a family trait. But what did Sara say about him never being able to inherit green eyes? He knew now why that memory disturbed him.

He dismissed the thought and telepathed, I'm *getting to the juicy details, I promise.* His amber eyes sparkled.

Not able to hold back any longer he whispered into her mind, hoping to pique her curiosity. *What if I told you that the Pudding Lane bakery wasn't just selling their famous pastries but was dealing with art stolen from the King?*

So, do you think Thomas Farriner Jr was instructed to dispatch King Charles I's paintings to Lord Buckhurst before setting fire to the bakery?

It's hard to say for sure, he replied, his voice tinged with suspense. *But anything was possible considering the tension and mistrust after the Civil Wars.*

Tilly nodded. *Lord Buckhurst was quite a character from what you've told me. Why would a King, betrayed by such a man with his mistress, and a murderer, pardon him unless he was expecting him to do nefarious deeds for him?*

Gabriel sighed, *The king would not have expected to pay for art that had belonged to his father and so the recovery of the art was an undercover operation Lord Buckhurst would have been ideally suited to. The vigilance and activity of the king and duke were extraordinary once the fire was underway. They took charge as though their lives depended on it.*

Tilly asked, *Do you think that was guilt?*

Gabriel answered, *Look at the newspapers before us. They report that the King was often overheard saying, "It is no wonder the plague spread so rapidly, look at the houses, so close together and filled with people. What we need is a great fire that will destroy most of the city and allow us to rebuild."*

Did these newspapers print the truth of things? Tilly asked.

Gabriel's voice echoed in Tilly's mind, *Does today's news report the truth? I don't think the royals expected the fire to take such a hold.*

Tilly looked up from her phone, *We are back to fake news,* she admitted with a shrug. *Stories with no real facts.*

A look of satisfaction crossed Gabriel's handsome features. *And yet you have proved, through that phone that the facts I gave you were true. Bakeries were used to store works of art. Thomas Farriner Jr was owed money by Lord Buckhurst.*

Gabriel felt Tilly's eyes watching him whilst conversing telepathically.

You've already said not to trust what you read. But even stories passed through word of mouth can become twisted and exaggerated, like a game we used to play called Chinese Whispers.

Gabriel raised an eyebrow in curiosity. *What is this game?*

One person whispers a message to another, who then passes it on to the next person until it comes full circle. But by the end, the message is never the same as when it started.

Gabriel nodded in understanding but couldn't resist adding, *Are you trying to say that even our conversations are like this game? That there may be errors in what I tell you. As an astralite I cannot lie.*

Tilly laughed and shook her head, *I trust what you tell me, Gabriel. With the knowledge you had at the time.*

He could sense that she thought she had the upper hand and held all the cards in her hand.

What do you mean? How do you know our news was fake?

He didn't like it when she appeared smug, as she did now.

You wouldn't know. but in 1986, London's bakers apologised to the Lord Mayor for one of their own, Thomas Farriner Sr., causing the fire.

As she held the phone for him. a picture of a colossal monument appeared on the screen, pointing towards the heavens like an accusatory finger. He couldn't ignore the symbolism of the accusing finger as he read about the six suicides linked to the monument and the turbulent path of shifting blame - from a rumoured Popish plot to the baker whose name would always be associated with false allegations. The injustice pained him when it might have been the baker's son who was to blame. He sighed, looked away from the accusatory finger and whispered into Tilly's mind.

I recall a book published at the time called 'The Examinations of the Business about the Fire of London', It contained the truth of the fire. He shared his thoughts and conviction that the aristocratic friends of the King instigated the fire with the help of the baker's son who dealt in art for Lord Buckhurst.

He became aware that Tilly was listening to him whilst seemingly distracted by something on her phone. Gabriel saw the phone as both a curse and a blessing. He resented the attention she gave it and that she chose the phone over his company, but it allowed her to find answers in an instant that would have taken him years of research.

She looked up and answered apologetically. *I am searching for the book online.*

I do not think you will find it, he telepathed, confident that the device she was addicted to which seemed to be an extension of herself, would not be able to find it.

Why?

The King commanded for it to be burnt.

That is weird, Another cover-up?

Gabriel answered that he was certain a chance wind didn't cause the fire. No competent baker, like Thomas Farriner Sr, could cause a fire and be allowed to continue to bake after the tragedy and he was allowed to continue. She still seemed distracted by her phone, and he felt hurt as she stifled a giggle and looked up from her phone.

What now? he asked

I find it amazing that your King Charles found the time to father at least twenty bastards and be the merry monarch the internet claims he was.

Gabriel answered confidently, *The merry monarch's disguise was a masquerade he could use for his apparently 'throw away words' which might have encouraged his ignorant, less intelligent, aristocratic friends, to start a fire or get others to do so. Ultimate-*

ly, Charles II got what he wanted- a new London and some of his father's art returned.

Confined within the four walls of the building, Gabriel had internet access and remembered the shock he got when he scrolled through images and videos of present-day London. The 17th-century city he remembered was a labyrinth of narrow, winding streets where houses jostled for space, so close that their eaves almost touched. Now it sprawled outward with wider roads and taller buildings and though Tilly had assured him it could still teem with people, during this pandemic it was as empty as the streets of London were when his family departed for Eyam. The reality of 21st-century London was that it appeared cleaner and architecturally more appealing and he wished he could roam its streets, but it was too dangerous for him to do so without Isaac. Would Isaac take him on a tour he wondered. Would Tilly turn the streets of London into a VR experience for him so that he could familiarise himself with it beforehand?

Tilly interrupted his thoughts.

I think we can call this battle a draw.

He had forgotten they were in competition.

She continued, *You know things I could never know about the 17th-century painting, but I was able to find out things of which you were unaware.*

Gabriel gave a rueful grin. Girls were the fairer sex.

37

FUTURE REALITIES

Tilly took the Lieve Verschuier painting back to its repository. As she looked around her, memories flooded back of her father's lessons on Hollar's drawings. The etchings depicted the city before and after 'The Great Fire of London'. She remembered that copies of Hollar's drawings of the results of the fire in London adorned all kinds of tourist paraphernalia nowadays. That was what people were interested in. The phoenix rising out of the ashes. When she did a London project for school her father took her on a walk in the parts of London affected by the fire, pointing out the architecture and identifying it on the printed copy of Hollar's etchings. She was sure there would still be copies in the gallery. She realised that etchings, as opposed to paintings, diminished the powerful reality of the fire and might have helped Gabriel more than a painting of the event. The epochal event meant the architectural changes to London were Charles II's greatest legacy, in her humble opinion. The architectural magnificence built immediately after the fire was the part of London she loved the most, perhaps because she had her father's undivided attention at the time.

She looked at Gabriel who had followed her into the repository. He was gazing at the Tree of Life tapestry, lost in thought, like her, but she doubted his thoughts would be about creating VR experiences of London. She knew she was becoming obsessive about VR, but, she reasoned, that it was better than other things she could be obsessed about. She was grateful to Gabriel for helping her develop her understanding of 17th-century works of art. Wrapped up in the descriptive element, she hadn't considered how interpreting a painting meant different things to different people.

Tilly spoke to Gabriel's mind.

I doubt you have a piece of art you would wish to revisit in virtual reality, but if you do, I could try and recreate it for you.

Without hesitation, Gabriel eagerly responded. She listened to his excited recollections of the family portrait, commissioned by his father after returning from the Netherlands to replace those destroyed by the Roundheads. The imagery of all the family gathered together, with Ida's delectable dishes and the rustling of satin dresses, flooded her mind from his. She could almost smell the clean freshness of the satin dresses and she saw the men adorned in their finest clothes and wigs, displaying their status with pride. Tilly could sense the joy and excitement in the air, wishing she could transport herself to that moment and relive it with him. It was a moment frozen in time. The images his mind shared with hers meant she knew exactly what she was looking for. It was just a matter of finding it.

She telepathed, *I understand your attachment to that scene and your faith in my abilities, but any modern interpretation of the 17th century would be a pale version of reality. Is that enough?*

Yes, it is enough, he whispered into her mind. *Your basement will be our reality. You can close your eyes and step into the world you have created for me. We can lose ourselves in virtual reality scenes that mean so much to us. Before COVID. Before the plague.*

Tilly smiled. She felt excited by the prospect of sharing their worlds realising he had seen the VR world she was creating for herself. Tilly had no time to process that thought as she heard footsteps on the stairs. Gabriel vanished.

Tilly began scrolling through her phone as she said aloud, "Now where could that family portrait be?"

"Who are you talking to?" Helena asked as she entered the room, concern etched on her face.

"Just myself," Tilly replied with a forced smile.

Helena's eyes darted over to her stepdaughter, unable to shake the uneasiness that settled in her stomach. Tilly seemed distant and disconnected, always scrolling through her phone and in another world. Sjaak had been pushing for her to get medical help, to demand Tilly be banned from the basement, claiming the child was always talking to voices in her head and that his friend Henry would have agreed. But Helena remembered how fiercely Henry had fought against medical intervention, dedicated to helping Tilly embrace her neurodiversity and self-regulate after she struggled with behavioural issues before her diagnosis.

Though she had to admit that since his passing Tilly had retreated into herself, lost in a dark cloud of grief. Helena wanted to believe that it was normal teenage behaviour after a bereavement and living through COVID not knowing if life would ever get back to normal. She was guilty of the same, though alcohol helped enormously.

Tilly's voice rose above the heavy silence, suggesting an ambitious immersive project using Hollar's drawings of London before and after the Great Fire. Helena hesitated, unsure if this was just another distraction or a genuine attempt at seeking a connection with her. She forced a small smile and tentatively agreed to look into it.

But as Tilly continued to talk excitedly about the project, Helena wondered if it might be enough to pull them out of their separate spirals of pain and loss. A fleeting moment of hope flickered in her heart, and she said, “There is an informative book called ‘The Man Who Drew London’ by Gillian Tindall with lots of background information that we could use to make it a worthwhile experience.”

As Helena began to climb the stairs she said, “I have made us ertwensoep for lunch if you are ready -I would appreciate your company.,”

"I've got to check something in the art gallery, but I will join you afterwards," Tilly promised.

Helena felt a wave of relief spread over her. Sjaak did not know her husband's brave, strong daughter at all.

38

WHAT LIES BENEATH

There was a clink of glasses and low voices.

Sjaak took a slug of wine. Holding his glass, he strolled purposefully towards the newly laid and solidified flagstones.

"They have made a respectable job of this," he said, stomping on the flagstones as if expecting them to loosen.

Kneeling, he prodded a finger into the grout between the flagstones. It was just as solid as the stones, and the floor appeared smooth with no discernible seams. Helena knew the new flagstones would need a pneumatic drill to remove them.

He said," Such a shame the old stones could not be kept."

"You have no idea what you are talking about Sjaak." Helena said, irritated by his constant negative attitude which insidiously contributed to her mood. "They look exactly the same and cost a small fortune."

The acidity of a perfectly chilled mouthful of wine crackled on her palate and she added, "The old flagstones were at least 400 years old and were dangerous!"

Sjaak straightened himself up, brushing non-existent dust off his trousers. He said, "You do realise something so historical cannot be kept quiet."

Helena nursed her glass of wine and made herself comfortable on a tub chair. "Yes, I do," she answered curtly.

Sjaak seemed oblivious to her irritation with him. She noticed him smacking his lips as he tasted the perfectly chilled Chablis, before saying, "A body preserved by saltpetre under the house and dating back to the 17th century will make headline news around the world."

Helena flinched, "Please tell me you have not shared that information Sjaak."

Sjaak looked aggrieved. "Have you told Tilly yet?" he retaliated. He collected the opened bottle of Chablis from the wine fridge.

Sjaak filled their glasses with a generous pour and returned the bottle to the fridge. With an air of satisfaction, he settled into the tub chair across from Helena and she nodded her thanks. She was irritated by his presence and interference in her life since Henry's death. She knew she owed him a debt of gratitude for dealing with everything in the Netherlands. But how dare he try to step in and help her with her moody, neurodivergent stepdaughter. He had no right to advise on something he had never experienced.

"No." she answered, "Henry planned to tell her."

She looked at him coldly, "His death has been enough for her to comprehend. "

Sjaak looked down at the table, and wouldn't meet her gaze, as he said, "She might have found it a distraction."

She noticed him shift uncomfortably before he added, "She might have been interested."

Helena took a mouthful of wine and put her glass on the table. She said in a loud whisper.

"Sjaak! Please do not tell me how to raise my stepdaughter."

He lifted his head, "I personally think hearing it on the news or seeing it online when it happened in her own home, might not be the best thing for her in her fragile state."

"Enough!" she said, picking up her empty glass and going to the wine fridge for a refill. Returning to the table she noticed his nervous twitch of the eyebrow as he helped himself to a custard cream from the biscuit barrel and said, "So, about this mummified body,"

Helena stared at him.

"Oh, I mean, it's incredible that they found one here. Mummification has been happening for thousands of years, but right here in this very room?"

Helena's eyes widened in shock, if he thought she would tell him anything else he was mad. But she quickly regained her composure and reached for her phone, effectively shutting Sjaak out of the conversation. He sat back in his chair with a sigh.

She turned to her photo album and the file labelled "Basement." She opened the photos of the mummified body. The first photo was of Henry's discovery of the open void. She remembered that the open void smelled of cinnamon and cloves. The scent lingered in the basement, even after it had been sealed shut and the void filled in. It seemed to resurface from time to time, a haunting reminder of what once happened within those walls.

She remembered Henry's infectious enthusiasm and delight at his discovery. She wondered if the discovery of Tutankhamun's tomb caused as much excitement. The builders initially brought the loose flagstone to Henry's attention, but he brushed it off. It wasn't until he stumbled over it later that night that he realised their warning was valid. He thought they were purposely looking for more work when they suggested new flooring and underfloor heating.

She remembered him telling her, "They are a canny lot. Nearly finishing the job and finding more things that need doing."

He laughed his irrepressible laugh and added, "Though I must admit, underfloor heating will solve a lot of issues."

Henry told her that once the flagstone was removed it exposed a void that appeared to be full of sacks. The smell was overpowering, and he was determined to find out where the smell was coming from. Later, that same evening, he texted her from the basement as she was filling the dishwasher. Tilly was on a school geography trip.

"Come down here. NOW."

She knew he went down to remove the sacks as he listened to his jukebox. It wasn't like him to summon her. She was curious. She descended the stairs and heard the voice of Peter Sarstedt drift up to greet her singing 'Where Do You Go To My Lovely.'

She smiled. He loved music from that era. She called out to him,

"What is it? What couldn't wait?"

She laughed. "I thought this was your private den."

Sitting on his haunches, with a large flagstone beside him, surrounded by sacks, large pieces of canvas, and what looked like white salt or sand, he was staring into a void and his face seemed transfixed.

"Come and see," he whispered as if he were in a church or somewhere holy.

She went over, and he moved back so that she could peer in. She knelt and looked into the hole. An odour she would usually associate with Christmas drifted up from the void.

"Cinnamon and cloves," Henry said noticing her wrinkling her nose.

A beautiful, well-preserved mummified face stared back at her. She sneezed and fell backwards in shock.

Henry immediately held her in his arms as he said soothingly,

"Sorry, darling, I didn't mean to startle you."

Lightly kissing her on the cheek, he said, "I thought that you needed to see it, as it was too hard to explain."

Letting go of her and standing up, he added, "I'll get us a drink."

He went over to the wine fridge and poured them both a glass of cold Chablis.

She instinctively picked up the glass she was now holding and was back in the present. She noticed Sjaak was standing behind her and staring at a photo of the mummy fully clothed and wearing an exquisite coral and gold necklace around her neck. The mummy even possessed all of her hair. He was staring at her with a worried expression on his face. She had purposely excluded him and decided not to share the photos with him. How dare he try to sneak a look. If he were right and it would make headline news, he would see the photos soon enough. He was untrustworthy. He lost their paintings for them. He didn't deserve to share their ownership of the mummy. She closed the phone and looked at him.

"What do you want, Sjaak?"

He struggled to speak, as though he had seen a ghost. "To be of help if you need it," he volunteered. "We could tell Tilly about the mummy together if that would help."

"You are not Henry, Sjaak."

She added, "I've told you, Henry planned to tell Tilly."

She continued, "He researched and had valuable information to share with her. Information about his family."

"You mean Tilly's family," he said purposefully.

She closed her eyes, trying to stop the tears that were threatening. "It was his to share. Not ours," she said, with finality and sadness in her voice.

"I seem to have upset a hornet's nest," he sighed. "I apologise, I should go."

She waited for him to leave, knowing he hoped she would ask him to remain. She didn't.

"I'll let myself out," he said resignedly.

Her voice was flat, "You do that." she said.

She poured herself another glass of Chablis and using the remote, she turned the shuffle mode on the jukebox and sat back in the tub chair, listening to her husband's music selection as tears ran down her face once more. She was confident Sjaak would know from recent experience, that it was not worth his while trying to reason with her.

The sound of running water suggested he was washing his glass. The noise of his shoes as he ascended the stairs echoed down to the basement. Helena sighed with relief as she heard the gallery shop doorbell rattle denoting his exit from her home.

39

THE CONSTCAMER FAMILY

Tilly revelled in the unexpected freedom of lockdown. With a triumphant grin, she tossed her schoolbooks into the recycling bin, having successfully persuading Helena that first-hand education within the family business was far more valuable than traditional schooling. Instead of trying to cover centuries of pockets of history deemed appropriate by the Department of Education, she would study 17th-century art and become an expert. Already she had applied to study for an online degree in VR. She intended to build a catalogue of immersive art experiences to make her father proud.

Fancy being able to study at home woohoo! She could work through the night if she chose and then sleep till late. Or work from the early hours and sleep in the afternoon. She searched online for 17th-century family portraits that could be included in her new studies and contribute to a project she would be able to submit online towards her degree. It wasn't time wasted and she was surprised to find so many of them. She uploaded the portraits onto the computer that fed the surrounding walls. The technology was so good that it adjusted the portraits to fit the walls. Magic!

This morning, she felt the familiar, welcome presence of Gabriel. She turned to see him looking at the paintings surrounding them as she scrolled through. Suddenly he gave a telepathic cry.

Stop!

Tilly nearly jumped out of her skin; his internal voice was so loud. Her gaze was drawn to the painting on the wall, its grandeur and complexity commanding her attention. It wasn't a mere family portrait as she had initially assumed, but a "Constcamer" - a room dedicated to displaying the most prized artworks of a collector. The artist, Dutchman Gonzales Coques, had captured a moment frozen in time from the 17th century, where four individuals gathered around a table adorned with riches and symbols of knowledge. Their refined demeanour and sophisticated interests made Tilly wonder about their identities and stories.

As she studied the scene further, her eyes were drawn to each figure's unique contribution - one man eagerly sharing a document with a woman, another younger man pointing towards recent acquisitions, while a third listened intently. Sitting at the table a young woman added her personal touch of beauty to the scene as she meticulously sketched feathers, shells, and ancient coins.

What secrets did this painting hold? What tales could it unveil about these enigmatic figures from centuries ago?

The painting had been enlarged to such a degree that Tilly could see the names of the books on the table. One entitled 'Harmonices Mundi' by Johannes Kepler was opened on a page explaining the musical harmony of the cosmos. Another book displayed was Hermes Trismegistus' 'Asclepius' showing the family's interest in alchemy. The constcamer was a showcase of the family's wealth, knowledge, and interests. Its purpose was to impress visitors and advertise the prosperity and sophistication of the family.

This is mind-blowing. Tilly whispered, not knowing what to look at next. The painting beckoned her towards the wall with its intricate details, revealing secrets and stories that a photograph could never capture. As her fingers delicately traced over the objects on the virtual table, she felt herself being transported back in time to an era when the 17th century reigned supreme. This canvas was more than just a piece of art, it was a living, breathing diary of the family's history. It was like scrolling through a Facebook profile - each portrait, painting, and object holding a tale waiting to be uncovered. And there, amongst the crowd of characters, she noticed a youth with curious amber eyes peering beyond the frame. It had to be Gabriel.

But then her attention shifted to an adolescent girl captured in a moment, her gaze meeting Tilly's as she delicately played with a coral necklace draped around her neck. It was as if she were inviting the viewer to share her joy of receiving such a precious gift. The painting captured more than just beauty and history - it promised an invitation to become part of its world. But it wasn't her world, it was Gabriel's.

Mathilde Gabriel whispered into Tilly's consciousness.

Tilly gasped. These people were Gabriel's family. She didn't belong here in such a private moment. Leaving the picture on display around the walls of the immersive room she went up to the gallery to see if she could find any other paintings by Gonzales Coques.

She found a couple and noticed that on the back of one of them were notes her father added. The notes included a biography of the artist, a list of his genres and paintings, and a reference to his work for Charles I and Charles II of England. Gonzales Coques, it seems, was also an art dealer. As were Tilly's parents, as were Gabriel's parents. Coincidence, serendipity, synchronicity. Tilly was excited by the painting lending itself to a fascinating VR experience exploring the different paintings it contained, books, artists, writers and the family. She thought of the collectables on display in the portrait and wanted to research and find out more about why they chose them.

Excited by the prospect she rejoined Gabriel in the basement.

It is as if they are waiting for me, Gabriel whispered into Tilly's mind.

I assume the portrait is of your family. Are you the young boy in the painting? Tilly replied telepathically.

Yes. My mama and papa are standing with my two older brothers, Harry, and James.

Tilly was fascinated to be able to put faces to the family members Gabriel told her about.

You look so much like your mother in the portrait Tilly said.

Gabriel smiled.

My father has recently returned from the Netherlands with Harry. He bought my sister Mathilde that coral necklace.

Tilly pointed to the young artist in the painting on the wall. *Who is she*? she asked.

That is Fran. An orphan that father took in. She was Dutch and deaf.

As Gabriel spoke, he pointed out the details he was referring to on the surrounding walls. Tilly walked up to the wall where Mathilde stood. She wore a beautiful sage green silk dress.

Tilly telepathed. *She looks delighted with the necklace. The artist has picked out every facet of it, as if he too is sharing her treasure with us.*

Gabriel replied enthusiastically, *She was delighted with it. It was her only necklace.*

He looked at Tilly who always wore the same silver heart-shaped locket. He asked, *Can you remember how you felt when you received your necklace, Tilly?*

Tilly stared at Mathilde's face. The sheer joy of receiving such a gift was reflected in her face and how she held it. Tilly thought of herself. She lived in a consumerist society and owned a jewellery stand for storing several necklaces. She suddenly felt ashamed and wished she had shown more appreciation for her locket when her father was alive. She felt more comfortable talking about Gonzales Coques and so she looked at Gabriel and asked.

Do you remember the artist?

Gabriel nodded.

Did your family deal with him?

Again, Gabriel nodded.

If we have that kind of provenance, it might be worthwhile for the gallery to put an immersive display of his work here.

Gabriel's amber eyes lit up and he smiled gratefully.

Tilly added, *Unfortunately, I cannot create a VR experience without the design experts, and they would require my stepmother's approval. These days provenance is everything.*

Gabriel appeared anxious and answered carefully.

The provenance that would matter more to visitors would be that my family, the family in the portrait, lived in this house. That is why I haunt this house, Tilly. It is my home. You are a descendant of my family.

Tilly's mind was reeling as she processed the words. A descendant of his family? It couldn't be true. And yet, as she looked at the painting again, the father in the painting stirred up memories of her father, adding to the confusion and conflict within her.

And what did that mean for her feelings towards Gabriel? She couldn't deny the magnetic attraction she felt with him and the deep telepathic communication they enjoyed but now she wondered if she misunderstood those feelings.

40

CONSCIOUSNESS

It was 7 am and Tilly woke with her mind in turmoil. She wanted to make sense of Gabriel's bombshell, but she was still grieving for her father and that took up all of her mind space and affected every decision she made. It was where she liked to reside, in her inner world, in his company.

She needed to speak with Isaac again. She did not need the distraction of Gabriel and the conflicting feelings his presence gave her. Putting on her warm dressing gown she crept down to the basement. She opened a curtain slightly and looked outside at the dovecote. She thought dovecotes housed a couple of pigeons like the one in front of her but when searching for Hollar's etchings of London in the gallery upstairs, she came across a print of 'Pigeons In A Dovecote' by Hollar. The dovecote in the print was exceptionally large, built to hold hundreds. *Why was it necessary when they had the whole sky and beautiful trees to nest in?* she wondered. There was no denying that the dovecote in the garden must have been grand in its original form, but it wasn't any longer. The crumbled walls offered shelter but lacked any sense of comfort.

On the other hand, trees radiated a comforting scent and their rustling leaves whispered secrets to each other. They were living beings, constantly growing, and evolving with each passing season. And if she were a bird, there was no doubt in her mind that she would choose the whispering trees over the grand but hollow dovecote as her home.

Today on the dovecote, a little robin was helping itself to a suet ball her stepmother had left on the bird table. Having no hands, it expertly used its beak to poke at the suet ball. Once it had a large lump of suet in its beak it tapped the piece against the bird table until it was of the desired size for swallowing.

The robin was the distraction she needed from the Groundhog days of realisation that her father was dead, and the subsequent stranglehold of grief. The robin fluffed up its feathers, trapping as much air in them as possible to stay warm. Pleasantly satiated it began to whistle a morning song.

Helping herself to coffee and a biscuit she headed outside and sat down on a bistro chair pulling her dressing gown sleeves down over her hands, before putting them around the hot cup of coffee. She took a sip of coffee and did the breathing exercises her father taught her, smiling to herself at his impression of a scouse accent and began to feel better.

Tilly followed the call of the robin's song and saw Isaac approaching in the distance, flying towards the dovecote. With each circuit around the garden, he used a pattern of swoops and turns, as if he were checking out every angle for danger lurking.

Tilly had noticed Isaac's take-offs were more energetically demanding than his landings. He landed with precision and grace, and she wondered whether that came instinctively or required lots of practice. She couldn't remember learning to walk as a baby but suspected she wasn't graceful to begin with. She watched as he braked before expertly touching down on the small bird table joining his feathered friend. The robin bobbed its head in greeting before hopping down into the lush kitchen garden full of tasty worms below.

Isaac began his necessary preening. *Good morning, Tilly. You are up early. Couldn't you sleep*?

Tilly's bleary eyes took in his well-groomed appearance and answered uneasily, *No.*

Isaac continued rearranging his feathers to insulate himself from the early morning chill. She wasn't sure why she asked the question. It wasn't the question she had intended to ask.

I was wondering. Why did I feel a jolt of electricity when Gabriel sat next to me?

Isaac fluffed up his bronze body feathers giving his bird form an air of importance. *It was merely a static discharge. You get it when you touch someone with a different electrical potential.*

Was it a feeling of familial love that transcends time? She asked.

Familial? You are asking the wrong question of one such as me Tilly though Gabriel's mother was certainly your ancestor.

I find his shared consciousness overwhelming at times, She admitted, but quickly changing tack, not wishing for Isaac to challenge him, she asked, *What is consciousness? Can you explain it to me in simple terms?*

That is certainly a preferred question, and I shall try. Can we agree that we exist, here and now, as consciousness in our different forms?

Well, you are a bird, Gabriel's a ghost and I'm a girl whose father has recently died. The only way we could communicate effectively is via our consciousness so as odd as all of those sound, I agree.

She took a custard cream in her hand, gently prying it open to reveal the creamy centre. With a small smile, she carefully licked the sweet cream from the centre of the biscuit, savouring each lick. She closed her eyes and let out a contented sigh. She wanted another biscuit but was rationing them so gave her full attention to Isaac who continued to preen himself as he telepathed.

Your electromagnetic sense in the brain enables your body's brain matter to connect to your consciousness. It gives you the ability to be aware and think. When you die your consciousness unplugs itself from the brain and re-enters the cosmic consciousness where you were before you were born. Consciousness is ultimately a pattern of vibrations or frequencies.

Tilly nodded her understanding. *You are saying that we do not die. Instead, we change our level of consciousness. Change the vibrational level we exist on.*

Isaac tilted his head. *May I continue?*

Tilly nodded for him to continue noticing that even the pigeon's tiniest movement showed off hypnotising flashes of iridescent purple on its neck. Humans drew the short straw when it came to beauty.

Consciousness has three parts, Isaac stated with confidence. Tilly could see him tracing imaginary lines in her mind's eye. *The conscious, the subconscious, and the unconscious.*

She couldn't help but put her hand to her head, feeling overwhelmed by the idea. But Isaac continued,

The conscious part of the mind encompasses our present thoughts and actions, while the subconscious operates behind the scenes and controls automatic behaviours like walking.

Isaac's orange eyes seemed to hypnotise her as they delved deeper into the topic of the subconscious and meditation. She couldn't help but think about her father and how he had taught her this practice from beyond the grave. She remembered his letter from Maastricht, which she kept safe in her memory box filled with items that reminded her of her father - things she couldn't bear to let go of. Why hadn't she learned about meditation in school? Isaac explained that it should be taught by those who have mastered the practice, not just any substitute teacher already having a bad day trying to deliver a subject they didn't understand. She remembered those schooldays as wasted days but now realised they could also be negative days if the teacher's inexperience put her off the subject matter.

Tilly's inner voice took on a worried tone as she asked, *Are we using only our conscious minds while we share consciousnesses like we three have been doing?*

She quickly added, *You can't access my subconscious can you?*" She looked at Isaac. *You can't access my unconscious and all the things I'd rather not remember or share, can you?*

When Isaac spoke to Tilly in her head his voice sounded to her like her father's voice. She knew she gave him that voice and it took on a gentle tone as he spoke into her mind,

No, I can't. No one can. What you think about is private. They are your thoughts, and they belong to you. It is your inner world. They are the essence of who you are. You can choose to share your thoughts or not to share them.

Tilly sighed with relief. She was so glad she learnt to speak telepathically. She hated to think of her stepmother overhearing her. She watched enthralled as Isaac took a drink of water.

Sometimes I have awful hateful thoughts about my stepmother. I sometimes wished it were her who died instead. I don't any more. I am luckier than her. A part of my father is in me because I am his child. My stepmother doesn't have that. I see the way that she looks at me. I know I look like him. I am all that she has left of him.

Is that all that was worrying you, Tilly? Your private thoughts?

Yes, Tilly admitted.

I have enough to do with my private thoughts Tilly. I certainly cannot read your thoughts, Gabriel cannot either. To be honest Tilly, anyone who says they can is lying.

Tilly could see Isaac nestling inside the dovecote as he added, *Do not worry. Did you find those horses?*

Yes, I did. Thank you. Tilly smiled. *It's a riding school, would you believe?*

Yes, I would believe.

One more question, Tilly ventured.

Isaac hopped outside and looked directly at Tilly. As he did so the flashes of iridescent colours on his body, and wings, once more caught the light of the early morning sun reflecting its heat and keeping his body at a comfortable temperature. Tilly gasped at the beauty. Isaac answered *I may choose not to reply but go on.*

Can you traverse planes of consciousness, visit parallel universes, and go to a different reality?

I can do some things as a bird that you can't. I live a different reality to yours, but I cannot visit parallel universes during a rebirth.

What about me? Can I travel to a parallel universe?

You cannot visit a parallel universe because you are in this universe. If you were to encounter your parallel self, one of two things would occur: either your existence would nullify theirs in that universe, or you would negate your existence, preventing any potential return to your original universe.

Tilly was relieved. She didn't want to visit parallel universes.

It is frankly too dangerous to mess with parallel universes Tilly. Cocking his head to one side as he stared down at her he added, *However, I believe that you can visit Gabriel's time on Earth and Gabriel can visit your family's past times on Earth.*

We can? She wasn't sure she wanted to know that.

The only way you can visit the past, such as Gabriel's time on Earth, is when you are in a dreamlike state or a meditative astral state. You will not be using your conscious mind but your subconscious mind.

Tilly sighed deeply, *After all we have spoken about this morning, I should know that already.*

You will be unable to alter your perception, but the memories of what you saw will linger upon awakening and becoming conscious. I'm afraid you cannot go back to a time when your father was alive. Does that answer your question, Tilly?

Tilly sighed, *Sometimes, I think you exist only in my head anyway. If it wasn't that I know Helena cleans the dovecote for you, and that Sjaak detests you I might seriously think I was imagining things.*

Tilly watched as Isaac hopped onto the top of the dovecote, leaving the bird table to a wren looking for its breakfast.

Did you know that Gabriel used to live here in this house hundreds of years ago? She asked.

Yes.

Isaac's piercing orange eyes locked onto Tilly's, and she could feel her father's presence in that moment. She took a deep breath and spoke from her heart, *Thank you for being here to listen, Isaac. I'm going to practice my meditation now.*

The weight of her words lingered in the air as if they held some deeper understanding that Isaac's teaching had given her.

41

FINDING ANSWERS

Gabriel's voice echoed in Tilly's mind, accusing and confrontational. She shifted uncomfortably in her seat, her eyes darting around the room as she tried to avoid his penetrating gaze. When she finally spoke, her voice trembled with uncertainty as she confessed that she needed time to process all of the information he had shared with her. She told him she had searched for evidence to support his claims but failed. Even the deeds to their family home were missing, adding another layer of confusion and frustration to the situation.

She knew Gabriel longed for her to be able to create the immersive experience of his family portrait so that it would feel even more real to him, just like the battle of Edgehill did.

Tilly telepathed, *I know that you can go back in time to when my father was alive. You could find out where he put the papers and deeds to the house. You could answer all these questions.*

She didn't feel she was asking too much of him. He was able to seamlessly move between the physical and astral planes, almost as if they were two homes he could easily visit. But she understood that travelling back in time while an astralite on Earth was an entirely new challenge. The astral plane was his happy place, a place where he felt no judgement, no fear, just pure, unconditional love. But she had searched for the documents with no luck. She needed his help. She heard caution in his inner voice as he answered her.

I will try and find those things out for you.

Tilly put the control station in front of Gabriel.

If you want sounds, music, smells, and an all-singing and dancing immersive experience you will need to tell me more about what you experienced on the days the artist painted the portrait.

Gabriel smiled gratefully and nodded his agreement as she continued,

I will need to study how to write and create the programme to include those things. The design team may help me if I can persuade them that it was a project my father decided on. If we prove you are one of my ancestors, I can't see it being a problem. If you are lying, I could be in serious trouble for wasting their time and expertise.

Gabriel's amber eyes stare directly into her green eyes, *I have told you before. I cannot lie.*

He had given her no cause to distrust him, but he was here one minute and gone the next. She was only asking him to travel back in time. Surely that wasn't dissimilar to what he did already? He was already dead. It wasn't like he could cancel himself out. It wasn't a parallel universe. It was just time travel.

She spoke into his mind, *Fine if that is true. Anyway, as for putting your family up on all of the walls so that they surround you I can already do that. I know you sneak in here at night to experience the Battle of Edgeware. The smell of smoke in the morning is a tell-tale sign, Gabriel. It will be safer if you sit with your family in this immersive room than attend a battle night after night.*

Gabriel shivered with excitement, *Will you do that?* He asked, his amber eyes pleading.

42

TIME TRAVEL?

Gabriel wasn't sure what time travel meant for someone like him. It seemed simple for someone like Tilly, who was still alive as she could sleep and dream of herself in a different time and place. He hadn't slept (as far as he was aware) since he died more than three hundred years ago.

He was restricted to haunting this house and could not travel further afield. He found that once he learnt how to use the internet, and Tilly allowed him to use her reader pass, he could access libraries online and learn about anything his 17th-century learning lacked. He was engrossed in the online library when his instinct, heightened since death, told him Tilly was watching him. His brow furrowed as he tried to concentrate and read further. He telepathed, without turning to look at her.

Isaac says I can't leave home without a rebirther, so thank you for allowing me to gain knowledge here on the internet.

He felt her take a step closer and heard the sympathy in her inner voice, *You must be bored haunting the basement and the gallery.*

Gabriel turned from the computer and glanced at her, noticing she wore his favourite sage green T-shirt. He telepathed, *I cannot understand how all of these books are free to read. Books were precious and expensive in my day. I noticed in your bedroom that you have treated your books without respect. Left on the floor, pages torn, your name written into the fore-edge of the book. Why would you do that?*

He felt Tilly flinch.

I didn't say you could go in my bedroom!. Didn't you read the sign on the door?

Gabriel swiftly changed the subject, *My research suggests there is such a thing as a wormhole that could take me back into the past.*

He felt Tilly's annoyance as she scowled at him before getting her own back by telepathing, *I've heard of those. I guess Isaac will tell us if a ghost can go through a wormhole.*

Hurt by her spite he answered, *I told you I am not a ghost. I am an astralite. But only those studying to be a cosmic being can survive a wormhole.*

She seemed to ignore him and began climbing the stairs, *I am going to my room. Do not enter my room in future without my permission. Got it!*

He didn't know whether he should ask Isaac for advice in case the pigeon advised against it. He wanted to be in Tilly's company forever and to have access to a virtual reality where he could be with his family. He had been reluctant to tell her she was a descendant of his family and didn't want her to see him as the weakling he imagined himself to be. He would have to do whatever she asked. He would have to use the wormhole. He was scared. He wanted to be sure that he could get back to this particular vibration. He needed a fool-proof way of going there and back. He would have to talk it over with Isaac.

He left the gallery and was about to materialise in the garden when he heard the abrasive screeching of a murder of crows. It sounded like a cacophony of grief. He found Isaac on the dovecote with some smaller birds. Three crows were on the grass surrounding what looked like a small dead bird. One of the crows seemed to be checking if it was dead by nudging it tenderly. Perched on the branches of a nearby tree, a group of sparrows peered down at the scene below. Two crows circled above, swooping down to dive bomb and squawk at Sheba, who was nonchalantly grooming herself on the grass below. The scene looked like a funeral for one of their fallen brethren, likely a victim of Sheba's hunting prowess. Gabriel was shocked by the level of emotional intelligence being displayed and looked to Isaac for confirmation if what he was seeing could be believed.

Isaac bobbed his head.

Sheba the cat killed a wren earlier. The wren's mate has been letting everyone know of the death and a murder of crows has taken over. They like to organise funerals.

Crows like to organise funerals. Are you serious?

Yes I am serious. Humans think they are unique in displaying grief, but they are not.

Gabriel felt Isaac's penetrating gaze and heard his inner voice speak to his mind, *I don't think you came out here to find out how to communicate with the birds in the garden. Did you want something?*

Gabriel wanted advice but as he looked at the scene in the garden he could see that the dead bird hadn't been hunted for food and suggested, *I will ask Tilly to put a little cat bell on Sheba so that no more birds suffer. Im sure the cat only wanted to play. She is well fed.*

He listened to the crows wishing he could understand what they were saying. He felt Isaac's piercing eyes watching him watching them and whispered internally, *Yes, some advice, I think. I might not take it, but I still need to hear it.*

Isaac replied, *Let us go into the basement out of respect for the funeral.*

They left the crows to the hastily arranged funeral, both reverted into their orb like forms and floated into the basement .Isaac vibrated, *Has Tilly asked you to find out where her father put his documents.*

Gabriel vibrated, *Were you eavesdropping?*

He watched the purple orb pulsate in reply as a single purple iridescent feather floated to the floor and a warm breeze tried scooping it up several times before letting it rest in a corner of the basement. *No. It was obvious she would ask you after my last conversation with her. All I would advise, before going down that route, is that he would not wish to make the discovery of those papers difficult for his family. However, they have a gallery that strangers access. Did he share a code with Tilly? I would have written in code.*

Gabriel hadn't thought about those things, but he knew, like him Tilly was interested in code breaking. He understood why Isaac would write his theories in code before sharing them with the world, but Tilly's father wasn't Isaac Newton. He didn't want to leave the basement and try and enter some wormhole he hadn't been cleared to enter. He thought of the basement as his second home. He had mastered travelling between the two and that was enough.

Isaac continued, *Has she searched in the places only she and he knew? Has she searched her dreams, her memory stores? Did he leave numbers on things that she hadn't noticed before his death?*

Gabriel hoped Isaac was right and answered, *I don't know.*

It is dangerous for you to try and go to another reality because you have already done that by coming here. You are an astralite and not a cosmic being. Even if you were a cosmic being you may have to stay there for weeks or months to find out what she has asked of you, and you may not even find the answers she seeks. The longer you are in another reality this universe will have moved on and if you manage to come back, things will not be the same as when you left. I could even be dead.

Dead? Gabriel asked alarmed.

I am a bird, Gabriel. Yes, I do have transformational powers that I have accrued from my years on the higher planes. However, as you can see from this morning's funeral, a predator might kill me. I might even be in my next life by the time you return. If you return.

What do you mean by "if?"

The purple orb glowed with an iridescence Gabriel hadn't noticed before. *Wormholes are unstable. They close very quickly. They are exits only. You can go back to the past, but I've never heard of any cosmic being who has dared to enter a wormhole, to return. It could be because they are happy to be back in the past. I don't know. We only understand the cosmos when we become a cosmic being. I wish to be a cosmic caretaker, not a wormholer, though I feel sure some cosmic beings are wormholers.*

Gabriel wished Isaac was right and that the papers were in the house somewhere, but he thought of one more option that his internet studies had suggested. *I thought I could send a part of me, in the way that a hologram can be split.*

The purple orb pulsated dismissively, *You are an astralite Gabriel, not a hologram. At your time of death parts of you could have been left behind to comfort the grieving but you have been dead for over three hundred years Gabriel. There is no one left to grieve for you. You lost holographic abilities once you entered purgatory.*

Gabriel's copper light dimmed. *How do I tell Tilly that I can't risk it?*

Gabriel couldn't read the purple orb's body language, but it seemed to roll back and forth as though irritated by Gabriel's dimness.

You don't. You tell her that her father would have left her clues. You tell her that a father who loved her as much as he did would have found a way. She needs to work that out. It will be in her subconscious somewhere. But don't forget Gabriel you know this house. You may know it better than Tilly. Nothing is stopping you from searching.

Gabriel suddenly realised what Isaac was telling him. The papers were in the house. They might be in code, but they were in the house. Gabriel knew the house. He could find the papers if he set his mind to do so. *Thank you Isaac I am sorry it has taken me so long to work out what I need to do.*

You got there in the end dear friend.

Gabriel felt pleased to be called a friend by Isaac. He had never had a friend before.

Now, where to search?

43

THE SEARCH

Gabriel entered the gallery. He went into the storage area where rows of chain link fences held 17th-century paintings on S hooks. He remembered Tilly saying that she found out about the artist of his family portrait from the back of one of these paintings. He held his hand above the first piece of art, and it dislodged itself from its hook and appeared in front of him. He flicked his wrist and the painting flipped over showing the painting's title, date, and number. Attached to the stretcher bar was a note with information about the artist and the painting. Gabriel read it briefly. It wasn't a painting that interested him. He held his palm in front of the painting, and it moved back to its original position on its S hook. He glanced at all of the paintings in the storage area and sighed,

This is going to take a long time.

After searching for a couple of hours he became engrossed in some of the paintings which depicted a world that he could never be a part of again. He yearned to step into one drawing of a bustling 17th-century Coffee House filled with lively discussions and warm camaraderie. To take a seat at the wooden benches, sipping coffee, smoking clay pipes, and reading newspapers while indulging in gossip like the men portrayed in the 17th century drawing. The drawing showed a servant pouring dishes of coffee out for the men. A maid, with a high lace headdress was serving behind the bar. He never reached an age on Earth when he could join friends he'd never had the opportunity to make in a coffee house as James often did. But Gabriel saw no harm in pretending now. He felt comfortable in the 17th century. He was used to it. He felt cheated out of the life he could have had but it was his fault. He was weak and chose suicide. Returning to Earth and being supported to view long buried memories from an unfamiliar perspective made him realise the contribution they made to his suicidal thoughts. Even his mother had been stronger than him. It was like she put up a protective barrier around herself and rarely let anyone in except for her beloved Henry and James. Harry would console him saying it was because James was a protestant like herself, and it was nothing to lose sleep over. Gabriel would soon meet a girl who would love him. If only he had met a girl. It had always been easier to talk to Sara or Mathilde than anyone else. If only he had had someone like Tilly to confide in when he was alive. It was as if a fragment of Mathilde's spirit resided in her and he was beginning to feel a brotherly love for her.

The past was a constant battle between regret and nostalgia, fuelled by the realisation that he was no longer alive and could never go back. He looked wistfully at the 17th century drawing and wondered if Tilly could create the immersive coffee house experience for him, to experience moments that were forever out of his reach.

He heard a noise behind him. He let the drawing remain in mid-air and became an orb of copper light. Tilly entered the storage area, carrying a painting. She almost dropped the painting as she gasped at the drawing suspended in mid-air. Gabriel quickly changed into his 17th-century self.

What are you doing here? She said in her head to Gabriel as she returned the Gonzales Coques painting to its storage spot.

Gabriel explained Isaac's advice, and Tilly agreed. She asked him, *Why did you choose the storage room?*

I wanted to check it off my list of places to search. Plus, you mentioned your father wrote on the back of these paintings. There could be clues hidden there.

Ahh ok. Not the fact that the paintings and sketches gave you a sense of nostalgia, she teased.

I didn't consciously do it with that in mind. Gabriel said defensively as she smiled knowingly at him.

Tilly telepathed, *We probably need to do this room together. Otherwise, you could still be here next week.*

She gave him a wry smile as he released another painting from its hook, turned it, noted nothing suspicious, returned it and continued as if he were competing with her. They completed the chain link fences.

He followed Tilly as she fetched herself a custard cream and a bottle of water and they began to search the storage boxes. A storage box full of files that bore numbers ending with 1667 suggested they were documents relating to paintings from that year. Tilly dismissed it but the year was important for Gabriel and he began searching through it, stopping abruptly when he came across a folder with the numbers 07291667 written on it. He left it in mid-air without opening it just staring at it.

What is wrong? You look as though you've seen a ghost. She joked.

She looked up at the folder floating in front of her. She stopped searching through the large storage box and sat back on her heels. Gabriel, consumed with shame, whispered into her mind; *It was the day that I committed Felo de se.*

Felo de se?

Suicide

She took the file from his hands and opened it, revealing plastic wallets containing documents. Gabriel could feel the tension in the air as she pulled out a sealed envelope and a birth certificate fell out. Her father's birth certificate dated July 29th 1967 — almost the same date printed on the front of the folder. Did he purposely write the wrong year? As she looked at the coded numbers inside the folder she said aloud the words "PRIVATE & CONFIDENTIAL". Gabriel knew this information was not meant for anyone else's eyes but hers.

44

FAMILY TIES

Tilly got herself a cup of coffee and opened the file which contained surprise after surprise. Like a gift that keeps on giving.

There were wallets containing information on business documents (deposited with a solicitor); a copy of his will (the original with the same solicitor); savings; investments; and insurance documents. All of her medical documents, which she really did not feel ready to confront, believing her father told her all that she needed to know. At least she knew where they were if she wanted to bore herself.

In one wallet she found a family tree that even predated Gabriel. Gabriel was certainly an ancestor. That felt weird and put an end to any romantic thoughts she may have still held. Here he was in front of her. A more messed-up teenager than she was. But he was meant to be ancient. With the family tree were words written by her father. It looked like mirror writing. Tilly remembered receiving the compact mirror and rushed to get it. Holding the mirror over the writing she read and copied out: 'Note to self: Noticed Sjaaks' fascination with my family tree. Find out why.'

Tilly felt that the suspicions she had about Sjaak must have been from a feeling she picked up on from her father.

Another wallet contained a plan of the original plot of land of the London house. It showed a stable yard to the side and more garden. It appeared that land had been sold and a neighbouring house built in its place.

There were deeds to a country home in Eyam. Gabriel was excited by these and was able to describe the home to her, from the plans. In the same wallet were solicitors' letters and photographs of the ruins of the house. Gabriel seemed overcome with emotion.

Is the country home still part of your father's estate Tilly? Would you be able to find my body and bury me with my family?

Tilly spluttered on a mouthful of coffee.

What do you mean? I don't know about a country home, and I have no idea about where you or your family are buried, Gabriel.

She glanced at Gabriel. He looked crestfallen. She wanted to put her arms around him and comfort him, but he was draining her energy, so she spoke into his troubled mind, *Get rid of the negative weeds that have taken over your mind.*

But you don't understand.

I think I do Gabriel. You are allowing the toxicity of your past earthly life affect your future. Let it go. Let it go.

Suddenly worried that she'd used too much 21st century psychobabble and hearing the song from the movie 'Frozen' become an earworm as she tried to forget her hurtful words she added, *Where is Isaac when we need him?*

Gabriel changed into a copper orb of light and was joined by an orb of purple light. The copper light vibrated and spoke telepathically to Tilly.

Please do not be afraid if we remain in our astral bodies Tilly. I think your stepmother would have something to say if she saw a pigeon in the art gallery with precious works of art. Unfortunately, even a rebirther of Isaac's status is unable to control his bowel movements when he is a pigeon.

Tilly looked to Isaac who remained static, seemingly unconnected. He was a proud pigeon and she imagined he would be annoyed with Gabriel for presuming to speak for his bowel movements. She waited to hear a scathing response from Isaac but it didn't happen. He seemed to be preoccupied.

You are full of surprises today, Gabriel. Tilly said. She sat on a chair, picked up a bottle of water and gulped down a mouthful.

The purple orb suddenly vibrated and spoke telepathically to both Tilly and Gabriel.

Is there anything I can do for you?

Tilly looked towards the copper orb darting about the room, and she really despaired of how she could help him.

I'm not sure there is Isaac. Perhaps we need to think things through together. We have found the documents we were looking for, but they have brought up more issues. Gabriel has announced that he wants me to find his body and bury it at Eyam in his family grave!

Isaac remained as a purple orb of light and spoke telepathically to Gabriel's consciousness alone.

I was busy consoling the wren family and I thought you were looking for these documents to support Tilly. I thought I could trust you to help Tilly on this occasion.

Gabriel answered Isaac sulkily, *I think that if my earthly body is not staked to the crossroads, I might find it easier to move on in my afterlife. I understood that my return was to help both Tilly and I move on.*

Isaac could not argue with Gabriel's reasoning, and he knew that for himself to become a cosmic being he was meant to help Gabriel to move on. But as a human he had borne many resentments towards his mother and colleagues, never allowing anyone to get too close to him. Humans were a constant disappointment. Supporting an astralite who had suffered an appalling life and had every right to hate the world was not something he would have chosen. How could this young astralite still be so naïve? Why wasn't he able to just ignore everyone as he had learnt to do? He didn't have the emotional intelligence required to help this young soul. It suddenly occurred to Isaac that he was being tested as part of his bid to become a cosmic being. Using his magnetic energy, he drew Gabriel's erratic orb towards him and caused his vibrational energy to send waves of peace. As Gabriel's energy softened, Isaac, who was still learning to master social etiquette, spoke into his mind.

You know that the earthly body you used was merely a shell that contained the real you. Like a hermit crab uses a shell. Im sorry, I would not have wanted your life on Earth. But you need to change the way you think. It would save us all a lot of trouble!

Tilly continued to search through the wallets. One wallet contained photos of the work done in the basement. She looked at the first couple of photos and decided they were boring. They were photos of the completed flagstone flooring. She guessed they were there for future reference for the underfloor heating.

She became distracted by Gabriel's light pulsating off and on (as he struggled with his anguished thoughts) and dropped the wallet containing the photos. They spread out on the floor in front of her. As she looked down at the photos beneath her, she could see that they told a story.

There was an underground burial pit. There was even a mummified body, wearing a faded green silk dress and a gold and coral necklace. It reminded her of Mathilde in the Constcamer portrait. She quickly swept them into a pile, picked them up and put them in the file.

Finding this file was quite a discovery. She did not feel she should share it with two pulsating orbs of light. She did not think it wise for Gabriel to see these photos. Both orbs of light seemed to be sparking at each other as she watched their lights fascinated.

She interrupted them as she spoke into their shared consciousness.

I need to share what I've found here with my stepmother. I need to find out if we still own land in Eyam.

She walked out of the storage room, carrying the folder, and made her way up the stairs.

45

SECRETS AND LIES

Tilly found her stepmother in the TV room. It was a room Tilly rarely went in now. Sometimes, in the past, when her father was alive, they might watch a Netflix film together as a family. Helena never suggested it any more. Neither did she. Everything she needed was on her phone. Tilly stepped into the room. The massive flat-screen TV hung on the far wall usually disguised as a piece of art, with minimalistic cream shelves surrounding it. Plush leather couches lined the other walls, tempting her to sink into their soft cushions if it weren't for their colour. She remembered her stepmother's insistence on the cream colour scheme and matching marble coffee tables, which her father had reluctantly agreed to.

Tilly could see that her stepmother was nursing a glass of white wine and staring at the TV live screen on the wall and hadn't noticed her enter the room. It was a news item. Suddenly, a photo of her father popped up on the screen. Next to him was a picture of an underground burial pit, like the one she had just found in his file. Another picture flashed up on the screen. It was a picture of the mummified remains of a young teenage girl. The newsreader announced that a study of the teeth by forensic anthropologists put the girl's age at fourteen years old. Tilly stared at the screen dumbfounded.

The newsreader went on: "The remains of the young girl were found encased in a substance called saltpetre. She was wrapped in rolls of tapestry, likely for preservation purposes. Other tapestries were also unearthed, possibly buried along with the girl's body."

Tilly stared in disbelief as more details of the mummified remains emerged. The photo of her father remained in the background reinforcing the fact that he had discovered something of such significance but had decided not to share the discovery with her. Had the discovery happened when he sent her and her stepmother away at that time?

"The tapestry pieces were remarkably preserved and estimated to be 17th-century originals. Worth a considerable amount of money. Other tapestries and paintings may have been recovered from the underground pit discovered under basement flagstones."

The TV screen proceeded to provide pictures of modern tapestries. Tilly assumed the producers of the news programme were treating viewers as if they did not know what a tapestry was. The newscaster continued:

"Radiocarbon analysis dates the remains to between 1647 and 1667. The likely candidate for the girl's identity is one Mathilde Stafford. It is believed that she perished from the plague."

Tilly dropped the folder she was carrying. Papers and photos that she removed from their wallets scattered about the floor. The movement caught her stepmother's peripheral vision, and she turned to see Tilly aghast, staring at the screen as the newscaster continued.

" Pneumonic plague can be transmitted by coming into close contact with a corpse or carcass, most likely through breathing in the droplets from their respiratory system. Additionally, bubonic plague can be transmitted by direct contact with the blood or body fluids of an infected corpse. This information has guided those who are handling the body, so they take necessary precautions to avoid transmission. However, as the corpse was mummified it is highly unlikely any fluids remain, and the family have allowed certain tests to be done on the mummy before reburying the body on the family estate."

Helena quickly pressed "pause" on the remote control.

Tilly disregarded the photos she wanted to show her stepmother and asked directly, "Why didn't my father ever tell us about this?"

Seeing the look on Helena's face told her that it was no surprise for her. She asked boldly, "Why haven't you?"

She looked at the tiny bird-like woman in front of her and shouted, "I am fourteen. I'm not a child. You are not my mother. I am nothing like you. I am stronger than you realise."

She watched as a picture floated down to land in front of Helena's foot. It was a photo of Henry, holding Mathilde's gold and coral necklace. At that moment, a copper orb seemed to hover above the photo before vanishing. Helena looked at Tilly.

"Did you see that?" She asked Tilly.

"Don't try and change the subject," Tilly said impatiently.

Tilly guessed Gabriel saw the photo. She knew his emotions would have to be addressed eventually, but in this moment, she needed her feelings to take precedence.

46

HELENA

Helena began picking up the photos while concluding that she needed to give up drinking during the daytime. She saw a flashing purple light yesterday as she was drinking. A copper-coloured light today. This wouldn't do. She would take it as a sign from Henry that she needed to cut down on her drinking. Damn the media, deciding to take people's minds off the pandemic with Henry's discovery. As she avoided eye contact with Tilly, tears threatened to spill over, highlighting the internal struggle within her. Part of her wanted to share everything she knew, while another part desperately wanted Henry to be the one to tell Tilly.

She said, "Your father wanted to tell you when he was ready to tell you. He implored me to keep it a secret. A TV documentary was being produced and he wanted you to participate in it. Before that could happen, he died Tilly. Nothing else mattered after that. Nothing."

She began to put all the photos of the find in the order she remembered. Then she talked Tilly through the discovery of Mathilde Stafford and the museum's involvement. In a corner of the room, an orb of copper-coloured light vibrated on and off.

She told Tilly that her father wasn't in Maastricht to tour the art fair. That was part of a bigger picture. He was employing Sjaak to assess the condition of the paintings and tapestry pieces found with the body and worth millions.

Helena and her stepdaughter went through the file together. The haunted, guilty look on Helena's face seemed to vanish. The file contained letters for each of them 'In the event of his death' As Helena read his handwritten note she smiled briefly before tearfully saying "He always said he wasn't meant for a long life. It is typical of him to leave us letters from beyond the grave so that he is still managing things."

Putting a wallet to one side she said, "I can follow up on what Henry was doing. I can inform the archaeological investigation team about the family tree. Thank you for finding the folder Tilly. I think Sjaak was looking for it to help me manage our finances, but he was looking in the wrong place. Mathilde, being yours and Henry's ancestor, will be particularly significant and might explain her burial site. Though it does appear a strange burial site. Who buried her and how did they know the properties of saltpetre?"

A knowledgeable copper orb pulsated in the corner of the room.

Helena found she was feeling purposeful once again, like she used to be, before her husband's death and she was enjoying the feeling. Sjaak had infected her mind, and she was glad he had returned to the Netherlands. She determined to cut all ties with him. She would approach Interpol and insist they collaborate directly with her.

Lost in her musings, she was jolted back to reality when Tilly demanded, "What else are you hiding from me? I know Sjaak has something to do with all of this. I don't know what, but I saw him searching through my father's boxes."

Helena sighed, "Before I do, please understand that anything I did or didn't do was to protect you. If you didn't know anything you would not be in any danger"

She got up, placed the photos carefully in the folder and placed it on the coffee table.

"Let's go into the kitchen and get something to eat."

Helena picked up the glass of wine, took it into the kitchen and emptied it down the sink. She turned to look at Tilly, whom she had always thought of as her daughter, her flesh and blood and felt ashamed for allowing her self-pity and grief to isolate her further from the parental care she needed.

She set about filling the cafetiere and Tilly went back into the TV room. Helena watched her leave with a mixture of anxiety and guilt, knowing that her stepdaughter was reeling from the bombshell she had just dropped on her. Thoughts of her deceased husband Henry, who would have known exactly what to do in this situation, only intensified her grief. She leaned against the kitchen counter and took slow deep breaths because her stomach, always first to react, was clutching in anxiety. She opened the fridge and grabbed mayo, turkey, and bacon, thankful for the technology enabling her to order groceries online delivered directly to the door during this scary time. The restrictions on life caused by the pandemic could be overcome to some degree but she missed the company of other people. She missed Henry, his physical presence. An urn of ashes couldn't tell her what to do in this situation no matter how much she talked to them. And she talked to them all the time. She ran some water until it was icy cold and splashed it on her tear- stained face and finished making her stepdaughter's favourite sandwich.

Taking a deep breath, she bustled into the TV room with a tray of sandwiches and a steaming pot of coffee, placing them on the marble coffee table. As she did so her eyes fell on her late husband's family tree chart and noticed a scrap of paper poking out from under it covered in Henry's secret code. "Why did he write this about Sjaak?" she asked, picking it up and wishing he had shared his concerns with her while he was still alive. Did he keep secrets from her to protect her? The thought sent a painful pang through her heart, but she pushed it away, not wanting to delve into that dark rabbit hole.

She took a sip of coffee, and, looking at Tilly, said hesitantly, "I am afraid I do have more to share with you."

Tilly picked up a sandwich as Helena continued.

"The lawyers had given the all-clear for the unearthing of Mathilde, hence the news article. However, I think the newscaster was speculating about works of art. They have no idea Henry unearthed a Bronzino and a Titian belonging to Charles I."

Tilly's sandwich fell from her hand, and a mixture of bread and mayo splattered onto the carpet. She coughed and sputtered, choking on a mouthful that had gone down the wrong pipe. Helena rushed to her stepdaughter's side, concern etched into her forehead.

"Are you okay?" she asked, full of love and concern, scanning Tilly's face for signs of distress.

But Tilly seemed to be staring at the copper orb in the centre of the room.

With a sigh of relief, Helena said, "You see it too?"

"I don't think my ancestors could have ever afforded to own those paintings," Tilly finally managed to say. "Please, tell me more."

Helena told her that Henry's lawyers sought provenance and authenticity so the paintings could remain in the Stafford family. Investigators were tearing through decades worth of royal documents, determined to uncover the true ownership of the priceless paintings. Should it be revealed that the precious works of art were stolen, they would be seized and returned to the crown.

"For generations, your father's family has unknowingly guarded these works of art. They did not steal them. These files you have found may contain evidence and if it is proven that the family hold rightful ownership, you will be allowed to keep the precious pieces, with the responsibility of ensuring their safety, maintenance, and safeguarding. However we would need to display these coveted masterpieces for all to see and admire, which isn't impossible, though a small gallery such as ours would not do them justice. I think Henry intended them to be on permanent loan to the National Gallery.

Helena cleaned up the mess on the carpet hesitating before deciding to share everything with Tilly. She told Tilly what she knew of Tilly's father's accident warning her that it too, might make world headline news in the future.

"There was an accident in Maestricht," she began, choosing her words carefully. "The local police were investigating, but Interpol stepped in to keep it quiet and catch the masterminds behind the heist. The media didn't pay much attention because they didn't know the true value of the stolen paintings." She paused before adding, "If too many people find out about their worth, there's a chance they'll never be recovered. Unless they're used as bargaining tools by the Camorra."

"The Camorra?"

"The Camorra, according to Sjaak, is a notorious Neapolitan crime gang, a bit like the mafia, but not as organised," Helena said quietly.

She saw a shudder of grief ripple through Tilly. Henry had not died in an accident but had been brutally murdered by the mafia. The truth was finally out, no longer hidden behind a facade of lies crafted by Sjaak, aided by herself. She watched as Tilly lifted her knees to her chest, curled herself up into a ball, and burst into tears. She moved across the sofa and held her, feeling her stepdaughter's stiff body relax as she spoke soothing words of comfort and stroked her hair.

47

SJAAK DISAPPEARS

Sjaak frantically rifled through the contents of his money belt, his heart racing with anxiety. He had to find the ferry ticket, the fake provenance papers, and most importantly, his passport. Without them, his carefully planned scheme would crumble.

But as he searched, memories of his heated drunken argument with Henry the night before his 'accident' flooded his mind. Henry claimed the art rightfully belonged to the crown under the 'bona vacantia' law as there was no will anywhere citing the art works as belonging to anyone. The only proof of anyone ever owning the paintings were the royal stamps on the frames of Charles I and the Westminster Palace art inventory. Though apparently Henry had discovered his family's inventory evidence of the paintings and supposed reference of letters to people involved in the restoration of Charles I art to the crown. Henry wanted to art to go on public display for all to see. Sjaak, however, insisted on the "finders equals keepers" rule and the fact that Cromwell sanctioned the sale of the paintings and so they did not belong to the crown at all. They had fought and the next day Henry was dead —a shock and a warning, but also a blessing in disguise.

As he reminisced, the familiar tingling sensation of walking into his studio and gazing upon the breath-taking Bronzino 's "Portrait of a Young Man" and Titian's "Venus and Adonis" flooded his mind. Both paintings had an intensity that took his breath away. The vibrant colours and intricate details were undiminished by any overpainting or damage, thanks to the saltpetre treatment and protective tapestries that had shielded them. He remembered gently wiping them down, restoring any minor imperfections with meticulous care, entranced by the beauty before him. A UV light would reveal every flaw, but there were none to be found. He savoured these moments, prolonging his time with the paintings as though he were a King basking in the presence of his royal treasures. Truth be told he didn't care that Henry was dead and he was glad the fakes he managed to recreate fooled the thieves. He was good at what he did. When things died down he would retrieve the paintings from the concealed wall in his attic space and install a secret display room in the new home he intended buying with the money he was owed.

Yet even in death, Henry held all the power. Sjaak desperately scoured through Henry's papers in his office, hoping to find some trace of the Stafford inventory which seemed to have vanished into thin air. These little touches added to the paintings provenance making the thieves believe his copies were the originals. He wasn't anything if not thorough.

With a sigh of defeat, Sjaak realised he had no provenance to accompany the works of art except for the forged papers Eddie had provided him with. No-one was as accomplished as Eddie, making his trip to London worthwhile and all thanks to the Dutch authorities allowing him to travel during COVID because he was repatriating Henry with his family. Everything had been risky, but he had come this far and couldn't turn back. The ignorant art thieves would be none the wiser —or so he hoped. Doubts and guilt gnawed at him, but he pushed them aside and focused on his ultimate goal: the million euros that would set him up for life and his own private gallery built for his eyes only.

All good to go. Schatje, recently returned from a long walk, courtesy of his neighbour, wagged her tail with excitement. His only regret was not discovering more about Francine. He felt sure he was missing something, But he had been warned. His life depended on keeping his mouth shut about what he knew about the theft of the paintings. Despite being told that buyers wouldn't touch something legitimately belonging to the Crown, they were still useful as bargaining tools if a prison sentence was threatening. The Dutch authorities would surely want them remaining on Dutch soil. The particular paintings were sold legally by the government of the day. Cromwell's government. It was all well and good having Charles I stamp on the frames but that meant nothing. As far as he could ascertain the paintings were bought by a Dutch nobleman and rightfully belonged in the Netherlands, not some little art gallery in London. With the promised money, he would become a Dutch nobleman himself, completing the circle. Helena had turned into an ungrateful lush and asked too many questions. He had paid his debt by organising Henry's repatriation. He had to keep his wits about him. His phone rang.

"Yes."

"When will you arrive in Rotterdam?"

"Midnight. Have you taken care of everything on your side- my dog included? The hotel must accommodate my dog." Sjaak's hands felt clammy, and he was grateful the caller could not see that his hands were wet from sweat.

The caller spoke calmly, "Yes. Do not worry Sjaak. Everything has been considered."

"Do you still have the paintings?" Sjaak asked, knowing that it was none of his business, but he needed to know if they suspected anything. He thought irritatingly of the number of times Tilly had interrupted his searches and Helena's strange question yesterday. They had suspicions about him. It was fortunate the forger had completed the job satisfactorily so that he could get the hell out of this quagmire he felt entrenched in.

"Of course, we do. They are our insurance. It was very good of you to publicly announce their existence and arrival in Maastricht Sjaak."

"It is not something that I am proud of, particularly as it ended in my friend's death."

"Then you should be more careful of what you say in my coffee shops Sjaak. In Maastricht, we all know how you love to boast."

Sjaak could hear the uncomfortable sound of a derisive snort of laughter at the other end of the phone. The caller continued,

"Besides, you might have a chance with his beautiful wife you tell everyone about in my coffee shop, or is she still out of your league?"

Sjaak wished he could end the call and never speak to them ever again, but he felt convinced that if he didn't deliver the provenance, they would suspect something was amiss with the paintings and find him, and he was certain they would kill him. He should never have followed up the clue he found in his studio after Henry's death. He had been too greedy wanting both the originals and a cut of the money the fakes would make, but it was too late. They knew that he knew, and he knew too much, and he could tell no one. It was laughable that Helena felt that Interpol would find them. He was far more scared of the organised crime syndicate than Interpol.

"Do you have the provenance that accompanied the paintings that you claimed you could provide?"

"Yes, but I don't understand your insistence on it. X-ray analysis will also confirm their authenticity." He was now sweating profusely, hoping that he had done enough to baffle anyone as to their authenticity.

"They may wish to use the provenance or destroy it, but they do not want any loose ends. It is of no concern to me, but it is to them Sjaak."

Sjaak held his nerve, knowing that the money would change his life. He put on a confident tone and said, "I am expecting what is due me in Rotterdam."

In a smooth voice, the caller said, "Good doing business with you Sjaak, and relax Sjaak. You will get what is due."

The phone went dead and Sjaak took one more look around the apartment that he had put on the market. Then, putting the apartment keys in the bowl he picked up Schaatje and left.

In Rotterdam Axel Jannsen, a suspected drug trafficker, put down his phone and said, "When he gets off the ferry with his baggage ensure you secure the provenance before you give him any money. Make it look like it is a proper transaction so that he suspects nothing. We will hang on to whatever documents he obtained in the goose chase we sent him on, the Comorra will not require it. It is merely a pawn in this game of chess. Then kill him and his dog and retrieve the thirty pieces of silver. We don't need the Comorra syndicate on our backs anymore, and he has a big mouth."

48

REBURIED

When Tilly first encountered Isaac, having fallen from the tree, she was sure that the pigeon grew in size to accommodate her fall. This time, Isaac told her it would be different as they would be travelling long distances. He could not inflate himself this time, as he didn't want them mistaken for an alien spacecraft. She would need to shrink in size. She stared at the purple orb of light in the basement. She was talking in her head to a purple orb of light. Was she going mad, she wondered, not for the first time?

This orb of light was telling her that she needed to shrink to the size and weight of a fairy (sadly without wings). Isaac would use his powerful wings to take both her and Gabriel on journeys that would take days in real time. However, these were astralites that she was travelling with, and they would use time dilation.

Many times, since her father's death, she found herself in places without knowing how she got there. She sometimes thought that grief was making her crazy, but shrinking in size might be a step too far for her grief-stricken brain. She telepathed into the group chat of shared consciousness, *I can't shrink!*

Yes, you can! Isaac and Gabriel replied in unison.

I would, if I could, I really would. She added, *As long as I could grow back to my normal size, just like Alice in Wonderland.*

She smiled at the thought. Then she telepathed, *But I know I can't.*

She looked from Gabriel to Isaac and telepathed, *You, Isaac, are a rebirther with special abilities that I don't have. And you, Gabriel, can make objects float in the air and goodness knows what else because you are a ghost!*

Gabriel shuddered and answered defensively, *I'm not a ghost. I'm an astralite!* he insisted.

Is there a difference? she asked rhetorically.

Yes. astralites are on a mission when they visit Earth. Ghosts are earthbound; they have never left. They cannot become an orb of light like you see before you.

Oh, forget it Gabriel! I don't want to know. I can't do this.

She took herself to the window seat and pulled the curtains around her. Poking her head out she said, *I'm sorry. It's too scary.*

The purple orb suddenly appeared inside the curtained idyl and vibrated as he spoke into her mind and the open group chat. Tilly nervously listened as Isaac suggested using the 360-degree drone camera her father had purchased. He offered to wear the camera himself to capture footage of their proposed journey. As he spoke, she felt relief wash over her. It was just the kind of thing her father would do for her.

She began attaching the tiny camera to Isaac and smiled as she watched the pigeon take off.

The software was loaded onto her laptop, ready to go. As she waited for Isaac's return, Tilly fiddled with the cables and programs necessary to prepare the 360-degree video, adjusting settings and calibrating the hardware to ensure they'd get a seamless experience when it came time to watch it in the gallery's VR room.

The moment finally arrived: Isaac landed with precision, carrying the camera containing an entire journey's worth of footage. Everyone gathered around the screen in anticipation as Tilly opened the program to begin piecing together their virtual reality adventure.

As the VR experience projected onto the walls surrounding them Isaac became a vibrating orb of purple light and telepathed them through the footage, *Once you have left your bodysuit behind, we shall fly to Culverhouse Crossroads.*

Tilly noticed Gabriel perk up on hearing the words "Culverhouse Crossroads" and looked closely at the footage. She knew this was the right thing to do for Gabriel if they were to help him move on. It meant they could rebury the bones with his beloved family and though both she and Isaac thought it a pointless exercise and a waste of time and energy they understood that Gabriel was not as mentally strong as they were.

Isaac vibrated to Tilly, *Gabriel will travel in your pocket, in his Astralite form, as an orb of light.*

Why? She asked.

He cannot travel on Earth in his 17th-century form, and he can only travel as an orb if I am with him.

Why? She asked.

Because it is not safe for him to travel alone from the place assigned to him. He has never rebirthed and so is vulnerable. People who believe in evil would use those evil beliefs to thwart him if they knew he did not have that protective shield around him. The shield protecting him is only around this particular house and land. Gabriel's consciousness is not strong enough to ignore the slings and arrows they would attack him with.

Gabriel nodded and began to concentrate carefully on Isaac's words.

When we get there, you and Gabriel will find his bones, and we will fly them to Eyam.

How will we get the bones? she asked as she watched the footage showing Culverhouse crossroads where Isaac, using his electromagnetic abilities, confirmed there were indeed bones buried there. Then, as Isaac told her, she remembered Gabriel's hands performing magic with the lavender and the paintings in the store room.

Isaac paused, *The only problem I can see is if they are not Gabriels bones.*

The copper orb nodded dejectedly.

Let's be positive. Tilly said, smiling reassuringly at Gabriel.

Isaac vibrated, *He will feel a connection with the bones if they are his.*

Is all of this safe? Tilly asked.

No, Isaac answered.

No?

That's why you have to do as I ask. You have to follow your father's precise steps in the meditation process to get to the higher vibrational level needed for astral travel.

She nodded, and he continued, *Those steps will also protect you from harmful energies that may try to prevent you from entering the dreamlike state.*

He warned, *Letting harmful energies in leads to madness.*

Tilly did not want to go mad. The pandemic, her Covid symptoms and most importantly the death of her father could all lead to a kind of madness that might make her imagine she could communicate with a pigeon and a ghost. Did it matter? If all of this was a figment of her imagination then it was a self- healing imagination because it was helping her to cope. She answered Isaac with conviction, *I have been following his steps precisely from the copy I have of them.*

Isaac vibrated, *Your father was very advanced in his journey, and so I have complete faith in those steps he prepared for you.*

I haven't been meditating for long, she argued weakly.

Isaac answered, *On your fourteenth birthday, Tilly, you were bestowed with powers that you may not have discovered yet. But fear not, I will help you understand and follow your father's instructions.*

She nodded.

You will need to follow his directions precisely so that your vibrational frequencies increase. This will take you into a dreamlike trance.

Tilly stared at him, open-mouthed.

Isaac explained, *Your vibrational energy will increase as if you are a spinning top. Then your higher self will leave your body.*

Tilly thought of her father's insistence that she learn to meditate properly. She guessed he was preparing her for a safe astral projection. He must have been concerned for her safety as well as her ability to be able to return from the astral plane. She could do this with his guidance.

She asked Isaac, *The meditation was written in code- was it written in code to protect me?*

Isaac answered. *Yes. We will follow his directions to the letter. It will be twice as powerful if we do it together.*

Tilly nodded, she was eager to get on with it before her confidence left her.

Once you are in a dreamlike state, you become sealed in a blue aura, and no one can harm you.

Tilly was confused, *Do I leave my body behind when I go on this journey?*

Isaac answered, *I'd liken it to when you are asleep.*

She looked at him questioningly.

He explained, *Your physical body is resting. Your consciousness is still active. Hence you will be able to imagine yourself small enough to sit on my back.*

Tilly took a couple of deep breaths and said, *But if I'm supposed to be meditating, won't my stepmother think I've passed out if I seem comatose for hours?*

Isaac answered, *Think of the last time you meditated. Where did you go?* he asked.

She smiled at him and said, *Oh, that's easy. I was talking to some birds in a tapestry tree as they made a nest.* She continued; *I imagined that I became a bird. My father appeared as a rose and surrounded me with the cross of protection.*

She added, *Then I imagined that I flew up into a thermal current with the birds.*

Afterwards, I went to sleep for a while and when I woke up, I felt amazing.

Isaac asked, *And how long did all of that take?*

It always takes 10 minutes, and I'm always surprised, as it seemed like hours when I was having the experience, Tilly said.

Isaac's purple light glowed vibrantly, *Exactly, time dilation exists in a dreamlike state. We might be gone a couple of days, but the earthly time will still be only ten minutes.*

Remind me why we are doing this. Tilly said, hands on hips, staring at Gabriel, with a grin.

Isaac answered, *We are taking Gabriel's physical body to join his family. Did you tell Gabriel that your stepmother is having Mathilde buried in the family grave at Eyam?*

Tilly shook her head and telepathed, *The land belongs to me.*

It does? Gabriel asked.

Tilly said, *Yes, my father left it to me in his will that we found. Everything has progressed so quickly since finding his documents. The moment Helena and I laid eyes on the crumbling remains of my father's country house, a serene calm washed over us. I felt a million miles away from the frantic motorway journey I had experienced moments before. My stepmother has agreed with me, it will make a marvellous Buddhist retreat centre, which is my plan. Being there felt like I had escaped civilisation for the afternoon. Thank you for helping me find the documents, Gabriel.*

The copper light glowed warmly with appreciation.

Tilly continued, *After our visit and because of our plans, my stepmother sent chartered surveyors to check out the ruin and the land. They found the burial plots. James was also buried there after his death (according to his wishes). The family grave even has a headstone.*

Tilly could sense Gabriel was anxious to see the plot and couldn't wait to start on the journey, but she had more to share with him.

The grave contained a sealed metal box with information on those buried and James's wish for Mathilde and Gabriel to join them (if possible). There is something else.

She could feel Gabriels concern and he asked, What *else can there be?*

She looked to Isaac for confirmation to continue and the purple light glowed brightly in approval.

Your brother wrote a confession to God in coded numbers and placed it in the metal box along with the family bible.

Have you read the confession? Gabriel asked.

No.

Tilly put the metal box in front of Gabriel. Both Tilly and Isaac left the window seat pulling the curtain closed behind them.

Gabriel put his hand over the metal box, and it sprung open. He took out the bible and looked lovingly at it. Tucked inside the cover he found the confession.

Gabriel read the cypher, easily translating it as he read. Then, putting his hand over Tilly's meditation candle he caused it to ignite and held the confession to the flame. The flame consumed it leaving only grey ashes. Molten wax splashed onto the grey ash and Gabriel caused the grey mess to run like an ink spill. He snuffed out the candle.

He knew his brother's secret, but he did not want anyone else to know of it. It was not the confession he expected it to be. James had tasked the priest with two duties: deliver the concoction to Gabriel and administer the sacrament of the Eucharist to three clerics imprisoned in the clink. The three clerics did not know it would be their last confession on earth. James was confessing to their murders.

Gabriel could not afford to dwell on the rights and wrongs of what his brother did to avenge him but any doubts he may have had of his brother's love for him were obliterated by that act. He made the curtains open. Tilly and Isaac joined him once again.

Tilly examined Gabriel's face, but his expression betrayed nothing. His inner voice was calm as he telepathed, *You mentioned that Mathilde's funeral is in three days.*

Yes, that's right.

She smiled thoughtfully; *We are also going to have a Buddhist farewell ceremony for my father the day afterwards. His letter to Helena stated that he wished for such a ceremony.*

Gabriel shook his head. *That doesn't give us much time.*

He seemed concerned.

Have you practised enough meditation, Tilly?

Have you been listening to me Gabriel? she asked. *I told you both that that was my concern, but we have to do it now or not at all..*

Gabriel answered *This is so important to me. We cannot afford to make a mistake. Are you sure that you are ready?*

She turned to Isaac for an unbiased opinion, knowing he could provide a clearer judgment than Gabriel who was consumed with emotions and the potential outcome of their journey.

Isaac was confident. *We have everything we need.*

A copper sphere of light appeared in front of both of them, before zooming into Tilly's jacket pocket. Tilly smiled. Gabriel was ready.

I guess we are ready, Tilly giggled nervously.

Isaac telepathed, *I will talk you through your father's meditation sequence until you enter another level of reality.*

He added, *As we end the meditation, you will be vibrating at a higher level of consciousness.*

Tilly re-lit her father's candle and turned on Arvo Pārt's "Spiegel im Spiegel." She closed the curtains around herself.

Isaac continued, *You will feel entirely rested and full of energy to enable you to complete the task.*

Isaac spoke the words of meditation into her mind and at the same time she said it internally, making it sound as though it was in stereo or as binaural beats. The powerfulness of it made her relax instantly. She imagined she was asleep and dreaming once more. Yet she felt wide awake. She found herself sitting astride Isaac's downy back as they glided through a thermal current. She felt ecstatic. She hated theme park rides. They were terrifying. This was entirely different. She was riding on the bronze, soft, downy back of an archangel pigeon. His iridescent wing feathers surrounded her and shone in the sunlight, shimmering green and blue. It was as if she were taking part in a VR game, and she was the heroine.

49

THE CIRCLE OF LIFE

A large white cotton sheet lay over the burial sites of Tilly's ancestors. The evening before Tilly knelt on the floor of the stable in Eyam, which had remained remarkably intact, though it had new doors and a roof hurriedly added by local carpenters and builders wishing for promised contracts in future. She reflected on the love she had received from her father and poured all of her love for him into the task before her and slowly a detailed mandala emerged onto the white cotton sheet.

Family members and her father's friends, excluding Sjaak, who seemed to have disappeared off the face of the earth, had all made the pilgrimage to Eyam to celebrate the life of Henry Stafford, and what was to be a new Buddhist retreat centre named after him. She was pleased Sjaak was not here and so was Helena. Helena's family in the Netherlands had found out he participated in the theft and in Tilly's father's death and that Sjaak's life was in danger. *Serves him right*, Tilly thought.

Everyone gathered and stood in a circle around the mandala. Tilly and Helena had sent out joint invitations asking everyone to bring roses or just rose petals with them but not funeral wreaths.

They both carefully placed the rose petals onto the mandala. As they did so Helena said aloud to the cosmos," I celebrate the place you held in my life Henry."

The colours of the petals were bright and vibrant against the earthy tones of the mandala. The heady scent of the roses filled the air as sunlight streamed in and Tilly paused to admire their work before releasing a gentle breath into the air. She said, "I celebrate the truths you taught me daddy."

The delicacy of the array of colourful rose petals contrasted with their ephemeral nature. Helena said, "I celebrate the colour you brought into my life."

Today the roses were intended for a ritual, paying tribute to the fleeting nature of life, but tomorrow, the sun might dry them out, the rain or wind might drive them away. The power of nature would direct their future course just as all things in life come and go. However, both Tilly and Helena were confident, that the intention of the ritual would remain with them always.

Tilly said, "I celebrate the growth you enabled in me like a tree that reaches out for the warmth of the sun."

Then both Helena and Tilly said together, "We celebrate the love you brought into our lives," as Helena slowly made her way around the circle, allowing each person to reach into the wooden box that held Henry's remains and take a pinch of ashes in their hands. Tilly watched everyone as they cradled the ashes for a moment before opening their hands and letting them drift down, like snow, over the vibrant mandala until it was completely covered in a blanket of grey.

Again both Tilly and Helena said together, "We celebrate the memories we made as a family and cherish the time that we had with you."

Tilly stepped forward with a basket of red rose petals, the deep burgundy hue a striking contrast to the grey ashes that blanketed the mandala. A sweet smell filled the air as if Henry himself had been there: the smell of his favourite roses intensified by the grief that everyone shared.

Both Tilly and Helena said together, "We celebrate the warmth of your presence even in death, and each time we reminisce about you it feels like a warm hug. We devote ourselves from this day forward to honouring your memory by offering each other love and support throughout this difficult period."

Helena and Tilly embraced each other in a genuine display of love and affection, and both felt the power of Henry's presence as if they were the three musketeers once more. Their tears flowed freely.

The petals cascaded over the mandala design like liquid silk, as the gentle notes of Morricone's 'Gabriel's oboe' filled the air until the entire mandala had been swallowed up by elegant petals. All around them, eyes glistened from an unseen emotion as they all said together, "As this circle has no end, neither shall our love for you. We celebrate the life of Henry Stafford and this intended retreat dedicated to his memory."

Helena and Tilly together slowly rolled over the cotton sheet, so that ashes and rose petals alike would lay upon the burial sites of Henry's ancestors. Tilly then rolled up the cotton sheet to take back to their home in London as a physical reminder of the ceremony in Eyam.

50

RETURN TO THE COSMOS

Mission accomplished, Isaac and Gabriel returned to Eyam, to watch the Buddhist ceremony for Tilly's father, then back to London. As Isaac alighted on the dovecote he was summoned before the cosmic council on the astral plane.

He had no time to say goodbye to anyone on the earthly plane. One minute a pigeon, the next a purple orb of light waiting outside the door of opportunities. As he waited, he could hear, all around him, the musical harmony of the spheres.

When Isaac entered the room, he saw multi-faceted light rays from the spheres of light that surrounded him. His senses were overcome with feelings of love, joy, and peace as the music and the light spectacle reached a crescendo.

Suddenly there was complete silence and a single silver orb of light vibrated,

Well, done, Isaac. We have studied your observations, and your mission was accomplished. Lights surrounding Isaac vibrated on and off in approval.

Your observations of the human condition and your ability to create solutions to their problems suggest your skills will be an asset to the universal condition. Added to that your research will support your eventual work as a cosmic caretaker.

Isaac sighed with relief. Perhaps he would be allowed to move on.

We can see that you were well received and admired by both astralite and rebirther.

He asked, *Has Gabriel returned? I thought that you wished us to remain on Earth for longer. Though I am relieved to be home.*

The silver orb vibrated. *Gabriel has remained on Earth for the time being.*

Isaac was glad and vibrated. *I am not surprised. Though thanks to Tilly, his bones were placed in the family grave. That meant everything to him. He did not deserve the burial he received. Thanks in part to the passage of time, Tilly found that the stake crumbled when she touched it and the bag of bones proved easy enough for me to carry to Eyam.*

The orbs syncopated their lights as if in approval and the silver orb vibrated.

Gabriel had never gotten over his time on Earth. It is easy for us to forget that the 17th century was a time of huge turbulence for the Earth. However, his ego still controls him, and he cannot progress until he is able to bury that ego. He needs more time.

Doesn't he need my help?

Not anymore. You have done more than enough. You were never meant to heal him but to give him the skills to heal himself. You did exactly that and your work with Gabriel is over. Tilly will help him by using VR to give him the experiences he missed out on. Now that VR exists, the genie cannot be put back in the bottle and so we will make use of it.

The assembly asked as one, *Was Mathilde buried with her family?*

Isaac answered, *Yes. Gabriel's earthly body is next to hers.*

And Tilly's father, Henry?

They had a beautiful ceremony the day after for Tilly's father's family and friends. Tilly will always grieve for the loss of her father. It is part of her current life.

The silver orb agreed. *She was more accepting of help from the astral plane than Gabriel was when he was on Earth. Gabriel had been taught by Sara to fear the faces he saw in his mind's eye. Tilly lives in more enlightened times.*

Isaac nodded.

The silver orb vibrated. *Thank you for your feedback, Isaac. it would seem that our use of micro-meteorites has a more beneficial effect on planet Earth. It would seem that humans are dealing better with mental health issues, though they are to blame for causing them in the first place. It is hoped that we will soon have no more young cavaliers to worry about on the astral plane. More souls might progress faster and need fewer rebirths.*

The purple orb nodded in agreement.

How did you fare on your other mission Isaac?

Isaac smiled to himself. He had found observing the flight of birds most interesting. *As for my observations and experiments with the flight of birds and how they might assist an astralite journeying around the cosmos-it was very useful. Their ability to transition between stable and unstable gliding is the key to agility in flight.*

Surrounding lights dimmed and Isaac realised that wasn't the mission referred to.

Isaac asked, *Do you mean the role of birds as messengers that tell us about the health of the planet?*

Indeed.

Isaac telepathed, *Air pollution is a concern. Bird deaths continue to be the first indicator that all is not well on planet Earth. A bird that sings is still a sign that all is well.*

And are they singing Isaac?

Isaac answered, *Most are. Humans are still to blame for the extinction of some species of birds and other animals. There is a concern that they are putting greed ahead of the safety of the planet through their use of untested vibrational frequencies and that is a problem, particularly for insects.*

The silver sphere spun around as if considering its reply, *Are you referring to those frequency effects on Earth's natural electromagnetic symphony, Schumann resonances I believe humans have named them. Though everything in the cosmos is made up of vibrations and light and if we started naming all of them we would never finish.*

Isaac nodded and continued, *Humans use untested technologies such as 5G which use high frequencies. They are not only harming other animals. They are destroying themselves. It is tragically laughable. They are progressing in science and medicine to treat the illnesses they cause.*

All orbs dimmed their lights.

The silver orb pulsated, *Your findings reflect those of others recently returned from Earth. Humans are still mostly ignorant of how the birds and bees give the first warnings of the effects of human interference with the electromagnetic shield that protects the planet and aids the birds and bees in their flight navigation.*

Isaac sighed. *Yes, not to mention how disturbing the frequency affects the mental and physical health of all creatures including humans.*

Isaac thought of his recent studies which had shown him that for centuries, humans thought of themselves as superior, particularly in terms of intelligence. However, his rebirths continually found increasingly complex abilities in the animal kingdom: problem-solving, tool use, language communication, and cooperative networks existing outside of human understanding.

Every time he imagined a new behaviour as 'uniquely human', animals invariably proved him wrong. Other animals respected the planet. Humans acted out of selfishness and greed.

Tilly seemed to care more for the plight of birds than Gabriel did but that was indicative of the evolution of human consciousness. He knew that not all humans shared Tilly's compassion and had not had as many rebirths as she had. He felt overwhelmed by the enormity of the task of the role given to humans as caretakers of planet Earth. He vibrated: *Humans may be doing too little too late.*

All spheres dimmed their lights.

The silver sphere vibrated, *That is a disappointment. Free will cannot be taken away from humans. A shift in consciousness is necessary once again. Maybe another micrometeorite is necessary with a DNA upgrade. But let us move on with today's agenda.*

Am I here to find out where I am to go? Isaac asked.

In a sense. Yes.

The room became filled with the golden light of unconditional love. Then a pulsating golden light took charge. *Isaac, we are pleased with what you have achieved on this mission. Apart from the small hole in an expensive suit, we believe that you succeeded.*

Isaac smiled. He knew they wouldn't have missed that incident with the cigarette. His damnable ego. All different coloured lights flashed on and off until the golden light shone brighter once more silencing them all.

The golden light vibrated. *Isaac, you are charged with another mission.*

Isaac sighed. He remembered the peace, the joy, and the love he was enveloped in when he was allowed to observe the solar system and he yearned to progress on his journey so that he might reside there forever, making observations and recommendations and becoming a caretaker of the cosmos. He was keen to use the knowledge he had gained to protect the fragility of the cosmos but understood that time was of the essence as far as Earth was concerned and Earth's plight would have a domino effect on the solar system and ultimately the whole of the cosmos.

As he stared ahead, his mind was overwhelmed by the knowledge that there were an estimated 1.75 million unique species on Earth. Would he have to live through the experiences of each one to truly understand the secrets of the solar system? And once he transcended, would he be able to protect this delicate balance, including planet Earth and all of its inhabitants? He felt a sense of responsibility settling heavily on his shoulders as he contemplated the weight of this new understanding.

He asked, *Do I have time to rest first?*

You have the equivalent of an earthly 24 hours. This is an urgent mission.

Can you tell me what I am rebirthed as?

Yes, I can, but as always, that will be done privately. Not with an audience, such as you have today. They simply wished to show their appreciation for a job well done.

Isaac looked around at the assembly of orbs gathered to shower him with the light and vibrational energy of the cosmos and he felt more at home than he had ever done.

I will see you in 24 Earth hours' time when you will have changed into your new embodiment for your next earthly assignment. And now, please meet the Rebirther who will accompany you.

A heady smell of roses filled the air and Isaac turned to greet the rebirther known on the astral plane as Henry.

THE END

or is it?

51

HISTORICAL FACTS

LUCASIAN PROFESSOR

Isaac Barrow was Isaac Newton's teacher and was the **Lucasian professor of Mathematics**. The Lucasian Chair of Mathematics is a distinguished professorship at the University of Cambridge in England and has been occupied by some of the most brilliant minds in history. Founded in 1663 by Henry Lucas, Cambridge's former Member of Parliament, and officially recognized by King Charles II in 1664, this position is revered as one of the most prestigious and coveted academic titles in existence. From Isaac Barrow, followed six years later by Isaac Newton to the 20th century's Stephen Hawking, each holder of this post has left an indelible mark on the world of mathematics and beyond.

THE COMETS

The Great Comet of 1664 was observed by Isaac Newton and Robert Hooke in England and Christiaan Huygens in Holland. It unleashed a flood of broadsheets calling upon readers to repent and reform. Another comet in the Easter of 1665 added to the panic as it was followed by observers shortly before the plague broke out in London.

The comet **NEOWISE** (C/2020 F3) was discovered on March 27, 2020 and became bright enough to be seen by the naked eye in July. However, it went unnoticed due to light pollution and did not make news. A group of researchers suggest that COVID-19 arrived on a meteor spotted over China in October 2019, a theory known as **panspermia.** This idea has been around since the ancient Greeks, but was popularized in the 1970s by astronomers Fred Hoyle and Chandra Wickramasinghe. While there is no evidence for this theory, it is more plausible than other theories such as blaming 5G for the pandemic.

THE PLAGUE

The **Great Plague of London** (1665–66) killed 100 000 people: almost a quarter of the population. It was the last major outbreak of bubonic plague in England.

Eyam is a small village in the Derbyshire Dales. It is often referred to as the plague village. In 1665 a bundle of flea-infested cloth arrived from London for the local tailor. Within a week the tailor's assistant was dead of bubonic plague. As the disease spread, it was decided to quarantine the entire village, led by the rector, the Reverend William Mompesson. 'Social distancing' precautions were introduced including families burying their own dead and relocation of church services to a natural outdoor amphitheatre. Infected families were advised to self-isolate. The plague lasted 14 months and the church in Eyam has a record of 273 plague victims.

Over three centuries later , history seemed to repeat itself with the outbreak of **COVID-19** pandemic putting communities around the world in a state of self isolation and social distancing.

CHARLES 1 ART COLLECTION

Charles 1 was a collector of magnificent works by many great artists including **Titian and Bronzino**. The two paintings of his collection referred to in this book - Bronzino 's "Portrait of a Young Man" and Titian's "Venus and Adonis" remain missing today.

Abraham van der Doort, the keeper of the King's collection in 1637, started making a list of all the artworks present in the Royal Collection. **This document still exists** and it documents the King's possessions and their respective displays at that time. Most of these works were sold and scattered after the King was executed in 1649.

Charles was a great patron of the **Mortlake tapestry workshops** and would acquisition cartoons as a guide for the weavers there.

Charles II did appoint a recovery committee for the repossession of Charles I art collection

THE CLINK

Since its inception in 860, the prison under the Bishop of Winchester's control underwent many transformations. In 1076, an archbishop introduced several forms of punishment including whipping with rods, solitary confinement, and silent isolation. The bishop also had authority to bring those accused of heresy or religious offenses before his ecclesiastic court. However, as the gaolers were poorly paid, they resorted to taking bribes from prisoners for better treatment. By the 16th century, the majority of inmates were deemed heretics going against the bishop's beliefs. The prison was destroyed during the Gordon riots of 1780 and never rebuilt. Today, visitors can explore the Clink Prison Museum on Clink Street, near where the original prison once stood in Southwark.

THE TOWER OF LONDON

Often victims ended up in the Tower for religious reasons. But the crimes varied. The majority of the prisoners were charged with high treason. Located within the walls of London's infamous Tower, the Little Ease cell was notorious for its oppressive conditions and use as a torture chamber. Designed for interrogation and extracting confessions, the cramped and uncomfortable space left prisoners with no room to rest or sleep. Combined with the psychological pressure from interrogators, this environment was meant to break even the strongest spirits. The cell was strategically placed in a dark and isolated area, adding to the mental torment of those held within. With no access to natural light or fresh air, this form of sensory deprivation only intensified the prisoner's suffering. Visitors to the tower will not be able to see the cell. It was torn down or walled up long ago.

BARTHOLOMEW FAIR

Endowed by King Henry I through a royal charter in 1133, the fair of St Bartholomew's Priory quickly became the most prominent event in London. Held annually on August 24th on the south-east side of Smithfield roundabout, the fair began as a simple cloth market. But over time, it expanded into a two week extravaganza that drew crowds from every corner of English society. From humble traders to aristocrats, all came to partake in the festivities. The Lord Mayor of London marked the start of the fair on St Bartholomew's Eve with great fanfare. By 1641, this once local affair had gained international notoriety.

As the years went on, the fair grew to include more than just trading. Sideshows of all kinds emerged, showcasing prize-fighters, musicians, wire-walkers, acrobats, puppets, freaks and even wild animals. It was a melting pot of entertainment and commerce.

However, not everyone approved of the fair's raucous atmosphere. In 1855, city authorities shut down the event for promoting public disorder and debauchery.

The song referenced in this book was first printed on a broadside in 1614, giving a glimpse into the diverse trades and activities that could be found at this early version of an English carnival.

Famous literary figures have also taken notice of the fair throughout history. Playwright Ben Jonson wrote a play about it in 1614, while Samuel Pepys documented his visits to the fair in his diary. Even John Evelyn, a renowned diarist himself, noted his experience at "the celebrated follies of Bartholomew Fair" on August 16th, 1648.

In Daniel Defoe's novel Moll Flanders (1722), the protagonist meets a well-dressed gentleman at the fair and in William Wordsworth's epic poem The Prelude (1805), he mentions the raucous noise and exotic sights of the fair, including Indians and dwarfs. Today, the fair has been revived as an annual celebration to honour St Bartholomew's Priory and Hospital, which turned 850 years old in 1973. Despite its tumultuous history, the fair remains a fascinating relic of early English culture and society.

THE GREAT FIRE OF LONDON

The Great Fire of London raged in the year 1666, consuming everything in its path for four long and harrowing days. The author painstakingly researched historical accounts and data to accurately portray the devastating effects of the fire and the rumours prevalent at the time. From eyewitness testimonies to detailed records, bringing this catastrophic event to life through Gabriel's eyes in the novel. The true extent of lives lost will never be known.

THE GRENFELL TOWER FIRE

On June 14, 2017, a high-rise fire broke out in the Grenfell Tower block of flats in London, lasting for 60 hours killing 72 people. The fire was caused by an electrical fault in a refrigerator and spread rapidly due to inadequate insulation and barriers. More than 250 firefighters, 100 ambulance crews, and other emergency services worked together to control the fire and rescue residents .A damning final report from the enquiry into Britain's worst residential fire since World War II blamed a litany of cost-cutting, dishonest sales practices and lax regulation for the blaze.

THE BATTLE OF EDGEHILL AND THE ENGLISH CIVIL WAR

The 23rd of October in 1642 marked a pivotal moment in English history - the **Battle of Edgehill.** As the first major battle of the English Civil Wars, it holds great significance and continues to be studied and re-enacted to this day. On one side stood the Royalist forces, fiercely loyal to King

Charles I of England. On the other stood the Parliamentarians, determined to fight for their beliefs and rights. With their armies numbering around 14,000 strong, the Royalists were formidable opponents. Their ranks included approximately 3,000 skilled horsemen and they were armed with 20 powerful guns. The opposing Parliamentary army was slightly larger at 15,000 soldiers, but not all were able to join the battle due to being stationed too far away from the field.

The clash between these two parties raged on for a single afternoon and evening, resulting in a stalemate. Both sides suffered heavy casualties, with a total estimated number of 1,500 soldiers killed or injured. Despite their early success with a bold cavalry charge led by Prince Rupert himself, the Royalists ultimately found themselves at a disadvantage when their main force pursued the enemy instead of remaining on the field to protect their vulnerable infantry.

This battle was a turning point in the **English Civil War**, as it showed that neither side would easily claim victory. King Charles I, who believed himself to be an absolute monarch with divine right to rule, had clashed with Parliament over issues such as taxes and religious reforms. This led to a long and brutal conflict between the 'Roundheads' (Parliamentarians) and 'Cavaliers' (Royalists), fought in over 600 battles and sieges across the country. The result was a divided nation torn apart by civil war which the Parliamentarians eventually won and Charles I was beheaded.

TYBURN

Nestled within the bustling city of London, the manor of Tyburn was once served by the parish of Marylebone. Its name derived from the Tyburn Brook, a small tributary that flowed into the River Westbourne. **The river Tyburn**, now hidden underground, used to wind its way through the city from Hampstead to Westminster, supplying water for London until it was eventually replaced by sewer systems.

However, Tyburn's notoriety lies in its association with capital punishment. For centuries, it was the main site of execution in London - earning the nickname "Tyburn Tree". The **gallows** stood near Marble Arch, where many religious martyrs and convicted traitors met their fate. Today, Tyburn may be unrecognizable as a place of terror and death. Instead, it is marked by a plaque at 8 Hyde Park Place - a stark reminder of its dark history. The last execution at Tyburn took place in 1783 and since then, the area has been transformed into a bustling hub of modern life.

Its past forever etched into its streets and buildings while all traces of the river are long obliterated, with one exception. Stand on Lambeth Bridge and look to the north bank. Here, at low tide, you will see the gate to a storm relief drain. Here, during times of heavy rain when the sewers overflow, the Tyburn's legacy still lingers as it spills into the Thames once more.

WIERWURT

Hidden within the dark depths of a small church in the remote village of **Wiuwert**, nestled in the province of Friesland, lies a crypt known as the Mummiekelder, or **Mummy Cellar**. Despite centuries passing since its creation in 1609, it still remains a mystery to scientists how the bodies within have been so remarkably preserved. The crypt holds the secrets of Wiuwert, a place shrouded in inexplicable wonder.

In the 17th century, a radical Protestant community named the **Labadists** was formed by French Roman Catholic Jesuit priest Jean de Labadie. His teachings gained significant followers in the Netherlands and they eventually settled in Wierwurt. One of these followers was **Anna Maria Van Schurman**, who sold her house and part of her library to join Labadie's sectarian group.

It wasn't until 1765 that seven perfectly intact bodies were discovered in the burial vault by carpenters while carving wood in the church above. Startled and afraid, they ran out in a panic from St. Nicholas Church. What was truly remarkable about these bodies was not only their state of preservation but also that they were still clothed as if they had just been buried there yesterday. Through various studies, it was concluded that these **mummies** were preserved naturally. During examinations at the former University of Franeker, two of the mummies unfortunately disintegrated, while another was reportedly smuggled to America, though no evidence has ever been found. Of the remaining four bodies, three date back to the 17th century - a young fourteen-year-old girl who succumbed to tuberculosis, a man who suffered a painful death, and an elderly woman who died of old age. The fourth body belonged to a goldsmith who was laid to rest in 1705 within the basement. Though their clothes have long decayed, the bodies of these four people remain remarkably intact. And for the goldsmith, his eyeballs are still preserved, a testament to the enduring mystery.

CONSTCAMERS

Constcamers were exactly as depicted in the story.

About the author

Introducing Ange Anderson, a visionary educational consultant who has revolutionized therapeutic and technological support for the neurodivergent community. Her innovative methods have been widely recognized and she has appeared on many podcasts worldwide. She has written several educational books published by Routledge. Her book on utilizing virtual reality as a tool for those with unique minds has been translated into Arabic expanding her impact to international markets. She is an esteemed advisor to a leading global VR company. VR was the catalyst for this book 'The Cosmic Caretaker'.

website: angeandersontherapeutic.co.uk

To leave your feedback :

1. Open your camera app.

2. Point your mobile at the QR code above.

3. The book's Amazon page will appear in your web browser.

4. Scroll down to the end of the page to write your review.

A personal note from Ange - "I greatly appreciate the time you took to read my book. It would mean a lot to me if you would share your honest feedback on Amazon and help new readers discover my books. Thank You"

Scan me!

Printed in Great Britain
by Amazon